ALSO BY AVERY ARUJO

Once Upon a Blue Moon

ONCE UPON A BLUE MOON

A WELCOME TO MOONRIDGE NOVEL

AVERY ARUJO

to every hesitant heart and wandering mind,
magic is in you... believe it

CHAPTER ONE

Hazel

I tap my fingernail against the edge of my cup. The tea's gone cold, dark and bitter at the edges. Kind of like my soul. Funny thing is, I'm a witch. Reheating it would take like three seconds, tops.

Not worth it.

I let out a heavy sigh. Three years of my life. Gone. All because Evan wanted someone more *normal*. I keep turning that word over in my mouth like there's a side of it that'll taste better. There isn't.

It's nearly three, and The Blue Moon Apothecary is dead quiet. Usually, I don't mind a slow afternoon, but today it just means I have more time to sit on my ass and brood. The floor needs mopping. Epsom salt coats every surface. There's a booger-green streak of something on the wall from this morning's bath bomb class. Seriously, what is that? I should clean it all up, but witchy depression is real today.

I snap my fingers, and the mop glides into motion across the floor as I check my phone for the twelfth time this hour.

Still nothing.

I reach for the teacup again just as the bell above the door jingles. La'Tasha breezes in with a white paper bag from the diner across the street, the grease smell hitting me before the door even closes.

"Girl, I know what you're doing." She drops the bag on the counter and eyes my teacup. "Put that divination tea down. He's a whole ass, and you don't need him."

I glance at the cup. The leaves have clumped into something that looks uncomfortably like a broken heart. Or possibly a sad turtle.

"I wasn't—"

La'Tasha lifts an eyebrow. *The* eyebrow. The one that has caught every lie that has fallen out of my mouth since second grade.

"Mmhmm. And I'm the Queen of England."

"At least you'd look cute in a crown." I set the cup aside and look into the bag. There's so much extra cheese it's basically load-bearing. "Ah! I love you."

"I know." She hops onto the counter and straightens the orange and yellow silk wrapped around her pineapple bun. The vibrant color makes her dark eyes sparkle behind her trendy leopard-print glasses. Her flowing orange blouse catches the light as she settles cross-legged, the fabric a stunning contrast against her mahogany skin. She's so effortlessly chic it's almost painful. "So, how were things while I was out?"

I shrug, reaching for the fries. The first bite temporarily relieves all of my sadness. "Sold three protection sachets and a dream clarity potion to Mrs. Fernsby. Her cat's having night-mares again."

"The cat is having nightmares? Or she's having nightmares about the cat?"

"It's Mrs. Fernsby. Does it matter?" I take a huge bite of my cheeseburger. Comfort food really is its own form of magic.

La'Tasha's fingers skim her bracelets, silver charms clinking in that familiar rhythm that's signaled bad news since second grade. "So, I have news."

I knew that was coming. "What kind of news? Oh God, please don't tell me you're quitting. Or moving. Tash, I can't lose you, too."

"No, I'm not quitting, and I'm not moving, but it is the kind of news that might make you spiral. I considered not telling you, but I'd be a terrible friend if I didn't." She gives me a pointed look. "But you have to promise you won't do anything stupid."

"When have I ever done anything stupid?"

She responds with a laugh so loud it startles the bundles of drying herbs hanging from the ceiling. "Let's see." She counts on her fingers. "The time in grade school when you enchanted all of Henry Lewis's socks so they would run away when he took them off—"

"That was hilarious."

"—the time right after Evan broke up with you and you enchanted his underwear to give him random wedgies throughout the day—"

"Funniest thing I've ever done and totally harmless." Though his butthole probably doesn't think so.

"—and let's not forget the time in high school when you tried to give yourself temporary mermaid fins for swimming and ended up with scales on your coochie."

Heat flushes my cheeks. "Fine. I occasionally make impulsive decisions that don't pan out perfectly."

La'Tasha softens. "Okay, you know I love your witchy ways, but your magic gets wonky when you're upset. And what I'm about to tell you might upset you."

I push aside my burger, appetite gone. "Just say it."

"I just saw Evan outside the diner." She pauses. "With Missy Lawrence."

My heart does a little stutter-step. "The new kindergarten

teacher?"

"Yeah."

I know there's more, and she's trying to spare my feelings because she's my girl. But I need deets. I need to know what I'm up against. "And?"

She runs her fries through a puddle of ketchup. "Well. They were looking pretty cozy."

I try to keep my voice casual. "Cozy how?"

"Hand-holding, laughing, sharing-a-milkshake cozy."

I'm up and moving to the window before I can stop myself. I push aside the crystal-draped curtains. Across the street, outside Midnight Stack, stands Evan in his usual pressed khakis and blue button-down. Next to him, Missy Lawrence looks as though she just stepped off a greeting card. She's all blonde and petite. Her sweet smile is probably as pure as it looks. How boring. He places a hand on her back. It used to be *my* back he'd place his hand on.

"She's so . . . . normal." The word tastes sour on my tongue.

La'Tasha appears beside me. She brushes one of her natural curls away from her face. "Normal is basic."

"Normal is what he wanted." I let the curtain fall back. "Not a witch who accidentally turned all of his white shirts into shades of purple and pink."

"That was one time."

"Tell that to his collection of formerly white button-downs." I drift back to the counter, a hollow feeling spreading in my chest. "Ugh. They looked happy."

"No spiraling."

Too late. My mind's already a whirlpool of everything I'm not. Unlike Missy, I'm not calm and collected. I'm not predictable. I am not small, cute, and blonde. I'm imaginative, but also a little obsessive and quick-tempered. She looks like someone who has never had incense stuck under her fingernails or potion stains on her palms.

Evan always did prefer clean hands.

I want to close the shop early and crawl into bed. "What's wrong with me, Tash?" The question slips out, small and vulnerable.

"Not a damn thing. Evan is basic. He wanted mediocrity. You're a witch with actual power and personality. You're unique. He needs someone who doesn't outshine him."

I catch my twenty-seven-year-old reflection in the vintage mirror behind the register. Bright green eyes, a constellation of freckles, wild curls escaping my bun. Average height and a few curves. I look like what I am. A slightly chaotic witch with a tendency to act first and think later. I begin to pace. "I'm going to end up alone, aren't I?" Jars rattle against shelves as the realization sets in. "I'm going to be the weird old witch of Moonridge. I'll be all alone, talking to my herbs and scaring kids. I'll probably have seventeen cats—"

La'Tasha chokes on her soda. "Um, you're allergic to cats!"

"Exactly!" I throw my hands up. "I'll be so desperate for companionship that I'll suffer through anaphylaxis just to be loved! I'll be forced to live on the outskirts of Moonridge in a decrepit house that farts out warnings when strangers approach. I'll be the cautionary tale for all future witches! 'Don't be like Hazel Thornton, girls. She was a sad, hopeless mess.'"

La'Tasha lets me rant as she reapplies her coral lipstick. She's seen it all before, and she knows exactly how this spiral ends.

We've been best friends since second grade. One day, she caught me levitating a pencil during math. In response, she mentally folded a sheet of paper into a perfect airplane and sent it gliding to my desk. She is the yin to my yang. She gets me.

I sink onto the stool behind the counter. The weight of my future as a wrinkly old witch handing out poison apples to pretty girls in the woods presses down on me. "What if this is it, Tash? What if I'm just too much? Too weird, too magical?" The words deflate me even more. "If I can't land a normal human guy like

Evan, who *can* I land?"

The silence stretches between us, filled only by the tick of the antique clock on the wall. La'Tasha reaches over and squeezes my hand.

"You know what?" I straighten up, something shifting inside me. "Maybe I just need a change."

La'Tasha's eyes narrow. "What kind of change?"

"Nothing drastic. Just a little lift. A makeover." The back shelves call to me, lined with more potent ingredients than the everyday herbs up front.

"Hazel Thornton." The way La'Tasha uses my full name tells me she's not about to be on my side. "What are you planning?"

"A simple enhancement spell." Down come jars of dried rose petals and cinnamon, and a small vial of amber liquid. I reach for the top shelf. Grandma Agnes's spellbook begins to hum the minute I touch it, ready to get to work. "Something to boost my confidence. Enhance my looks. Make me feel desirable again."

La'Tasha leans against the counter, hand on her hip. "Girl, you're already fine as hell. And you know what happens when you try to work magic when you're hyper-emotional. You'd be better off driving drunk."

"I'm fine. Really. Plus, it's not that kind of spell." I grab my mortar and pestle. "It's more like magical lip gloss. Just add a little glow. Maybe lift things up a bit?" I gesture vaguely at my chest.

"Absolutely not." La'Tasha's up faster than I can say magical moisturizer. "Remember Jenny Whitaker's prom makeover? Green skin, purple polka dots? No digital photo filter could have saved that train wreck."

"That's because I used swamp moss instead of Irish moss. Rookie mistake." I set more jars on the workbench. "Besides, that was in high school. I know what I'm doing now. I have years of practice under my belt."

Or something.

"This isn't about using the right ingredients," she says flatly.

"This is about you obsessing over Evan. You're trying to change who you are for a man who rejected you. Do you really want someone who doesn't appreciate you for you?"

"It's not—" I start, then stop. We both know I'm about to tell a lie. "It's about control," I finally admit. "If I look better, I feel better. And if I'm happier with my appearance—"

"Changing your appearance won't change your heart," La'Tasha interrupts. "And your heart? It's pretty damn awesome already." She pauses. "And, girl, your titties are just fine."

"Aww, thanks!" I give her a quick hug. "I'm still going to do it, though."

She sighs in exasperation while I crush rose petals and cinnamon, adding a drop of honey for sweetness and a pinch of crushed pearl for shimmer. The rhythm of spellwork steadies me. I'm good at turning intention into magic.

"This isn't about Evan," I say, but we both know it kind of is. "It's about me feeling good about myself."

"Magic isn't a bandage, Hazel."

"Says the woman with flawless skin and body for days." I try a wink. "Trust me, this is totally harmless."

I add a dash of powdered vanilla bean and two drops of rosewater. The mixture goes a peachy shade of pink, which honestly looks kind of beautiful.

I close my eyes and focus. "Confidence bloom. Beauty shine. Make the best of what's already mine." I stir clockwise with my finger. The heat from the mixture seeps into my skin.

La'Tasha leans in, her shoulder brushing mine. "At least it's a pretty color. Smells nice, too."

"See? Totally safe." I transfer the glowing liquid to a small crystal vial. "I'll just dab a little on my pulse points and—"

The shop door slams open. I fumble the vial, catching it against my palm.

Blake Carter fills the doorway.

This is not the man I ordered. This is six feet three of annoyed werewolf. His dirty blond hair is going in about four directions, like he hasn't combed it since last weekend. Flannel shoved to the elbows. Jaw set. He looks like he came over here specifically to fuck something up.

"What the hell are you brewing in here, Thornton?" He stalks in, nostrils working overtime as he sniffs out the place. "I've been trying to work across the street and it feels like someone's beating a bass drum inside my skull."

I pull myself up to my full height, which puts me somewhere around his collarbone. "Hello to you too, Blake. Thank you for checking on my well-being. I'm fine. You can go now."

He doesn't blink. "Something's wrong with the energy coming off this place. It's been building for twenty minutes. It's bouncing all over the street."

"Mmm-hmm. Thanks for the dramatic weather report. Just working on a spell. It's what we do here."

"What kind of spell?"

"A simple one." I keep busy, refusing to make eye contact.

"Simple." His eyes drop to the vial. "It doesn't feel simple. By the way, you still owe me for those pipes."

"I told you I'd pay by the end of the week."

"It's been two weeks."

Has it? With the whole Evan situation I've genuinely lost track of what week it even is.

"I've been busy," I say, gripping the vial a little tighter.

His nostrils flare. "Jesus. What is that smell? It smells like a dog pissed on a rosebush."

Funny he says that. I literally watched him pee on a rosebush in high school after he got into Brian Kowalski's dad's whiskey at a party after winter formal and half-shifted because he could not, in fact, handle his alcohol.

"Trust me. It smells fine to anyone with a normal nose."

La'Tasha steals a fry from my bag and settles back, watching us like we're a new episode of *The Real Vampire Wives of*

Obsidian Hills.

Blake steps closer and looks at the vial like it might confess something. "You're working beauty magic. Really?"

My face goes hot. "What's your issue with beauty magic?"

"Nothing. If you're thirteen and having a sleepover." He steps closer. The scent of sawdust and sweaty man pits hits me, and honestly, it does something to me that I am not going to think about right now. "Aren't you supposed to be a serious witch?"

The jar of dried chamomile on the counter rattles.

"What I do in my shop is none of your concern," I say, keeping my voice even, "unless you've developed an interest in magical cosmetics."

Blake's mouth does that thing. That fucking smirk I've hated since he first hit me with it in the fifth grade. "Right. Because that's going to solve all your problems."

The way he says it makes my temper spike. "At least I'm not afraid to admit what I am."

He folds his arms across his chest and cocks his head. "I'm not afraid of anything."

"Could've fooled me." I nod at his flannel, the work boots, the way he keeps his wolf side caged like it's something dirty. "When's the last time you shifted? Publicly, I mean? You've got your pack on lockdown, too. They're only allowed to be wolves in the woods. What are you so afraid of? That they'll start publicly marking fire hydrants like you did in high school?"

His entire body goes rigid. Bingo. Still a sore spot after all these years.

"That's different."

"Is it?" I cross my arms, mimicking his stance. "At least my magic doesn't come with an identity crisis."

Blake rolls his eyes. "Seriously. Are you going to pay me for fixing your plumbing?"

"Fine." The march to my register is probably a little over-dramatic, but I don't care. I slam my business checkbook onto the counter. "How much?"

"Two hundred and forty-five dollars." He follows me, looming over the counter. "And maybe consider using less caustic ingredients in your potions."

"Maybe consider using pipes from this century," I snap back, scribbling out the check. The pen tears through the paper. "Damn it."

I rip out the ruined check and start over, aware of Blake's impatient breathing. The guy has gotten under my skin since second grade when he told me witches were just humans with better imaginations. Obviously, nothing has changed. He still treats me like I'm some kind of emotional tsunami.

And okay, sometimes I am. But that's beside the point.

"Here." The check crumples as I shove it into his hand. "Now you can quit bugging me about it."

He takes it, our fingers brushing for a half-second. A static shock zaps between us, making us both pull back.

"What was that?" he demands.

The wind picks up outside, rattling the windows. Crystals on the shelves begin to hum in eerie harmony, and the hair on my arms stands on end. Even the dust motes vibrate in the thickening air. Pressure builds around us.

Blake's head snaps up. "Do you feel that?" His entire body goes still like he senses danger. "What's happening?"

I sense it too. A humming beneath the floorboards. A vibration that makes the herb bundles hanging from the ceiling start to tremble. "I don't know."

Then the door bursts open, wind tearing through the shop. Papers fly. Dried herbs scatter. Several jars crash to the floor. Herbs and shards of glass float around us, then spin into a funnel of sparkly light.

"No!" I lunge to catch the vial, but it smashes against the floor. The pink mixture splatters, but instead of spreading across the floor, it rises like steam, glowing brighter. Below us, something pulses. The energy in the room spikes.

"What did you do?" Blake shouts over the growing wind.

"Nothing! This isn't me!"

The glowing pink mist dances around our feet, then coils up our legs like it's searching for something. It's drawn to us. Lured by the magic in my veins. And by the wild, restless energy humming under Blake's skin. Cold pressure pokes around my ribs, like something is searching for the core of my power. Testing. Tendrils reach toward Blake, latching onto his ankles and then his wrists.

"What is it doing to me?" His face turns pale as another tendril wraps around his waist. "Make it stop!"

"I'm trying!"

I reach for the containment charm on my necklace, but my fingers won't respond. It's like the pink mist has temporarily paralyzed me.

The air around us crackles, lifting my hair and raising goosebumps across my skin. I feel weightless. Untethered.

And then I'm rising. So is Blake. Which, under literally any other circumstances, would be cool. Not today. What's worse is, the pink mist has grown and seems to have become almost vampiric. My skin prickles like tiny teeth are nibbling at my entire body. Blake's expression flickers between rage and panic.

"Hazel!" La'Tasha's voice sounds distant, muffled by the roar of magic that envelops me.

For a moment, Blake and I hang suspended, our gazes locked. His blue eyes are the last thing I see before the world explodes in brightly colored confetti. I'm hit with a sensation like being turned inside out and then snapped back into place like a human-shaped rubber band. We both crash to the floor.

And then there's nothing but silence.

***

I wake to the worst headache of my life. My body feels wrong. Heavy. Stretched in weird places. There's a ringing in my ears, and my mouth tastes like burnt onions and whiskey.

"Ugh," I groan, but the sound that comes out is deep, rough. Not my voice at all.

I strain to sit up, my muscles protesting. I blink rapidly, trying to clear the haze from my vision. Slowly, the world around me starts to sharpen.

I focus on the hands in front of me. They're large and rugged, with skin roughened by hard work. The knuckles are prominent. The nails squared-off and slightly grimy. Yeah, these strong and hairy digits are most certainly not mine.

"What the—" I stop, touching my throat as that strange voice emerges again.

Across from me, my body lies sprawled on the floor, auburn hair fanned out, freckles sharp against pale skin. It sits up slowly. It stares at its hands, then touches its face, eyes widening in horror.

Then it looks up. And locks eyes with me.

This is so trippy!

"What did you do?"

My voice says it, but the tone, the edge of panic? That's all Blake. The horrible truth smacks me in the head. I look down. Red flannel. Blue jeans. Black work boots. My hands tremble as I reach up, brushing short hair that isn't mine. I trace my fingers over a stubbled jaw.

Oh gods. I'm wearing Blake Carter.

This is bad. This is so, so bad.

"Oh no," I whisper, and Blake's voice comes out instead of mine. It's rumbly and all kinds of wrong. "This isn't happening."

Blake—in my body—shoves to his feet and immediately wobbles in my boots. There's something deeply unsettling about watching my own face reshape into an overly panicked expression.

"Fix this." He makes my voice sound all forceful and commanding. Gotta admit. I sound kind of hot when I'm bossy. "Fix this right now."

"I don't know how it happened." I stand too, which takes longer than it should. Blake's body is *a lot* of body. "The spell wasn't supposed to do this."

"Well it did." He throws my arms wide. "Look at me. I'm in a dress. I have—" He looks down. Looks away fast, my freckles going red. "I have boobs! Jesus, this isn't happening."

"Believe me, I'm not thrilled either." I take a step forward and nearly pitch sideways. Running Blake's body is like driving a semi when you've only ever ridden a bike. Nothing responds the way I expect. "It's probably temporary."

"It better be." My voice, his growl. The combination is unsettling, like a golden retriever doing a Rottweiler impression. "I've got a job site to get back to. I can't show up looking like—" He gestures at my body. "This."

"What's wrong with how I look?" I put my hands on my— Blake's—hips, feeling bizarrely defensive.

"Nothing! That's not—" He runs my hands through my hair, messing up the bun even more. "We need to fix this. Now."

La'Tasha, who has been standing frozen in shock, lets out a strangled laugh. "Well," she says faintly, "you definitely changed your appearance."

"Not helping, Tash!" I take a deep breath, trying to think. "Okay. Body-swapping spells are serious magic. This shouldn't have happened from a simple attraction potion."

"Well, it did, so un-happen it!"

"It's not that simple!" I glance around at the scattered ingredients. The shattered vial. "Something else was at work here. Did you feel it? That pulse beneath the floor?"

Blake frowns with my face. "I felt something, but—"

"There was magic here that wasn't mine," I insist. "Something really powerful."

We stare at each other, taking in the impossible situation. Me in Blake's body, Blake in mine. The grumpy werewolf and the chaotic witch literally seeing life through each other's eyes.

"This," Blake says in my voice, low and dangerous, "is precisely why I hate magic."

The irony isn't lost on me that he's saying this while being trapped in a body that was made to perform magic. Not to mention, werewolves aren't exactly mundane. But now doesn't seem like a good time to point that out.

La'Tasha stands looking at us. "Looks like you two have a problem."

That's an understatement.

CHAPTER TWO

Blake

My dumb ass never should have stepped into this shop. I should be getting ready to grab drinks with my pack, but instead, I'm stuck in a witch's body. This is not at all what I had planned when I woke up today. I'd take a cave full of hungry vampires over this shit. How am I supposed to do anything? She has way too much hair, and these hands are far too small and delicate to be of any use—lavender nail polish and all. Her skin is really soft, though. It feels kind of nice. It's weird not to feel a beard when I—

"Stop touching my face!" Hazel barks. That's way too much drama coming from my mouth. She stands stiffly in my body, arms dangling like she doesn't know where to put them.

"I'm not," I start, then catch myself mid-swipe across her cheek. I can't help it. Her skin is weirdly calming.

No. No, it's not.

"I'm trying to process this nightmare." I step forward and nearly topple. Okay, definitely not used to wearing heels. Werewolf drag isn't usually my thing. I right myself and instinctively cross my arms, then immediately uncross them. Heat floods my face. I just touched her boobs. I have boobs! And don't even get me started on what's missing downstairs. It's all empty, and . . . Ohmigod. I have literally lost my dick.

"Look what you did!" The growl comes out in Hazel's sweet voice. I sound less like a wolf and more like a kitten with a grudge. How can I possibly act as alpha when I sound like this? "Your stupid potion did this."

"My potion wouldn't have done this!" Hazel paces in my body, each step clompy and forceful, like my legs are too heavy. She's going to strain my hamstrings if she keeps this up. "That was basic magic, not . . . not body-swapping Voodoo!"

"Excuse you. Voodoo is a religion, not a type of magic," La'Tasha points out while trying not to laugh at us. "Just so everyone's aware."

"Not the point, Tash!" Hazel throws my hands up in frustration. I wince as she nearly knocks over an entire shelf of potions.

"Be careful with my body," I snap. "Don't go breaking my arms with all your flailing."

"I don't flail!" She flails as she says it.

"Both of you need to calm the hell down." La'Tasha steps between us like a referee. "Fighting isn't going to fix this. Hazel, think. What could have made your spell do this?"

Hazel stops mid-stride and scratches the top of my head until the short blonde strands stick up in every direction.

Great. Now I look electrocuted.

It's weird to see my own face scrunch in concentration. Is that really what I look like when I'm thinking? Because it kind of looks like I'm holding in a fart.

"I don't know," she admits. "The wind came out of nowhere. The floor was vibrating. And there was that pulse . . ."

A strange sensation creeps up my spine—Hazel's spine. It starts as a tingle, then becomes an itch. An intense, maddening itch right in the middle of my back where I can't easily reach. I arch against the counter, trying to scratch it like a bear against a tree.

"What are you doing to my body?" Hazel asks, alarmed.

"It itches," I mutter, twisting to reach the spot. "Everything itches. How do you live in this skin? It's so sensitive."

"Don't scratch!" She takes a step toward me, then freezes. A horrified expression suddenly appears on my face. "Oh my God."

"What now?" I ask, still trying to relieve the itch.

Her eyes—my eyes—grow wide. "What happens when I have to pee?"

It takes me a second to catch up. Then it hits me. "Oh."

"I'm going to have to touch your wiener," she says, gesturing vaguely at my crotch. Her embarrassment turns my face bright red. "I don't want to!"

"Well, I'm going to have to deal with . . ." I wave at Hazel's crotch area, "Whatever you've got going on down there, too. So I guess we're even."

La'Tasha snorts, covering her mouth. "Sorry. Not funny. Definitely not funny."

Hazel shakes her head and looks as if she's struggling to breathe. Is she having a panic attack? "I can't. I can't do this."

"It's basic anatomy," I say, trying to sound calm while fighting the urge to scratch every inch of this hypersensitive witch skin. "It's not a big deal. We'll figure it out."

La'Tasha claps her hands. "Focus, people! Bodies are bodies. You'll manage. Simply sit while you pee and don't touch it. Easy. Besides, you've both got bigger problems than peeing right now."

"Okay, okay." Hazel does her best to refocus. She takes a deep breath. "Let's think this through. We need to figure out what caused this. Then we reverse it. Simple."

"Simple," I echo, not believing it for a second. Nothing involving Hazel Thornton has ever been simple.

"The floor," she says, staring at the spot behind the counter. "I felt something. From under the floor."

She steps forward, lurching in my body like she's piloting a mech suit. She stops, head tilted in a very un-Blake-like gesture of curiosity.

"There's something . . ." she murmurs.

I sense it, too. A pull. Subtle but insistent, drawing me toward the same spot. It's like a magnet tugging at my sternum.

La'Tasha watches us with narrowed eyes. "What are you two sensing?"

"Something's under there," I say, moving closer to the spot behind the counter. An old rug with a pentagram printed on it covers part of the wooden floor.

We both reach for the edge of the rug. Our hands touch, and something sparks between us. It doesn't hurt. It's almost like a jolt of recognition.

"Did you feel that?" she whispers.

I nod. Together we pull back the rug.

The floorboards underneath look pretty normal at first. They're just old, worn-out wood with stains from years of spilled potions. But then I see it. A red, pulsing glow shines through the slats in the floor. It's almost rhythmic.

"We need to open this," Hazel says.

I grab a letter opener off the counter and jam it between the boards.

"Be careful with that," Hazel warns. "It's silver."

"Why do you have a silver letter opener when you know there are werewolves around?" I ask, working the blade into the crack.

"It was my grandmother's." Her shoulders—my shoulders— square up. She's willing to fight about it. "And werewolves don't typically go around licking my office supplies."

Fair point. I work the blade deeper, noticing the wood start to give. With a loud crack, one board pops up, then another. The glow intensifies, bathing our faces in an eerie red light.

"Holy shit," La'Tasha breathes, peering over our shoulders.

There, nestled in a hollow beneath the floor, lies an amulet.

For a moment, none of us speaks. It looks ancient. Older than the building. Maybe older than the town. A blood-colored stone glows at its center, ringed by runes that shift and curl around the light.

"That's . . ." Hazel starts, then stops, my voice failing her.

The light pulses. So does my heart. The beats are in sync.

That can't be good.

"It looks like the Wolfsbane Amulet." La'Tasha stares in awe. "I thought it was just a legend."

Hazel stares at the pulsing red stone. "Grandma Agnes told me there was something important buried under the shop. She said it was to fight off evil and to keep the peace between witches and wolves."

"How so?" I ask, shifting uncomfortably in a body that will never feel like mine.

"I don't know. I thought it was just a story she told me to keep me entertained." Hazel reaches toward it, then pulls back when the light flares brighter. "She said there was something that was extremely evil and it could make werewolves . . ."

"Aggressive. And the witches had to bind it to weaken its influence," La'Tasha finishes, her face stoic. "My grandfather told stories, too. About wolves who couldn't control their shifts during the early days of Moonridge." She walks over and grabs a thick book from the shelf behind us, flipping through pages. "Here. 'Archaeological discovery, 1847. Unearthed artifact caused increased territorial disputes among local wolf population.'" She glances up. "It just says the item was 'contained by local practitioners.'"

The amulet pulses again, and my chest—Hazel's chest—throbs in response. "If it was bound and contained, why is it glowing now?"

"Maybe whatever they did to bind it is wearing off," Hazel says, backing away from the hole in the floor. "Or maybe our swap somehow . . ." she gestures between us.

La'Tasha turns another page. "Oh no. Listen to this. 'Effects noted to intensify during lunar cycles.' Blake, when's the next full moon?"

My stomach drops. "Five days."

Goosebumps prickle along my arms—her arms—and I wrap them around myself. I suddenly feel even smaller in this body. "So that thing can control werewolves?" I find myself backing away from the glowing amulet.

"I don't know about control, but according to the history books, it definitely enhances werewolf aggression." La'Tasha looks directly at me. "If the power binding was somehow reversed . . . that would be bad."

"Especially during a full moon." I begin to pace. Full moons always make our aggression worse. If this thing intensifies them . . .

The amulet pulses brighter, as if responding to my thoughts. Dizziness washes over me and I grab the counter for support.

"It's definitely active," Hazel says, looking equally unsteady on her—my—feet. "The magic that swapped us must have triggered it somehow."

"Or maybe the amulet is what triggered your swap." La'Tasha counters. "Which would make sense. The spell you cast was a simple enhancement spell. It shouldn't have triggered body displacement. We don't know what this thing is capable of." She gestures at the amulet. "It's ancient. The magic is way older than any of us. What I don't understand is why it's suddenly active."

"Great question." Hazel stares at the amulet. It's strange to see myself looking worried. "We need to make sure it stays contained until we can deactivate it."

"Agreed," La'Tasha says, already turning toward a shelf of supplies. She grabs a jar of what looks like salt and a bundle of herbs. "We'll contain it with salt and then sage the shit out of it."

I've never been big on witch magic. I prefer to rely on wolf strength and pack bonds, but even I know that a salt circle is Magical Containment 101. I step back to give them room.

La'Tasha scatters salt in a wide ring around the amulet,

chanting low and steady. She strikes a match and lights the sage, waving smoke through the air.

Nothing happens.

"It's not working." Frustration leaks into Hazel's voice—my voice. "It should be responding to the containment. Maybe we should try black salt." She points at a shelf behind my head. "Will you grab that for me?"

I grab a bottle of what looks like black sand from the shelf and hand it to her. Our fingers brush for half a second—

The amulet blazes with blinding red light. The floorboards groan beneath it, jars rattling across the shelves. We both jerk back. Something pulls at my chest, almost as if there's thread hooked into my ribs, tying me to the amulet and to Hazel.

"What the hell was that?" Hazel stumbles back. My face—her face now, I guess—is twisted up in total confusion.

La'Tasha stares at us and the now-pulsing amulet. "Every time you two touch . . ." She points at both of us. "It's like it gets stronger."

The glow's gotten brighter. It throws shadows against the walls that move in time with the thumping in my chest. Well, Hazel's chest.

"It's getting stronger," I whisper. Red light seeps between the floorboards like spilled blood.

Hazel begins to pour salt around it, but a burst of energy blows it back in her face. "It's resisting!" She bends and pokes at the edge of the amulet, then tries to jam a fingernail beneath it. "It's fused to the floor. Like it's become part of the foundation."

Great. Just great. The magical junk causing all this chaos isn't just turned on, it's actually grown into the floor. The shit-tasticness of this day just won't quit.

Suddenly, a howl fills the air. It's far off, but I'd know it anywhere. There's a note of distress in it that makes the hair on the back of my neck stand up. Well, Hazel's neck. Damn this is going to get old.

"The pack," I say. I'm instantly alert. Years of instinct make me tense, ready to rally.

Hazel hears it too. She snaps my head toward the sound. "That's your brother, isn't it? Calvin?"

I nod, surprised she can tell. Then I remember. She's in my body. She has my wolf senses. She could hear a mouse fart in the basement below us.

"Something's wrong." That's the howl for *someone needs to get the alpha*. The alpha is me.

I have to go.

Now.

I stand, wobbling slightly on Hazel's feet. The instinct to respond to my pack's call wars with the reality of being trapped in the wrong body. "I need to go."

"You can't go like that," La'Tasha points out. "You're in Hazel's body. They'll think you're a witch interfering in pack business. Not a good thing if the amulet is active again."

She's right. My pack is already on edge with the full moon coming. Some of the older members still blame the witches for the territorial disputes years ago. There's not a lot of trust between witches and wolves. If I show up looking like Hazel, I might make things worse.

But I can't just ignore that howl. Calvin wouldn't call unless it was serious.

"I have to go with you," Hazel says, reading my thoughts. "I'm in your body. They'll listen to me."

"No," I say automatically. "You don't know how to act like me. You'll give us away."

"And you know how to act like me?" She crosses my arms over my chest. "Face it, Blake. We're stuck with each other until we figure this out. Your pack needs you, and right now, I'm your best chance of helping them."

Another howl slices through the air. Every instinct screams at me to run toward it, to lead. Protect. Instead, I'm trapped in a witch's body, dependent on her help.

I clench my hands—her hands—into fists. "Fine. But you follow my lead. Don't try any magic. Don't talk unless you have to. And for God's sake, stop playing with my hair."

Hazel drops my hand from my hair, looking sheepish. "Deal. But you have to stop scratching my body. You're going to break skin."

It dawns on me that I've been absently scratching my—her—arm, leaving red marks. "Your skin is ridiculously sensitive."

"No, you're just too rough with it," she counters. "Try to act more like me. Smile occasionally. Use your hands when you talk. Don't walk like you've been riding a horse and have a massive stick up your butt."

"I don't walk like that," I protest.

La'Tasha snorts. "You absolutely do."

The howl comes a third time, making my decision for me. "We don't have time for this. We need to go figure out what's going on with the pack. We'll have to deal with all of this . . ." I gesture at the glowing amulet and our swapped bodies. "Later."

Hazel nods, setting my jaw in what she probably thinks is a hard line. "I'll try not to ruin your reputation, if you promise not to ruin mine."

"Deal." I hold out Hazel's hand to shake on it, and she takes it with my larger one.

The contact sends another jolt through us both, and the amulet flares in response. We pull apart quickly.

"That's not good," La'Tasha says, looking between us and the amulet. "You two touching seems to enhance it somehow."

"Then we don't touch." Hazel steps away from me. "Not until we figure this out."

Not touching sounds like an excellent plan to me. The less interaction I have with Hazel Thornton, the better. Even if I am stuck wearing her skin like a costume that doesn't fit right.

"I'll stay here." La'Tasha begins to pull books from the shelves.

"I'll see what I can find on body-swapping spells and this amulet."

"Thanks, Tash," Hazel says with a grateful smile. She does the heart sign with her fingers and I almost barf.

"Can I ask that you please don't do that gesture while wearing my skin? I would literally never do that."

Another howl pierces the air, cutting off her snarky response. That one was closer. My packmates are moving toward town, which means whatever trouble is brewing, it's headed this way.

"Let's go." I move toward the door, trying to adjust to the unfamiliar sway of Hazel's hips. "And remember. You're me, I'm you. Just until we sort this out."

"Got it, Captain." Hazel straightens my posture and adopts a more serious expression. "I'm Blake Carter, grumpy werewolf extraordinaire."

I roll Hazel's eyes so hard I'm surprised they don't get stuck in the back of my head. "And I'm Hazel Thornton, hyper-emotional witch who bursts pipes because she can't keep her magic under control."

"Hey!"

"If the pointy hat fits," I mutter, pushing open the door to face whatever new disaster awaits. Hopefully, this one comes with instructions.

CHAPTER THREE

Blake

Calvin's howl just about rips me in half. It's sharp and urgent. Desperate. I stumble toward the park. My borrowed feet still haven't figured out how to walk in these ugly-ass boots. Hazel stumbles ahead of me, looking like a penguin trying to walk on stilts.

"Slow down," I hiss, jogging to catch up. "You look like a drunk bear in my body."

"You're not exactly gliding either, princess." She adjusts her stride to something a little less clunky. "This is so intense! I can hear everything. And the smells . . . good lord, there are so many smells."

We round the corner to Moonridge Central Park, and it's an absolute shit show. Mason writhes in the grass near the old oak. He's stuck somewhere between human and wolf. He just turned nineteen and is barely six months into his powers. He's still learning to control the shift. And failing. His body jerks at weird, unnatural angles. Fur ripples over his skin and his fingers stretch into claws, then snap back. He's fighting it, but it's a losing battle.

Calvin circles Mason in his coffee-colored wolf form. He looks ready to lunge the second things go to shit. Leo hovers nearby in his human shape with worry all over his face. He's got a tight grip on his tranquilizer gun. The one I mandated after Mason's last bad shift two weeks ago. We've still got five days until the full moon, but the new guys always struggle when it's this close.

"Mason, buddy, you gotta breathe," Leo says. He keeps his voice soft even though he's stressed the hell out. "In through your nose, out through—oh shit!"

Mason lunges toward Leo. A blur of teeth and claws. Leo counters, colliding with a park bench. The tranquilizer gun hits the grass and Mason takes the chance to bolt. Calvin moves, slamming into Mason with a heavy thud, driving him back to the ground. A deep growl rumbles from Calvin's throat. The sound would normally make the younger wolf submit immediately. But Mason keeps fighting, eyes wild. It's like he's possessed. This isn't normal wolf behavior. Even newly turned wolves don't act like this. Unless . . .

"The amulet," Hazel says. "It has to be affecting him."

Calvin's head snaps in our direction, ears pricked forward. Recognition flashes in his eyes, then confusion as his gaze shifts between 'Blake' and the witch beside him.

Mason takes advantage of the distraction, twisting free from Calvin's hold. He scrambles up, foam flecking his half-wolf jaws. He charges toward a young mother and child who stand frozen in terror near the playground.

"Stop him!" I shout, but the words come out in Hazel's voice. It holds none of the alpha authority that would normally make any pack member freeze on the spot.

Hazel looks like she finally understands the problem. She straightens my shoulders and yells, "HEY!" It's not bad. But it's also not enough. Mason slows for half a second, then charges forward.

Leo scrambles for the tranquilizer gun, fumbling with the safety. "I got it, I got it," he mumbles, then immediately drops the dart. "Nope. Guess I don't got it."

Calvin tackles Mason barely a second before he reaches the mother and child. Mason bucks and growls before breaking free. He's a wiry little shit and difficult to hold onto. Two more pack members move in, trying to box him in.

Calvin shifts back, drops to the grass, and yanks on the jeans he'd stuffed behind the oak tree near the fence line. "Blake, why aren't you shifting? And what the hell is she doing here?" He nods toward me in Hazel's body. "We've got a situation. No witches needed."

Before Hazel can answer for me, Sheriff Ben Harlow's cruiser screeches into the parking lot, lights flashing. Mason turns toward the lights, and the mother seizes her opportunity. She scoops up her child and sprints toward the safety of the courthouse across the street.

Mason howls, a sound of frustration and pain that makes my—Hazel's—ears ring. He somehow manages to evade the wolves who circle him and lopes toward the trees.

"Head him off!" I yell at Leo, forgetting again that my voice carries zero authority while in this body.

Calvin shoots me a suspicious glare as he pulls his T-shirt over his head. "Since when do you give orders to our pack, Thornton?"

Right. I'm supposed to be Hazel. I'm supposed to act like a witch who thinks werewolves are nothing more than stinky, rowdy boys.

"I just—" I start, but Leo is moving again, trying to intercept Mason with all the grace of a coked-up elephant on ice skates. He trips over his own feet, sprawling face-first in the dirt.

Instead of trampling him, Mason skids to a halt. He sniffs Leo's prone form with sudden interest. Something in his posture shifts. There's less aggression now. It's more confusion mixed with curiosity.

Hazel sees it too.

"Leo," she says, voice gentle. "Stay still. Talk to him. He

recognizes you."

Calvin starts forward, running a hand over his dark brown beard. "Blake, what are you—"

"Trust me," Hazel says. Confident but not domineering. It makes Calvin pause.

Leo, still flat on his stomach, tilts his head up to look at Mason's snarling face inches from his own. "Hey, Mase," he says. His voice is remarkably steady for someone who's inches from getting his face bitten off. "Not having a great day, huh? Me neither, bud. Dropped my sandwich in a puddle this morning. Had to eat the soggy vending machine sandwiches Ben keeps in the station. You know the ones that are always at the back of the store. They're supposed to be fresh, but they taste like they were soaked in water and salt before being packaged up?"

While Leo rambles about terrible sandwiches, Mason's growling quiets.

"That's it," Hazel encourages.

She handles my pack with an ease that makes my jaw clench. My fingers—her fingers—dig into my palms. How is she better at being alpha than I am?

Sheriff Harlow approaches, his right hand resting on his Taser. His eyes scan the scene as he shakes his head. "Carter." He nods at Hazel, thinking she's me. "This pack of yours is becoming a problem."

"It's under control, Ben," Hazel says, mimicking my clipped tone remarkably well.

"Like hell it is," the sheriff growls. "That boy nearly attacked a mother and child. If this happens again, I'll have to take action. I can't keep giving you all passes."

Heat shoots through me. "So, what? You gonna take in a nineteen-year-old kid because he's having trouble with his shift?" The second the words leave my mouth, I regret it.

Everyone stares at me like they're in shock. Hazel Thornton, the fun and flighty witch, doesn't talk to authority figures like that. And she definitely doesn't defend werewolves. I'm going to blow our cover if I don't get a grip.

Calvin steps between me and the sheriff. "We've got this handled. Mason's new to shifting. It won't happen again."

Leo has moved on from sandwich stories to describing his ideal first date. Apparently, it involves a haunted amusement park and margaritas and karaoke afterward. His gentle voice seems to be doing the trick. Mason's human form has settled back into place, the half-shift gone. Now he's just a scared kid sitting naked in the dirt.

"Leo," Mason croaks, sounding disoriented. "What happened?"

"You went a little wolfy at the wrong time, buddy," Leo says. He sits up and pats Mason's shoulder with a reassuring smile. "But it's cool. We all have bad days." He pulls his hoodie off and drops it across Mason's lap. "Gotta keep the dong covered in public, dude. Rule number one. Always have something to cover the boy parts."

Sheriff Harlow's expression softens slightly. "Get him home," he tells Calvin. "And keep your wolves in check. The town council meeting is tomorrow. People have concerns."

"What concerns?" I demand.

Before he can answer, a melodic voice cuts through the air. "The reasonable concern that maybe Moonridge has been a little too . . . welcoming to certain species."

We turn to see Bianca Mayweather gliding toward us, looking like she stepped out of a wellness magazine. Her white yoga pants and flowing tunic are spotless despite the park's dusty paths. Her long black hair is pulled into a sleek ponytail. She carries herself with poised certainty. Someone who's never doubted her place in the world.

"Ms. Mayweather." Sheriff Harlow nods. He straightens his posture. "I didn't expect to see you here."

"I was leading my sunset yoga class when we heard the commotion." Her eyes are sharp as they scan each of us in turn. When they land on me, she cocks an eyebrow. "Hazel, what a surprise. I didn't think werewolves would be your thing."

Bianca steps closer, and my borrowed skin breaks out in goosebumps. What is this reaction? It's like I'm standing too close to a live wire. Across from me, Hazel jerks slightly in my body, her hand moving to rub the back of her—my—neck. She feels it, too.

"Just trying to help," I manage, attempting to sound like the Hazel I know. A bit flippant, a bit defensive.

Bianca turns her attention to Sheriff Harlow. "Ben, this is the third incident this month. The mothers in my wellness circle are frightened to bring their children to public spaces when the wolves are around. Perhaps it's time to consider more proactive measures."

"Like what?" Calvin asks, his voice tight.

Bianca's smile sticks to her face as she turns to face him. "Increased patrols would be a start. Perhaps a curfew for pack members. Or, if these incidents continue . . ." She lets the sentence dangle.

"Banishment isn't on the table." Hazel stretches my voice to a commanding tone. "The pack has been here as long as the town has. We own a good chunk of the land in Moonridge. This is more their—our town than anyone's."

Bianca regards her with mild surprise. She clearly thinks she's speaking to Blake. "I'm simply concerned for public safety, Mr. Carter. Surely you understand that your pack's unpredictability puts everyone at risk."

A squeezing sensation crawls up my spine—Hazel's spine— tickling at the base of my skull. Mason shudders. He grabs his head like he can feel the same thing.

"Hazel?" Leo notices my discomfort. "You okay?"

I nod, but I'm not. It feels like someone just found a dial inside me and cranked it all the way up.

Hazel's eyes go wide. She feels it too.

"The amulet," she mouths to me.

Calvin helps Mason to his feet, and drops a protective arm around his shoulders. "We're taking him home," he says. "Blake, you coming?"

Hazel hesitates and looks in my direction. We need to get back to the apothecary, but Calvin's suspicion is cranked up to a level ten and grows by the minute.

"We should go," I say to Hazel, trying to sound like I'm making a suggestion rather than giving an order. "The . . . tea I was brewing might boil over."

Hazel nods with my head. "I'll stop by later," she tells Calvin. "Get Mason settled first."

Calvin's brown eyes narrow. "Since when do you let a witch tell you what to do?"

"I'm not—" Hazel starts, then catches herself. "I make my own decisions. It's just good sense."

"Blake's right," Leo chimes in, oblivious to the undercurrents. "We should get Mason home, and you two can . . . do whatever you're doing." He waggles his eyebrows suggestively, then immediately looks mortified. "Not that you're doing anything! I mean, unless you are, which is cool! Live your truth! I just . . . Yeah, I'm making it worse, aren't I?"

"Yep," Calvin and I say simultaneously.

Calvin and Leo guide Mason toward the truck. Before we can follow, Bianca steps closer, her designer perfume almost gags me. It's like horse piss mixed with peaches and lavender. "I'm looking forward to our meeting tomorrow, Hazel. I have so many ideas for how my wellness products could enhance your quaint little shop."

The what? I glance at Hazel, who's trying to signal something from behind Bianca's back.

"Right," I say cautiously. "The meeting."

"I think customers would respond wonderfully to my supplement line being featured at the apothecary," Bianca continues. "Natural wellness is the future, don't you agree?"

"Except your supplements aren't magic," I reply. I recall overhearing Hazel complaining to La'Tasha a few weeks ago about Bianca's attempts at getting her to join some sort of MLM sales scheme. "And from what I hear, they're mainly just laxatives with fancy packaging. But I'd be happy to send customers your way if they're ever constipated."

Hazel winces, and I realize I've probably been too blunt. Too late now.

Bianca's perfect smile hardens. "Oh, look at you. Such a sense of humor! But my products are backed by science, unlike some of your . . . creative concoctions. I only want to help elevate your business model, dear."

"My business model is fine." I realize I'm using a little too much bite. I try to soften my tone to something more Hazel-appropriate. "I appreciate the offer, but I'm not looking to become part of your . . ." Shit, what had Hazel called it? "Your MLM empire."

"Multi-level marketing is simply collaborative entrepreneurship." Bianca's smile never wavers as she speaks. "But we can discuss the details tomorrow. Ten o'clock, yes? I'll bring samples of the new immunity booster. It's perfect for the upcoming fall season."

Before I can answer, Hazel steps forward. "We should go," she says in my voice, gruff and authoritative. "Hazel has a bunch of inventory to do."

Bianca's gaze shifts between us. She's calculating something. "Of course. Don't let me keep you. Though I must say, Blake, I didn't realize you were into witchcraft."

"There's a lot you don't know about me," Hazel replies, somehow making my face look almost convincingly stern.

We turn to leave, but Bianca calls after us, "Oh, and Hazel, I think it would be a good idea for you to think about what I said regarding the pack situation. You're a well-respected member of the community. Your voice at that meeting tomorrow carries a lot of weight. Especially if you care about public safety."

So, basically, side with her against the werewolves, or face consequences. I don't trust this woman. I kind of want to hang out in this body for a little longer just to fuck with her. Neither of us speak as she walks off to join her minions who have congregated at the edge of the park.

"So, tell me about this meeting with Bianca the Wellness Queen."

Hazel sighs, scratching my chest. Must not be used to having so much body hair. "She's been after me for months to stock her products. She has all these bullshit weight-loss pills, 'detox' teas, immune boosters. They're all basically just vitamin C and sawdust with a markup. She runs this whole wellness empire and has most of the human women in town selling her stuff in some pyramid scheme. She comes in at least once a week to try to get me to join her MLM. She talks about 'synergy' and 'alignment' and makes it sound like I'm failing as a business owner because I won't join her cult." Hazel puffs out a breath.

As we leave, I catch Calvin tracking us, posture tense, eyes clocking every step. Behind him, Leo helps a shaking Mason into the truck.

I glance over my shoulder and notice Bianca is still watching us. "Something is off with her."

Hazel follows my gaze. "What are you tracking?"

"Don't you think it's convenient that she just happened to show up tonight when all of this went down? And not only does she show up, but she also has a lot of thoughts on how the sheriff can control the situation."

"I do find that awfully suspicious." Hazel considers. "And you're right. She does have a weird energy, but I just chalked it up to her being annoyingly assertive."

"We need to keep an eye on her. Something isn't right."

Calvin's truck crawls past. His gaze cuts toward us and he

stares a little too long. He knows something's up. My brother is no dummy.

"Your pack's struggling," Hazel says quietly. "I could feel it. If what my grandma said was true, the amulet's basically werewolf poison. It stirs up aggression and fucks with your mind. And from the way Mason just lost it, that thing's super dangerous. Especially for the new guys."

"Then let's fix it. Before things get worse."

My pack, this town, even the stubborn witch whose body I'm trapped in, are all under my protection now. I won't let them down. Even if I have to do it while dickless and wearing a bra.

CHAPTER FOUR

Blake

Sunlight streams through unfamiliar curtains. My head pounds and for about one second, I think I'm in my own bed after a night of too many beers. Then my hand lands on my chest and finds two boobs that shouldn't be there, and reality hits like a bucket of ice water to the nuts.

Yep. Still in Hazel's body.

"Motherfucker."

I sit up too fast and a curtain of auburn curls drops into my face. They smell like lavender and vanilla. How does she deal with this much hair? I wonder if she'd be super pissed if I shaved it all off?

Last night, after the park incident, we came back to the apothecary and tried to figure out how to reverse the body swap. Nothing worked. La'Tasha finally made us get some rest. Hazel took the couch downstairs and I got the bed. At least we didn't have to sleep in the same room.

I swing her legs over the side of the bed and take a look around. It's exactly what I'd expect. There are more plants in here than actual furniture. Dried flowers hang from the ceiling, an inspirational quote is written in loopy writing over the headboard, and crystals cover nearly every surface. It's very Hazel.

I need a shower.

The thought is quickly followed by the realization that in order to do that, I'll have to see Hazel naked. Touch her body. It feels like crossing a line. Should I ask for permission first? Technically I'd just be cleaning the body I'm currently stuck in, but still . . .

"Get it together, Carter," I mutter to my reflection. "It's just a body."

A very nice body, my traitorous brain replies.

"Shut up," I growl at myself.

Did she have these same thoughts this morning when she had to shower while in *my* body? Did she *like* my body? Did she touch my . . . Why does that turn me on? And why does being turned on feel so weird? It's like—

Focus!

The bathroom is as cluttered as the bedroom. Lotions and mysterious bottles line every surface. The pink shower curtain is covered in flowers. I turn on the water, then stand frozen, unsure how to proceed.

I rip off the pajamas and pull back the shower curtain. The mirror across the room gives me a full view of Hazel's body, and my breath catches. She's beautiful. Curves in all the right places, skin pale and scattered with freckles. I've always thought she was pretty, in an objective, annoying-witch kind of way, but seeing her like this . . .

"Nope." I pull the shower curtain closed and slam my eyes shut.

I have the foresight to not wash her hair. It would take all day to dry, so I lean back and wash everything real quick with honey-scented soap.

So that's what she uses. It's nice.

I towel off and head to the bedroom, but getting dressed is another disaster. I dig through her drawers like a burglar until I find underwear that is more than just a piece of string covering my butthole, and consider that a win.

But the bra defeats me.

I try three times and then chuck the thing across the room. This is humiliating. In my own body, I can run a full electrical panel. I have lifted a two-hundred-pound beam by myself with a bad knee. But for whatever reason, I can't figure out how to hook together two pieces of fabric.

Sorry, Hazel. Today we're flying free.

I throw on a faded pair of jeans, and a bulky, soft rainbow-striped sweater, then head downstairs. It's crazy how much lighter I am in this body. My feet barely make a sound on the wooden steps.

The apothecary is quiet in the morning. Pale light comes through the stained-glass windows and throws colored patches across the shelves. It smells like old wood and dried herbs.

Hazel's already there. She looks ridiculous in my body, stumbling around the counter. She's got my flannel and jeans on. She even tried to style my hair, but it sticks up in the back like she gave up halfway through.

"You're up," she says. My voice sounds way too gentle coming out of her mouth.

"Yeah." I just stand there at the bottom of the stairs. "This is so fucking weird."

"Tell me about it." She gestures to my body she's wearing. "I feel like I'm an ant stuck in a bear's body."

Her analogy makes me snort. "At least you don't have to figure out how to wear a bra."

Her eyes—my eyes—widen. "Please tell me you're wearing a bra. I can't have my boobs flopping all over town!"

"I tried! Those things are designed by sadists. How do you hook it behind your back without dislocating something?"

She sighs and shakes her head. "We'll figure it out later.

Right now, I need to show you how to run the shop so you can pass as me. La'Tasha texted. She's still researching but hasn't found anything useful yet. She'll be here later."

For the next twenty minutes, Hazel gives me a whirlwind tour of the apothecary. She shows me where everything is kept, which potions are ready to sell, and which customers might come in today. I don't know what any of this stuff is and none of it is categorized. How does she expect me to remember all of this?

"Mrs. Fernsby's in here almost every day. She'll probably want more dream clarity potion for the cat." She points to a small blue bottle. "Just remind her to only use one drop in the water bowl. Not the whole bottle like last time."

"A cat needs dream clarity?" I can't help but snort.

"Don't judge. Just smile and take the nice lady's money." She points to another shelf. "The protection sachets are there. They're a big seller since the full moon is coming up."

"Do they actually work?"

She looks at me with a look that's a cross between annoyed and almost amused. "Yes, Blake. They work. Teeth and claws aren't the only way to handle something."

The bell above the door jingles before I can even respond. Calvin strides in. He looks tense.

"Blake. What the hell? I've been looking all over for you." He gives me a short nod. He clearly thinks he's talking to Hazel. "Sorry to interrupt your . . . whatever this is."

Hazel straightens, trying to act convincing. "Hey, Calvin. What's up?"

"We've got a situation at the Thompsons' site. The foundation is shifting, and we need to reinforce it before the whole east wall collapses." He hitches his right thumb over his shoulder. "I need your help. Now."

Hazel shoots me a panicked look. She knows about as much about construction as I know about potions. Nothing.

"Can't it wait?" she asks, clearly stalling. "I'm kind of in the middle of something here."

Calvin's eyes narrow. "Since when do you put off work for

a witch?" His eyes dart between us. "What's going on with you two anyway? First the park, now this?"

I speak up, trying to sound like Hazel. "We're just discussing . . . a payment plan for the plumbing work. Nothing weird."

"Right," Calvin says. He's not convinced. "Whatever it is, it can wait. We have a crisis on our hands. Leo's trying to hold things together, and you know how that usually goes."

I can picture it all too well. Leo tripping over a saw and cutting off a toe. Accidentally nailing his own thumb to a wall.

Hazel sighs, looking at me helplessly. "I guess I have to go."

"Guess you do," I reply. Panic edges its way up my throat. She's leaving me alone in her shop? With her customers? Her potions?

She must see the fear in her own eyes, because she offers a reassuring smile. I get the gesture, but it doesn't quite know how to make itself work on my usually stern face. "You'll be fine. Just be nice to people and try not to break anything. I'll be back as soon as I can."

"But what if someone wants a potion? Or asks about ingredients? Or—"

"Just say I'm out of stock, or offer a protection sachet instead. Everyone loves those." She moves toward the door where Calvin waits impatiently. "And Hazel? Don't touch my mead brewing in the back room. It's . . . temperamental."

Calvin frowns. "Since when do you make mead?"

"Let's go," Hazel says quickly, pushing past him. At the door, she turns back, looking worried. "Good luck."

And just like that, I'm alone in a witch's apothecary with absolutely no idea what I'm doing.

Yep. This is going to be great.

***

The first hour alone in the apothecary passes in a blur of anxiety. I keep expecting something to explode, or for me to accidentally sell poison to someone instead of perfume.

Nothing about this shop makes sense. Dried herbs hang from the ceiling. Crystals seem to be sorted by function instead of color and I don't know what any of them are supposed to do. The tiny drawers have symbols on them instead of words. It's a nightmare.

And the shop won't stop making noise. Bottles randomly clink together, wind chimes move on their own, and I'm pretty sure that stuffed crow on the shelf just gave me the stink eye.

"It's not real," I mutter to myself. "Just a regular stuffed bird."

The crow blinks and I decide to ignore that corner of the shop entirely.

The bell above the door chimes. My heart leaps into my throat. Well, Hazel's throat. A middle-aged woman with silver hair pulled back into a ponytail steps inside. Greta Sanderson? She carries a small wicker basket of flowers.

"Good morning, Hazel," she says cheerfully. "I brought those moonflowers you asked for. Picked precisely between midnight and 1:00 AM, just like you asked."

I have no idea what moonflowers are or why they need to be picked at that specific time, but I nod and try to channel my inner Hazel.

"Great! Thanks." I try to make my face do some sort of bright, customer-servicey-like smile. My cheeks seize up like they want to file a complaint. Is this what being perky feels like? I feel like a total idiot.

Greta tilts her head. "Are you feeling alright, dear? You look constipated."

"Just a headache," I lie, taking the basket from her. "Too much, uh, magical stuff yesterday."

"A cleansing bath might help. Lavender, sea salt, and a pinch of rosemary." She points at a jar on the shelf. "That protection powder worked wonders for my garden, by the way. Not one rabbit's gotten through."

I nod again, not trusting myself to speak about products I know nothing about. Every second that passes, I'm more convinced she's going to figure out I'm not Hazel. What if she asks about the specific properties of moonflowers? What if I'm supposed to read her aura or bless her chakras or whatever the hell witches do with their regular customers?

My palms—Hazel's palms—begin to sweat.

"So that'll be the usual? Fifteen dollars for the moonflowers?" she asks.

Money. Right. I nod and fumble with the ancient cash register, pressing buttons randomly until the drawer springs open with a loud ding. I hand over a few bills, and the woman leaves, though not without giving me another curious glance.

"One down," I mutter. "How many more to go?"

The answer comes sooner than I expect. The bell jingles again, and this time a whirlwind of color and energy bursts through the door. A petite young woman with sun-kissed skin and wild black curls practically dances into the shop. She's a collision of patterns. Floral top, striped skirt, and dangly polka dot earrings all somehow working together.

"Haaaazel!" she sings, rushing toward the counter. "Buenos días, mami, ¿qué es la que?"

I freeze. Who the hell is this and what did she just say? She moves through the space like she owns it, so she's clearly no stranger here. The energy rolling off her makes my skin prickle. This feels like someone handed a lightning bolt a triple espresso and dared it to sit still. I don't know what to do. She scares me. Do I hug her? Shake hands? Hide behind the counter until she goes away?

"Um, hi." I do my best to channel Hazel's usual warmth while frantically searching for clues about who this hurricane of a person might be. She's kind of familiar. I must have seen her around Moonridge before. Hard to say, though. I don't get out much.

"¿Qué es la que?" she repeats.

I smile and shake my head.

"Oh, someone hasn't been practicing her Spanish. You said you wanted to learn. You can't learn without practice. Mi abuela always said—" She tilts her head, studying me with bright, curious eyes. "Something's wrong. You seem different today. More . . . rectangular. Your aura is completely off! It's all orange and wonky instead of its usual sparkly pink swirls!"

Great. The pinwheel in human form can see auras.

"I'm just having an off day," I say carefully.

"I brought you a surprise!" she continues, thrusting a plant pot toward me. Inside is what appears to be a normal cactus, except it appears to be . . . glowing?

"Is that . . . ?" I start, not sure how to finish the question.

"Mood de cactus." She waits, and I don't know how to respond. "A mood cactus! I enchanted it myself. When you're happy, it glows yellow. When you're sad, it turns blue. When you're angry, it glows red and shoots tiny spines at whoever pissed you off!" She beams proudly. "Isn't it amazing?"

The cactus pulses with an ominous red light. I duck because I don't know why it suddenly turned red and I don't feel like getting shot with cactus spikes. "That sounds . . . dangerous."

"Only a little! The spines aren't poisonous." She sets the plant on the counter. "Probably."

She turns and waves at the stuffed crow like it's a person. "Hello up there! I'm Coco. Oh, wait, you already know that." She turns back to me. "Sorry, I've been talking to all the shop guardians lately. They get lonely just sitting there all day."

The crow's a shop guardian? Is it actually alive?

"So, what are we brewing today?" Coco hops up on the counter. "Something dangerous? Something sparkly?"

"Actually, I was thinking of just restocking some basics," I hedge, hoping to avoid brewing anything.

"Boring!"

She swings her legs around and drops behind the counter. Before I know it, she's pulling jars from shelves. "Mrs. Parker told me this morning that her husband's snoring is on her last nerve. Let's make her an enchanted pillow that will drown out the sound!"

She grabs a bunch of herbs and starts grinding ingredients together with zero chill. I'm not even sure she knows what she's doing. She adds what looks like glitter to the mix. "Hand me that blue bottle with the silver stars!"

I reach for it but knock over three others in the process. One's full of purple, bubbling liquid. It tips onto the counter and starts sizzling right through the wood.

"Oops! Not that one!" Coco yelps. She dumps sand over the spill. The bubbling stops, but now there's a smiley-face-shaped hole at the edge of the counter. "That's weird. It usually makes heart shapes."

"Maybe we should—" I start, but Coco's already holding a glowing crystal over a pile of herbs. The air crackles with energy causing the hair to rise on my scalp. Is she about to summon a lightning bolt or something?

"Fire!" I yell as the herbs start to smoke.

"It's fine! That just means it's working!"

I collapse against the counter, breathing hard. How does Hazel manage this chaos every day?

The shop door bangs open, and La'Tasha strides in looking like a breath of fresh air. Her hair frames her face in dark curls, and she wears a bright, flowy, flowery dress. She takes one look at the mess and just sighs. She's obviously dealt with this a thousand times. She grabs a spray bottle from under the counter and spritzes the smoking herbs. The fire sputters out.

"Fire-suppressing rose water," she explains, giving me a pointed look. "Essential for days when Coco's here wreaking havoc."

"La'Tasha!" Coco bounces over to hug her. "How are you? We're making enchanted ear plugs!"

"I can see that." La'Tasha surveys the hole in the counter and the singed herbs. "Having fun, Blake?"

I give her a look that I hope conveys just how not fun this has been.

"Blake?" Coco tilts her head, confused.

"Figure of speech," La'Tasha says smoothly. "Hazel's just channeling her inner Blake today."

"Ohhh." Coco nods sagely. "That explains the square aura. You know, you should really try some cheese-flavored joy juice. I made a batch last night that will turn that frown upside down!" She reaches into her bag and pulls out a bottle of something neon orange that seems to be . . . giggling?

"No, thanks," I say, taking a step back.

La'Tasha steps in. "Coco, why don't you go check on the herb garden? I think the sunflowers need watering."

"But it rained last night."

"They're, uh, really thirsty flowers."

"Fair point!" Coco sets down the giggling potion and skips toward the back door. "Don't start any fun magic without me!"

As soon as she's gone, I collapse against the counter. "Who the hell is that?"

La'Tasha laughs, adjusting her glasses. "That's Coco Montoya. You've never met her?" La'Tasha starts cleaning up the mess with practiced efficiency. "Powerful witch, just needs focus."

I look at the hole in the counter, the singed herbs, and the still-giggling potion Coco left behind. "That was her being focused?"

"You should see her on a bad day." La'Tasha shrugs. "But hey. Her stuff works, even if her methods are a little chaotic."

I wipe the sweat from Hazel's brow. "How does Hazel work with her without losing her mind?"

"Hazel actually likes her energy. Says it balances her out."

"This is impossible. I can't pretend to be Hazel all day. Especially not with Hurricane Coco blowing through here."

"Well, you better figure it out," La'Tasha says, nodding toward the window. "Because your ten o'clock appointment just pulled up. She's got her white lady power suit on and everything. She looks ready for business."

I turn to see Bianca Mayweather stepping out of her pristine white SUV, a sleek briefcase in hand and a permanent smile drilled to her face.

My stomach sinks. Could this day get any worse?

Bianca glides into the store like she's the CEO of apothecaries. Her expensive perfume hits my borrowed nostrils before she's even fully through the door. It's floral with an undercurrent of something bitter. She sets her white leather briefcase on the counter with a precise click.

"Hazel, darling. So good to see you."

La'Tasha gives me a sympathetic look before slipping behind a shelf, pretending to reorganize jars while obviously eavesdropping. I don't blame her.

"Bianca," I manage, hoping I sound more like sunny Hazel and less like grumpy Blake. "You're very punctual."

"I believe that success is built on reliability." She opens her briefcase and begins to arrange her samples in a precise line across the counter. Look at her claiming the space like she already owns it.

"And speaking of success, I've brought the newest additions to my Celestial Wellness line. These are absolutely flying off the shelves with my other retailers."

I scrutinize the tiny bottles. They look like normal vitamins you can get at any drugstore. The only difference is that these have fancy labels with cosmic designs and names like "Starlight Serenity" and "Cosmic Cleanse."

"What do they do?" I ask, picking up an alleged vitamin-infused drink. The liquid inside shifts strangely. It kind of looks like a jellyfish in a bottle.

Bianca's smile never wavers. "That one is Lunar Lift. A proprietary blend of adaptogens and mood enhancers. It promotes energy without the crash of caffeine."

For someone who runs a construction company, I've sat through my fair share of sales pitches with vendors. I know exactly what she's trying to do.

"Sounds . . . interesting," I say noncommittally.

Bianca leans closer, invading Hazel's personal space. Her voice drops, low and hypnotic. "Change can be frightening, Hazel." She reaches out and touches my arm without permission. Her grip is firm, possessive even. "But I'm here to help you make the right choices."

I slowly wrench my arm out of her grip. "I'm just not sure it fits with what we sell here. The apothecary focuses on more traditional remedies."

"That's exactly why this partnership works!" Bianca steps back. She studies me. Her lips try to smile, but her eyes remain dark and vacant. "Your rustic approach paired with my modern wellness science? We'd own both markets. The old and the new. Tradition and innovation."

The way she says 'rustic' makes it sound like she's describing a backyard outhouse instead of a business.

"I don't know," I shift against the counter. "My customers expect certain things."

"Your customers expect results," Bianca counters smoothly. "And my products deliver. Take Cosmic Cleanse, for example." She holds up a bottle of pale blue liquid. "It detoxifies the body within twenty-four hours, removing impurities and leaving you feeling lighter, cleaner."

La'Tasha coughs behind her shelf. I know exactly what she's thinking. It's probably just a laxative with glitter in it.

"I appreciate the offer," I try again, "but I don't think—"

"I understand your hesitation," Bianca interrupts, her voice softening into velvet. "But this could be good for not only your business, but also for Moonridge. Think about what's happening right now. The tensions, the fears. There's a lot of darkness brewing around town and people need solutions they can trust to help get them through the sleepless nights."

"What do you mean?" If she knows something about what's happening with the amulet, maybe I can get her to slip up.

Bianca's eyes fix on mine, dark and sharp. For a moment, I swear they flash red. "The werewolf pack is unstable. You saw what happened in the park yesterday. People are afraid. They want protection."

"The pack isn't dangerous," I say automatically, then catch myself. Hazel wouldn't be quite so quick to jump to our defense. "I mean, they've never caused problems before."

"Until now. Which is why my Protective Aura supplements would be perfect for your customers." She pulls out another bottle, this one a deep purple. "Ancient wisdom enhanced by modern science. It creates a subtle energy field that discourages aggressive entities from approaching."

I stare at the bottle. "You're saying this will keep werewolves away?"

"I'm saying it offers peace of mind in uncertain times." Her eyes widen, doing their best to draw me in. I ain't buying it. "And as a valued member of the community, you should be offering every protection possible to your customers. Unless you have some reason for not wanting to protect them?" She pauses, studying my face. "I saw you with Blake yesterday. The two of you looked awfully cozy. I thought witches and werewolves hated one another."

"Hate is a strong word," I say. "We've known each other since we were kids. We've always been hot and cold with each other."

More cold than hot, but she doesn't need to know that.

"Are you really willing to put your customers' safety at risk over a little childhood crush?"

"I would hardly call it a crush." I look at her pointedly. Oh, to be in wolf form right now. I'd totally pee on her leg.

"These wolves are dangerous." She crosses her arms. "Something needs to be done, and you seem unwilling to acknowledge that."

The accusation hangs in the air between us. Heat flashes through me. This woman is talking shit about my pack to stoke fear, and I can't even defend them properly without blowing my cover.

"My customers and the other humans in Moonridge are perfectly safe." I do my best to keep Hazel's voice steady. "The werewolves have been part of this community since the beginning."

"Things change," Bianca says simply. "Allegiances shift. And smart businesswomen adapt."

She runs a perfectly manicured finger along the counter, stopping at the smiley-face left after Coco's potion disaster. "Speaking of adaptation, it seems your charming establishment could use some . . . modernization. New countertops? Better organization?" Her gaze sweeps over the cluttered shelves. "My pop-up display would actually improve the aesthetic in here."

I bristle at the criticism. Sure, the apothecary is chaotic, but it has character. It feels alive in a way Bianca's sterile wellness brand never could.

"I like it the way it is." I cross Hazel's arms over her chest. The movement reminds me again that I'm still braless. Great.

Bianca's smile tightens almost imperceptibly. "Sentimentality is charming, but not profitable. Let me be direct, Hazel. The town council meeting this evening will address the recent werewolf incidents. As a respectable business owner, you'll be expected to take a position."

"And?"

"I've got a lot of pull with the members of our little town. If you back my wellness line, people see you as someone who cares about the community. It makes your vote on the werewolves look a lot more credible, no matter which way you go. Don't you want to be seen as reliable? It might finally kill those 'bumbling witch' rumors everyone's always whispering."

I straighten Hazel's shoulders. "I'm not sure I understand what you're getting at."

Bianca's smile grows. She definitely smells blood in the water. "I'm simply pointing out mutual benefits. A small display of my products, a percentage of sales, and a strong ally on the council during these troubling times. It's completely reasonable."

I glance toward La'Tasha, who gives me a subtle head shake. She knows Hazel would never touch this deal. But I'm not Hazel. Bianca is connected to the amulet. I'd bet on it. Making an enemy out of her right now is just a bad move. I'm about to do something that'll probably get my ass kicked later. But I've got to try.

Keep your enemies close. Right?

"Fine. We can do a trial run," I say. "One small display. Two weeks. Then we talk again."

Bianca's eyes light up. "Wonderful! I knew you'd see reason. I'll have my assistant bring over the display this afternoon." She starts shoving samples back into her briefcase. "You've made a wise choice, Hazel. Together, we'll keep Moonridge safe. Think of the healing we'll bring to this community."

She hits those last few words a little too hard.

"Just so we're clear," I say, keeping Hazel's voice as level as I can, "I make my own decisions on the council. I'm not promising anything about the werewolf situation."

"Of course, dear." Bianca snaps her briefcase shut. "We all make our own choices. And we live with the consequences. I'll send someone over later with the stand."

She scurries out of the shop, leaving behind the lingering scent of her perfume, and I'm left with the distinct feeling of having been outmaneuvered.

The moment the door closes, I sink against the counter. "Shit."

La'Tasha emerges from behind the shelf, her expression

horrified. "Tell me you did not just agree to let that woman set up shop in here."

"It's just a small display." My voice lacks conviction. "A trial run."

"She's going to kill you." La'Tasha stops for a second. "Well, I guess if she kills you in her body, she's basically killing herself. So maybe not. But she's going to be pissed."

I sink onto a stool behind the counter, suddenly exhausted. "I didn't know what else to do. I didn't want to completely piss her off. There's something weird about her. Did you see how her eyes flashed when she was talking about protection? And why is she so hyper-focused on me and my pack?"

La'Tasha nods slowly. "Yeah, I caught that. And that perfume she wears? It's not just perfume. It's some kind of influence enhancer. Makes people more suggestible."

"Great. So I just got magically manipulated into a business deal."

"Looks like." La'Tasha pats my—Hazel's—shoulder sympathetically. "But hey, at least you made it through your first customer interactions without blowing up the shop. That's progress."

As if on cue, Coco bursts back in from the garden, trailing dirt and carrying some type of wriggling plant. "Hazel! I found a dancing dandelion! Can we use it in a potion? I'm thinking something that makes people float when they're happy!"

I drop my head into Hazel's hands with a groan. At this rate, I'll be lucky if there's a shop left for Hazel to come back to.

CHAPTER FIVE

Hazel

I'm drowning in smells. Blake's nose picks up everything. As soon as I step out of the truck, I'm assaulted with the sharp tang of fresh-cut lumber, the loamy smell of freshly dug earth, and the sweaty bodies of at least six different men. And weirdly, a ham sandwich that must be in someone's lunchbox at least fifty feet away.

Even the dirt has layers of scent. How does Blake function like this? It's like walking around with your nose directly connected to everyone's armpits.

I follow Calvin to a half-finished foundation wall. It's a mess of concrete and wooden beams, with what looks like the beginning of a house rising up from the dirt.

I stride over, shoulders back and chin up, making my steps confident and heavy to mimic Blake. Men nod respectfully at me. The deference in their nods catches me off guard. People rarely treat me like I'm important.

"So what's the problem?" I ask, trying to sound gruff and authoritative.

Calvin cocks an eyebrow. "The problem? The east wall is shifting. The soil underneath wasn't compacted properly, and now we're getting settlement issues."

I nod and paint a concerned look on my face to make it seem like I understood any of what he just said. "Right. Settlement. Bad."

"We need to shore up this section before we pour any more concrete." Calvin points at a hole that looks completely normal to me. "I was thinking we could add some helical piers, maybe three or four along this stretch."

Helical whatsies? I nod again. "Good plan."

"So you're okay with the expense?" Calvin asks. "It'll add about five thousand to the budget."

Shit. Money decisions. I have no idea what's reasonable for construction stuff. Five thousand sounds like a lot, but maybe it's pocket change in building-a-house terms?

"If that's what it takes to do it right," I say, trying to sound decisive.

Calvin slaps me on the back. "That's what I thought you'd say. Quality first."

"Let's get started then," I say, looking around at the worksite. "What do you need me to do?"

"Help me move these support beams into position. Then we'll get the jacks set up."

Calvin leads me to a pile of massive wooden beams that look impossibly heavy. He picks one up like it's nothing, muscles flexing under his T-shirt.

Oh crap. I'm supposed to do that too.

I bend down to grab a beam and brace for the strain. But when I lift, it comes up so easily I almost fling it over my shoulder. Whoa. Blake's body is strong. Like, *scary* strong.

Okay . . . that's kind of hot.

"Careful," Calvin cautions as I wobble, adjusting to the unexpected power in these arms.

For the next hour, I help move lumber, hold things in place, and pretend I know what's happening. It's like being a really strong, really confused assistant. I overcompensate for everything because I'm still not used to the power in these limbs. Calvin keeps giving me concerned looks when I accidentally bend a nail with my thumb or leave finger dents in a wooden beam. Still, my muscles move with practiced ease. Blake's body seems to know what to do even when I don't. His muscle memory does half the job.

But the smells and sounds are still a distracting issue. Every nail gun shot explodes in my ears. Every whiff of sweat or exhaust from the cement truck hits like a punch. How does he filter all this out?

"Yo, Blake! Heads up!"

I turn just in time to see Leo trip over nothing, fumbling with an armful of tools that go flying in every direction. A heavy wrench spins through the air directly toward my face. Without thinking, I snatch it one-handed, inches from my nose.

Leo's eyes widen. "Whoa. Nice catch."

I stare at the wrench. Talk about badass werewolf reflexes.

"Sorry about that," Leo says, gathering up the scattered tools. "You know me. Two left feet. Calvin's got me running supplies while Mason's out. Probably safer for everyone if I stay away from the actual building, right?"

He laughs.

I don't. A low growl vibrates deep in Blake's chest. My lips pull back, and I notice that my teeth are way sharper than they were a minute ago. Every instinct screams at me to put him in his place, and for one genuinely terrible second, I'm not the one driving this body.

Leo freezes. The smile drops from his lips. "Blake?"

I clamp my mouth shut. What the hell was that?

"Sorry," I grunt. My voice sounds like gravel. "Just, be more careful."

Leo's already backing away. "Yeah, totally. My bad."

I turn away, heart pounding. My hands—Blake's hands—won't stop shaking. Where the hell did that come from? What other instincts are going to take over without warning? For a split second, I lost control. The wolf owned me. And it wanted to dominate. Is this a normal everyday thing? Or is it the effects of the amulet?

Calvin appears beside me. "What the hell was that?"

"What?" I try to sound innocent.

"You nearly wolfed out on Leo. Over a dropped wrench?" Calvin pulls me away from the others, behind a stack of lumber where we can't be overheard. "What's going on with you? And don't bullshit me."

I swallow hard and spit out the first lie that enters my head. "Just stressed about the pack stuff."

Calvin's eyes narrow. "We've got that under control. We'll go to the council and speak our piece and it'll be good. And I don't think you're telling me the whole story."

I feel threatened, and that makes me feel like I need to pee. "That's it. I swear."

"No, it's not. You smell different."

Shit. He can tell that it's me just by scent? Stupid magical nose powers.

"Different how?" I fight to keep panic from my voice.

He leans closer, sniffing subtly. "Like Hazel Thornton."

My heart skips. "I was just in her shop. Makes sense her scent would be on me."

"*On* you, sure. Not coming *from* you. It's like you bathed in vanilla and lavender." Calvin crosses his arms. "What's going on between you two? You were with her last night at the park, and then you left with her. Now you're acting . . . Wait, did you two . . . ? Are you . . . ?"

I force a laugh. "Nothing's going on. I was helping her out with a plumbing issue. That's it. I'm acting weird because I'm just dealing with a lot right now."

"Is it the full moon making you freak out? It's still four days away, but . . ."

Thank you, werewolf biology, for giving me an excuse! "Yeah, maybe that's it. Making my wolf side more touchy."

Calvin studies me for a long moment. I do my best to look casually broody and wolfish instead of panicked and witchy.

"Maybe you should take it easy," he finally says. "We can handle things here. Go home. Get some rest."

"Yeah. Good idea. Sorry about Leo."

"Just make sure you apologize to him. Kid looks up to you, you know."

Great, now I feel guilty for something Blake's body did automatically. "I will."

As I turn to leave, Calvin adds, "And Blake? Whatever's going on with you and the witch . . . be careful. Things are tense enough in town right now."

If only he knew how tense things really are. I wave and head toward Blake's truck, trying to wrap my head around what just happened. That growl, that flash of aggression . . . it was primal and powerful and scary. Is that what Blake deals with all the time? A wolf always lurking under his skin, ready to take over when provoked?

No wonder he's so controlled, so careful. He has to be.

Maybe Blake Carter isn't just a grumpy werewolf. Maybe he's a werewolf working really, really hard not to be dangerous.

And I've been judging him for it all this time.

I keep thinking back to what I did to Leo. He could have been hurt.

Leo's by far my favorite of the werewolf pack. He's never without that goofy smile or some terrible joke. And he's defi-nitely easy on the eyes. He's tall and lean, with tawny skin and long, wavy hair he always keeps in a top-knot. After my grandma died, he showed up at the shop every single day for a week with donuts. Sweet, harmless Leo.

And I almost tore his ass up.

***

I drag Blake's exhausted body through the apothecary door. The little bell jingles like it's laughing at me. Every muscle aches in ways I never knew possible. Who knew werewolves could get sore? Blake's body is strong, sure, but it still burns after hours of hauling lumber. My brain feels raw, too. There are too many smells and too many sounds. Being Blake Carter is a full-contact sport, and I'm losing.

"Oh good, you're back." My own voice hits me from behind the counter. Blake looks trashed. He's got my hair pulled back in a tight ponytail. Something I'd never do. It's way too tight and makes my ears look huge. "How was the job? Anything still standing?"

"Barely," I drop onto a stool. "Your brother thinks you're going moon-crazy because I nearly wolfed out on Leo for dropping a wrench."

Blake sits up straighter, one eyebrow cocked. "What do you mean 'wolfed out'?"

"I growled at him. Like, for real, extra-scary growling. With teeth." I scratch at the beard I suddenly own. "It just happened! He was being clumsy, and I just completely lost my shit."

Blake sighs. "That's the protective instinct. It kicks in when pack members are in danger. Even from themselves."

"Well, it's exhausting." I look around the shop. It's weirdly organized. The counter's neat, and the products are all lined up. Even the herbs seem to have a system. "What happened in here? Did a cleaning fairy go nuts?"

Blake looks almost proud. "I had some time between customers. Thought I'd straighten up a bit."

"You reorganized my entire shop?" Emotions war in my chest.

"It can't be reorganized when it wasn't organized to begin with," he counters. "How do you find anything in this chaos? I couldn't even locate basic ingredients without searching through seventeen different drawers."

"How did you even know how to organize things? You know nothing about magic." I want to be more pissed about this than I am.

"Coco was here today. I had to make her focus on something so she didn't burn the shop down. We did it together."

I sigh. This is *my* space, *my* carefully curated chaos. And he fucked it up. But as I look around, I have to admit . . . it actually looks good. The herb bundles are arranged by magical properties instead of alphabetically, which, honestly, makes more sense. The crystals are grouped by their metaphysical properties rather than just by color. Even the potion bottles are organized by potency and purpose.

"You put the protection sachets next to the cleansing herbs," I say with grudging approval.

"They're used together most often," Blake says defensively. "Made sense to keep them close."

Damn it. He's right. I've been reaching across three different shelves every time Mrs. Robertson comes in for her monthly spiritual cleanse.

"And you moved the moon water to the temperature-controlled cabinet," I add, hating how impressed I sound.

"It was sitting in direct sunlight. That stuff's supposed to be stored in cool, dark places, right? Keeping it in the dark will up its shelf life."

I've been meaning to move it for months, but kept forgetting. I hate that he did it before I could. I walk over to the herb wall, running my fingers along the newly organized bundles. I search for my usual protection spell ingredients, expecting to catch a misstep, or a missing ingredient, but nope. Chamomile, sage, and protective stones are all right here, within arm's reach.

"How did you know to group these together?" I ask, moving to the herb wall.

I grab for rose petals and find them next to the cinnamon and vanilla. Everything I need for love magic in one spot. When I turn toward the dangerous ingredients, they're gone from their usual scattered locations.

"Where did you put the mercury and nightshade?"

Blake points behind the counter. "Locked cabinet. Now they're Coco-proof."

I open the cabinet and find everything organized by potency level, with the most dangerous items in a separate, warded box. My mouth falls open.

"I hate that this is better," I mutter, part irritated, part amazed.

I catch him smiling. It's a small, pleased expression that looks foreign on my usually animated features. "You have good instincts for magical organization. Your system just needed some . . . refinement."

"Don't get smug about it," I warn. "This is still my shop."

"I know. I just . . ." He gestures around the room. "I couldn't work in the chaos. Everything kept shifting. I'd put something down and it'd be gone two minutes later. Coco said it was because they 'wanted to be with their friends', whatever that means, and then she explained how things should be stored with elements that complement them, so we did it, and then everything stopped shifting. Except for that crow. It definitely relocated itself at least twice."

I laugh. "The crow does that. It's protective magic. It moves to wherever it thinks danger might come from."

"So it's alive?"

"Enchanted," I correct. "There's a difference. Mostly."

Blake shudders. "Your world is weird."

"Coming from the guy whose body tried to maul a friend over a dropped wrench? That's rich."

We share a look. Part exasperation, part understanding. Maybe our worlds aren't so different. Just different kinds of complicated.

I'm about to admit that maybe his organization system isn't entirely terrible when I spot something that makes my head want to explode. Next to the front counter sits a large, sleek display stand with mint-colored bottles plastered with cosmic-themed labels.

Bianca's products.

How did I not see that when I walked in?

"What. Is. That." Each word comes out like a separate sentence.

Blake follows my gaze, and my face turns sheepish. "About that. Bianca came by for your meeting. I might have agreed to a small trial of her products. Just for two weeks!"

Blake's body temperature rises. "You let that woman put her magic laxatives in my shop? After I've been fighting her off for months?"

"I didn't know what else to do!" Blake throws my hands up in exasperation. "She kept pushing, and I was trying to act like you. I thought you might say yes to keep the peace."

"When have I ever kept the peace? You said yourself that I'm a hyper-emotional threat to society." I stomp toward the display, hands clenched. "I can't believe you did this."

"Well, I can't believe you nearly wolfed out on Leo! Do you know how long I've worked to control those instincts?" Blake fires back. "If my pack stops trusting me because you can't handle basic werewolf control—"

"Oh, and you're handling witch life so well? Did you or did you not completely change the layout of my store without asking AND let a pushy MLM boss set up shop here?"

We glare at each other. It's bizarre staring into my own angry face, seeing my green eyes flash with someone else's frustration.

Blake breaks first, my shoulders dropping. "Being you is

impossible. Everything in this shop seems to have a mind of its own. Coco nearly burned the place down while making some enchanted pillow thing. Every customer wants something different. Today, Mrs. Fernsby wanted a potion that would let her experience her cat's dreams. And then some teenager wanted acne cream that would make her 'glow from within,' and a man asked if I had anything for 'bedroom stamina' with a wink. A wink! That's going to haunt me forever."

A laugh escapes me, deep and rumbling. "Welcome to my life."

"It's not just retail. It's magical retail. Everything's alive or dangerous or both." He gestures around helplessly. "How do you do this every day without losing your mind?"

The lost and frustrated tone of his voice brings me down a notch. "The same way you handle having super-strength and enhanced senses that never shut off, I guess. You just do."

We fall silent, a new understanding hovering between us.

"I almost broke a support beam today," I admit. "I forget how strong you are. And the smells! My God, the smells. How do you function when you can literally sense what everyone had for breakfast?"

"Years of practice," Blake says. "I've spent my whole life learning to filter it out, and keep the wolf in check."

"When it almost took over today?" I say quietly. "It was really scary."

He nods. "That's my daily reality. One slip, one moment of lost control, and people look at you like you're a monster. Which is why we need to get this amulet locked down before it makes things worse. If the entire pack gets aggressive, it could get really bad really quickly. I don't want anyone to get hurt."

I've never thought about it that way. I've always seen Blake as uptight, rigid, unnecessarily stern. But maybe that control isn't a personality flaw. It's survival.

"Being in your skin is hard," I admit. "Maybe I've been

judging you too harshly."

Blake looks surprised at the concession. "Being you isn't exactly a walk in the park either. You juggle so many elements, so many people and their needs. It's impressive."

We both collapse against the counter, equally exhausted.

I gesture toward Bianca's display. "What the fuck am I going to do about that?"

"I'm sorry. I should have found a way to say no."

An idea forms as I study the display. "Actually, maybe this isn't so bad."

"How so?" Blake looks confused.

"If she's connected to the amulet somehow—and I think she is—having her come around more often could be useful. We can watch her. See if she gives anything away."

Blake makes my eyebrows rise. "To be honest, that was exactly what I thought."

"So we're on the same page?"

The door bursts open, bell jingling. La'Tasha rushes in looking like she's about to burst.

"You're not going to believe this." She slaps a folder down on the counter and pulls out an old newspaper page, all yellowed and sealed in plastic. "I was digging through the library archives for anything on the Wolfsbane Amulet. I found this."

I lean in, and my breath catches. It's a grainy black-and-white photo from the Moonridge Gazette. It's from seventy years ago. The headline reads:

Local Witches Celebrate Harvest Moon

But it's the people in the photo that catch my eye. Two women stand side by side. One is unmistakably my grandmother Agnes. She's much younger, but I'd recognize those playful eyes and that determined set to her jaw anywhere. Beside her is a woman who looks eerily familiar. She has sharp, hawkish features and a smile that's all teeth and no warmth.

"Is that . . . ?" I can't even get the words out.

"Bianca," Blake confirms, leaning closer. "But the caption says . . ."

La'Tasha points to the text beneath the photo. "'Agnes Thornton and Ravena Blackwood prepare for the annual harvest festival.'"

"Ravena Blackwood?" I repeat. The name sparks a memory. "Grandma used to mention a Ravena. She said she was brilliant but dangerous. She left Moonridge after some kind of falling out."

"Left, or was kicked out?" Blake questions.

"I don't know. Grandma didn't talk about her much." I stare at the photo, at the woman who is undeniably Bianca Mayweather. "But if Bianca is actually Ravena . . ."

"Then she's a witch," La'Tasha finishes. "Possibly an immortal witch who's been hiding her identity, pretending to be human, and stirring up anti-werewolf shit all over town."

"While trying to weasel her way into my shop. Where the amulet happens to be buried."

Blake and I share a look. This isn't just about our body swap anymore. Something bigger is at play.

Blake taps the photo. "I have no doubt that she's behind this. We need to find out why and what she's planning."

I nod, surprised by how right it feels to be aligned with him instead of against him. "And figure out what her connection to my grandmother means."

"And how to get you back into your own bodies," La'Tasha reminds us. "Because no offense, but you two as each other is getting on my nerves."

She's right, but weirdly, being Blake doesn't feel quite as impossible as it did this morning. Don't get me wrong. I want my body back immediately. But after today, I think I understand the werewolf a little better.

And judging by the thoughtful look on my face across the counter, maybe he's starting to understand me, too.

CHAPTER SIX

Hazel

Town Hall smells like armpits and bad news. I swear every soul in Moonridge jammed their way through these doors tonight, and the ones who couldn't squeeze into seats are huddled along the back wall like pissed off sardines. A large guy toward the end cracks his knuckles and then crosses his arms. He's looking right at me. Was that a threat? Did I take a wrong turn and end up at the fight club instead of the town hall meeting?

I push through the crowd with Blake's wide-ass shoulders. People step aside and nod at me. It's kind of disorienting. Do they respect me? Well, not me. Blake. No one has ever respected me, and I'm pretty sure it all started that day in fourth grade when Mrs. Jenkins refused to let us have recess because Billy Porter got diarrhea and pooped on the slide, and then I turned her hair bright blue to impress the other kids.

Blake's nose is doing its usual thing where it picks up every scent in the room. Someone needs to wash their butt. Badly. Seriously, how do I turn this thing off? The combination of armpits, freshly eaten dinners and sweaty booty makes me want to barf.

I grab a seat in the back and glance down at my phone. Blake should be here tonight, but he texted saying there was an emergency at the apothecary shop. Apparently, Coco dug up some kind of plant and enchanted it to give hugs to anyone who needs them. It wrapped itself around a customer and they can't get it off. Not exactly what we need right now. I make a mental note to rein her in.

The council table is packed with familiar faces. Mayor Peterson's toupee is crooked as always. Dude needs some better glue. Mrs. Henderson hasn't stopped knitting since she sat down, and Melanie Perkins and Dr. Whitman just walked in together. Um, why do they look suspicious? Are they hooking up? Oh-em-gee! I have to tell La'Tasha about this.

My own chair is empty (probably for the best). There's no way Blake could sit up there and convincingly play me without someone noticing he's a six-foot-something werewolf trapped in my sundress.

And then there's Bianca. Front row, all white, completely unbothered. Ravena Blackwood dressed up in a wellness brand eager to fuck shit up. I want to stand up and out her right now, but I've got nothing more than an old photograph and a hunch to back me up. The pack is already being treated like they're trying to give everyone in town rabies. Throwing accusations while in Blake's form would just make it worse for them.

The mayor taps his gavel. "This emergency meeting of the Moonridge Town Council will now come to order."

The room settles.

"We've had several incidents over the last three weeks involving members of the local werewolf pack. Yesterday's situation in the park raises serious safety concerns."

Across the room, Calvin's jaw is set, but that's the only tell that he's bothered. He doesn't move. Doesn't react.

Sheriff Harlow leans forward. "We need to address this before someone gets hurt. Parents are calling my office non-stop. They're afraid to let their kids outside."

The mayor nods gravely. "We've always prided ourselves on peaceful coexistence in Moonridge. But something has changed."

"If I may, Mayor Peterson?" Bianca/Ravena raises one perfectly manicured hand. When he nods, she stands, smoothing her white skirt. "I think we need to look at every possible cause. This aggression? It's not typical werewolf behavior."

If I didn't know better, I'd think she actually gave a damn.

"What are you suggesting, Ms. Mayweather?" Mrs. Henderson's knitting needles pause mid-stitch.

Ravena wrinkles her nose like she's about to deliver sad news. "I hate to cast unwarranted blame. But has anyone considered magical interference? Werewolves are particularly susceptible to certain forms of witchcraft, and we'd be remiss not to at least ask the question."

This bitch! She's blaming the witches. After I—okay, Blake— let her set up a product display in *my* shop, gave her a foothold in *my* space, she's standing in front of this entire town and pointing the finger in my direction now.

The room fills with whispered agreements.

"Now hold on," calls out Jim Rodriguez from the back. "The witches have been part of this community for decades. Just as long as the wolves. They've gotten us through some very difficult times."

"Things were different in the past," Mrs. Block counters. "These young witches today, they're experimenting with things they don't understand. They're too careless. My dog turned purple after that Coco girl walked by with one of her potions!"

"Purple puppies sound lovely," Mrs. Henderson mutters, not even looking up from her knitting.

"I will admit," Mr. Garcia, who owns the hardware store, interrupts, "strange things have been happening. And they all seem to center around the apothecary."

"Or around the full moon," Calvin says, standing up. "Which

affects werewolves naturally. This will pass. It always does. We have a couple of newer wolves in the pack and the first few shifts are always tough for them. We don't need magical interference to explain normal pack behavior. Seriously. We have this under control."

"Normal pack behavior?" Mrs. McCready's voice could curdle milk. "Was it normal for that boy to nearly attack a mother and her child?"

Calvin's jaw tightens. "Mason is nineteen and still learning control. Like I said."

"And that's a serious accusation against the witches." Sheriff Harlow frowns at Ravena, which makes me feel like I at least have him on our side.

"I'm not accusing anyone specifically." Ravena's tone stays gentle, which is somehow worse than if she'd just come out swinging. "But we do have a thriving community of younger witches in Moonridge, and perhaps someone is experimenting with spells that are producing unintended consequences. As Mrs. Block pointed out, this new generation doesn't always seem to have the same level of discipline as those who came before them."

She lets that little poisonous tidbit hang there, and half the room nods along like she just spit gospel.

Mr. Garcia stands up. "My nephew saw Hazel Thornton arguing with Blake Carter the day before the first incident. Said there were sparks flying between them. Actual sparks! And remember the marshmallow debacle from a few weeks ago?"

"That we stopped—" I catch myself half a second too late.

Heads turn.

"Blake." The mayor looks genuinely surprised. "Would you care to address Mr. Garcia's statement?"

Every person in the room is looking at me. I clear my throat and try to remember how Blake holds his jaw when he's being authoritative. "Hazel and I were dealing with a plumbing issue at her shop. Any sparks came from the pipes. And from what I understand, the marshmallow situation had outside causes. The witches handled it."

I think that landed okay.

"Interesting." Ravena tilts her head with the slow patience of someone who is always three steps ahead. "I'd like to note that young Mason was seen near the apothecary shortly before his episode. Perhaps something there triggered him?"

I open my mouth.

"My son saw Blake Carter leaving that shop yesterday looking completely out of it!" Mrs. Simpson, PTA president, is already on her feet like she's been waiting her whole life for this moment. "What if she's enchanted him?"

The room picks that up and runs with it.

"The pack's never been unstable before!"

"What's she brewing in that shop?"

"I knew they shouldn't have made her Virtus Suprema!"

"She made my underwear give me wedgies!"

That voice. I'd know that whining tone anywhere.

I search the crowd and find him. Evan. Sitting with Missy Lawrence, her hand resting possessively on his arm. They look comfortable together. Settled. Like they've been a couple for months instead of weeks.

I wait for the stab of jealousy. The familiar ache of loss that has haunted me for the last few weeks. Instead, there's just complete indifference. I'm literally unbothered. When did that happen? Just twenty-four hours ago, I was obsessing over him and thought my life wouldn't go on. Is it because I'm in Blake's body? Am I reacting in a way that he would? When we switch back, will I start obsessing again?

The mayor bangs his gavel repeatedly. "Order! We will have order!"

When the noise dies down, Sheriff Harlow speaks. "Blake, the issues are with your pack. As Alpha, do you want to address any of these concerns?"

The question catches me off guard and my tongue becomes dead weight. How do I answer that? *I'm actually Hazel trapped in Blake's body because of ancient magic caused by a whacked out amulet.* I'd be carted off to the werewolf loony bin.

"Uh. No. Nothing to add," I say stiffly. "I agree with what Calvin said . . . about the pack."

Bianca watches me with calculating eyes. "Perhaps we should consider a temporary restriction. For safety's sake."

"What kind of restriction?" Calvin demands.

"A pause on magical activities," Bianca suggests smoothly. "Just until we determine what's causing these incidents. Purely precautionary."

"You can't just ban magic! That's not how this works!" I blurt out, forgetting, once again, that I'm supposed to be Blake.

Everyone stares at me. Oops.

"Since when are you pro-magic?" Sheriff Harlow asks suspiciously. "If I remember correctly, you started a petition a couple of years ago to declare a set number of days each month as 'magic-free' days."

He what?

I backpedal quickly. "I'm not . . . I didn't say I was pro-magic. I just meant . . . you can't just ban something like that."

Calvin gives me a look that clearly says *What the hell?*

Mayor Peterson clears his throat. It sounds like he's gargling boulders. "It's not a total ban on magic. Just a pause. A breather until we get a handle on things. Any protective wards need to stay up, obviously."

"I think that's reasonable." A smug twitch hits the corner of Ravena's mouth. "I'm sure Miss Thornton would agree to this small sacrifice for the greater good. Where is she, by the way? I'd have thought she'd be here. She is Virtus Suprema. Isn't she supposed to attend these meetings?"

The heavy door at the back thuds open. Blake staggers in looking frazzled. One side of my hair is totally bird-nested, and there's a smudge of something purple on my cheek.

"Sorry I'm late." The voice is too gruff to sound like me. He's annoyed. Magical retail is clearly eating him alive. "What'd I miss?"

The timing couldn't be worse. Everyone turns to stare at my body, now inhabited by a very uncomfortable werewolf. I look a whole-ass mess. Great job, buddy. Really selling the 'powerful witch' vibe.

"Miss Thornton," the mayor says, "we're just talking about a temporary hold on new spellwork. You know. Given recent events."

Blake's gaze finds mine across the room. I try to send a "keep your mouth shut" look, but it doesn't land.

"What does spellwork have to do with recent events? And what recent events?" He cocks a hip and crosses his arms. We need to work on his body language if he has to pass as me for much longer.

"The werewolf incidents," Mrs. Henderson explains. "There's concern that magical interference might be at play."

"That's stupid." He places his hands—my hands—on his hips. "Hazel—I mean, I— or the other witches, would never do anything to harm the pack. Or anyone else. We aren't the problem."

"No one's saying you are," Ravena says, her voice the kind of smooth that makes you want to agree with things before you've thought them through. "But for everyone's peace of mind, we're proposing a pause on new magic. That's not too much to ask. Right?"

Blake starts to snap back. I'm already on my feet.

"As the pack rep, I'm behind this." I cut across him before he can make it worse. "It's a smart move. I'm sure Hazel gets it."

Blake looks at me like I just asked if I could wax his ass.

The vote is a landslide. Calvin votes no as does Mrs. Henderson, for some reason. Everyone else is too spooked to think straight, and Ravena is watching it all happen with the patient expression of someone who already knew how it would all play out.

"It's settled." Mayor Peterson taps the gavel. "No new spell-work in Moonridge for two weeks. Meeting adjourned."

I push through the chairs to get to Blake, then grab my own arm to steer him into the corner before he says something I can't fix later.

"What the hell?" he hisses in my voice. "You just let them ban your magic!"

"Shh!" I glance around nervously. "They didn't ban *my* magic. They banned *new* spells. We can find a loophole."

"It's still wrong. You're letting them pin this on the witches when it's her."

I push down the arm he's pointing in Ravena's direction.

"We don't have enough proof. And you're being an ass." I step closer, Blake's height finally giving me the advantage in an argument. "We have to strategize."

He's clearly frustrated. "Strategy or not, it feels like giving up."

I lean forward "Don't you see? Someone wants us to fight. They're spreading rumors, turning the town against witches and wolves to cause a diversion. To pull us further apart. They expected us to fight back and make a scene tonight. It would've given them an excuse to crack down even harder."

Blake's anger fades. I see the understanding hit.

"And we both know who's behind it."

We look across the room where Ravena stands, accepting congratulations from concerned citizens, a smile of satisfaction playing on her perfect, blood-red lips.

Blake nods. "You're right. Fighting each other is exactly what she wants."

"And we need to figure out why before things get worse."

"So what's our next move?"

"We lay low, play along, and dig up dirt on our witch in white. We need to prove she activated the amulet and then find out why. And we need to stop it before the next full moon. That's when energy is at its highest, and a lot of witches use that time of the month to perform major rituals."

And if we don't stop her, I'm not sure Moonridge will survive what comes next.

***

"This is a fucking disaster."

Blake is still pissed.

I pace the back room, every step pulling a creak out of the floorboards, and try to organize my thoughts into something that isn't just pure panic. "The whole room was eating out of Bianca's hand. She walked in there knowing exactly how it would go, and we showed up with nothing. We need to get ahead of her before she makes her next move."

La'Tasha sits cross-legged on a cushion, scrolling through her phone. "At least they didn't vote to run you out of town with pitchforks. Progress, amiright?"

Blake leans against the workbench, arms crossed over my chest. He's not handling having boobs very well. He keeps accidentally squishing them. "We should've just dumped the photo on the table. Called her out right then."

"And said what?" I stop. "Hey, neighbors, Bianca is actually a ninety-year-old witch named Ravena who's apparently figured out how to opt out of aging? That would've landed great."

"Better than letting her strangle your magic one ordinance at a time!" Blake argues. "I can only imagine what she'll cook up next."

"They didn't kill her magic," La'Tasha points out, not looking up from her phone. "And they only banned *new* spells. And it's only for two weeks."

"Two weeks is all she needs to cause serious damage." Blake's still pissed that I let them do this. "The full moon is in a few days. If the amulet keeps affecting werewolves . . ."

He doesn't need to finish the sentence. We all know what happens when werewolves lose control.

La'Tasha looks up from her phone and smirks. "Maybe this will make you feel better. They only banned Hazel from doing magic. They didn't say anything about me or Coco."

Blake and I both turn to stare at her.

"What? I'm just saying." She lifts her phone. "The official proclamation that was just posted online specifically says *Hazel Thornton* is banned from using any new magic. *I'm* not Hazel Thornton."

A grin tugs at the corner of my mouth. "That's true. And physically speaking, neither am I."

"Don't," Blake warns. "The plan was to lay low, not find technicalities."

"Whatever." The word comes out as a low growl from somewhere in his chest. "But she's right. The order's specific. If Tash can still work, we won't lose ground."

"Yeah, if I don't go blind first." La'Tasha looks like she lost a fight with the library. "While you two were playing politics, I was doing the actual work. Do you know how hard it is to find someone who's been deliberately scrubbed from public record?"

She spins the laptop around. It's full of wall-to-wall browser tabs. "I searched 'Ravena Blackwood' in the town archives first. Nothing. Then just 'Blackwood,' which turned up a property deed from 1962. A house on Elm Street." She pauses. "It just so happens to be the same house Bianca is renting right now."

"Convenient," Blake mutters.

"Right? So I cross-referenced the address with old phone books and census records. Most of it's been digitized, but there are holes in the timeline that don't feel accidental, like someone went through with a very targeted delete button. Took me three hours of digging through archives nobody has touched since the nineties, but I finally found this."

The laptop slides across the table toward me. On the screen is a grainy newspaper scan, nearly seventy years old.

Local Witch Banished from Moonridge.

"But check this shit out." She leans over and clicks another tab. Same headline, completely different text underneath. Then another. "Three versions. Same heading, different story."

Blake squints at the screen. "They don't match."

"Exactly. Someone has been editing the record." She clicks through the versions. "The first one has details about what she was trying to do. The second is deliberately vague and the third never mentions her at all."

I point to a line in the original article. "'Attempting to harness lunar energy for the purpose of binding supernatural entities to her will.' And look at this. The ritual was supposed to take place at the site of an ancient artifact buried beneath the old trading post.'"

"The trading post that used to be where the apothecary is now," Blake says grimly.

"Exactly. She wasn't just kicked out for no reason. She was trying to use the Wolfsbane Amulet, and your grandma stopped her."

"But why the exile?"

"The article's vague on the specifics. Whatever she was up to, the Regency decided it was dangerous enough to kick her out for good. And your grandma's the one who sealed the deal."

Blake reads over my shoulder. His breath—my breath—is warm against my ear. "It says Agnes Thornton's the one who found her out. She's the one who exposed the whole plan."

Unease prickles up my borrowed spine. "She's been planning revenge this whole time. That's why she's been so hellbent on setting up shop here."

"But why now?" La'Tasha asks. "Your grandmother's been gone for five years."

I think about the amulet pulsing beneath the floorboards. "Because she needed something that was here. Something that could hurt both witches and werewolves."

"The Wolfsbane Amulet," Blake says grimly. "She's using it to make the pack look dangerous, turning the town against us. And now she's limiting the only people who might be able to stop her. Witches."

"It's basically a supernatural divide-and-conquer strategy," La'Tasha agrees. "Get the two most powerful groups in Moonridge fighting each other, then swoop in to . . . what exactly?"

"Revenge?" I suggest. "Finish what she started nearly sixty years ago? Maybe both?"

Blake pushes away from the workbench, pacing now. It's weird watching my body move with his stiff, militaristic stride. "We need to contain that amulet before the full moon. If it keeps amping up werewolf aggression, someone will get hurt."

"Or worse," I add quietly.

I notice Blake adjusting a crooked picture frame then straightening the throw pillows on my reading chair to keep himself occupied. What's he thinking?

La'Tasha flips open one of her grandmother's old spell books, pages crackling with age. "I think I found something that might work." She points to a hand-drawn diagram of intersecting circles. "A binding spell designed specifically for ancient artifacts."

I peer at the faded ink. "What does it need?"

She runs her finger down a list written in the margin. "Salt for purification, silver for containment, and . . ." She squints at the writing. "Moonstone charged under a waxing moon. When's the last time you charged your moonstone?"

Blake looks confused. "You charge rocks?"

"Crystals," I correct automatically. "And I charged them a week ago."

La'Tasha nods, making notes. "Then we have everything we need."

She continues outlining the spell components, but I find myself distracted by Blake. He's absently braiding a small section of my hair while he listens. It's such a gentle, unexpected gesture from someone I've always seen as harsh and unyielding.

"What?" he asks, catching me watching him.

"Nothing." I look away and smile. "Actually . . . you're braiding my hair."

He looks down at his hands—my hands—as if surprised to find them working on their own. The half-finished braid lies against my shoulder, intricate and careful. "Force of habit. I used to braid my little cousin's hair when she visited."

"You did?" I can't form the image in my head. Blake, comforting a little girl? Something warm unfurls in my chest at the thought. It doesn't track against the Blake who tormented me when I was a little girl.

"She lost her parents young." His voice—my voice—goes soft. "Hair brushing calmed her down when she had nightmares. Made her feel safe."

I smile, suddenly seeing him in a new light.

Our eyes meet across the room. The silence stretches until Blake clears my throat and drops his hands.

"I'm sorry." He quickly steps back. "I shouldn't mess with your body without asking."

"No, it's . . ." I'm not sure what to say. That it's okay? That I'm seeing layers to him that I never noticed before? That maybe there's more to Blake Carter than the rigid pack leader? "It's fine."

The moment shatters with the explosive sound of breaking glass from the front of the shop. We all freeze for half a second, then leap into action. Blake is first through the door. I'm right behind him, with La'Tasha at my heels.

The front window of the apothecary is shattered. Glass glitters across the wooden floor like little diamonds. Cold night air rushes in through the jagged hole causing the hanging herbs to sway and the wind chime to tinkle.

In the middle of the glass is a brick. It's old, edges worn to a dusty red.

"Stay back." Blake grabs the broom and sweeps a path through the shards, then crouches next to the brick. There's a folded piece of paper underneath it. He picks it up, and I watch my own hand shake a little as he opens it.

"What does it say?" La'Tasha's voice has gone tight.

Blake turns the paper around so we can see it.

Leave Moonridge or suffer.

I take the note with unsteady hands. The letters are neat and written in dark ink.

Blake moves to the broken window, scanning the dark street. "I don't see anyone. Whoever it was got away quick."

La'Tasha backs away from the window. "This isn't some random drunk with a brick. This is personal."

I look around my shop. Glass lies scattered across the floor and cold air rushes through the jagged hole where my window used to be. The herb bundles swing in the breeze like wind chimes. My sanctuary. Violated.

"Any bets it was Ravena?" Blake says with certainty, but his eyes continue to scan the darkness outside, every instinct alert.

"Or someone working for her." La'Tasha peers out through the broken window. "They could still be out there."

Blake's werewolf instincts take over. I move to the door, double-check that it's locked, and then check the rest of the windows. "This is my home." My voice—Blake's voice—comes out rougher than intended. "I was raised here, and I'm not leaving because some witch with a grudge throws a tantrum."

"Neither am I," Blake agrees, grabbing a large piece of cardboard and some duct tape to cover the hole. "My pack has been here for generations. This is our territory."

After he's covered the broken glass, he takes my hand—well, his hand—and squeezes. His thumb brushes over my knuckles, a gesture so unconscious I don't think he realizes he's doing it.

Warmth spreads through me. It feels right.

"Look. We're in this together," he says quietly.

"I know." When did Blake Carter become someone I could depend on? "But we kind of have to be. We're literally wearing each other's bodies."

"Anyway," Tash says, breaking the quiet with a tired half-smile. "I'm going to go mix up that containment spell. Because crazy, brick-throwing witches don't exactly wait for a formal invite."

I nod. I'm still holding Blake's hand. I drop it and walk over, collapsing into my favorite chair. It's not nearly as cozy in his body.

"You scared?" Blake asks.

I consider lying. I could put on a brave face and pretend that I've got this. Just one more fucked up hurdle life likes to throw at me. But after everything we've been through, pretending feels pointless. "Terrified," I admit. "You?"

"A little." He moves closer. Even though he's in my body, he still feels solid. Like a wall between me and the rest of the world. "But I'm not running. This is our town."

Our town. Not his pack's territory or my little shop. Ours.

And no one threatens this town. Not my shop, and definitely not—I realize this with a sudden, sharp clarity—my werewolf. Especially not while he's stuck wearing my skin.

CHAPTER SEVEN

Hazel

I've never been great at following rules. I like to think of them more as guidelines rather than hard stops. I'm also really good at finding loopholes. But this time, with Ravena on the hunt and the full moon closing in, breaking the "no new magic" rule isn't just about rebellion. It's about survival. She forced this rule for a reason.

Which is exactly why I'm in the process of packing a picnic basket while trying to convince Blake that swapping supernatural skills isn't optional. Yes, it means spending an entire day alone with a brooding werewolf who's currently wearing my face, but the benefits outweigh the risks of us strangling each other.

"You know this is a terrible idea, right?" Blake says. Again. I'm still not used to my voice being all negative and gruff. "If anyone catches us using magic, we're screwed."

He picks up the sandwich I just wrapped and sniffs it.

"That's why we're going to Amethyst Beach." I tuck bottles of water and cans of soda into the cooler. "It's outside town limits. No magic ban there."

"You're really good at finding loopholes, aren't you?"

"I'm gifted, what can I say?" I flash him a grin and wiggle his bushy eyebrows. "Besides, you need to know at least basic protection spells. I can't do magic while in your body anymore than you can morph into a wolf while you're in mine. What if Ravena attacks while you're alone? You need to be able to defend yourself in my body."

Blake crosses my arms over my chest. "Well, what about you? There's no way you'd be able to control my wolf form. Look what happened with Leo."

"Exactly my point." I close the cooler with a snap. "You teach me wolfy stuff, I teach you witchy stuff. Win-win."

He sighs, defeated. "Fine. But if we sense any other people around, we're out of there."

"Yes, oh cautious one." I toss him my keys. "You're driving. I'm still not used to these big-ass feet."

On our way out, I give Mr. Garcia from the hardware store a quick "thank you" for coming so quickly to fix the broken window. That's the thing about Moonridge. We don't always get along, but we're always quick to help out our friends and neighbors.

The drive takes thirty minutes, winding through forest roads that curl away from town. Blake handles my old Jeep like it's made of something breakable, shifting gears carefully, hands at ten and two. I can't decide if the fact that he's so cautious is comical or endearing.

I catch myself stealing glances. It's cute the way he bites my lower lip when he's focused. Watching someone else move around in your body is something I'll never get used to. Are these tics I didn't know I had or are they all his? Will they stick when we switch back?

I finally break the silence. "My hair is really on your nerves, isn't it?"

"Why do you say that?"

"You keep pushing it behind my ear."

His cheeks—my cheeks—flush slightly. "It keeps falling in my face. How do you stand it?"

"I mean, I've had it my whole life. I guess I just got used to it." I run a hand through Blake's short hair, feeling the bristly softness under my fingers. "This is so much easier to manage, though."

"How would you feel if I shaved off your hair?" he asks and I can't tell if he's joking.

"I would murder you."

"You couldn't. Because then you'd be stuck in my body forever." He winks at me.

"Don't even think about it. I look horrible with short hair. I don't have the right bone structure."

"You could just throw one of the nine hundred scarves you have over your head." His lips twitch into an almost-smile. "Your closet is like a textile factory exploded."

I roll my eyes and we lapse into comfortable silence again.

Amethyst Beach lives up to its name. I've been up here several times, but it always takes my breath away. The sand is a pale lavender due to the fact that it's comprised mostly of amethyst rather than silica. Light reflects off the tiny amethyst fragments, enhancing the purple color. The lake is glassy and clear all the way to the rocky bottom near the shore, and pine trees press in close along the edges, blocking out everything else.

"Wow," Blake says, stepping out of the Jeep. "I've lived in Moonridge all my life, and I've never been here. We always go to Skipper Lake on the other side of town. We train there a lot."

"You've seriously never been here?" I grab the cooler and a small backpack stuffed with magical supplies.

"No. We grew up being told it was a 'witch spot', so we stayed away." He takes in the surroundings, a sense of wonder crossing his face.

"This is my favorite place. It's where I come when I need to get away and think. The natural magic here is incredible, too.

Feel it?"

He scrunches my forehead as he concentrates. "I feel something. Kind of staticky?"

"That's it." I'm impressed he can sense it so quickly. "The amethyst in the sand amplifies natural energy, too, which makes it perfect for practicing."

We find a quiet spot at the edge of the lake, tucked behind a cluster of driftwood. I spread out a blanket and unpack the basics. Candles, a bowl, dried herbs, and a few crystals. Sitting cross-legged proves a challenge. His legs aren't as bendy as mine.

Blake eyes the setup like he has no idea what he's even looking at.

"Let's try something." I pick up a selenite crystal and hold it out. "Take this."

He accepts it cautiously, like it might explode. "Now what?"

"Just hold it. Think about it getting warm."

"That's it? No chanting? No waving herbs around?"

"Just focus on the crystal with intent. Like you're studying it with your heart."

Blake eyes the crystal, skeptical. "That makes zero sense."

"Just trust me. Hold it and concentrate on it."

He goes still, brow furrowing in focus. At first, nothing happens. Then, a faint glow builds between his fingers, soft and steady.

"What the hell?" He nearly drops it. "I didn't do anything!"

"Actually, you did." I grin at his shocked expression. "You acknowledged the crystal and it responded."

Pride feels different in Blake's chest. It's not the flutter I'm used to, but something hot and solid. It's weird how almost every emotion lands differently. Happiness pools warm and low behind my sternum. Nerves don't flutter, they churn, like I swallowed a live fish. And arousal . . . that's a whole different storm I'm not ready to talk about right now. Let's just say morning wood is a weird thing to experience.

"Let's try something that you can actually use to protect

yourself," I suggest. "A simple shield spell."

For the next hour, I guide him through the basics. I teach him how to create a protective barrier around himself, then we move on to how to sense when magic is nearby, and finally how to channel energy through different objects. He's a surprisingly quick study. These concepts took me years to perfect when I was a kid. I wonder if it's because he's inside a body that has already perfected these skills?

"You're doing it wrong," I say, as he struggles with a containment spell. "Your hands need to be like this." I reach out to adjust his posture. Our fingers brush, and a spark jumps between us. Not the metaphorical spark people mention in romance books, but actual, visible static that crackles in the air. We both jerk back.

"What was that?" Blake asks, shaking out my hand.

"I don't know." But I have my suspicions. Each time we touch, something happens. Like our borrowed bodies recognize each other and are trying to snap back to their rightful owners. "Maybe we should avoid direct contact."

"Probably smart." But he doesn't move any further away. In fact, he leans closer, studying the bowl of herbs I've set between us. "What's this one for?"

"This helps with protection against mind influence." I scoot around to his side of the blanket, careful not to touch him as I arrange the herbs. "If Ravena tries to mess with your head, this will help block her."

He watches intently as I demonstrate. We sit close enough that I can smell my own shampoo on my hair—his hair now. Which means he showered (good) which also means he's seen me naked. (Good? Bad?) When was the last time I waxed? Did he notice?

I've certainly seen him naked and have not been shy about exploring. I wonder if he's done the same. Why does that turn me on? Nope. Can't go there. I don't need to pop a boner in his body while he's right here.

"Now you try." I slide the bowl toward him, our fingers brushing as he takes it. The spark jumps between us again, and this time I don't pull away immediately. Neither does he.

"Like this?" he asks, but he's looking at me instead of the herbs.

"Better."

Blake attempts to recreate the pattern I showed him, but his movements are stiff, too controlled. After three failed attempts, he growls in frustration.

"This is pointless," he mutters. "I can't do this. I'm not a witch."

"You can do this. Come on." I nudge his shoulder with mine. "You're overthinking it. Magic isn't about perfect technique. It's about feeling."

"Werewolves don't exactly specialize in feelings. We specialize in control. Feeling too much usually results in bad things happening."

"And that's problem number one." I grab a handful of sand, letting the purple grains slip through my fingers. "You're trying to control the magic instead of working with it. Magic is like . . . like cooking. You can follow a recipe exactly and still end up with something that tastes bland. Or you can understand how the ingredients work together and create something amazing."

He stares at me for a long moment, my green eyes searching my—his—face. "Is that how you see it? Because from where I'm sitting, your magic looks like controlled chaos at best."

The words sting more than they should. I thought we were having a nice day. "Maybe that's how it looks, but there is a method to my madness."

Most of the time.

"Really? Because before I organized it, that shop of yours was one sneeze away from a magical disaster. Coco nearly burned it down twice."

"But it's *my* shop. Maybe it was disorganized for you, but I knew where everything was. It's been that way for years. Gran liked it that way. It gave it personality. It felt alive." I don't know why I'm getting defensive. Maybe because he's hit a nerve. "Not cold and rigid like your construction office, where everything has to be in exact spots. It's like you're afraid if one little thing is out of place then someone dies."

"No, people don't die in my office because I take precautions," he snaps. "I'm prepared and a step ahead of any potential disasters. Unlike you, who seems to think consequences are optional. Case in point." He gestures at both of our bodies.

We glare at each other, a bizarre mirror image of frustration. The fight drains from me instantly. Why are we doing this again? We need each other right now.

"You're right." The admission feels raw. "I'm not always careful enough. That's how we ended up in this mess in the first place. I haven't handled my breakup with Evan well. I was making that enhancement potion because I saw him with Missy, and it made me feel inadequate. If I hadn't been so emotional, maybe the spell wouldn't have gone haywire when it mixed with the amulet's energy."

Blake is quiet for so long that I would think he got up and left if he wasn't sitting right in front of me. When he finally speaks, his voice—my voice—is soft. "I understand feeling inadequate."

I scoff unexpectedly. "You? Mister perfect and in control feels inadequate?"

He nods, a lock of my auburn hair falling across his forehead. "When my father died eight years ago, the pack leadership fell to me because Calvin was living on the West Coast. I was twenty years old and terrified. Everyone expected me to be just like him. Confident. Decisive. But I wasn't. I faked it for years, hoping no one would notice how scared I was of messing up. It was too much responsibility and the only way I could make sure nothing went off the rails was to stick to the rules."

I stare at him, seeing everything differently. All those times he seemed controlling, he was just scared of failing his pack. One wrong move, one moment of weakness, and people he loves could get hurt.

"I didn't know it affected you like that." All this time, I've seen his control as coldness. He always just seemed so arrogant. But I guess it's not that at all. I reach toward him instinctively, then stop myself before we spark again. "You've been carrying all of this alone?"

He nods, and something breaks in my chest. This strong, seemingly unshakeable man has been holding up the weight of his pack's lives while convinced he's not strong enough to do it.

"You're not your father," I say quietly. "You're your own person. Maybe you can let the real Blake shine through. You can still be protective without being so rigid."

The air between us changes, charged with a newfound understanding.

"Try the spell again, but this time, don't try to control it. Just feel it. Guide it."

Blake takes a deep breath, my chest rising and falling with the motion, and tries again. This time, the herbs arrange themselves in a perfect protective pattern, glowing softly with contained power.

"Whoa! I did it." He glances up, and his smile makes my face glow in a way it hasn't in days.

"You did." I can't help but smile back. "You're a natural."

The pride that swells in my chest catches me completely off guard. I'm proud of him. Not just that he succeeded, but that he trusted himself enough to let go of his control issues and try again. That he let himself be vulnerable enough to do it in the first place.

"We've been at this for too long. Now it's your turn." Blake stands and brushes sand from my jeans. "Time for wolf lessons."

I groan, but get to my feet. "Please tell me it doesn't involve leg humping or sniffing butts."

"Only on special occasions," he deadpans, and I'm startled into a laugh that booms from Blake's chest.

He leads me to the edge of the forest, where pine needles cushion the ground in a soft carpet. "The first thing about being a werewolf is learning to track. Not just with your nose, but with all your senses."

"Like this?" I take an exaggerated sniff, pulling air deep into Blake's lungs.

"Not quite." He steps behind me. He's close enough that I can feel the heat from my own body on my back. "Close your eyes." His voice is closer than I expected. "Don't try to smell it all at once. Focus on one scent, then separate it from the others."

I close my eyes, hyperaware of his proximity. In this body, I can hear his heartbeat—my heartbeat—picking up speed.

"What do you smell?" The question is barely a whisper.

"Everything. It's still very overwhelming."

"Focus. Pick out the individual scents."

I inhale again. "Pine. Dirt. Something sweet. Maybe sap?" I concentrate harder. "Animal turds somewhere nearby . . . And you."

"Me?"

"Your body. I mean, my body, but your scent on it. My soap and . . . home." The admission slips out before I can stop it.

There's a pause, a shift in the air between us. "Good," Blake says finally, his voice slightly rougher. "Now, open your eyes, but don't focus them on anything in particular. Let your peripheral vision do the work. Movement is easier to spot when you're not staring directly at it."

I try, softening my gaze until the forest becomes a blur of greens and browns. Suddenly, I catch it, a flicker of movement about twenty yards away.

"Rabbit," I whisper.

"How do you know?"

"The way it moves. Quick. Nervous." I'm surprised by my

own certainty. "And it smells like damp fur and . . ." I sniff again "Fear?"

"Exactly." There's pride in his voice. "Now track it, but don't chase it. Just follow."

For the next hour, Blake teaches me how to move through the forest with a wolf's awareness. How to place my feet silently, how to use the wind to mask my scent, how to listen for the subtle sounds that betray presence. A heartbeat. A stuttered breath.

It's exhilarating. Blake's body responds with instinctive grace, moving in ways I never could in my own skin. I feel powerful, connected to the world in a completely new way.

"This is amazing," I say, balancing easily on a fallen log that spans a small stream. "I can feel everything."

"That's the wolf sense," Blake explains, watching me from the bankside. "It's always there, under the surface. Most of us spend our lives learning to dial it back so we can function in the human world."

"Why would you want to dial this back?" I leap from the log to a rock, landing on one foot which would have been impossible in my own body. "It's like having superpowers!"

"Those same instincts can make you dangerous. Especially when you're angry or scared." His expression grows serious. "The amulet seems to be amplifying that exact instinct. Especially the aggressive side of our nature based on what happened with Mason. There's a part that sees threats everywhere and wants to eliminate them."

I jump back to solid ground, landing beside him. "Is that why I freaked out on Leo?"

Blake nods. "Your reaction was natural. For a wolf. Especially when it comes to pack members. Leo's clumsiness triggered that instinct. You felt like you needed to correct it to not only protect the pack, but also protect him from himself."

"But you control it so well."

"Years of practice." He steps closer, placing a hand on my

back.

His hands—my hands—rest just above my waist, and electricity shoots through both our bodies. The contact feels like coming home.

I go still under his touch.

"You're tense," he says, rubbing his hand up my back. He starts massaging my shoulders and I almost melt.

"Is this okay?" His fingers linger, thumbs brushing against my collarbone.

I nod. "It's your body."

"But you're inside of it and I don't want you to feel weird."

"I don't."

He pats me on the back and I turn to face him. I want to stay right here, in this moment where we're close enough that I can see the flecks of gold in my own eyes as he looks up at me. It's a strange feeling being physically taller than someone while knowing that, in reality, I'm the shorter one. It's also extremely disorienting to feel all melty for someone who's wearing my face.

"Did I do okay?" The question comes out softer than I meant.

He doesn't step away. "You're a fast learner."

A twig snaps somewhere in the forest, yanking us from the moment. We both freeze, instantly alert.

"What was that?" I whisper, ready to track whatever it was.

Blake shakes his head slightly, eyes scanning the trees. "It sounded too heavy for a rabbit or deer."

I sniff the air, sorting through the forest scents until I catch it. It's human, but smells both sweet and sour. Like something unwashed covered in body spray. Ravena? One of her followers?

"Someone's watching us," I murmur, barely moving my lips.

Blake nods almost imperceptibly. "I sense them too. We need to leave. Casually."

We start walking back toward the beach, my every sense on high alert. The hairs on the back of Blake's neck—my neck now—stand up. Something's wrong. The forest has gone too quiet.

There. A flash of movement to our right. Something pale among the trees.

Wolf instincts kick in and I suddenly feel the need to protect him at all cost. He's trapped in my smaller, more fragile body, and if something happens to him while he's defenseless . . .

I push him behind me, Blake's body moving without being told. Wolf programming will never cease to amaze me.

Blake starts to protest. "Hazel, I can—"

"No." I push him back, using Blake's larger frame to shield my own body. If someone wants to hurt him, they'll have to go through me first. "Stay back."

My heart pounds against Blake's ribs as I scan the treeline. I've never felt anything this fierce, this primal. I would kill to protect him. The realization should scare me, but it doesn't. I want to fight.

"Who's there?" The growl builds until it rumbles through the forest like a challenge.

Nothing. Just silence and the sense of being watched.

"Protect," Blake whispers behind me, pressing something into my hand. It must be the charm we made earlier, activated by that single word.

I squeeze it, feeling a sort of magic pulse through Blake's fingers. It's unfamiliar but not entirely foreign. A shimmering barrier forms around us, barely visible except where sunlight catches its edges.

From the trees, something flies toward us. A rock, or maybe another brick like the one that smashed my shop window last night. It hits the barrier and bounces off, falling harmlessly to the ground.

"It worked," I breathe.

"Run," Blake says, tugging my arm. "While the shield holds."

We sprint back to the beach, not stopping until we reach the Jeep. I fumble with the keys, hands shaking with adrenaline, while Blake keeps watch.

He places a hand on my shoulder. "I can't sense them anymore."

I sit there for a moment, hands shaking, adrenaline still coursing through Blake's larger frame. "Do you think it was Ravena?" I ask.

"Or one of her followers." Blake's voice is quiet, thoughtful.

Then we hear it. A group of boys burst from the trees, laughing hysterically.

"Where did they go?" one of them asks.

"You scared the shit out of them," another one says.

And I'm about to return the favor.

Anger surges through me. I step away from the Jeep, planting Blake's feet wide, letting his full height work in my favor. "Hey, you little shits!"

The four boys freeze mid-laugh, their heads whipping toward me. Fear floods their faces as they take in Blake's imposing frame moving in on them.

"Holy shit, that's Blake Carter. He's the alpha werewolf."

I stride toward them, Blake's long legs eating up the distance in no time. They scramble backward, bumping into each other. The acrid smell of fear and—is that urine?—fills the air.

"You could have hurt us." Another step closer and they huddle together like cornered rabbits.

The tallest boy's voice cracks. "We're sorry! We didn't know it was you, or we wouldn't have—"

"You shouldn't have done it at all." I let Blake's voice drop to a dangerous rumble.

The short, pudgy one tries to look unbothered, but fails. "We were just messing around."

I glare at them, watching them shrink further. One of them shifts his weight nervously, confirming my suspicion about the urine smell.

"Well, it wasn't funny. If I catch you up here again, I'm going to wolf the fuck out on you. Do you understand?"

Four heads bob frantically. Tears threaten in the smallest boy's eyes.

"Now go home. And I'll consider not telling your parents."

They bolt. Feet slipping on pine needles as they race around the lake to where bicycles lean against trees. Within seconds, they're streaking down the forest path like their lives depend on it.

Blake appears beside me, shaking his head with amusement. "Wolf the fuck out? That was pretty impressive. I might have to use that."

My borrowed heart still hammers against Blake's ribs. "I seriously thought it was Ravena after us."

"I did too." Laughter starts as a chuckle but builds until we're both doubled over. "But the more I think about it, she'd probably do more than throw rocks at us."

"True." The absurdity hits me all over again, and fresh laughter bubbles up.

When we finally catch our breath, Blake's expression on my face grows thoughtful. "So, like, when did we stop being enemies?"

I lean against the side of the Jeep. "I don't think we were ever really enemies. We just decided we hated each other in second grade and never got past it."

He steps closer, forcing me to look down to meet his eyes. "And now?"

The words slip out before I can stop them. "Now I'm kind of afraid."

"Of what?"

"Of what happens when we get our bodies back. What happens to . . ." I gesture between us, unable to name it yet.

His expression softens. "I don't know. But I know I don't want to go back to the way things were before. To bickering all the time. To pretending we don't . . ."

"Care about each other?" I finish.

"Yeah." He almost smiles. "Care about each other. I actually think we could be friends. I kind of like us like this."

"Good." Not gonna lie. This makes me feel a little giddy.

Blake turns to look at me, studying my face—his face—with an intensity that makes my stomach do that weird fish-flipping thing again. He squeezes my hand and kicks off that spark of recognition.

I wonder what else those sparks might ignite, given the chance.

CHAPTER EIGHT

Blake

We sit in silence, both leaning against the Jeep. The late afternoon sun hangs low over Amethyst Beach, painting the lavender sand in shades of amber and gold. Despite the lingering adrenaline, I don't want to leave yet. Maybe it's the serenity that this place brings me. Or maybe it's the company. Whatever it is, it's so peaceful here. I want to enjoy it a little bit longer. I'm not ready to deal with all the Ravena shit that waits for us back in town.

"Let's stay." The words come out in Hazel's voice, but the determination is all mine. "Those little assholes are gone now. It's nice up here. I'm not ready to leave yet. And we should eat that food you packed. Seems a waste to leave it."

A hint of a smile tugs at my—her—lips. "Blake Carter, choosing relaxation over kicking ass? Who are you and what have you done with the grumpy werewolf I know?"

"I'm right here and I'm wearing your skin," I deadpan, and she laughs, a deep rumble.

"Truer words."

We gather the cooler and what remains of our magical supplies, then find a spot closer to the water but still sheltered from anyone who might drive up. The sun hovers above the horizon, setting the lake ablaze with reflected light.

I spread the blanket while Hazel unpacks the sandwiches and water bottles. It feels domestic in a way that causes a flutter in this chest.

"This is nice." Hazel hands me a sandwich. "When was the last time you just sat and watched a sunset?"

I sink my teeth into the sandwich. Peanut butter and blackberry jam. Simple but perfect. "Can't remember. There's always something that needs doing."

"The never-ending to-do list of pack leadership?"

I nod, chewing thoughtfully. "The pack comes first. Always has."

"That sounds lonely." She cocks her head and gives me a look I'm pretty sure my face has never made before. Ever.

"It's just how it is." I shrug. "My dad was the same way. He used to say a good alpha never asks for what he can't give."

"What does that mean?"

Trying to organize thoughts that I rarely put into words is difficult. "It means if I expect loyalty and sacrifice from the pack, I have to give it first. Can't ask them to put the group before themselves if I'm not willing to do the same."

Hazel hums thoughtfully. "That's a lot of pressure to put on yourself."

"Says the head witch in charge who also runs the town's only magical supply business while also managing a town full of supernatural politics."

She smiles, but there's a sadness to it. "Not the same thing. You're responsible for lives. I just make potions and occasionally enchant the mayor's hairpiece when he pisses me off."

I snort. "You do more than that. You're the heart of the magical community here. People depend on you."

"Maybe." She picks at the crust of her sandwich. "But I don't feel like I deserve it. I'm a mess. If I didn't have La'Tasha to keep me grounded, the town would have exploded by now. This isn't even something I got to choose. It was expected of me."

"When your grandmother died?" I ask gently.

She looks at the sunset rather than at me. "Yeah. It's in some formal decree. Thornton witches are to always serve as Virtus Suprema. It should have gone to my mother, but my parents died when I was four."

My chest blooms with pain. "How did they die?"

"We were visiting one summer. They'd left me with Gran, and had gone out to dinner. On their way back it was raining. They missed a turn coming around a bend up by Skipper Lake."

I vaguely remember when she moved to Moonridge, but as a kid, I'd been shielded from the details of why. Four years old and orphaned. Wow. I'd had no idea. "I'm sorry."

"It was a long time ago." She takes a sip from the thermos. "Grandma Agnes raised me, taught me everything about magic, about the shop. She was amazing. She could be tough as nails but also soft when it counted."

Imagining Hazel as a little girl, orphaned and alone except for her grandmother, is almost too much. Sorrow sits in my chest. It's an emotion I'm not used to feeling.

"What were they like? Your parents?"

A small smile touches her lips—my lips. "My memories are very vague. Most of what I know about them came from things my grandmother told me. Mom was brilliant. A powerful witch who could do pretty much anything. Most witches are stronger in certain areas like herbs, crystals, potions or whatever. But Grandma said my mom could do it all effortlessly. Dad was human but loved magic. He called it 'science we don't understand yet.' They were disgustingly in love, according to Grandma."

The way she talks about them, with such love for people she barely remembers, makes my borrowed heart ache. She's spent most of her life alone. Now she carries the weight of the entire town on her shoulders and she has no family around to help support her. No wonder she felt lost after Evan dumped her. The promise of stability, of no longer being alone was ripped away. I understand it more than I want to admit. Looks like we've both been so focused on taking care of everyone else that we forgot we might need taking care of, too.

"After they died, Gran was my everything," she continues. "When she passed, it was like losing everything. Suddenly, I was alone, running a business I wasn't sure I was ready for, trying to live up to this legacy. Then this past summer with the whole Virtus Suprema title finally landing on my shoulders . . . It's a lot, you know?"

Her voice catches slightly, and something twists in my chest.

"I just feel like everything I love gets ripped away from me. It's like I'm cursed. Must be because of some childhood trauma."

"Well, your parents died when you were four years old," I say quietly. "That had to be traumatizing. And then you lost your grandmother, too, who was the last of your family."

She nods. "It was a rough few years after Gran passed. But then Evan came along, and I thought maybe things were starting to look up for me."

That guy. I don't know him well, only that he's some smarmy accountant I'd occasionally seen her with around town.

"How long did you two date?"

"Just a little over three years. He moved to town a couple of years after Grandma died. He seemed so stable and I definitely needed stability. He was like an anchor when everything else was chaos." A shrug. "I needed that in my life. I thought he was the one, you know? Someone who'd stick around. But it turns out, he didn't want a witch. He wanted a version of me that doesn't exist."

"His loss." I'm surprised by how much I mean it.

Hazel looks at me—at herself—with surprise. "That's not what I expected you to say."

"What did you expect?"

"I don't know. Maybe how you can understand why he wanted something more normal. That witches are too much trouble. Maybe how magic complicates everything? Or at least that's what you told Ryan Carlisle in high school when he wanted to date me."

I shake my head. "That was high school. I was an idiot back then." *And I wanted to date you, but didn't think you'd want anything to do with me.* I definitely can't say that part out loud.

"Magic is part of who you are," I continue. "Just like my enhanced senses and pack duties are part of me. Anyone who asks you to be less than who you are at your core is an idiot."

She stares at me for a long moment, then bursts out laughing.

"What?" I ask, confused.

"It's just funny hearing that from you. Mr. 'you're hyper-emotional and your magic is unpredictable.'"

Heat climbs up my—her—neck and spreads across her cheeks. "I never said you should not be you, though. Just . . . more careful."

"Potato, po-tah-to." But she smiles as she says it.

We fall silent and I find myself stealing glances at her. Yes, I'm looking at my own profile, but somehow it looks different. Like her presence inside of it has changed something. The way she tilts my head when she's thinking, the gentleness in my usually stern features.

"You're staring," she says without looking at me.

"I'm watching the sunset," I lie.

"Through my face?" She turns toward me, and the smile playing at my lips makes my heart skip.

"Maybe." I lay on my back and place my hands behind my— okay her—head. "It's strange, seeing myself through your eyes. You make my face look . . . softer."

"Maybe that's just how you look when you're not trying to intimidate people."

She nudges me and then lies down next to me.

"I didn't know," I say finally. "About your parents, I mean. I didn't realize how much you've been carrying alone."

"We all have our heartaches." She picks at a callus on my

palm. "You have the pack, all those expectations."

"It's different, though. I at least have family here. I have Calvin, and a couple of cousins. You have . . ."

"No one?" She finishes my thought. "I know. But I'm not totally alone. I have La'Tasha. She's been my best friend since second grade. And Coco, in her own chaotic way. The shop."

"Not the same as family."

"No," she agrees softly. "But we make do with what we have, right? Sometimes we have to make our own families."

The simple truth settles between us like the last rays of sunlight. We all make do. We all carry weights we never asked for. Hazel just does it with more color and laughter than I ever could.

"You know," she says quietly, "this is the longest conversation we've ever had without arguing."

"It's kind of nice," I admit. "I guess it's hard to have heart-to-hearts when you're busy trying to prove you don't need anyone."

She sits up and stretches. My back pops and I know that had to feel great.

"Do you? Need anyone?" The question is soft, careful.

I sigh. "I'm starting to think maybe I do."

I want to reach for her hand and tell her she doesn't have to carry everything alone anymore. But we're sitting in each other's bodies, and I don't know if what I'm feeling is real or just some side effect of this magical chaos.

When did this happen? When did I start to like her? Or did I ever stop? Did I just push aside my childhood crush and pretend to despise her simply because I thought she'd never like me back?

These thoughts terrify me. A werewolf and a witch. It's not just unconventional, it's unheard of. What would the pack think? And more importantly, what happens when we get our bodies back and she doesn't need to rely on me anymore? What if I get my body back and these feelings disappear with it?

***

The drive back to Moonridge passes in comfortable silence. I find myself taking the long way through town, still not ready for the day to be over. Neither of us mention how I decide to take the scenic route past the old mill instead of the direct path home.

She turns to look at me as we pull up to the apothecary. "I meant what I said earlier. I don't want this to end." The words hang in the air between us.

"The investigation?" I ask, though we both know that's not what she means.

"This." She gestures between us, then lets her hand fall to her lap. "Whatever this is we've found today. The talking. The understanding. The friendship."

I turn off the engine, but neither of us moves to get out. "It doesn't have to end."

"But, what if . . ." There's something vulnerable in her voice—my voice—that makes my chest ache. "What if when we get our bodies back, when this crisis is over, we go back to petty arguments and avoiding each other at all costs? What if we only tolerate each other now because we're in the other's body?"

"I've wondered that, too," I admit. "But I don't want to go back to the way it was."

She looks at me then, my blue eyes searching my face—her face—in the dim glow of the dashboard lights. "Same."

The moment stretches, but eventually the glow of lights from inside the apothecary reminds us that La'Tasha is waiting. That the real world, with all its complications and threats, is still there.

"Come on," Hazel says, reaching for the door handle. "Let's see what Tash found."

When we step through the door, La'Tasha is on the floor behind the counter, surrounded by stacks of old leather tomes, yellowed newspapers, and a small cauldron putting out a smell that is definitely not soup.

"Don't touch that," she warns without looking up. "It's detecting magical signatures."

Hazel peeks at the concoction before settling into a chair. "Did you find something?"

La'Tasha has dark circles under her eyes, and her normally neat curls are frizzed at the ends like she's been mindlessly twisting them between her fingers.

"Oh, I found something, and you're not going to like it." She points to the cauldron. "This is a detection potion. It identifies the type of magic used in spellwork."

"Okay." Hazel's voice turns careful. "What's it detecting?"

La'Tasha reaches for a small vial of what looks like water and adds three drops to the mixture. The liquid swirls, then steam rises. Slowly, the steam turns to clouds that change color. First pale pink. Then deeper rose. Then deep, crimson red.

La'Tasha backs away from the cauldron like she's afraid it might explode. "She used blood magic," she whispers.

"No." Hazel shakes her head, my voice coming out strangled. "That's not . . . she wouldn't . . ."

"But it is," Tasha confirms. "And she did."

I know enough about blood magic to know what that means. This is the kind of thing that separates good, ethical witches from those willing to cross lines. I've heard stories from older pack members about witches who dared dabble in blood magic, and how it corrupts everything it touches. If Ravena's willing to use blood magic, she's desperate. She's past the point of caring about consequences. Moonridge is definitely in danger.

"Are you absolutely sure?" Hazel's voice comes out strained through my throat.

"I've run the test three times." La'Tasha's hands shake slightly as she sets down the vial. "Same result every time. Someone, likely Ravena, used blood magic to activate the amulet. Which explains why she was able to activate it so easily."

Hazel stares at the glowing spot on the floor where the amulet rests. "But how did she activate it? Wouldn't she have had to be here to do it?"

La'Tasha nods. "My guess is she cut herself and let a few drops of her blood drip onto the floor one of the many times she was here pushing for product placement. This would have connected her to the amulet. Then, she was able to activate it through a ritual from somewhere else."

"That's . . ." I struggle to find words that match the gravity of the situation.

"Bad. Really bad," La'Tasha says. "We're in some shit here. I think we might want to call the Sortium."

Hazel snaps to attention. "What? No. Not yet. If they find out that I did a spell that made us swap bodies, it would be very bad for me. I'm still on probation."

"I know, but I think we might be in over our heads here. We should at least consider pulling in some of the elder witches for help," La'Tasha says.

Hazel paces, shaking her head. "Not yet. We can figure this out."

La'Tasha stands. "Hazel, come on. This is serious. This is the type of magical threat that requires you as Virtus Suprema to alert the higher-ups. This is dangerous."

"How dangerous?" I say, trying to pull La'Tasha's focus away from Hazel.

"It's the kind of magic that requires sacrifice." La'Tasha's voice is barely above a whisper. "Small spells might just need a few drops of the caster's blood."

I feel sick. "And bigger spells?"

La'Tasha can't meet my eyes. "Usually means something, or someone, has to die."

The silence that follows is deafening. Hazel starts pacing again, a nervous energy that makes my movements sharp and agitated.

"So we're not just dealing with a witch holding a grudge," she says finally. "We're dealing with someone who's willing to kill to get what she wants."

The implications weigh heavy in the air. If Ravena used blood magic to activate the amulet, she's playing a game far more dangerous than we realized.

"Would it be strong enough to cause our body swap?" I ask.

"Definitely." La'Tasha moves to her stack of folders, pulling one free. "Blood magic can enhance any spell tenfold. It could easily have interacted with your potion and the amulet's energy to cause something this dramatic."

Hazel grows even more agitated. "So we're dealing with a very desperate, very dangerous witch."

La'Tasha reaches for a manila folder. "Yes. Which is why I think you need to consider reporting this."

Hazel stares out the window, but doesn't answer.

"I need to show you something," La'Tasha finally says. "I've been going through old town archives, looking for any trace of Ravena over the years." She opens the folder carefully, revealing several old photographs. "These are from the Moonridge Historical Society. Pictures of various incidents around town over the last fifty years."

I lean closer, studying the first black-and-white pic that shows a crowd gathered around what looks like a building fire. "The old mill fire?"

"Nineteen seventy-eight," La'Tasha confirms. "Destroyed the entire east wing. They never figured out what caused it."

Hazel joins us, peering over my shoulder. "I don't understand. What does this have to do with—"

"Look closer," La'Tasha interrupts, pointing to the crowd of onlookers. "Third person from the left."

I squint at the grainy photo, focusing on a woman with blonde hair styled in an elaborate bouffant. Something about her profile seems familiar, but . . .

"Oh my God," Hazel whispers, recognition dawning.

"Is that . . . ?" I start.

"Ravena," La'Tasha confirms. "Or Bianca. Or whatever she's

calling herself."

The realization hits like ice water in the face. "She was here. In 1978."

"I need to do some more digging, but I have a hunch that this isn't the only time she has visited Moonridge since she was banished."

"But what was she doing?" Hazel asks.

"That's the million-dollar question," La'Tasha puts everything back in the folder. "We can assume she has an agenda. She likely wants revenge for being banished. But a lot of time has passed between then and now. What else has she done, and what is she planning?"

"And why now? Why the big move with the amulet?" I ask.

Hazel shakes her head in disbelief. "Of course. Grandma Agnes. She was the one who originally caught Ravena and had her banished. Grandma was very powerful. Ravena likely didn't have the power to push back. As long as she was alive, Ravena couldn't make her big play."

I think about the changes in Moonridge over the past few years. The growing tension between supernaturals, the increasing separation between communities that once worked together.

"So she was waiting for the right moment," I realize aloud. "And now she's trying to turn the town against us so she can finish what she started all those years ago. Breaking the pact between witches and werewolves leaves the town magically imbalanced."

Hazel's eyes—my eyes—meet mine across the room. "There has to be something with those MLM supplements. What if she's using them as a way to get humans on her side. What if she's building an army of followers. You saw how quickly they all fell in behind her at the meeting the other night."

The pieces slot together, painting a picture that makes my blood run cold. Ravena hasn't just been nursing a grudge; she's been methodically planning revenge against the entire town. She's had plenty of time to plot the perfect revenge.

"So what's her endgame?" La'Tasha asks the question we're all thinking. "What happens when the full moon rises and the werewolves lose control?"

"Chaos," I answer grimly. "The pack will be blamed for any violence. The town council will have no choice but to take action against us."

"And if she can manage to get the rest of the witches banned from using magic to help stop it, there's no one to keep her from taking over," Hazel adds. "She could position herself as the only one able to protect the town."

La'Tasha shivers visibly. "By the time people understand what's really happening, Ravena will already be in control."

"We need to stop her," Hazel says. "And I agree. We may need help from the Sortium, but before we call them, can we please try to get Blake and me back in each other's bodies first?"

La'Tasha nods. "Okay."

I find myself moving closer to Hazel, a protective instinct driving me. "Body swapping issues aside, how do we prove what she's doing?"

"First, we need to confirm it's really her," La'Tasha says. "That photo is circumstantial. We need more evidence that ties Bianca to Ravena."

Hazel snaps her fingers—my fingers—a gesture I've never made in my life. "The B&B! If she's been coming back to Moonridge for years, she must have stayed somewhere. The Moonridge Bed and Breakfast has been around forever."

"But Mina Cartwright only bought the B&B a few years ago," I point out.

"Yes, but Mrs. Holloway owned the place for at least forty years prior," La'Tasha says. "And she kept meticulous records. She was the town's historian. I'm sure there must be old-school, handwritten guest books going back decades."

"So we visit Mina tomorrow," Hazel says decisively. "See if she can help confirm our suspicions and maybe give us something concrete to take to the sheriff."

I nod, but my mind is racing ahead to potential problems. "We have to be careful. Ravena isn't stupid, and I know she's been watching us. We have to stay alert."

"We'll go early in the day," Hazel decides. "While Ravena is busy with her pathetic excuse of a business and all of her evil plotting."

I nod and look again at the crimson liquid bubbling in the cauldron. Blood magic. If Ravena is willing to go that far, what else is she capable of?

"We should sleep together tonight." The words slip out before I can stop them, and suddenly the air in the shop feels charged.

Hazel's eyes—my eyes—widen slightly. "Sleep together?"

"Not like that." I roll my eyes and do my best to force away the heat rising in my face. "In the same room. For safety," I add quickly. "Tactically, it makes sense."

"Tactically," she repeats, but there's something in her voice. A warmth that makes me think maybe she doesn't want to be apart either.

"Uh-huh," La'Tasha says with a knowing smirk. "Tactical."

Hazel's expression on my face is unreadable for a moment, then softens. "He's right. If Ravena comes after either of us, we're stronger together."

La'Tasha looks between us, then winks. "No funny business now. I'll cast protective wards on my way out since you're power-less and I don't trust Blake to not turn you both into chickens."

As La'Tasha gathers her things, I catch Hazel's eye across the room. Something passes between us. An acknowledgment that tonight isn't just about safety from Ravena. It's about not wanting to be apart. And maybe a little bit about this strange, impossible thing growing between us.

For the first time since this chaos started, I don't feel over-whelmed. I experience a completely different feeling.

Hope.

CHAPTER NINE

Hazel

The drive to Moonridge B&B winds us through the heart of town. People wave as we pass, so naturally, my dumb ass waves back like I'm the homecoming queen in a parade.

"Stop that," Blake says. "I don't wave like that. People are going to think something's wrong with me."

"Sorry. Force of habit." I place his hands in my lap. His lap. Whatever. "How do you usually wave?"

"I don't."

Right.

I roll my shoulders and massage my neck. I woke up with a crick in it after sleeping on the floor. Blake insisted I take the bed, but I refused. I know my back. He would have been in pain all day. Wait. Am I chivalrous? If I were a real man, would I be considered a gentleman?

I'm kind of impressed with myself.

"You okay?" he asks.

"Yeah." I turn to look at him and immediately wince.

He made me braid his hair—my hair—to keep it out of the

way. He looks like he's about to lead one of Ravena's yoga retreats, and let me tell you, the severity of it all is absolutely not doing my round face any favors. I'll let it slide today, but once we're back in our own bodies, that braid is getting exorcised.

The B&B sits at the edge of town, tucked behind towering maple trees along a circular drive at the end of Maple Street. The house is a stone-gray Victorian with striking black trim. It's both elegant and a little dramatic. Kind of like Mina, the proprietor. Flower boxes spill over with bright blooms, putting her famous green thumb on full display. The place radiates warmth and welcome. She's the ultimate at making everything feel like home.

As soon as we climb out of the car, the smell of fresh baking hits us like a perfectly planned assault. Cinnamon, butter, vanilla, and some sort of berry mingle together in a perfect symphony of deliciousness. My stomach growls audibly.

"Someone's hungry," Blake says with a smirk.

"It's not my fault. Your body is a bottomless pit," I shoot back. "I ate enough for two people this morning, and I'm already starving again."

"I'm a growing boy," he says proudly.

"And I hate you for it. If I ate like this while in my body, I'd be the size of your truck."

A basket of flowers props open the front door. We step into a foyer filled with antique furniture and fresh-cut bouquets. A sign directs us to the kitchen, where we find Mina Cartwright kneading dough on a flour-dusted counter. She has her fiery red hair pulled back in a loose ponytail. Smudges of white flour pepper her freckled cheeks. The kitchen is a cozy chaos of baking supplies and cookbooks. She seems to be in the middle of at least three different projects, but despite the mess, there's obviously an order to it.

"Blake Carter, as I live and breathe!" Mina's Scottish accent lilts with delight when she sees us. "And Hazel, too! To what do I owe this honor?" She eyes us curiously. Usually, it's Mina coming to visit me at my place, not the other way around. I can't tell you the last time I was over here. I really should make more of an effort to maintain friendships outside of the apothecary.

"Morning, Mina." I do my best to sound all gruff and Blakeish. "Hope we're not interrupting anything."

"No, not at all." She wipes her hands on her apron as she comes to greet us. "You're lookin' a bit frazzled there, big man. What's got your knickers in a twist this time?"

Blake shifts beside me, clearly uncomfortable with Mina's assessment even though she's not addressing him directly. I fight back a smile.

"Just tired," I mutter. "Ya know. Pack stuff."

"Oh, pack stuff, is it?" Mina's eyes twinkle as she turns to Blake in my body. "And Hazel, love, you're lookin' particularly stern today. Look like you've been takin' grouchy lessons from Mr. Broody Pants here. What's wrong?"

Blake clears my throat awkwardly.

"Just worried about . . . town things."

"Town things and pack stuff. Very specific troubles you two have," Mina says, laughing.

"Well, you're in luck. I've just pulled a batch of raspberry scones from the oven, and nothin' fixes pack stuff and town things like oodles of butter and sugar."

She ushers us to a small table by the kitchen window, quickly setting out plates, jam, clotted cream, and perfectly golden scones that steam when you break them open. The smell is heavenly, and I have to stop myself from diving face-first into the plate.

"Been meanin' to check in on you and your wolves, Blake," Mina says, pouring us each a cup of coffee. "Heard about those incidents with your pack. Sounds like you've got your hands full."

I nod, trying to look present and engaged while also stuffing half a scone into Blake's mouth.

Blake nudges me with my bony elbow. "Slow down," he whispers. "You look like this is the first time you've eaten this month."

I casually wipe my hand across my furry face and chew. This hunger is seriously intense. If I could somehow manage to unhinge my jaw and eat the entire plate of scones at once, I would.

"You think, uh, maybe they're rebellin' because you're too strict with 'em?" Mina continues as she sits across from us.

I don't respond because I forget she's actually addressing me because she thinks I'm Blake.

"Just a word of advice if I might," she continues. "Maybe consider lightenin' up a bit. You keep them on a tight leash. Poor Leo was over here the other day helpin' me install a porch light and almost had a heart attack when he realized he was going to be late for a pack run at the lake."

"Gotta keep in shape, right?" I say, trying to sound offended while secretly loving this. I'm glad I'm not the only one who thinks he's too much of a tight-ass. "And I can't have them falling out of line. A good wolf is a disciplined wolf. And I kind of like being a hardass for no reason."

Blake makes a choking sound and kicks me under the table.

"Don't give me that," Mina wags a flour-covered finger at me. "Ya know you're allowed to have fun now and then. I've known ya since I moved here. The only time I see ya is when you're workin' or runnin' drills with your wolves. I've watched ya stomp around town with that permanent crease between your eyebrows for the last six years. Can't be healthy for any of ya."

She reaches over and pokes the spot between my—Blake's— eyebrows. "Look at that crease. It ages ya about ten years. You're too rigid, love. I know your type. I had an ex just like ya. Well, without the wolfy bits."

I bite the inside of Blake's cheek to keep from grinning. "I appreciate the advice," I manage.

By the look on his—my—face, Blake seems to be taking this as a personal criticism. I wish he could see it's all for his own good.

Mina pats my hand with motherly affection. "You're a sweet lad. You've got a good heart under all that growling. Just let it show more often." She turns to Blake in my body. "Don't ya think so, Hazel?"

Blake looks me directly in the eye and raises his eyebrows. "Oh, absolutely. Blake is wonderful. Great guy, really. Biggest heart I've ever seen. And I kind of think he's fine just the way he is. Perfect, even. I mean, look at that sweet face. And that body! He wouldn't have an ass like a dump truck if he just sat around all day."

Mina's eyes dart between us like she completely missed something.

"Speaking of hidden things," I say, before Blake can jerk off his own ego any further, "we actually came to ask you about something."

Her eyebrows lift. "I'm all ears."

"Have you noticed any unusual guests lately? Or maybe remember anyone from years past who resembles Bianca Mayweather?" I do my best to keep my tone casual while stuffing another scone into Blake's bottomless gut. Sweet Jesus, these things are good.

Mina tilts her head, considering. "Can't say I have. Why do ya ask?"

Blake leans forward. "We think she might not be who she says she is."

"That wellness woman? Always dressed like she's afraid of gettin' dirty?" Mina snorts. "Never trusted her. She's takin' the hand out of her customers' if you ask me. You know, she's tried to set up a stand here? More than once. I finally had to tell her if she comes back again, I'd get a restrainin' order."

"We believe she might have visited Moonridge before, under different names," I explain. "We're trying to confirm it. We think she may have stayed here."

Mina raises an eyebrow. "Well, Mrs. Holloway, who owned this place before me, kept records of everythin'. Meticulous woman, that one. She documented everythin' in these big leather books."

My pulse quickens. "Do you still have them?"

"Of course! They're all in the basement. Couldn't bring myself to throw 'em out. Part of the B&B's history, you know? I keep meanin' to take them to the historical society, but just haven't found the time." Mina stands, wiping her hands on her apron. "You're welcome to have a look through 'em."

She disappears briefly, returning with a large ring of antique keys.

"The basement door is through that hallway past the laundry room," she points. "Third key from the left should unlock it. Just mind your step. And I'll warn ya, it's a bit creepy down there. All cobwebs and old trunks. I don't get down there much."

"Thanks, Mina." I take the keys from her.

"Take your time," she says, already returning to her dough. "I'll be up here if you need anythin'."

We head toward the basement. Blake still looks bothered by the ego bust Mina gave him.

"She's not wrong," I say quietly. "About lightening up I mean."

"I'm not a total asshole, you know?"

Yep. His feelings are hurt.

"She wasn't calling you an asshole. It's just that Mina knows you care about people. She just wants you to let them know it, too. You don't have to be a rigid military drone to be a good alpha."

Something vulnerable flickers across my features. "What if they see my caring as weakness? What if they stop respecting me?"

"Or, what if they respect you more?" I counter. "What if they've been waiting for permission to be something more than perfect soldiers?"

I can tell he's mulling this over.

"And she didn't say all that to be mean," I point out. "She sees the good in you. Okay?"

He nods.

"Cool. Now let's go do what we came here to do." I unlock

the basement door, and we're immediately hit in the face with cold, damp air. A narrow staircase descends into dusty darkness.

"Ladies first." I step aside and gesture toward the stairs.

Blake rolls my eyes. "Hilarious."

The stairs creak under us, loud enough that I half expect something to answer back. It's exactly as bad as Mina promised. Dim and musty and absolutely packed. Old furniture is shoved against more old furniture. Several stacked boxes look like they're about to topple over. And a row of mannequins? Interesting.

Something furry brushes my forearm. I scream. Which is hilarious because it comes out of Blake's mouth in Blake's tone. I've never heard a sound like that before. I look down to see a dead mink draped around one of the psycho mannequins. Gross. People seriously used to wear those?

"There." Blake points past a rocking horse and the ugliest holiday decorations I've ever seen. An entire corner is stacked with leather-bound books, each spine stamped with gold lettering. "Those must be the ledgers."

They're surprisingly well-preserved. Mrs. Holloway clearly took her record-keeping seriously. Blake lifts a book marked '1970-1975' from the shelf.

"Guess we'll start here."

I clear off a card table that looks like it gave up on life a year ago. Blake sits and opens the book.

"Oh wow." I lean in. "This is—okay, this is a lot."

The pages are meticulously organized. Handwritten notes appear along with guest information. Including Polaroids taped to the pages.

"Who takes pictures of their B&B guests?" Blake asks, flipping through the pages. "Kind of creepy."

"Someone who doesn't trust her memory?" But even as I say it, I'm reading the notes under the photos, and it's more than memory. Occupations. Reasons for visiting. Personal observations. Mrs. Holloway wasn't just running a B&B. She was watching. Writing things down. Keeping a record of everyone who passed through.

"She was the town historian," I say. "This tracks, actually."

"Or she was keeping tabs on strangers," Blake says.

"Could just be customer service. Making sure she remembers details about previous guests." I don't buy it even though the words came from my mouth. It's almost like she was running some kind of sting operation.

We work forward through the decades. I'm starting to think we've driven across town for nothing when Blake goes completely still next to me.

"Found her." He points to a photo in the 1978 ledger.

It's of a younger woman with blonde hair styled in an elaborate bouffant, wearing large round glasses that can't quite hide her sharp, distinctive features. But it's not just the face. It's the eyes. Even in the faded Polaroid, those cold, dark eyes are unmistakable.

"That's her." I lean in for a closer look. "Same disguise as the photo La'Tasha found."

Blake reads the entry. His voice gets quieter with each line. "Lydia Fairchild. Historian. Researching local folklore. Shows a particular interest in unusual incidents. Spent considerable time at the library. Left abruptly after one week."

"And?" I ask.

He flips the page and there's a follow-up note. Different ink. Clearly added later. "Fire at old mill, two days after Ms. Fairchild's departure. Timing suspicious."

We sit with that for a second.

"Coincidence?"

"Maybe," Blake says. "But very suspicious."

He snaps a photo with his phone to document what we found.

The next several ledgers are dead ends, but 1988 provides another jackpot. Another photo. Another entry. This time I spot her immediately. The hair is different. Short and dark, cut in a severe bob. But the face is unmistakable.

"Sabrina Moore," Blake reads. "'Vacuum salesperson.' Stayed two weeks."

"What was she up to this time?"

Blake shifts in his seat as he reads. "'Ms. Moore claims to sell vacuum cleaners but has made no sales attempts. Not once did she ask me if we need new vacuums here at the inn. Seems to be more interested in walking the neighborhoods, but she never takes anything more than her purse with her. Peculiar indeed. She asks unusual questions about local families, particularly those with children. Paid in cash. No forwarding address provided.'"

Blake's jaw clenches as he reads the next sentence. "'Miller children (ages 6, 8, 11) went missing for 48 hours. The day after Ms. Moore's departure they were found unharmed by the fountain in town square. No memory of their disappearance. Parents report their children seemed 'different' for weeks afterward.'"

Horror fills my gut. "Their memories were wiped. Was she testing some kind of memory manipulation on them?"

Blake's hands—my hands—clench into fists on the table. "On children? That's disgusting. And bold."

I force myself to breathe through the rage building. "What kind of monster experiments on kids?"

"Someone who sees humans as disposable. But what I don't understand is why no one recognized her. Her disguises are shit."

I have to agree with him there. I've seen better wigs in the bargain bin at the costume store.

"She probably wore some sort of shielding charm," I realize. "See that necklace she's wearing? It's in all the photos. My guess is it probably holds some type of glamor magic to shield her identity. She just didn't realize it wouldn't work on photos."

By the time we reach the 2002 ledger, Ravena's increasing boldness and sophistication are in high-res.

"Clara Blackwell, journalist," I read from the entry. "Claims to be writing about small-town America for a national magazine." Auburn hair. Tailored jacket. Same necklace. And those predatory eyes; her only other constant.

Mrs. Holloway's notes are much longer this time. *Questions about town governance, emergency protocols, community tensions, maps of flood-prone areas.*

When Blake reads the follow-up entry, his voice turns hollow. "'Worst flood in Moonridge history occurred three days after Ms. Blackwell's departure. Dam failure of unknown cause resulted in significant property damage and temporary displacement of 200+ residents. Emergency response overwhelmed. Community tensions reached critical levels.'"

"She's obviously behind these tragedies. It's like she was testing us."

"Seeing how we handle crisis," Blake agrees grimly.

I lean back in the wobbling chair and look at the ceiling, which is just cobwebs and darkness. The basement suddenly feels smaller, the shadows deeper. She has no limits. How many of Moonridge's tragedies were orchestrated by her?

"There's more," Blake says quietly, pointing to an entry in the next ledger. September 2015. Honey-blonde this time, and wide-framed glasses. She looks like an owl playing dress-up.

"Vanessa Lake, consultant for Natural Remedies," I read, my voice dripping with annoyance. "Stayed one month."

Her longest visit yet.

Mrs. Holloway's notes run long. She claims that "Ms. Lake" was very interested in local herbs and natural medicine. "Claimed to be developing medical products 'specifically suited to Moonridge's unique magical population'. She showed particular interest in werewolf biology, diet, and seasonal behavior."

Blake goes still again.

I keep reading, "During Ms. Lake's stay, local werewolf population saw a surge in illness including fatigue, irritability, difficulty maintaining human form under stress."

"That was the year I kept getting sick," Blake says. His voice has changed.

"And my dad—" He stops. Shakes his head and then starts again. "The doctors never figured out what was wrong with him. He died soon after."

"It was her," I breathe. "I'd bet anything she was testing something on you."

Blake stares at the photos spread across the table, his hands shaking slightly.

"It feels like it's more than revenge." The words leave my throat like broken glass.

"It's like she's preparing for war," Blake says quietly.

I thumb through the rest of the ledger. The last entry is dated 2019. "That's all I can find."

"I'd say that's more than enough." Blake stands and stares at the back wall. "She's been escalating. Each visit, the incidents got more targeted."

The basement's shadows seem to press closer, filled with the ghosts of all Ravena's past experiments.

"And each time, she's focused on something different," I add.

He turns to look at me. "This isn't just about revenge for being banished. This is methodical. It's like she wants to take over."

"And I would venture to guess the amulet's the final weapon in her arsenal." My head spins with this new information.

"Take pictures of everything so we have it as proof. Send what you can to La'Tasha as backup."

As Blake photographs the evidence, I do one more pass through the last book to make sure I didn't miss anything.

"Why did she wait so long to come back?" I wonder aloud.

"Probably because she needed to be able to get access to the amulet. You're a good witch, but I'm sure that Moonridge's magical defenses aren't as strong without your Grandma Agnes." Blake finishes snapping photos. "She needed to make sure she could access the apothecary."

He's right. My grandmother was much more powerful than

me, and she had a personal tie to Ravena. She was the one who banished her.

"We need to show the council what she's been doing." I help Blake put the ledgers back in order.

"Do you really think this is enough proof?" Blake asks. "Old B&B records showing similar-looking women? They'll think we're paranoid. And she'll likely have a rebuttal. We need to hit her with something unexpected."

"Right. We need to catch her in the act," I say, determination kicking in. "Force her to reveal herself."

We head back upstairs, both of us lost in thought. The warm, bright kitchen feels jarring after the basement's musty gloom. We step into the kitchen just as Mina pulls another tray of scones from the oven.

"Find what ya were lookin' for?" She sets the tray on a cooling rack.

Blake nods making that ugly-ass ponytail sway. "We did. Thank you."

She wraps several scones in a checkered napkin and places them in a basket before handing them to me. "Here, take some for the road."

I gladly take the basket, already tempted to dive in.

"Take care of Hazel and that pack of yours." Her kind, knowing eyes search Blake's face. "And for heaven's sake, let yourself have fun for once. Ya gotta take care of yourself, too."

Her words loosen something in this chest I wear. I know the words are meant for Blake, but they ring true for me, too. "I'll try," I promise.

Mina smiles, patting my arm. "Good. Because life's too short for all that broodin', even for werewolves." She winks, then turns to Blake in my body. "Maybe brew this one some chamomile tea? Might take the edge off."

Blake manages a smile. "I'll keep that in mind."

"Thank you again," I say.

Mina smiles at us both. "Any time, love. You two take care of each other, yeah?"

As we step outside, the gentle August breeze feels cleansing after the basement's stale air. The sun is higher now, warming the colorful flowers that dance beside the sidewalk.

Then I spot it.

A sleek white SUV parked down the street, its windows tinted dark enough to hide whoever's inside.

"Blake," I whisper, nudging him subtly. "Look."

His eyes track forward.

"That's her car, isn't it?"

The tinted windows stare at us, and Blake's muscles coil in response. My hands clench into fists. I'm overcome with the need to get him somewhere safe.

"We should go." My voice comes out rough. "Now."

But Blake doesn't move. "No. She wants us to be scared. I'm not going to give her that."

"Well, I *am* scared," I admit, surprising myself with the honesty. "Not for me. For you. If something happens to you while you're trapped in my body . . ."

We both glare in her direction.

I see you. We know what you're doing. I think.

As if responding to my thoughts, the SUV's engine purrs to life. It pulls away from the curb with deliberate slowness, like it's completely unbothered that we clocked her presence.

"She definitely knows we're onto her."

Blake's expression on my face is grim. "Then we'd better move fast. Before she decides we're too dangerous to keep around."

CHAPTER TEN

Hazel

We haul ass back to the apothecary. And why do I feel like we're in a spy movie? I know we're trying to act tough and unbothered, but we're both scared shitless. We've passed two white SUVs since leaving the B&B, and both times I almost pissed my pants.

She knew we were there.

We thought we were getting ahead of her. But she's watching us. Which means she knows we're onto her and is already covering her tracks and planning her next move. She's probably sitting in her fancy-ass car sipping martinis and cackling her evil villain laugh.

Blake keeps checking the rearview mirror while white-knuckling the steering wheel. He's going to get whiplash if he doesn't calm down.

"You think she followed us?" I ask.

Blake shakes his,—okay my—head. "No. I think she just wanted us to know that she knows that we know."

"Well, that's comforting."

We pull up behind the apothecary, using the back entrance just in case Ravena decided to stake out the front. As soon as I enter, I'm hit with the scent of fresh coffee and sugary sweets.

"La'Tasha must be stress-baking," I mutter as we slip through the back door.

Sure enough, we find her in the small kitchen area, surrounded by books, munching on what looks like lemon bars and scrolling through her tablet.

"Oh good, you're back," she says without looking up. "I was starting to think Ravena had kidnapped your asses."

Blake sets down the basket of Mina's scones and I immediately grab one.

"Did you get my texts?"

"I did." La'Tasha's eyes brighten when she looks up. "You two hit the lottery."

I stuff the scone in my face and then immediately reach for a lemon bar. "We need to compare notes."

She slides her tablet across the table. "Look at this." On screen is a grainy newspaper clipping with a headline that makes my stomach drop:

Strange Lights Over Wolf Ridge Precede Livestock Deaths.

"Wolf Ridge?" Blake asks, leaning closer. "Where's that?"

"That's what the north side of town used to be called," La'Tasha explains. "It was renamed Miller's Hill in the '80s."

I study the blurry photo that is featured with the article. Three dead cows scatter the field, their bodies positioned in what looks like . . . "Is that a ritual pattern?"

"Looks like it to me." La'Tasha points to the date at the top of the article. "And look at the date."

Blake removes the elastic from the ponytail from hell and lets my curls out. He immediately starts scratching my head. "Is it supposed to mean something?"

La'Tasha pulls out her phone and shows me a photo Blake sent. "It was two days after Lydia Fairchild checked into the B&B."

My stomach knots up. "So, obviously a blood magic ritual."

"Most likely." La'Tasha scrolls to another article, but pauses before showing it to us. "Hold on to your panties. It gets worse."

Blake and I exchange glances. "How much worse?" he asks.

"Remember the 1988 incident you found? When she was calling herself Sabrina Moore?" La'Tasha's finger hovers over the screen.

"The missing children one?" Blake scoots closer to get a better view.

"Yep. Three kids went missing for two days. I'm thinking memory manipulation?"

I knew it.

"Which requires . . ." La'Tasha lets the sentence hang.

"Blood magic," I finish, voice hollow.

"But what is she after?" Blake asks. "We know she has a grudge, but what's the end game?"

La'Tasha pulls up a map of Moonridge. "That's what I was trying to figure out. I started messing around. Went all forensic and shit and started plotting dots and lines and I noticed something." She taps the screen, and red dots appear.

"These are all the incidents." She has all five of them labeled with their respective dates.

"And? They look random," Blake says.

"That's what I thought." La'Tasha's finger hovers over the screen. "Until I literally started connecting the dots."

She draws a line from the north dot to the east. Then east to south. South to west. West back to north.

My breath catches. "No."

"What?" Blake looks between us.

"It's a pentagram." The words taste like ash in my mouth.

Blake looks at the map. Looks at me. "What does that mean?"

"Five points of power." My voice shakes. "Each incident is a focal point. She's been constructing a ritual workspace. Right under our noses."

"A workspace for what?"

La'Tasha puts her finger on the center of the pentagram, where all five lines converge.

The apothecary.

Nobody says anything for a second.

"A big-ass ritual from the looks of it," La'Tasha says.

"With the apothecary—and Wolfsbane Amulet—at the center."

None of us moves for what feels like forever. La'Tasha finally breaks the silence by reaching under the counter and pulling out an ancient book. It looks like it's literally being held together with string and a prayer.

"What is that?"

"My great-great-great-grandmother's diary." La'Tasha opens it with careful hands. "She was one of the founding witches of Moonridge."

Blake runs a finger over the worn leather cover. "How far back does your family go here?"

"The beginning." La'Tasha is already turning pages, looking for something specific. "Morehouse witches helped build this town. Carter wolves, too."

Blake cocks his head. "Carter wolves?"

"Your ancestors helped found Moonridge." She finds the page. Smooths it flat. "August 15th, 1902. The tension between wolf packs and witch covens has reached a breaking point.'"

She keeps reading. "'Last night's confrontation at the Moonstone Circle. Nearly ended in bloodshed. Again, we find ourselves manipulated by outside forces.'"

"Again," I say.

La'Tasha glances up, then back to the page. "'Elder Carter proposes a Binding Pact. Something to bring us together as a community and ensure our continued safety from dark forces that seem to plague our community. The other werewolves and several witches are skeptical.'" She pauses. "'Though, Elder Carter sees it as the only way forward to unity.'"

Blake doesn't say anything.

"Your great-great-great-grandfather sat down and drew up the terms himself," La'Tasha says.

"The Pact of Moonridge." I always thought it was just administrative. A handshake formalized on paper. "I didn't know it was—"

"It's not a formality." La'Tasha reads from the journal. "'The Binding Pact would draw from both wolf and witch magic. So long as our kinds do not turn against each other, the wards will hold. Moonridge remains protected.'"

"The town's protection depends on us working together," Blake says slowly. "That's why she's been trying to drive us apart."

"Exactly." La'Tasha closes the journal. "This pattern has repeated throughout history. Someone starts shit, weakens the alliance, then makes their move."

"And we walked right into it," I groan.

"Not entirely." Blake reaches for a scone. "We're working together now. She didn't count on the body swap forcing us to cooperate."

La'Tasha points at us with a half-eaten lemon bar. "That was her mistake. She wanted to create chaos but accidentally made you two a team."

I snort. "At least there's that."

Blake smiles. "I mean, we do make a decent team. When we're not driving each other crazy."

Heat spreads beneath my ribs and I can't help but smile.

"You said this has happened before. Do you know when? And how often?"

Before she can respond, the bell above the front door jingles.

La'Tasha checks her watch. "I thought I flipped the sign."

I tilt my head toward the door, reminding Blake that he's supposed to be me. Supposed to greet customers when they come in. He immediately adjusts his stance and moves to greet whomever it is. I poke my head around the corner and see Silvie Harper, her daughter in tow. Silvie looks worn thin. Dark circles under her eyes. The little girl is pale and wide-eyed. She clutches a threadbare stuffed rabbit.

"I'm sorry," Silvie says quickly. "I know it's after hours, but Hazel, we need your help."

Blake glances at me, a brief flash of panic crossing my face before he composes himself. "Of course. What's going on?"

Silvie gently nudges her daughter forward. "This is Emmy. She hasn't slept properly in days. Not since . . ." Her voice drops to a whisper. "Not since she saw what happened. At the park."

My stomach drops. The wolf incident. The little girl must have witnessed Mason's attack.

"She keeps having nightmares," Silvie continues. "She's afraid to go to school. Afraid to play outside. I've tried everything. Nightlights, monster spray under the bed, sleeping in her room with her. Nothing helps."

Blake crouches down to the child's level, brushing a stray curl out of my face. "Hi, Emmy. That's a nice rabbit you have."

Emmy clutches the stuffed animal tighter but remains silent.

"Does your rabbit have a name?" Blake is soft and patient. I can't help but smile.

"Hopper," Emmy whispers, barely audible.

"Hopper. That's a good name. Is Hopper scared, too?"

A tiny nod.

"You know what? I used to be scared of monsters when I was your age," Blake continues. I can't imagine him being afraid of anything. "Every time I heard a scary noise, I'd hide under my blankets."

Emmy relaxes a little. Her fingers loosen around Hopper's ear. "What did you do?"

"My grandma made me something special. It's called a dreamcatcher. A magical one that kept the scary things away." Blake glances up at me, then back to Emmy.

"Would you like me to make one for you and Hopper?"

Emmy nods eagerly.

Blake steps behind the counter, completely confident. He gathers dried lavender, then a wooden hoop, blue thread, and small crystals that glint in the late-evening sunlight that flows through the front window.

Emmy drifts closer. Kids always know when something is about to get interesting.

"These crystals are special," he says, holding up a crystal so she can see it. "They glow just enough to remind the bad dreams they're not welcome."

He begins weaving the thread. To my surprise, the pattern isn't half bad. La'Tasha throws me a look, one brow raised. I shrug. How was I supposed to know he had secret dreamcatcher skills?

"The most important part . . ." He ties a final knot. "Is this." He holds out the half-finished dreamcatcher to Emmy. "I need you to hold it and think about the happiest place you know. Where do you feel the happiest?"

Emmy places a finger to her chin in exaggerated contemplation. "Grammy's garden. With the butterflies. And cookies and chocolate milk."

"Perfect." Blake guides her small hand to hold the center of the web. "Close your eyes and picture your Grammy's garden. All the colors. The butterflies. And those yummy cookies and chocolate milk."

As Emmy closes her eyes, I feel a prickle of magic in the air, and it's coming from Blake. He's using the basic energy manipulation I taught him, channeling it through Emmy's happy thoughts and into the dreamcatcher. The crystals glow briefly and then audibly pop after a few seconds. Emmy's eyes expand in wonder.

"What was that?" she gasps.

"That was your happy place. Now it's caught in the web. And it'll be there to protect you when you fall asleep," Blake explains. "When you hang this above your bed, it will catch all the scary dreams and only let the happy ones through."

He finishes up by attaching a few sprigs of lavender and then hands the completed charm to Emmy. She accepts it with joy.

"What do we say, Emmy?" her mother prompts.

"Thank you," Emmy says, smiling for the first time since they arrived.

"You're very welcome," Blake responds. Then, to the mother, "Have her hang it where she can see it from her bed. The lavender will help her relax, too."

While Silvie pays and thanks Blake profusely, I stand back, seeing him through new eyes. There's a gentleness there I never expected from stern, rule-following Blake Carter. I see patience. Understanding. Two things I wouldn't have guessed he possessed. Feelings bubble up that make my borrowed heart flip-flop.

"You're really catching on to this whole magic thing," I say as he packs up the remaining supplies and places them back where he got them.

"I just so happened to read a chapter on dreamcatchers the other day during a slow period. I guess it came in handy." He doesn't look at me. Is he embarrassed?

"You were amazing with her," I say quietly.

He shrugs. Keeps tidying. "She was scared."

"You made her feel safe." I lean against the counter. "How did you know what she needed?"

He's quiet for a second. "Because I was her when I was a kid." He sets down the lavender. "I spent most of my childhood terrified. Convinced something bad was coming and nobody was going to be able to stop it."

"What were you scared of?"

He exhales slowly. "My mom had a hard time with all of it. The pack stuff, I mean. Dad's shifts. The whole life that came with marrying a werewolf. She drank. It got worse around full moons. Dad would leave to keep the peace, thinking if he wasn't there she'd have less to be upset about." He pauses. "What actually happened was she'd just drink more."

My heart clenches. "I'm sorry."

"One month, Dad took Calvin and me to our aunt's to get us out of her way. Mom got drunk, decided she wanted us home, and came to pick us up." His voice breaks. "She crashed on the way to get us. Died instantly."

I squeeze his hand. I don't dare try to speak.

"After that, everything set me off. I was sad, then angry. Constantly on edge. The nightmares were nonstop. My emotions were a wreck. Honestly, I think that's why I started shifting so young. I couldn't regulate anything. Anyway, my cousin Olivia was a therapist. She worked with me. Taught me how to calm myself and regain control."

His confession leaves me speechless. It explains so much.

"Thanks for telling me that." I squeeze his—my—hand. I want to hug him so bad right now, but I don't want to make him uncomfortable. "You're a natural with kids."

He glances up, a hint of pride in my green eyes. "Thanks."

La'Tasha clears her throat. "I hate to interrupt whatever this is, but we still have a psychotic witch to deal with."

"Right." Blake nods, all business again. He begins to pace. Something I've learned helps him think.

"We need a plan. If Ravena's been building this pentagram of power points around the amulet, we need to disrupt it somehow."

"Or use it against her," La'Tasha suggests. "The full moon is in two days. If she's planning something big, that's when she'll make her move."

I'm about to respond when a crash from outside the shop cuts me off.

We all freeze.

"What was that?" I move toward the door.

"Hazel, don't," Blake hisses, grabbing my arm. The familiar spark jumps between us at the contact. Before I can reach the door, it flies open. Mason stumbles in, half-shifted and bleeding, caught between human and wolf. His eyes glow an unnatural yellow. Claws extend from his fingertips. His shirt is torn.

"Blake," he half-growls, spotting me. "Help . . . me."

"Mason? What happened?"

He staggers forward, knocking over a display of tarot cards and crystal spheres. They shatter across the floor.

"Can't . . . control it. She's in my head."

"Who's she?" I step closer, carefully maintaining distance.

"Lady . . . in . . . white." His words slur, his mouth struggling with human speech.

"Tells me to . . . hurt the . . . witches." He convulses. The sound that comes out of him isn't human. When he looks up, Mason is no longer there.

"Where is she?" His nostrils flare. "The Thornton witch. I can smell her."

I put myself between him and the work room, waving behind my back for Blake and La'Tasha to move. Now. Quietly.

"Mason. Hey. Look at me. This isn't you."

He lunges for the counter. Claws out. I catch him and shove him sideways. He flies into the tincture shelf. Glass scatters across the floor. I'm pissed about the glass but really impressed by how strong I am. Still.

"Go!" I shout toward the back room.

Mason doesn't stay down. He circles back. Eyes locked on the work room behind me.

"The witch dies." His voice has gravel in it. "All of them die."

"Not a chance."

He charges. Blake's body moves before I tell it to. I step to my right. Grab his arm. His own momentum sends him ass over elbows into the door.

"Mason, stop." I get in front of him again. "She's controlling you. Ravena is controlling you. This isn't—"

A feral roar fills the space. Mason feints toward me. Dives past. He's headed straight for them.

Blake stands frozen in my body. Eyes wide. Mason barrels forward. Time slows down.

I feel Blake's heart pound in my ears. The wolf inside rises up. *Protect.*

I clear a fallen chair and hit Mason from behind. We go down hard together.

He's strong. Whatever she's got in him, it's got teeth. But Blake's body is stronger. I use the weight of it to pin him flat.

"La'Tasha—"

"I know!" She's already behind the counter. Grabs a jar of black salt. She pours a circle around us without hesitating.

The glow hits.

Mason goes board-stiff, then drops. The light in his eyes flickers. Fades. His face contorts one more time and then eases into stillness. Pupils pull back. Brown replaces yellow. He's back.

"What . . . happened?" he mumbles, confusion replacing the rage that consumed him minutes ago.

I ease my grip cautiously. "You're safe now. The salt is blocking the influence."

La'Tasha crouches just outside the circle. "What do you remember? Before you came here."

He has to think about it. "I was home. Just resting after work." His throat moves. "Then she was just there. Not there-there. Inside my head, there. Bianca. The lady in white. She said the witches were planning something against the pack. Said the only way to stop it was—" He stops. Shakes his head. His eyes go wet. "I tried to fight it. I couldn't. It was like being locked in a room inside my own head. I'm so sorry."

"Nothing to apologize for." I help him sit up. "I need to tell you something about Bianca."

Blake has started pacing the edge of the circle. The light coming through the window makes my hair look like it has gold streaks in it. It looks good! I'm so happy I went with the highlights last week. I need to remember to ask for that same color next time.

"Hazel? Hello? What's wrong with you?"

I zone back in. "Huh?"

Mason looks between us, eyebrows raised. "Why did you call him Hazel? That's your name."

Blake and I look at each other.

La'Tasha sighs. "It's a long story. We had a little magical incident the other night. Currently, Blake is in Hazel's body, and Hazel is in Blake's. That's the short version."

Mason blinks slowly. "That's . . . weird." His eyes dart between the two of us. "But it explains a lot."

"What I was saying is," Blake gives me a stern look, "She was able to mentally control Mason. This isn't good. If she's able to control him, she might be able to control the rest of us."

"She can." Mason looks up at us from within the salt circle. "Or she plans to. I heard her say that I was the first, and the others will soon join me. She's planning to control the entire pack at once. She wants us to act as her weapons."

"She wants to make you hunt us. Maybe even humans." My throat goes tight.

Mason offers a small, defeated nod. "She showed me. What she wants us to do. All of us."

Blake doubles over like he's been punched. "My pack."

"Blake." I reach for him, but he jerks away.

La'Tasha looks between us. Terror fills her face. "The full moon is in two days. If you two are still swapped when she takes control . . ."

The implication hangs in the air. If I'm still trapped in my body when Ravena activates her control, will I be the one forced to hunt? Can I even survive a shift?

Blake stands up abruptly. "She's going to make us destroy everything we've sworn to protect."

"Not if we stop her first," I say.

"How?" Blake turns to face me. "How do we fight someone

who can control minds? Who's had half a century to prepare? Who knows every weakness we have? She's twelve steps ahead of us."

The questions hang in the air.

He's right. How do you win against someone who's been planning your downfall since before you were born?

CHAPTER ELEVEN

Hazel

I sit crouched between La'Tasha and Blake, all eyes still trained on Mason. Mason sits cross-legged across from us, looking all dejected. Like a kid in time-out. It's been thirty minutes and he hasn't freaked out again, so I think the containment circle is doing its thing.

I'm still all ramped up. Like I want to strip naked and run circles around the house. Or maybe the entire block. Do I have the zoomies? Is that a thing for werewolves? Before I can ask, my stomach rumbles with an internal fart. It's so loud it almost rattles the shelves. All eyes turn to me, and my face goes beet red.

"I know you ain't about to fart on me." La'Tasha slides a foot to the left.

"No, I'm hungry," I lie.

"I know my stomach. That wasn't hunger. That was a full-on gas bubble. That's what you get for stuffing yourself to the gills with all those carbs and sugar."

I stand and excuse myself, leaving them alone to assess Mason.

"How long will the salt circle hold him?" Blake asks when I reenter the room.

La'Tasha inspects the iridescent barrier. "As long as the circle isn't broken, and he stays inside, it should keep Ravena out."

"So I'm a prisoner now?" Mason's voice is resigned. The werewolf who broke into the shop all teeth and claws now looks like a wounded puppy.

"Not a prisoner." I crouch down to his level. Blake's knees crack in protest. Why does his body make so much noise? "It's just that inside that circle is the only place we know for sure Ravena can't reach you."

Mason nods, running his finger over a knot in the wood. "What about the others? We can't all fit in this little circle. She's not just after me."

Blake cracks my knuckles and it makes me wince. "Do we have enough containment salt to protect the entire pack?"

I do some quick mental math. "That's a lot of salt. And we only have two days."

"One and a half, technically," La'Tasha points out, which earns her a glare from both me and Blake.

"Thanks for the reminder," I mutter.

Broken glass crunches under my feet—correction, Blake's size-twelve feet—as I sweep up the remnants of our battle. The normally comforting smells of herbs and incense mix with the sharper scents of blood and sweat. Mason's blood. My sweat. Or technically, Blake's sweat. Ugh. This body-swap situation isn't getting any less confusing.

"Even if we can protect the pack, Ravena still has the amulet's power," Blake points out. "And something tells me she has a backup plan."

La'Tasha clears her throat. "There's something I didn't get to tell you before Mason burst in." She hurries into the back room, returning moments later with her ancestor's journal. "You two are going to want to sit down for this."

Blake and I exchange glances. His expression on my face is wary, matching exactly what I feel. How much more is there? I pull up a stool, testing it to make sure it'll hold. Blake's body weighs a ton compared to mine, and I've already broken two chairs since the swap.

"What exactly are we sitting down for?" I ask.

La'Tasha perches on the edge of the counter, ankles crossed. She looks at us like it's storytime. "A history lesson."

Even Mason leans forward in his salt circle, eager to hear what she has to say.

"As I mentioned earlier," La'Tasha begins, "my ancestor, Marigold Miller, wrote about things that went down in Moonridge in the late 1800s." She flips carefully through the brittle pages until she finds what she's looking for. "I found this entry particularly interesting. 'April 18, 1870. The council met today to discuss the increasingly troubling relationship between Samuel Carter and Rose Thornton.'"

My heart skips a beat. "Carter? Thornton?" I glance at Blake. His expression matches mine.

"Your ancestors," La'Tasha confirms.

"Wait. Our families were connected over a century ago?" I move to look over her shoulder.

"Yep. Samuel was part of the original Carter pack. And Rose was a witch from the Thornton line, as you probably already guessed, but you know how I like to state the obvious."

"And what about them?" Blake asks.

La'Tasha chooses her words carefully. "They were together. Romantically."

"A werewolf and a witch?" My voice comes out rougher than intended. "And in 1870?"

"It was a whole scandal." La'Tasha turns the page slowly. "The vibes between witches and wolves were pretty rancid in those days. I'm still digging for the receipts on why, though, because it doesn't make sense. The settlement started out peaceful. Witches and werewolves and humans got along just fine for the first hundred years or so. Like today. But something went sideways and turned them against each other. By this point in time, these two groups hated each other. But here goes Rose and Sam falling in love anyway."

It's like Romeo and Juliet but with fur and potions. "What happened to them?"

Something in La'Tasha's expression tells me this isn't a love story with a happy ending.

"Let's just say there was a whole lot of mess. The witches thought Rose was betraying her kind by hooking up with a fur daddy, and the werewolves accused Samuel of divulging pack secrets for a little nae nae. But it sounds like they refused to stop seeing each other. They were totally smitten."

She traces a perfectly manicured orange fingernail along a particularly long passage. "According to Marigold, Rose and Samuel really believed witches and werewolves could work together. They were out here trying to be a whole power couple for the people."

"So what happened?" Mason sits close to the edge of the circle, fully invested in this story of starcrossed lovers.

"There was another witch involved," La'Tasha says. "And this is where it gets all crazy soap-opera-like. The witch was Adeline Blackwood. And *she* had *her* sights set on Samuel before Rose came into the picture."

"Blackwood? As in one of Ravena's ancestors? Seriously?" I roll my eyes so hard I'm practically checking out my own ass. Well, Blake's ass. "Has there ever been someone with the last name Blackwood who lived here and wasn't a total pain in the ass?"

La'Tasha cocks her head and raises an eyebrow. "The Blackwood witches have a long history in Moonridge. And according to Marigold, Adeline did *not* take rejection well."

"Shocker!" Blake is just as annoyed with the Blackwood bloodline as I am.

La'Tasha reads from the journal, slow and dramatic, her tone that of someone reading a very serious story. "'Adeline's rage at being rejected has taken a dark turn. I fear she delves into magics best left untouched. Yesterday, Eliza found a slaughtered rabbit near Adeline's cottage, its blood drained in the pattern of ancient binding runes.'"

"History repeating itself." Blake throws up his hands. "If ever there was a case for generational psychosis, this is it."

"Like ancestor, like descendant." La'Tasha flips to the next page. "But Adeline didn't stop at small animal sacrifices. She was committed. She spent months studying Samuel, learning his habits, his weaknesses. And then she found an artifact. Something called the Moon's Tear Amulet. And you already know this is when the real mess starts."

I exchange glances with Blake. "Would this happen to be our Wolfsbane Amulet?"

La'Tasha nods. "These magical artifacts get renamed through history, but yeah, it's gotta be the same one."

"So what did she do with it?" Mason asks, his face pale in the dim light.

"Everything went south at the Midsummer gathering." La'Tasha reads again, her voice somber. "'Samuel arrived late. His manner strange, eyes wild.'"

I glance at Mason in his salt circle, remembering the wild look in his eyes when he burst into the shop.

"'When Rose approached him, he seemed not to recognize her.'"

"Just like with Mason," Blake says quietly. "He looked right through me earlier."

"'Then Adeline whispered something in his ear, and he changed.'"

Goosebumps scatter across my arms. "He transformed?"

"Partially," La'Tasha confirms grimly. "Just like Mason did. Half-human, half-wolf, completely out of it the way it sounds."

Mason makes a soft sound of distress from his circle, and I realize he's seeing his own experience reflected in this century-old tragedy.

"What happened next?"

"This says he ended up wolfing out on one of Rose's friends. A witch named Eleanor. He didn't totally take her out, but he hurt her bad enough that blood was spilled and trust was shattered."

"Let me guess," Blake says, his voice tight. "The witches blamed Samuel and demanded justice."

"Oh, they wanted him *gone* gone," La'Tasha reads. "'The council called for Samuel's execution. Only Rose's desperate plea reduced the sentence to permanent exile. She swore he would never set foot in Moonridge again, that the attack must have been caused by external magic. No one believed her except Marigold, who had seen Adeline's smug satisfaction as chaos erupted.'"

Mason shifts uncomfortably in his salt circle. "So they drove him out? Even though it wasn't his fault?"

"Look, fear is one hell of a drug," La'Tasha says simply. "And Adeline played her cards well. She planted dark magic receipts up in Rose's cabin to make it look like our girl had planned the attack. The werewolves believed that Rose only pretended to love Samuel. That she was using him to take them all out."

"What happened to Rose?" I ask, dreading the answer.

La'Tasha's finger traces down the page, and her voice softens. "Sounds like Rose just faded. Over the next few months, she went downhill fast. And Adeline was always up in her face, too, bringing over these 'teas' and 'tinctures' that were supposedly for her health, but Rose's health just kept getting worse and worse. By wintertime, she was gone. Most people were out here claiming she died of a broken heart, but anybody with half a brain cell and some common sense knew Adeline was the one who really pulled the plug."

The shop falls silent except for the ticking of the old clock above the register.

"So Adeline killed her. For revenge." Blake runs his hands over my face. "She drove Samuel away, killed Rose, and kept the communities divided."

"Yep. But karma came for her ass." La'Tasha flips to the final page. "After Rose died, Adeline started acting like she was the 'protector' of the people against 'wolf treachery' and convinced the council to put all these restrictions on the pack. But Marigold said she was still never satisfied."

"Because Samuel was still alive somewhere," I guess.

La'Tasha nods. "Exactly. She was still pressed over him. That obsession was *deep*. She spent literal years trying to track him down while she was busy bossing everyone around in Moonridge, but she never caught a lead. Meanwhile, the Carter pack finally got fed up with the nonsense and started forming alliances with other supernaturals and even some humans. By the time Adeline realized she was losing control, it was too late."

"What happened to her?" Mason asks.

"She tried one final, hopeless ritual to drag Samuel back to Moonridge. But the magic said 'no ma'am'. It backfired. Catastrophically." La'Tasha closes the journal gently. "The book is a little fuzzy on the specifics, but whatever stunt she was pulling ended up taking her out—along with her whole little fan club."

"And the amulet? The Moon's Tear?"

"It vanished in all that magical mess. It popped up again years later as the Wolfsbane Amulet."

Suddenly it all makes sense. "So Ravena is not only seeking revenge, but she's also trying to finish what Adeline started."

"With one key difference," La'Tasha adds. "She's had fifty years to prepare. And she's not just pressed over one wolf. She wants control of the entire pack."

Blake stands suddenly. "This is all fascinating history, but how does it help us now? We still have a power-hungry witch with a magical artifact and a town full of potential werewolf weapons."

La'Tasha holds up her hand. "There's more." She turns to the back of the journal and removes a slip of ancient paper. "Marigold believed the tragedy could have been prevented. She wrote this prophecy about what might happen if history repeated itself."

She unfolds the paper carefully. "'When evil rises again, wolf and witch will unite in love, and the ancient wounds will heal,'" La'Tasha reads, and the words almost knock me off my feet.

I can't look at Blake. Can't bear to see whatever expression might be on his face—my face—right now. Because the truth is, something has been building between us. Something that started with forced cooperation and has grown into . . . what? Trust? Attraction? Something deeper?

My mouth goes dry. "That sounds a lot like . . ."

"You and Blake," La'Tasha finishes simply. "A descendant of Samuel Carter. A distant cousin from Rose Thornton's line. It's like you're destined to play out their love story all over again."

The silence that follows is deafening. I stare at Blake, trying to process what La'Tasha just revealed. Samuel Carter and Rose Thornton—our ancestors—were lovers torn apart by jealousy and fear.

And now us.

The thought sends a million worms loose in my chest. What would have happened if we'd known all along that members of our families once loved each other enough to defy their entire communities?

"Are you saying," Blake finally speaks, each word careful and measured, "that Hazel and I are supposed to fall in love to break some ancient curse?"

"I'm not saying you have to start looking at wedding venues," La'Tasha says, setting the journal aside. "But there's a reason you two got body-swapped instead of, say, turning into frogs. The amulet's magic recognized there was a connection between you. Even if you didn't."

My heart pounds. "But we don't have *that* kind of connection."

Even as I say it, I know it's not entirely true. Being in Blake's body and being forced to spend time with him has shown me a different side. The softer, more vulnerable Blake. The version of him that I actually enjoy being around.

"Maybe not yet." La'Tasha looks at us with knowing eyes. "But the potential is there. Ravena must see it. That's why she's working so hard to keep you apart."

"Because history repeats itself," Mason murmurs from his circle. "She's Adeline all over again."

"But there's a difference this time," La'Tasha points out. "We know what her crazy ass is up to. And you two are already working together to stop her. Something Samuel and Rose weren't able to do before it was too late."

Blake paces again, my body moving with agitated energy. "This is a lot to process."

"Tell me about it," I mumble. "Finding out your ancestors had a tragic romance is one thing. Being told you're supposed to fall in love with your lifelong frenemy to break a curse is a whole other level of weird."

"Lifelong frenemy?" Blake looks at me with raised eyebrows and a smirk. "Is that what I am to you?"

"Well, what would you call it? We've been at each other's throats for years."

"Professional opponents?" he suggests with a shrug.

"That's just a fancy way of saying frenemies."

I smile. An understanding passes between us. This is about more than ancestral curses or prophecies or childhood grudges. It's about who we are now. Who we've grown into the last few days. And about protecting the place and the people we love.

"We need to stay focused on two things," La'Tasha says, killing my love story vibe. "We need that containment salt to keep the pack safe, and we gotta find a way to shut that amulet down for good."

"And Ravena," Blake adds, determination hardening my features. "We need to deal with her directly."

Mason shifts in his salt circle like his butt has fallen asleep. Poor guy. He can't be comfortable. "How much of this containment salt can you make before the full moon?"

La'Tasha purses her lips, doing the math in her head. "If we're both in here pulling all-nighters and working around the clock? We could probably get enough for maybe fifteen, twenty wolves. And that's if we're really pushing it."

"There are thirty-two in the pack," Blake says. "We need to prioritize who gets protection first."

I run a hand over Blake's face, the stubbly beard still throwing me. "So, the youngest wolves, and anyone who's shown signs of being susceptible to the amulet's influence."

"Like me," Mason says.

I nod slowly. "And while we're making salt, we need to figure out how to neutralize the amulet."

La'Tasha drums her fingers on the counter, nails clicking. "The tricky part is getting to it. It's under the floorboards. And it's wrapped in about fifty layers of magical security. Granny Agnes wasn't messing around when she locked it down."

"Gran never did anything half-assed." A profound sense of admiration blooms in me. "But she also taught me that every magical lock has a key."

"So we need to find that key," Blake concludes. "And soon."

Mason's stomach growls loudly, the sound echoing in the quiet shop. He looks embarrassed. "That really is hunger. Not . . ." he waves in my general direction and La'Tasha busts out laughing. "Sorry. Haven't eaten since . . . well, I don't actually remember."

"I'll get you something," La'Tasha offers, heading toward the kitchen. "You're going to be in that circle for a while."

While she rummages for food, I move closer to the salt circle, crouching down to Mason's level. "How are you feeling? Really?"

His eyes meet mine with raw vulnerability. "Scared. I can still feel her, you know. Like a shadow that's just outside, trying to get back in."

"We won't let her take control again." I lean closer to the circle. "I promise."

"How can you be sure?" His voice cracks slightly. "She's so strong, Blake. I mean, Hazel. Sorry, this is confusing."

"Tell me about it." I offer him a half-smile. "But here's what I know. Ravena might be powerful, but she's also desperate. Desperate people make mistakes."

Blake joins us, kneeling beside me. "Hazel's right. And we have something Ravena doesn't expect."

"What's that?" Mason asks.

"Each other," he says simply.

I look at Blake and realize that I don't want this to end. Not the body swap. I definitely want *that* to end. But this closeness. This partnership. This feeling of being truly seen by someone who gets all my flaws and chooses to stand with me anyway.

"Yeah." I meet Blake's gaze across the salt circle. "We do."

La'Tasha returns with a plate of sandwiches and a bottle of water, carefully placing them inside the salt circle. "Eat up."

Mason accepts the food gratefully, tearing into a sandwich with wolfish hunger. Between bites, he asks, "So what's the plan? How do we stop Ravena before the full moon?"

I look to Blake. An understanding passes between us, a trust that feels both new and strangely familiar.

"Tomorrow," Blake says, "we need to secure as many pack members as possible. I'll contact Calvin, explain what's happening, and decide which pack members are most at risk. We'll get them the containment salt."

I nod. "While you do that, La'Tasha and I will work on making more salt and researching ways to neutralize the amulet."

"And me?" Mason asks.

"You need to stay contained. We'll get you somewhere more comfortable, though," I promise him.

"There's something else we should consider," La'Tasha says, her expression serious.

"What?" I ask.

"The prophecy. What if that's literally the key to breaking the amulet's power?"

An uncomfortable silence falls. I steal a glance at Blake and my cheeks flush pink. He looks as flustered as I feel.

"Let's focus on what we know will work," Blake says diplomatically. "Containment salt and research first. Prophecies and . . . other complications can wait."

"Agreed." I'm grateful for the out. "We don't even know if that prophecy is reliable. It was written over a century ago."

La'Tasha gives us both a knowing look but doesn't push. "Fine. Then we should get started. That salt isn't going to make itself."

As La'Tasha begins gathering ingredients, I feel a strange sensation in Blake's chest. Anxiety? Hope? I can't tell. I catch Blake watching me, his expression thoughtful behind my green eyes.

"What?" I ask softly.

"Nothing." There's a hesitation that tells me it's not nothing. "Just thinking about Samuel and Rose. What they tried to do."

"Bridge the divide," I murmur.

He nods. "They were ahead of their time."

"Or maybe," I say, suddenly feeling very bold, "we're exactly on time."

The moment stretches between us. Then La'Tasha drops a jar of dried herbs, the clatter breaking the spell.

"Oops! My bad. Clearly my grip is not gripping today."

Blake clears my throat and straightens up. "I should call Calvin. I'll ask him to come over first thing in the morning. And then I think you and I need to take a little road trip."

"Road trip?"

"I think we need to go check out Ravena's business. See if we can find any clues as to what she's cooking up."

"Sounds dangerous. But you're right. It's our best chance at finding answers."

As Blake steps away to make the call, I watch him with new

eyes. Would falling for him really be so bad? Was this meant to happen all along?

Samuel and Rose tried to bridge the divide between our kinds and failed. But maybe, just maybe, Blake and I can succeed where they couldn't. Maybe we can heal all that generational trauma. Create something new.

Maybe we're exactly what Moonridge needs.

CHAPTER TWELVE

Blake

We need to move Mason somewhere safe." My voice is still jarringly high. I don't think I'll ever get used to sounding like her. "We need to get him out of the middle of the shop, but somewhere Ravena can't reach him."

Hazel nods. "Agreed. The salt circle is working, but we can't keep him trapped in the middle of my shop forever."

"I have a basement in my house," La'Tasha offers. "It's lined with protection herbs and crystals. I could reinforce it with more salt. He'd be more comfortable somewhere he can move around and stuff. And it'd get him out of here in case the po-po come looking for you two heathens."

"We need to know exactly what she's planning," I say.

"And you're going to get that by breaking into her store?" La'Tasha raises an eyebrow. "You realize that's illegal, right?"

"What other choice do we have? I'm not above a little breaking and entering," Hazel counters with my deeper voice.

"Look at you. My little criminal best friend."

I crack my knuckles and Hazel grabs my hands to stop me. That spark hits again. "She'll likely have magical protections in place."

"Which you can handle," Hazel says, pointing at me. "You've been practicing the protection spells I taught you. And I can use your super-sniffer to find any magical traces." She taps the side of my nose.

She hands me a black corded necklace with an onyx stone attached. "Concealment charms. They'll help us get past non-magical security measures."

I check the clock. "It's almost midnight. Things should be quiet, and her staff should all be long gone."

La'Tasha grabs her purse. "Fine. I'll babysit wolf-boy here while you two commit felonies." She pats Mason's shoulder. "Come on, kid. Let's get you somewhere safe."

I watch the two of them leave and I'm hit in the face with a ball of fabric.

"Wear this," Hazel says. "My usual color palette is a little too bright for recon work."

I catch the sweater, noting how big it is. "Wait. Is this mine?"

A blush creeps across my cheeks—her cheeks—as she shrugs. "I found it last winter. You'd left it in my basement after fixing my frozen pipes. Forgot to return it."

Did she just keep it, or did she wear it, too? Did she think of me when she did? No. I can't think of that right now, so I shove the thought into a corner where I can't reach it.

"You could have brought it by the shop," I say.

"I could have. But I didn't want to."

The admission hangs between us. I smile. I pull the sweater over my head and it hangs like a dress. I feel ridiculous. Definitely cozy, though.

***

Bianca's Wellness Boutique glows white in the moonlight at the edge of Main Street like some giant, square-shaped marshmallow. The lights are off, and not a car in the parking lot.

All clear.

We dart across the street and down a side alley to the service entrance in the back. Hazel tests the door handle, glances around one last time to make sure no one is lurking in the shadows, and then puts every ounce of wolf muscle into it, twisting it free with a quiet crunch.

I wince. "So much for not leaving evidence."

"Please. None of this will matter if Ravena is able to mind-control your entire pack."

Fair point.

We slip inside. Boxes of supplements and wellness products line the shelves. The air is full of some lemon-scented chemical stank that sticks to the back of your throat like peanut butter. I hope Hazel isn't prone to migraines, because this shit could trigger one.

"This way." Hazel points toward the main store area.

The boutique is eerily perfect. White shelves filled with pastel-colored bottles line three of the four walls. A juice bar with gleaming countertops and a wall-length menu complete the room.

"We should check her office," I suggest, pointing to the hallway beneath a motivational quote written in perfect calligraphy. 'Fuel Your Soul. Find Your Glow!' Who comes up with this shit? It's so "look at me, I'm a wellness girlie" it makes my butthole itch.

We walk past several consultation rooms to the end of the hall where we find an office with her name on a plaque outside the door. Hazel moves to break the doorknob, but I stop her, reaching into her pocket and pulling out the pocket knife I'm never without.

"Are you trying to get frisky with me? Now is not the time."

"Very funny."

I manage to pop the lock without busting it and push the door open. The office is a cavernous white void. It practically glows in the dark. Everything is white. Not a paper out of place.

Hazel stops. She sniffs the air, head tilted. "Something's under the floor. Does this place have a basement, or a lower floor?"

I kneel, pressing Hazel's hands against the white tiles. A faint vibration hums against her palms. "You're right. There's a space beneath us. Lots of crazy energy coming from down there."

I step out of the office, and then I hear it. A key in the front door.

"Someone's coming." Hazel grabs my arm. "Hide!"

We nudge the door closed and then duck behind the desk just as the front door opens. The distinctive sound of Bianca's heels clicks across the tile floor. But she's not alone. Another, heavier set of footsteps accompanies her.

"It's all working out just fine," Bianca's voice drifts through the partially open office door.

We both freeze.

"The werewolves are almost fully under my control and they're becoming more aggressive by the day. And with the magic ban in place, the witches can't interfere."

"You're sure they suspect nothing?" The voice is deep. Unfamiliar and cold.

"The Thornton witch is useless. Idiot girl. She's not even half the witch Agnes was, which has made my job so much easier."

I feel Hazel tense beside me.

"They're so busy fighting they're completely clueless as to what is happening right under their noses."

She's lying. She knows we aren't fighting. She's been following us. Or having us followed. Who is this person she's talking to?

"Tomorrow's council meeting will seal their fate," she continues. "The youngest wolf is under my control. I'll make sure he shows up at the meeting. I'll set him loose, and . . . By the time the full moon hits, the entire town will be in chaos and the last piece of the puzzle will fall into place."

I glance in Hazel's direction. We have to give Mason extra protection tomorrow. Just to make sure she can't get to him. I won't let her continue to use him as a weapon.

A drawer opens and then closes. "Once the pack is gone, the town's magical defenses will collapse. The binding that protects Moonridge requires both wolf and witch magic to maintain."

"And the amulet?" the man asks.

"Almost at full power. The recent blood sacrifice fully activated it. The wolves will be powerless once I free it."

What—or who—did she kill to power that thing?

"By the time the full moon rises in two days, it will have enough energy stored to power the ritual."

Fire boils in my chest. So it's not at full power. Maybe we can deactivate it before the full moon.

The man makes a satisfied sound. "Finally. After all this time."

"Fifty years I've waited for this," Ravena says, her voice dropping to a near whisper. "Fifty years planning, watching. Now Agnes is gone, and her granddaughter is too useless to stop us."

Hazel's—my—jaw clenches.

Ravena continues. "The collection points are established at each corner of the pentagram. All we need now is for—"

A crash cuts her off. I turn to see a horrified expression on my face. Hazel accidentally knocked over a container of pens.

"What was that?" Ravena's voice ricochets down the hall.

Footsteps head our way. Quick. Purposeful.

I grab Hazel's arm and pull her toward the window on the other side of the room. It's locked.

"Use my knife to try and get it open," I whisper. "I'll distract them."

They're right outside the door now. I can hear them whispering.

I try to remember the hand gestures for the cloaking spell. Circle first, then triangle? Or was it the other way around? Shit. My luck, I'll do the wrong thing and end up blowing my face off my skull. My brain is a static-filled mess. These hands feel like tiny, clumsy mittens.

"Breathe," Hazel whispers, her larger hand covering mine. I hate how calm she is. "Feel the energy."

The office door explodes against the wall.

"Ventus obscuro!" I screech. It's more of a question than a command.

But it worked.

A gust of wind erupts. Wild. Uncontrolled. The room is a blizzard of invoices and wellness brochures, a chaotic paper-cut waiting to happen.

"Hold it steady," Hazel's hands are on mine, forcing the energy into a funnel.

We shove the cyclone toward the door, picking up a few manila folders and a paper cup along the way. A focused, churning wall of recycled office supplies. Ravena and her accomplice are a dark blur on the other side.

Then comes a low, guttural chanting from the other side.

"She's casting something," Hazel whispers.

A pulse hits us. A wave of ice-cold static that crawls over my skin. Probing. It's invasive.

"The spell won't hold much longer," I gasp. I can feel it slipping. Like Ravena is sucking what little power I have right out of my hands.

"There!" Ravena shouts, the detection spell pinpointing our location despite the chaos. "Behind the desk!"

Our barrier collapses. Paper drops like dead birds.

Hazel leaps forward and grabs the edge of the heavy wooden desk.

"Push," she says as she shoves a shoulder against it. There's a teeth-grinding screech. I will it to float forward and somehow, some way, I make it happen. The desk flies forward. It slams into Ravena and her guest, knocking them to the ground. Hazel grabs my hand. We jump. We land. And we run.

I turn back and see Ravena's face, twisted with fury and recognition.

"You," she breathes.

But we're already past her, sprinting for the door as she struggles to free herself from under the desk.

"She knows," I pant as we turn the corner. "She knows it was us."

We sprint through the store. Hazel stumbles. A cardboard display of "Organic Soul-Cleansing Tea" scatters. We're like a couple of drunk wrecking balls. Behind us, the air starts to hum.

"She's casting something big," I gasp as we reach the back door. "We need a shield!"

I try to visualize the barrier. My focus is shot. Hazel's hands tingle. The power is there, but it's like a garden hose with a kink in it.

"Like this," Hazel says, taking my hands in her larger ones.

The energy snaps into place. A shimmering, soap-bubble shield pops into place. The blast hits. The force sends us flying through the back door and into the gravel of the alley. My teeth rattle in my skull.

"Run!"

We don't stop until we're ten blocks away, safe in the shadows of the library. My lungs are full of glass. I slide down the brick wall, my butt hitting the cold dirt with a thud.

"That was . . . way . . . too close."

Hazel drops beside me. "We got out. We're safe."

But there's a slight tremor in that deep voice. I reach for her hand, needing the contact. Needing to feel safe just as much as she does.

"Hey," I say softly, squeezing her fingers. "We're okay."

She gazes at our joined hands, and something shifts in her expression. "I thought she had us. I thought I'd failed you."

The words hang between us.

"No," I whisper, my thumb tracing over her knuckles. "We're in this together. No one is failing anyone."

Hazel nods, barely winded. When we survive this, I'm forcing her to start running. She has zero lung capacity. How does she live like this? "But we got what we came for. We know our suspicions were correct."

"Yeah, but we still don't know how to stop her."

"True. But we need to make sure Mason goes nowhere near the council meeting tomorrow," I say.

"She mentioned something about collection points. I feel like they're tied to the pentagram. If I'm right . . ."

"We might be able to disrupt whatever ritual she's planning." I feel the first real sense of hope since this whole mess began.

"We're gonna figure this out," she says softly.

When I look up, the hope in her eyes makes my breath catch. I can almost see her in there. And I know that she feels what I'm feeling.

We're falling for each other. Despite the body swap. Despite years of careful distance, and poking at each other's last nerve. We're falling. And I'm not sure I want to catch myself anymore.

CHAPTER THIRTEEN

Hazel

We explode through the apothecary's back door like demons are chasing us. We thought we were safe but then Blake swore he saw a white SUV turn the corner, so we hauled ass down the alleys until we got here. I've definitely had enough cardio for the week. I'm glad I'm not in my body. Blake sounds like my lungs are about to claw their way out of my chest. I fumble with the deadbolt, my fingers shaking so hard it's like I'm trying to solve a Rubik's Cube while riding a jackhammer. For a moment, we stand frozen in the dark entryway, struggling to catch our breath.

"We . . . we good?"

My voice is a pathetic, thready whisper. I don't even know why I'm whispering; it's not like she's right outside the door. Is she? I look through the peephole just to be sure.

"We have to be extra careful now." My words come out shaky. "She's going to double down on us."

Blake turns to face me. In the dim light, I see raw, jagged fear in my eyes. It's something I've never seen before. It's haunting, seeing yourself look that terrified.

"Yeah," he says, still trying to catch his breath.

I stumble into the main shop area. Everything looks wrong. The shadows are too long, the air feels heavy. It's like nowhere is safe anymore. I feel like we're just roaming targets.

We just sit there. The silence is thick. That weird, post-adrenaline, brush-with-death intimacy where you're just glad you still have all your limbs and everyone is still breathing.

"I choked," Blake mutters. He's staring at his hands—my hands—like they've betrayed him. "That protection spell . . . I fumbled the gesture. If I hadn't been such a klutz—"

"Hey. Stop." I interrupt, turning to face him. "You did fine. Your instincts were solid. You just need more reps. Being a witch isn't as easy as it looks in the movies. It takes lots and lots of practice."

He shakes my head, copper curls are plastered to his forehead with sweat. "A real witch wouldn't have needed practice. If you'd been in your own body—"

"If I'd been in my own body, I wouldn't have been able to shove that desk across the room, or break that lock. Or run that fast. We both did what we could with what we have."

His shoulders drop, the rigid line of them softening as he releases a breath. "I guess we make an okay team."

"Better than okay." Something fierce and protective rises in my chest at his self-criticism. "We got what we came for, didn't we? Information."

Blake nods, moving to the kitchenette to fill two glasses of water. He hands me one, and our fingers brush. The now-familiar spark jumps between us, making us both flinch.

"I wish it would stop doing that," he mutters, though I'm not entirely sure he means it.

I gulp down the water, letting the cool liquid soothe my parched throat. "So, council meeting tomorrow. That seems to be when Ravena's making her big move."

"And we need to make sure we're a step ahead." I roll Blake's shoulders, trying to shake off the tension that never seems to leave this body. "We have to find out what's at the corners of the pentagram."

I move to the register, pulling out the old town map I keep under the counter. I spread it out across the surface, our heads bent close together as we study it. He stands close, and I have to fight back the desire to kiss him.

"If the shop is the center . . ." I place my finger on the spot, snapping out of my distracted state, "then the five points would be . . ." I tap locations forming a rough star around the apothecary.

Blake stares at the points I've marked. "These are all significant places in town. The old mill, the Moonstone Circle, Whispering Falls, the town hall, and—" he pauses, frowning. "My construction office?"

"Your office?" I look up, surprised. "Why would that be a point?"

"It's built on the site of the original Carter family home." Blake shrugs. "But what would that have to do with anything?"

I stare at the map, half hoping the answer will just appear. My brain hurts, and I'm tired of playing this game. I want my boobs back, I don't want to smell like wolf anymore, and I want Ravena to crawl back up Satan's asshole where she belongs. I will admit, though. I'm gonna miss being able to pee standing up. It's so convenient.

"We need to check these places out tomorrow," Blake says, bringing me back to reality. "See if we can find whatever she's set up there and figure out what she did. Deactivate anything we can find."

"But the council meeting is tomorrow evening," I remind him. "We don't have time to investigate all five locations. That will take us well into the evening. We don't know where exactly these things are hidden. Just the general area."

Blake paces, his movements stiff and awkward. "Should we

even bother going to the meeting? Ravena will be there. She knows we were at her shop. She'll twist any accusation we make into paranoia."

I chew my lip, thinking. "Let's wait and see what we find tomorrow. If we can find something concrete, then we can show the council. If not, well . . . I don't want to think about that."

"We need help," Blake says. "We can't do this alone."

"La'Tasha." Obviously. "And I think it's time to bring Calvin into the loop."

Blake nods slowly. "You're right. He's my brother, and he deserves to know what's happening."

I glance at the clock. 2:00 AM. No wonder I'm dragging ass. The adrenaline is wearing off and I'm about to crash out.

"We should get some rest. Tomorrow's going to be rough. Help me set up some protection wards in case Ravena decides to pay us a visit."

Blake nods. "Show me what to do."

As we move around the shop laying protections, I catch Blake watching me with an expression that makes me feel self-conscious.

"What?" I ask.

"Nothing," he says, but his smile—my smile—is gentle. "Just . . . I like seeing you move so confidently. It suits you."

"Whatever, princess. You were checking out my ass, which is technically your ass. You're so conceited." I give him a wink.

"I have done many squats and deadlifts to get that ass," he deadpans. "I kind of miss it."

"I'm not gonna miss it," I say. "It farts a lot. You are really, really gassy."

He turns away from me. "Can we not? We were about to have a nice moment."

"Just saying. You might want to get a colonoscopy or something. Or change your kibble."

He rolls his eyes and I nudge him with my hip. "Sorry, I'll stop now."

After we finish laying the protection wards, we trudge up the narrow stairs to my living quarters above the shop. I've lived up here since I was sixteen. I could move to the main living quarters downstairs, but I haven't been able to bring myself to clear out Gran's things in her room. It just doesn't feel right.

I push open the bedroom door. It's weird seeing my sanctuary through Blake's eyes. The colors seem different, muted somehow. But not the scents. The peony-scented candle fills my nose and immediately makes me long for simpler days. I just want to curl up with a book and turn the rest of the world off for like seventy years.

"I'll sleep on the floor again," I announce, pulling a rolled-up sleeping bag from the closet.

He doesn't do that annoying "alpha" thing where he insists on the floor just to be chivalrous. He's practical. He knows this massive frame would look like a folded-up lawn chair if I tried to sleep in my twin bed in my current state.

I unroll the bag while he's digging through my dresser. Any shred of modesty we had left died about three days ago. It's hard to get shy about someone seeing you naked when they're literally wearing your body parts. Been there, seen that.

"Your pajama game is tragic," he says, pulling out an oversized tee with a cartoon cat that says *Catty Bitch* in pink, cursive letters.

I let out a wheeze of a laugh. "La'Tasha gave me that. She thinks she's a comedian because I'm deathly allergic to cats. It was a 'get well' gift after Mrs. Fernsby brought her cat in so I could treat him for sleep paralysis, and he rubbed all over me before I could get away. I was covered in hives for days."

"She's brutal. I love it." A smile tugs at my lips—his lips—as he pulls the shirt over my head. It hangs down to mid-thigh on my smaller frame, making him look weirdly vulnerable. He kicks into some lounge pants that are about three inches too long and puddle around his—my—ankles.

I grab a plain T-shirt and sweatpants from his bag. Practical.

Functional. Just like him.

The wards hum softly from downstairs. The sound is comforting, like distant wind chimes. We move around each other in a weird, silent dance. But it's not as awkward as I thought it would be. It feels, dare I say, very domestic. Somehow, it feels strangely right. I sit on the edge of the sleeping bag, and I'm hit by a wave of exhaustion so powerful I swear I could fall asleep on a pile of gravel right now. Blake perches on the bed, almost childlike among the mountain of pillows I keep on there.

"Do you think we'll be back to normal before the full moon?" Blake asks, breaking the quiet.

I absently run my fingers along the edge of the sleeping bag. "I hope so. The thought of transforming into a wolf . . ." I shudder. "No offense, but I don't think I'm ready to sprout fur and fangs."

He chuckles. "It's not so bad, once you get used to it. Though I admit, the first time is intense."

"How old were you?" I ask, genuinely curious. "When you first shifted?"

"Thirteen." His voice goes quiet. "It wasn't long after my mom died. I hated everyone and everything. Calvin and I were fighting, like brothers do, and I got really pissed. The shift just happened. Scared the hell out of both of us."

I turn onto my side in the sleeping bag, facing him in the darkness. "That must have been terrifying."

"It was." He's quiet for a moment. "What about you? When did you first do magic?"

"Four years old. Right after my parents died. I made all the flowers in the funeral arrangements expand and fill the space. Grandma Agnes said it was my way of bringing life back into a room full of death."

"That's beautiful," Blake says softly.

"That's one way to put it. I also accidentally set the tablecloth on fire trying to light a candle for them."

Blake's quiet laughter drifts across the room. "I guess magic and grief don't mix well."

"No, they don't." I'm quiet for a long moment, thinking about four-year-old me trying to bring my parents back with flower magic. "Do you think it's weird that we both had to learn control so early?"

"Maybe that's why the body swap worked," Blake says after a moment. "We understand each other in ways we never realized."

The words hang heavy between us.

"Blake," I start, then stop, not sure how to voice what I'm thinking.

"What?" His voice is gentle, encouraging.

"Do you think it's true? The prophecy La'Tasha found?"

I can hear him shift in the bed, possibly turning to face my direction. "Which part?"

"The part about . . ." I take a shaky breath. "About a witch and wolf being destined for each other. The only thing that can heal a broken Moonridge?"

The silence that follows is so complete I wonder if he's fallen asleep. "Would it scare you if it was true?"

"It terrifies me," I admit a little too quickly.

"Why?" His voice is barely audible.

I close my eyes, gathering the courage to tell the truth. "Because I think my feelings for you are changing. Prophecy or no prophecy."

Another long silence. Then I hear the bed creak as Blake sits up.

"Me, too," he says, and there's something in my voice that makes my breath catch.

"I . . ." The word comes out too high. I clear my throat and try again. "I didn't think you liked witches. Or at least, not this witch."

"I didn't think I did either," he admits. "But that was before."

"Before what?" I ask a little too quickly.

"Before I saw you through different eyes. Literally." A small smile flickers across his face—my face. "Being in your body, seeing how you live. How you think. It's changed things. And seeing how fine my ass looks through your eyes."

I laugh. "No, seriously. What changed?"

I know I sound needy, but I need to know what I'm working with. I will not let myself get hurt by another man. Not so soon.

He looks down, fidgeting with the edge of the quilt. "The way I see you. The way I think about . . . us. When all of this is behind us."

The word 'us' hangs in the air, heavy with possibility. I can't help but smile.

"I didn't expect this," he continues when I don't respond. "But seeing how you handled Mason, how fiercely protective you are . . . it made me realize how strong you really are. Not just magically, but here." He taps my chest, over my heart.

His hand stays there, palm flat against my chest, and suddenly I can't breathe properly.

"I think my biggest fear," I start, "is that we switch back and our feelings revert. What if what we feel for each other now is only because we're in the other's body? What if it has something to do with the spell? And once it's broken, these feelings go away?"

"I've wondered that, too, but I don't think they will." He takes a deep breath. "I think we've both changed. It feels like we're finally seeing each other clearly."

"Yeah, well. Seeing you with Emmy was eye-opening. I always thought you were all rules and growling, but you were so gentle with her. That dreamcatcher was impressive, by the way."

"I had a good teacher." His smile is shy, almost boyish on my face.

"You're a natural with kids," I say. "I wouldn't have guessed that about the big, bad wolf."

"There's a lot you don't know about me," he says quietly.

"I'm learning." And I am. I'm learning that beneath the stern pack leader is a man who braids little girls' hair and is fiercely protective of those he's close to. A man who cares deeply, even when he tries to hide it.

Then Blake yawns, the moment breaking as exhaustion catches up with him. "We should sleep. Big day tomorrow."

"Yeah," I agree, suddenly uncertain where this leaves us. Are we friends now? Something more? Or just two people thrown together by circumstance?

As if reading my thoughts, Blake adds softly, "We'll figure this out, Hazel. All of it. The body swap, Ravena, and . . . whatever we are now. It'll all work out."

I nod, not trusting Blake's voice to remain steady if I speak. *Whatever we are.* It sounds promising and terrifying all at once.

I stare at the ceiling, wondering how we got here. One minute we're escaping a murderous witch, and the next we're having feelings talks. How did everything get so complicated?

And why does complicated feel like exactly where I want to be?

CHAPTER FOURTEEN

Blake

Sunlight streams through Hazel's gauzy curtains, and stabs me in the eye. My heart does a frantic little tap-dance against my ribs—well, her ribs—the second my brain boots up and remembers last night.

I think my feelings for you are changing.

Those words have been on a loop all night. I even dreamt about them. What's happening to me? I don't feel things. At least not like this. Is it the hormones? Is this what girls feel like when they have a crush? I'd never tell anyone this, but it's kind of fun.

The sleeping bag on the floor is a crumpled mess. Hazel's probably already downstairs, being productive and mapping out how we're going to kick Ravena in the tits while I'm up here having a crisis over whatever it is we admitted last night.

I sit up and stretch. Her shoulders don't have that familiar, satisfying *pop* mine do, but there is this dull, thudding ache in her lower back.

I untangle myself from the sheets and dig through her dresser for something that won't make me look like a toddler who dressed herself for the first time. I settle on a tee with a cartoon owl that says *'Hoo's the Boss?'* God, her taste in puns is tragic.

I follow the scent of coffee and find Hazel and La'Tasha in the work room, huddled over the town map we marked last night before Mason burst in. Hazel raises her head as I enter.

"Morning." She's testing the vibe. "Sleep okay?"

"Yeah. Good." I head straight for the caffeine.

"So, what's the deal?" La'Tasha asks, looking between us. She definitely smells the tension.

"We need to check those collection points," I say quickly. "We need to see what Ravena's rigged up and dismantle them."

Hazel nods, jaw tight. "But we need reinforcements. Calvin needs to know what's happening. The entire pack is in danger. I'm thinking I should drive over and convince him to come back here so we can talk to him."

"He's hardheaded. Maybe I should go. I know how to speak to him," I counter.

"He'll be more likely to listen to your body, even if I'm the one driving it," she says.

I hate that she's right. My brother respects me as pack leader, even when we disagree. He might dismiss Hazel as just another witch, but he'll at least hear me, or what looks like me, out.

"Are you going to tell him about the body swap?" La'Tasha asks, measuring herbs into a mortar.

Hazel and I exchange glances. "Yes," we say simultaneously.

"He needs to know everything if he's going to help us," I explain. "No more secrets."

"Not to change the subject," La'Tasha says, "but I think you should know, we're dangerously low on protection herbs. I need to go out back and see if there are any I can harvest from the garden. Blake, you'll need to help out with customers and restocking while Hazel's gone. Think you can manage witch duties for a bit?"

"He'll be fine," Hazel says, lifting my confidence. "Blake's getting pretty good at the basics."

I feel a flush rise to Hazel's cheeks and take a large gulp of coffee to hide it.

"Yeah, I'll manage," I say when I've recovered.

Hazel grabs her jacket—my jacket—from the back of a chair. "I'll find Calvin and bring him back here. I'll be quick."

"Be safe," I reply, watching her leave.

La'Tasha watches me. "So," she says, grinding herbs like it's a competition, "are we not talking about the obvious tension between you two?"

I turn and busy myself by arranging bottles on the counter. "There's no tension. Just two people sharing an extremely weird situation."

"Uh-huh." Her tone makes it clear she doesn't believe me for a second. "And I'm secretly a mermaid."

"Focus on the herbs, La'Tasha," I sigh. "Romance is the least of our problems right now."

Even as I say it, I can't help but wonder if that's really true. Because according to that prophecy, love between wolf and witch might be the only thing that can save us.

***

A woman with purple-streaked hair approaches the counter with her toddler. "Do you have anything for itchy skin?" The kid's arms are covered in tiny red bumps that look like mosquito bites on steroids. I've been manning the register for two hours, and so far, I've managed not to blow my cover as Hazel. Thankfully, today's customers don't ask for anything that requires actual witchcraft.

I point to the shelf behind her. "Grab the calamine with chamomile. Pink bottle, silver cap. Right there. Looks like something you'd find in your grandma's medicine cabinet."

Her face deflates with relief. "You're a lifesaver. This little guy touched something in the yard and has been scratching like crazy."

I snatch the bottle and ring it up. "Apply it three times a day. If he's still digging at his skin tomorrow morning, bring him back and we'll break out the heavy-duty stuff."

Behind me, La'Tasha grinds like her life depends on it. She's been at it all morning, creating batches of containment salt while I handle the front. The air smells like basil, sage, rosemary, and cinnamon. It's a weird combo, but I kind of like it.

The bell above the door jingles as the woman and her itchy toddler leave. I turn back to cataloging spell petitions when the bell dings again. I look up and freeze.

Evan Marsh stands in the doorway. Pressed khakis, pink polo shirt, and a smug smile that makes me want to wipe it off his face.

"Hazel." His voice drips with fake warmth. "You look well."

I bite back several responses that would definitely blow my cover. "Evan. What brings you to the apothecary?" The words come out clipped, Hazel's voice tighter than usual.

He steps closer, glancing around like he's making sure we're alone. I can smell his awful cologne. It's one of those overly fabricated scents that tries too hard to be masculine and sophisticated.

"I wanted to talk to you." His voice drops to what he probably thinks is an intimate tone. "I thought you should hear this from me first, before town gossip gets to you."

"Hear what?" I dread whatever's going to come out of his mouth next.

Evan straightens like he's about to deliver an important speech. "I've been dating Missy Lawrence for a few weeks now. It's getting pretty serious."

The way he watches me makes it painfully obvious what he's up to. This egomaniac expects me to be jealous. Burst out in tears. He came here hoping to see Hazel crumble at the news that he's moved on. What a fucking dick.

I force a smile. "Congratulations. I'm sure you'll be very happy together."

He blinks. Raises his eyebrows. He clearly didn't expect *that* response. "Oh. So. You're okay with it?"

I lean against the counter, all cool and unbothered like. "Why wouldn't I be? We broke up weeks ago."

"Right, of course." He shifts, smile faltering before he rallies. "It's just that I know how you felt about me, and I didn't want you to be blindsided."

Every word out of his mouth makes me want to shift into wolf form and pee on his shoes.

"Was there something else you needed?" I ask. It takes effort to keep Hazel's voice level instead of letting my growl show through.

Evan's expression shifts and he glances over his shoulder. "Actually, yes. I was hoping you might have something that could . . . enhance, uh, things between Missy and me? In, uh, the romance department?"

Is he serious? I stare at him, slack-jawed.

"So you want a love potion?" I clarify, just to be sure I understand him correctly.

He winces at the term. "I wouldn't call it that. Just something to add a little spark. Make our connection stronger. Maybe make me irresistible. *Especially* in the bedroom."

The man has the sex appeal of a donkey in a tutu. I want to tell him that there's no magic in the world that could make him sexy, but I bite my tongue. Seriously, though. What did Hazel ever see in him?

La'Tasha appears at my side, having abandoned her salt-making to witness this train wreck. Her voice turns dangerously sweet. "Hi, Evan. So nice to see you."

He nods. "Hello, La'Tasha. I hope you're well."

"Mmm hmm. Did I just hear you ask my friend here for a magic spell to make you sexy? A love spell even? AFTER you dumped her for being a witch? And now your ass comes in here asking if she can spice up your sex life with the 'normal' girlfriend?"

Evan has the decency to look embarrassed. "It's not like that. I just thought, since Hazel is so good with herbs and natural remedies . . ."

An idea forms in my mind. Something petty and perfect. "You know what? I have just what you need. La'Tasha, can you help me whip this up real quick?"

La'Tasha follows me to the workroom, looking like she'd rather stay behind and melt Evan's face off his skull. "What are you doing? I don't want to give that trifling man anything but a kick in the nuts and a piece of my mind."

"I want to give him a tonic that makes him fart every time he kisses Missy."

Her mouth drops open and she holds back a laugh. "Oh, Blake Carter. I didn't know you had it in you."

"Oh, I have a petty side," I say with a shrug. "I just don't get to let it out very often."

"This is brilliant," La'Tasha whispers, already reaching for ingredients.

We work together, La'Tasha grabbing bottles while I measure and mix according to her instructions. The potion turns a pleasant pink color with tiny bubbles that pop and release a scent like strawberries. The final ingredient is a pinch of what La'Tasha calls "reverberation powder". Meant to build then redirect energy in unfortunate ways.

We return to the front, where Evan waits, looking at his watch impatiently.

"This will most definitely spice things up." I hold out the bottle with a beaming smile. "Just add two tablespoons to your drink before your date. The effects will be explosive."

His face lights up as he takes the bottle, already handing me his card. I can almost sense his boner. He seriously thinks he's going to get something good out of this. "You're amazing, Hazel. I knew I could count on you."

La'Tasha takes his card and hands it back to him. "This

one's on the house. Consider it our gift. Congrats on your new relationship."

We watch him leave and then burst into laughter, high-fiving across the counter.

"Being petty feels good," I say. I almost wish I could be there to see the new girlfriend's face when she kisses him and he rips ass. "Should I feel bad for giving him that?"

It takes La'Tasha a minute to catch her breath. "Nah. The man had it coming. Hazel's going to love this when she hears about it."

"Love what?" asks a familiar voice—my voice—from the doorway.

I turn to see Hazel standing there with Calvin. She raises an eyebrow, eyes dancing between La'Tasha and me. "Was that Evan I just saw walking out of here?"

Before we can explain, the bell jingles again. Mina Cartwright bustles in, carrying a basket covered with a checkered cloth.

"Morning, loves!" she calls. "Brought some fresh scones to brighten your day."

She sets the basket on the counter, the warm smell of butter and berries filling the air. But despite her cheerful entrance, I notice the worry lines creasing her forehead.

"Everything okay, Mina?" I slip back into Hazel-mode.

She sighs, pushing a strand of red hair behind her ear. "Not really, pet. Had three cancellations at the B&B this week. Folks are gettin' spooked by all this werewolf trouble."

Calvin stiffens, jaw tightening.

"They're sayin' it's not safe to visit," Mina continues. "In the six years I've owned the B&B, I've never seen people so afraid. Not even back in Scotland when we had that banshee invasion. One couple even asked if we have 'wolf-proof locks.' As if such a thing exists!"

Shit. This isn't just about Hazel and me, or even just the pack and the witches. It's about Moonridge itself. The businesses. The families. The entire community is being torn apart by that witch and her fear-mongering.

"We're working on a solution," La'Tasha assures her.

Mina nods, but her worried expression doesn't fade. "I hope so, dears. This town and the B&B is all I've got. I poured my life savings into it."

An idea hits. "We could use some help," I say. "What are you doing today?"

CHAPTER FIFTEEN

Hazel

Mina's eyes dart between us. She knows there's something way bigger going on than a few canceled B&B bookings.

"No plans today now that my guests have all left. What do ya need?" She removes one of the scones she brought with her and bites into it.

"You might want to sit down for this." La'Tasha pulls up a couple more chairs. "This is some crazy shit."

Mina settles into one and crosses her legs. "Love, I grew up in Scotland with banshees and Nessie. Crazy is my bread and butter."

Calvin forgoes the chair, choosing to lean against the counter instead.

I take a deep breath and lock eyes with them both. "I'm not Blake. I'm Hazel. And that . . ." I point across the room, "is Blake. I was doing a spell on Monday, and things went haywire. We ended up swapping bodies."

The silence that follows is so empty I can hear conversations on the street two blocks away. Mina looks utterly confused and Calvin stares at us like I just asked him to get naked and run down the street.

Calvin shifts against the counter. "So, you're telling me, that my brother is standing right there, in Hazel's body, and Hazel is wearing Blake like a . . . like a human costume?"

"That's a weird way to put it, but essentially yes," Blake confirms.

Calvin studies both our faces, his expression cycling through disbelief followed by horror. "How is this even possible?"

"Magic." La'Tasha shrugs. "The old, chaotic kind that only Hazel seems to be able to pull off."

I'm almost offended at that comment.

Mina looks at us in disbelief, and then, unexpectedly, delight. A bubble of laughter escapes her lips.

"Well, that explains a few things!" Mina uncrosses her legs and leans forward to get a closer look. "I knew somethin' was off when I saw ya both at the B&B. Blake bein' all chatty, and Hazel lookin' like she wanted to crawl out of her skin!"

Calvin isn't laughing. His eyes narrow as he studies us. "Prove it."

Blake immediately bursts out with, "You used to make me check under your bed for monsters until you were thirteen, and you still sleep with a nightlight."

Calvin's face goes white, then red. "Okay, that's . . . that's—" He looks as though he might faint. He sits next to Mina.

"And remember when Dad taught us to ride bikes?" Blake continues. "You crashed into Mrs. Peterson's roses, and I took the blame. I still have the scar on my left shoulder where the thorns got me when I helped you up."

"Wow." Calvin leans forward and puts his head in his hands. "Wow. Okay."

"And you've been livin' like this for four, almost five days?" Mina asks, her voice still filled with humor. "Poor things. You pair have been through the wringer. That must be so confusin'."

"You have no idea," I mutter.

Calvin shakes his head, and Mina starts to laugh again.

"It's not funny," Calvin says. "How are we supposed to deal with this? How do we fix it?"

"We're working on that," Blake assures him. "But first, we need your help with something."

Calvin folds his arms, both hands firmly planted in his armpits. "I still need a minute. How did you get yourself into this shit?"

Mina leans forward. "I was wonderin' the same thing. What kind of spell could do this?"

So we tell them. Everything. About the spell I attempted. About Ravena and the blood magic and attempted mind control on Mason and what she plans to do with the pack.

"She's made this pentagram around town," La'Tasha adds. "We think she may have performed rituals there that will help charge whatever spell she has planned for the full moon."

"We want to try and find and destroy them. Weaken her. But we need to do it before the council meeting tonight. That's why we need your help."

Calvin's face has gone from pale to gray, and Mina's playful smile has been wiped off her face.

"Let me make sure I understand this," Calvin says slowly. "That weird yoga lady with all the supplements is an evil, likely immortal witch? And she's been planning revenge for almost sixty years? And she can control werewolves' minds and plans to use us as her personal army during the full moon?"

"Yeah," Blake confirms. "Pretty much."

Calvin stares at the map spread across the table. His eyes dart between the five red dots marking Ravena's collection points. "And if she succeeds? If she drives the pack out of town?"

"Moonridge loses its magical protection," La'Tasha explains. "The Binding Pact requires both wolf and witch magic to maintain the town's defenses."

"So she gets her revenge and turns Moonridge into what?" Mina says, her Scottish accent thick with disgust.

"That's the question of the day," I say.

"What an absolute cow." Mina spits. "Somethin' about her always felt off. She's always so polished. When she tried to lecture me about the 'excessive carbs' in my desserts, I nearly bent her over and showed her where to stick her wellness advice."

Calvin pushes back from the table. "Don't you think we'd be better off focusing on protecting the pack rather than driving all over Moonridge looking for spell items that we don't even know for sure exist? Why don't we just get everyone out of town until after the full moon?"

"And go where?" Blake asks.

"I dunno. Dapple Glen? It's only an hour away. Plenty of woods around for us to run during the full moon. We can't stay if that means becoming her weapons—"

"We don't know how far she can reach," I interrupt, surprising even myself. "What if all the wolves go to Dapple Glen and end up turning and attacking everyone there? It would be even more catastrophic. I won't let that happen to you guys."

Calvin studies me. "You really care about the pack," he says, wonder creeping into his voice. "Even though you're not actually a werewolf."

This catches me off guard. Why wouldn't I care about the pack?

"Yeah," I say. "I do."

"Can I ask a question?" Mina says, removing her cardigan and placing it on the counter. "Before we start makin' battle plans, I need to know. Are you two alright? Really alright? This must be incredibly difficult for ya both."

The question catches both Blake and me off guard. With all that's been happening, I haven't really bothered to do a mental health check.

"It's . . ." I start, then stop, not sure how to explain.

"Weird," Blake finishes. "Everything feels different. Food. Colors. Even emotions feel different."

"But not bad different," I add quickly, surprising myself. "Just . . . new."

Calvin shakes his head in amazement. "I can't even imagine. How do you know which thoughts are yours and which hitched a ride in your new body? Can you do magic? Oh, shit. Have you two hooked up? Did you literally have sex with yourself?"

Blake rolls his eyes. "Okay, first of all, no, we haven't hooked up. We've been too busy dealing with getting our bodies back and stopping Ravena."

"But do you want to hook up? I think I might want to see what it's like. See how good I am." Calvin has obviously fully accepted that we've swapped bodies.

"Oh, one hundred percent," La'Tasha chimes in. "I would totally want to know how good I am. I mean, I know I gotta be good, but I just want that confirmation."

I hold up a hand. "Can we not?"

Blake sends me a grateful glance before continuing. "To answer your question, yes, I've been able to do magic, but I'm not very good at it. It's like the body possesses the power but the soul doesn't. And I don't have all the knowledge. It's like we merged in a way and I only have basic abilities."

Calvin whispers something to La'Tasha and they both burst out laughing. I pull us all back to what we're all here for in the first place.

"So, here's the plan. We need to search these areas for anything that might have been set up by Ravena to help with her ritual. The council meeting is tonight," I add. "If we can gather evidence from these sites that prove she is up to something, maybe we can stop her from convincing the council to banish the pack. And if we're lucky, banish her instead."

Calvin rubs his jaw, eyes locked on the map. "So we need to

hit all five spots in . . . ?" He checks his watch. "Seven-ish hours?"

"We can do it if we split up," Blake says decisively. "Calvin and I can check the Old Mill and the construction site. He knows the mill's layout, and the construction office is on Carter land."

"And Mina and I can take the Moonstone Circle and Whispering Falls," I say. "I don't think it's safe to search around the fountain just yet. It's right at the entrance to Moonridge. Someone will see us. We can check that spot out later tonight if we need to."

Mina's eyes light up with excitement. "Oh, this'll be fun. I hike the falls weekly. Know every path and hidin' spot."

I love that she's so eager to jump into supernatural detective work.

"Are you sure you want to get involved?" I ask her. "This could be dangerous."

Mina snorts. "Pet, I once faced down a kelpie with nothing but a fryin' pan and a dish towel. Ravena Blackwood doesn't scare me." She pats my arm—Blake's arm—with sisterly affection. "Besides, someone's got to keep an eye on ya until you're back in your proper packaging."

"Tash, are you good to watch the shop?"

"Yeah, for sure," La'Tasha says, going back to the work table. "I look too cute today to be out messing with nature. Coco should be here soon. I'll put her on salt making duty. I'm going to go back to my place and check on Mason. Take him some breakfast, and pick up some fresh clothes for him from his house."

"This stays between us," Blake adds firmly. "All of it. The body swap, Ravena's plans, everything. If word gets out—"

"Mass panic," Mina finishes. "I understand. My lips are sealed, loves."

"And I don't even want to know what will happen if the Regency finds out I made Blake and me swap bodies. I barely passed their trials." I glance over at La'Tasha as she grabs her bag. Our eyes meet and she nods.

Mina pats my shoulder. "Secret's safe here."

"We should move quickly," I say, checking Blake's watch. "The council meeting is at eight. That should give us plenty of time to get back here to debrief beforehand."

We gather bags for collecting evidence and a couple of protection amulets. Blake shows Calvin how to handle the magical detection tools, and then we're off.

"Ready?" Mina looks ready for an adventure. She's tied her red hair back and changed into a pair of jeans and hiking boots she grabbed from her truck.

I nod. "Let's go witch hunting."

"That's usually my line," Blake says with a smile. "Be careful."

"You too," I reply, wishing I could say more.

Then Calvin clears his throat, and the moment breaks.

***

The forest path to Moonstone Circle is wet and mucky from this morning's brief rainfall. Every step kicks up a symphony of smells. Pine tar mixed with damp earth mixed with decaying leaves. Mina hikes beside me, her red hair catching sunlight in flashes between the trees like little flames.

Mina casts a sideways glance at me. "You're awfully quiet over there. Thinking about how to stop our evil wellness coach, or something else entirely?"

I clear Blake's throat. "Both, I guess. There's a lot happening at once."

"Like bein' stuck in a werewolf's body?" Mina suggests. "Or perhaps feelins for said werewolf?"

A root snags my boot mid-step, and I nearly face-plant. "Who said—"

She chuckles. "Oh, love, I've seen the way you look at him. It's like watching one of those romantic comedies where the couple can't stand each other until they're forced together by circumstance."

Warmth climbs up Blake's neck, and I'm grateful Mina can't see my expression. "It's more complicated than that."

"Because of the prophecy?" Mina asks as if she's simply inquiring about my day.

I stop dead in my tracks. "How do you know about that?"

She shrugs, adjusting her backpack. "La'Tasha mentioned it while you two were whispering in the corner. Somethin' about a witch and wolf unitin' in love to break an ancient curse? Sounds quite romantic, if you ask me."

"It's not romantic," I protest, continuing up the path. "It's pressure. Like we're supposed to fall in love because some old prophecy says so, not because we actually want to."

"And do you? Want to?" Mina asks.

Do I? The honest answer scares me almost as much as the threat Ravena poses to all of us.

"I think I already have," I admit quietly. "And that terrifies me."

"Why?" Mina's voice is gentle, encouraging.

I voice my deepest fear. "Because what if it's just the body swap? What if these feelings disappear when we get back to normal? What if I only think I care about him because I'm literally inside his skin?"

"And what if it's real?" Mina counters. "What if bein' in his body just let you see what was already there?"

"I don't know," I admit. "And even if I did, what if Blake doesn't feel the same way when all is said and done? What if he gets his body back, and he's no longer tied to me and he's like, 'Later, loser'?"

We reach a fallen log across the path, and I help Mina over it. She gives me a knowing look. "I don't think he'd be that cruel."

The path narrows, forcing us to walk single file. Pine needles cushion our steps, making our approach almost silent.

"Can I tell ya a story?" Mina asks from behind me.

"Of course. Is it a Scotland story? I love hearing your stories about the shit you would get into when you were a little girl."

"It is a Scotland story, but not from when I was a girl." She takes a deep breath. "I was engaged twice before I moved to Moonridge." She pauses, letting that sink in. "Twice! Each man worse than the last, though I couldn't see it at the time. The first was handsome but lazy and mean. Expected me to work all day, then come home and serve him like he was a king."

I wince. "Sounds charming."

She sighs. "The second was wealthy and controllin' and couldn't keep his willy to himself. Decided my best friend was more his speed."

We emerge into a small clearing. Sunlight streams down through the pines surrounding us.

Mina continues. "Both times I knew in my gut somethin' wasn't right. But I ignored it because I was so afraid of bein' alone."

Her words hit too close to home. How many times did I swallow my opinions around Evan? Dimmed my magic because it made him uncomfortable, or apologized for being "too much"? I totally get what she's saying.

"You changed yourself for them."

She glances at me sideways. "Aye. Made myself smaller, quieter. Less outspoken, less passionate about what I truly loved. Less me. Sound familiar?"

I sigh. It does. "Evan always hated when I'd use magic unless it directly benefited him. He'd get so pissed when my emotions would get out of whack and my magic would spike. Told me I was a ticking time bomb. Completely out of control and unskilled."

"And you believed him?" Mina asks gently.

I think about Blake learning magic, about the wonder in his eyes when he managed his first shield spell. "At the time, yeah. I know my magic can be erratic when I'm hyper-emotional. But I also know I'm good at it when I'm focused. And now I know someone who thinks my magic is kind of amazing."

We continue on, her words sinking in.

"Is that why you left Scotland?" I ask.

She nods, and sadness flickers across her face. "One of the reasons. I needed a fresh start. Decided if I was goin' to be alone, I'd at least be happy and unapologetically me while doin' it."

"Is that when you bought the B&B?" I ask.

"Aye. Best decision I ever made. Moonridge is home. It's like it was calling me across the Atlantic. In Scotland, I felt so alone, but now? Now I have all of you. My weird little family." She catches up beside me as the path widens again. "So, my advice to ya, pet? Listen to what your instincts are tellin' ya. They usually know before your brain catches up. If they're pointin' ya toward the grumpy werewolf, then maybe that prophecy is onto somethin'. You'll never know unless ya give it a go."

We round the final bend, and the Moonstone Circle comes into view. It's a ring of twelve standing stones each at least seven feet tall, arranged in a perfect circle around a massive central stone. It's kind of like our own little Stonehenge. This used to be the place where everyone in Moonridge would meet during full moons to watch as the witches recharged the protection shields around town. It was a whole thing. The witches would do their ritual. The wolves did their full moon run. I kind of wish we still did it. Maybe, when all this is over, Blake and I can propose it. It might be a nice way to bring the community back together.

"Beautiful, isn't it?" Mina whispers. "Even with evil witch magic mucking it up."

I nod. The place always feels charged with all that old, beautiful magic, but today the air feels different. Wrong. I step carefully between two of the outer stones. Blake's enhanced senses immediately pick up the smell of something rotting. Like an egg left in the sun in the middle of a strawberry patch. My nose wrinkles.

"Ravena's been here."

Mina stays at the edge of the circle. "What do ya need me to do?"

"Stay back and keep watch," I tell her.

I move slowly around the circle, following the scent. It grows stronger near the central stone, a massive slab of granite with symbols carved into its surface. The markings are old, weathered by centuries of rain and wind, but among them I spot fresher scratches. Runes that seem fresh and out of place.

Crouching down, I examine the base of the stone. Partially buried in the soil, is a small leather pouch. The smell is overwhelming now, making my nose burn and my stomach roil.

"Found something," I call to Mina. I should probably take pictures before I touch it. I fumble in my pocket and pull out my phone, snapping several angles of the pouch and its placement. I carefully dig it out with a stick and pick it up with a protective cloth.

The pouch is about the size of my fist, tied with red thread knotted in a complex pattern. Inside is a mixture of bloody fur and what appears to be powdered bone. My stomach turns. "It looks like some sort of offering, but it could also be a conduit. I need La'Tasha. I can't sense the type of magic she used when I'm walking around as Blake."

Mina steps closer, her face pale beneath her freckles. "Should we destroy it?"

"Not here," I warn. "Breaking it in the circle might release the energy. We need to take it away from the stones first, then try to neutralize it."

As I start to rise, I catch Mina stepping closer for a better look. Protectiveness surges through Blake's body. Mina is human and I don't know what might happen if she touches this.

"Stay back and don't touch!" The words come out sharper than intended. "Seriously. It's not safe."

Mina blinks, then a knowing smile spreads across her face. "There he is."

"What?" I ask, confused by my own reaction as much as her response.

She steps back obediently. "Blake's body must be enhancin' your protective instincts. You care about people the same way he does. Your confidence is there, it's just enhanced. All this is helping ya find your voice."

I stand there like I lost the ability to move. Is that true? I don't know how to respond, so I ignore what she said and put the bundle of fur and bone in the containment bag La'Tasha made.

"All done?" Mina asks, interrupting my thoughts.

I nod, rising to my feet. "One collection point hopefully disrupted, one to go."

As we trudge back to the truck, my brain won't shut up. Mina's right. I've spent a lot of time making myself small, like I'm trying to fit into a carry-on bag so I don't inconvenience anyone. But in Blake's skin, I feel like I deserve to take up the space I'm actually entitled to.

The problem is, I'm not sure which of the bravery and confidence is mine or if it all belongs to the meat-suit I'm borrowing. What happens when the "rightful owner" gets back behind the wheel? Am I going to shrink back down, or is this new, confident version of me here to stay?

CHAPTER SIXTEEN

Blake

Calvin keeps checking me out as we climb into Hazel's Jeep. And I get it. If someone tried to convince me that they were someone trapped in a body that isn't theirs, I'd roll my eyes and call bullshit. But here I am, all small and soft and cute, about to go witch-hunting with my brother.

"You really expect me to call you Blake?" Calvin asks as I struggle to adjust Hazel's seat. We may have swapped bodies, but I don't like the way she has things positioned. "While you look like that?"

The glare I send his way doesn't intimidate him. "Yes, because it's still me. Inside. We went over this."

"Right." He drums his fingers on the dashboard. "And you proved it with the nightlight story, which, by the way, was a dick move. And for your information, I keep the nightlight on so I don't stub my toe or something when I get up to pee in the middle of the night."

I turn the key in the ignition. "Uh-huh. Sure."

"I'm thirty-three. I'm not afraid of monsters," he says, turning to look out the window.

"Would you have preferred that I mention how you were

constantly trying to hump visitors' legs when you were a new pup?" As I adjust the rearview mirror, I catch a glimpse of Hazel's green eyes and still feel a jolt of surprise.

Calvin winces. "Yeah, okay, I get it. You're Blake." He settles back in his seat, a hint of a smile creeping in. "Nice shirt, by the way."

"Thanks. I picked it out myself."

That earns me a chuckle.

"Let's hit the Old Mill first," I announce as I pull onto Briarwood.

Calvin nods, his expression growing serious again. "I still can't believe any of this. The hawk-looking, fake-vitamin-pushing, yoga-ho is an ancient witch? Seriously? I just thought she was some weirdo wellness influencer from the city looking to expand her brand. She's super committed to the whole evil villain thing. She's been at this for sixty years? Really?"

"Some people hold grudges." I swerve around a pothole. "Others plan multigenerational vendettas."

Calvin goes quiet, and a knot forms in Hazel's stomach. Guilt, probably. I know it's more than just the body swap bothering him. There's a tension that's been building between us for years. We're close, but I've always suspected he resents that I became alpha when he's the oldest. We've never really talked about it. I want his respect, and I never wanted to drag him into this mess.

We can talk about that later. We have bigger things to worry about now.

The Old Mill appears around the bend. The entire easternmost section is charred and blackened from the fire that shut it down years ago. Despite the damage, the structure is still impressive. It was once the profitable heart of Moonridge's logging industry. Now it's just a historical landmark that school kids visit on field trips. And since the buildings themselves aren't open to the public, it's the perfect place for a witch to hide her evil magic stuff.

"I brought flashlights." I reach into the back seat to grab

them. I'm getting really good at this whole trespassing thing. Twice in one week. "And obsidian stones for protection. Take one of these."

Calvin nods and takes the stone. His mind seems elsewhere as we approach the safe side of the mill. We'll start here. I don't want to go poking around in the burned section unless we have to.

The front door creaks open with very little effort. It seems the historical society isn't big on security. Inside, dust motes dance in the shafts of sunlight that poke through broken windows. The air smells of mildew and mouse shit. Hazel's witch instincts immediately pick up something. We walk through several rooms, the pull growing stronger. I stop when we reach the back room. Magic was definitely performed nearby not too long ago. The entire place feels charged with it.

"Something's here." A faint pulse hums throughout the battered room. "I can feel it."

Calvin raises an eyebrow. "Witchy senses prickling?"

"Something like that. Let's check the basement."

As we search for the basement entrance, I decide it's time to get his opinion on something.

"So," I start, trying to sound casual, "what do you think about this prophecy thing? The whole 'wolf and witch unite in love' business?"

Calvin runs his hand over an old mill wheel. "You mean the prophecy that apparently means you and Hazel are destined to be soulmates?"

"Yeah. You think destiny is actually a thing? Or is it just . . . I dunno, cosmic peer pressure? I'm asking because, honestly, my brain is short-circuiting over all this."

Calvin tilts his head as he processes the question. "Does it even matter? If you're into her and she's into you, who cares if some dead witch wrote it down in a notebook a hundred years ago?"

"Because what if the feelings aren't real?" I finally say it. The big scary thought. "What if it's just magical brainwashing? What if Ravena is just pulling my strings and making me *think* I care?"

Calvin gives me the same kind of look you'd give someone who said the pile of shit you just stepped in was a melted pile of chocolate. "Dude, come on. You've looked at Hazel Thornton with doughy eyes since you were in grade school. Long before all this bullshit. The magic body swap didn't create any of these feelings. It just kicked the door down so you'd stop pretending they weren't there."

I pretend to examine a dusty control panel. "No way. We hated each other."

Calvin grunts, his voice dropping an octave. "You're not fooling anyone. You've had a thing for her forever. You just hid behind that whole 'werewolf-vs-witch' rivalry because it was easier than admitting the truth. And you were afraid of what people might say."

A wildfire hits my cheeks. Do I blush this easily in my own body? "That obvious, huh?"

"To anyone with a working set of eyeballs." Calvin finds a door half hidden behind a stack of old crates. "Think I found the basement."

We descend creaking wooden stairs, but my mind is still upstairs with our conversation.

"Am I a total idiot if I actually try to make a go of it?" The question feels weirdly heavy in my mouth. "With Hazel, I mean. Once we're . . . unscrewed."

Calvin stops at the bottom of the stairs. He's actually being serious now, which is even more uncomfortable. "Look, you deserve to not be miserable for once. If she makes you happy, then go for it. Not because some prophecy said it's so. Because you want to. And screw what everyone else thinks."

The sincerity catches me off guard. "But witches and wolves are sworn enemies. That's what we've always been taught. Witches bad. Wolves good. Where's this sudden acceptance coming from?"

He sighs, scratching his beard. He looks so much like our dad right now, it almost hurts. "That rivalry is antiquated and has never been law. It's just magical prejudice. And look, I know you took on the alpha role because I was too busy chasing my dreams. Running off to college, staying on the West Coast, falling for Jace . . ."

The name of his ex-fiancé hangs in the air between us. When Jace left it nearly broke him.

"That wasn't your fault."

"But it is." His voice is firm. "You stepped up because I left after Dad said he didn't approve of my 'lifestyle choices,'" Calvin continues. "You carried the pack, the business, everything. While I was off trying to build a life that eventually fell apart anyway."

His bitterness catches me off guard. I stop pretending to examine the dusty mill equipment and turn to look at my brother. I can actually see the regret weighing him down. The heartache is palpable.

"You know—"

He holds up a hand, cutting me off. "I need to say this." He takes a deep breath. "I feel like I'm responsible for all the weight you carry. I feel like you didn't get to live. You never got a chance to be young and take risks with your heart because you were too busy holding the pack together after Dad died."

Is that what I've been doing? Holding everyone together while falling apart myself?

"It was my choice," I say. I don't think either of us really believes that.

"Was it? Or did you do it because it was expected of you?" His voice is gentle but firm. "Look, I'll admit that I was pissed to find that you were named alpha. I'd lost Jace, and I felt like I'd lost my position in the family as well. But you deserve it. You also deserve to be happy." He takes a deep breath. "All I'm saying is, maybe it's time you considered what you want, not just what everyone needs from you. You don't have to be everything to everyone else. It's okay for you to take care of you sometimes."

I have to lean against the damp wall. "I don't know how to do things for myself anymore. It's been so long since I even tried to let go of pack responsibilities and just live a little." I swallow hard against the boulder growing in Hazel's throat. "And if the prophecy is real, and Hazel is meant to be mine . . . it could change everything."

"Good." Calvin squeezes my shoulder. "Some things need to change. It's called growth."

Before I can respond, a small pulsing in the air tugs at my attention, a faint magical tug that Hazel's body recognizes instinctively.

I point toward a corner draped in shadows so thick they look like velvet curtains. "Over there. Behind those crates."

Calvin helps me shove them out of the way. Behind them is a circle of blackened stones that look like they were charred in a barbecue grill. They're arranged in a rough star pattern, and directly in the center is a small leather pouch.

"Bingo," Calvin whispers.

I crouch down, careful not to disturb anything. The magical hum coming off this thing makes every last hair stand straight up. Pretty sure I look like I stuck my finger in a light socket. "Take some pictures so I can dismantle it before my hair floats off my head."

While Calvin fumbles with the camera, I squint at the layout. Five points. Just like the collection spots we've been tracking across town. I take the protective cloth and pick up the tightly wrapped bundle, inspecting it.

"Definitely wolf fur," I note, gesturing to wisps of gray hair poking from the pouch. "And flower petals, maybe?"

Calvin bags the charm, shoving it into La'Tasha's protective container with a look of pure disgust.

"This is recent. The ground is still warm." I stand up, feeling a strange mixture of triumph and dread in Hazel's chest. "This confirms what we suspected. Let's just hope that by removing this, we can weaken whatever it is she did."

We climb back upstairs, the evidence secure in Calvin's backpack. Sunlight seems harsher now as we emerge from the basement.

"We should get to the construction office," I say, squinting. "See if she's tampered with anything there, too."

***

Hazel's Jeep bounces along the road toward the construction office, each pothole jolting me back to the conversation in the mill basement. *You deserve to be happy.* Happiness always seemed like something for other people, something I could worry about after the pack was safe, the business stable. And somewhere along the way I just got comfortable with the way things were. There was always a "later". And it never quite arrived.

"You're awfully quiet over there," Calvin says, breaking into my thoughts.

I snort, navigating around a fallen branch. "Maybe it's the estrogen."

"Sure, blame the hormones." He grins, but his eyes stay serious. "Actually, I've been meaning to ask . . . have you ever thought about it? Being with someone, I mean. Not just casual dates, but seriously. I don't think I remember you ever really being with anyone. Not seriously at least."

The question catches me off guard. Have I? I've dated. Plenty. But never with anyone that felt worth pursuing.

"Not really," I admit, hands tightening on the wheel. "It was never really a priority for me. The pack always came first."

Calvin sighs, shaking his head. "That's what I mean, dude. You've spent so long putting everyone else first."

"Like a witch with a temper?" I try to joke, but it falls flat.

"If that's what does it for you." Calvin chuckles. "But seriously. I know Dad wanted this for you, but I know he didn't expect you to put your life on hold forever."

Calvin's mention of Dad hits harder than expected. Eight years gone, but I can still hear his voice. *The pack needs strong leadership. We're responsible for keeping the town safe. If we fail, or if we lose control, people could die.*

"It just feels like Dad had it easier," I mutter, hands tightening on the wheel.

"How do you figure?"

"He had Mom. Even with all her problems, he had someone there for him. And he had us." The admission feels strange. "I don't understand how he balanced it all."

Calvin goes quiet for a moment. "But he did."

"I don't know how to do both," I confess. "Be what the pack needs *and* still have something for myself."

"Maybe that's the point of all this." Calvin suggests. "A reminder that you can't be everything to everybody. A reminder to let go of who you *think* you need to be."

I hadn't thought of it that way. If Hazel and I were together, I wouldn't be dividing my attention. I'd be multiplying my support. A partner, not just a lover.

"Huh," is all I manage to say.

As we near the construction site, Calvin claps me on the shoulder, and it nearly buckles under his werewolf strength.

"For what it's worth," he says, "Hazel's tough. If she can put up with you in your own body, maybe she's tougher than we think."

I park in front of Carter & Co. Construction, the familiar sight of our family business, oddly comforting even in these strange circumstances. The red brick building has stood here for three generations, built on the site of the original Carter family home.

"1-9-8-6-2 is the code," I tell Calvin as we approach the front door.

He gives me a look. "I know the code, dude."

Right. Sometimes I forget Calvin has a life here again. That leaving for college didn't mean he'd abandoned Moonridge, even if my father acted like it did. And he came back stronger. Proudly and openly gay. He returned a new person, living his truth, knowing exactly what it might cost him. But he stayed. Made this his home again. I admire that.

We step into the office and the smell of sawdust and coffee pulls me back to the present. Plans cover the drafting tables. Invoices sit piled in wire baskets. Everything looks normal. I don't sense anything off.

"Picking up anything?" Calvin asks.

I shake my head.

Calvin walks toward the back. "I'll check the workshop, you search your office?"

I nod, and he heads through the connecting door to the building's larger back section. Alone, I check drawers, look behind filing cabinets, searching for any sign that someone has been in here.

But I don't find anything.

As I search, I think about what Calvin said, about not always putting others first. How many years have I spent doing exactly that? Taking on extra pack responsibilities when I was barely out of my teens. Running the business after Dad died. Always being the responsible one, the dependable one, the one who never falters.

It's exhausting.

And for what? To prove I'm worthy? To make sure no one sees any weakness in me? Dad never ruled through fear or perfect strength. He was loved because he was human. Or as human as a werewolf can be. He had flaws. He made mistakes. He lived.

Have I been living? Or just existing?

Calvin is right. I've been so busy being what everyone needs that I've forgotten who *I* am. What *I* want.

And what I want, I know without a doubt, is Hazel. Her fire. The way she just says things, unfiltered, even if it might offend someone. She's a little hyper-emotional, sure, but I appreciate the way she never backs down, even from me.

Looking around this sterile office, I realize this is exactly what I don't want my life to be. Functional but empty. The door to the workshop opens, and Calvin returns, shaking his head.

"Nothing back there. You find anything?"

"Nope. Place is clean."

Calvin studies my face for a moment, then nods as if confirming something to himself. "You really should tell her."

"Tell who what?" I hedge.

"Hazel. How you feel. How you've always felt about her." He leans against the doorframe, arms crossed. "Prophecy or not, she deserves to know."

My mouth goes dry. "I have. Kind of."

Calvin's eyebrows raise. "What do you mean kind of?"

"It came up the other night. We were talking about how we don't want to go back to how we were. The bickering I mean."

Calvin gives me a knowing look. "All good things, but did you tell her you've had a crush on her since you were eleven?" When I don't answer, he continues. "You need to remember that these feelings you have aren't new just because you've never told her about them. You need to be honest about everything. And if she rejects it, then at least you know. If there's one thing I learned from Jace, it's that regret lasts a lot longer than rejection."

The mention of his ex-fiancé makes his voice crack slightly. I know how badly Jace hurt him, but even through that pain, Calvin has never regretted loving him.

"I just don't understand how we got to this place." I suddenly feel very overwhelmed.

Calvin considers this carefully. "I think this whole body-swap mess is the universe's way of forcing you two stubborn idiots to see each other clearly for once. Might as well take advantage of it."

He has a point. Being in Hazel's body has shown me sides of her I never would have seen otherwise. "You're right. When this is all over, when we're back in our own bodies, and Ravena is dealt with, I'll tell her everything."

Calvin rolls his eyes. "Or you could tell her today, before some other magical disaster pops up."

"One catastrophe at a time," I say, smiling. "Let's get back to the apothecary. The others should be returning with whatever they found, too."

As we lock up and head back to Hazel's Jeep, I feel lighter somehow. The weight of unacknowledged feelings finally being lifted from my shoulders. For the first time since this whole body-swap nightmare began, I'm actually grateful for it. Without it, I might never have seen what was right in front of me all along.

Hazel Thornton. Witch. Nemesis. And possibly, if a centuries-old prophecy and my newly acknowledged feelings have their way, my future.

CHAPTER SEVENTEEN

Hazel

The roar of Whispering Falls drowns out everything except the words Mina spoke earlier. The water cascades over moss-covered rocks, spray catching rainbows in the late afternoon sun. All the forest scents are on full display, invading my nostrils with no apology.

And there it is again. The scent of rotten eggs and strawberries.

"She's been here, too."

Mina adjusts her ponytail, squinting against the spray coming off the falls. "How can ya tell? All I'm gettin' is wet rock and moss. Smells like the scum on my gran's old tadpole pond."

"Gotta love the werewolf nose." I tap the side of Blake's face. "It's like having supernatural smell-o-vision. There's definitely magic here. The same kind we found at the circle."

We pick our way carefully along the slippery rocks that form a natural path beside the falls. The constant mist has turned everything slick, but my feet—Blake's feet—find purchase on rocks that would have sent me tumbling. His body knows these mountain trails in ways mine never could. Little werewolf perks. Who knew?

Mina plants her walking stick against a rock and almost slips. My reflexes spring into action. She grabs my forearm, and it takes her a minute to steady herself.

"You okay?" I ask.

She nods. "Dizzy spell. I've been gettin' these migraines lately. Haven't had them since I was at uni. Must be all the stress. Sometimes I get vertigo. I might need to sit for a spell."

"You okay to wait here while I explore ahead? I don't need you falling and getting hurt."

"Yeah. I'll be fine. Just need to rest a bit. Ya might already know this, but there are little caves along the trail closer to the top. They're not very deep, but they'd be perfect for hidin' away magic trinkets."

I nod, focusing on following the strawberry-egg-fart scent. It grows stronger as I make my way up the trail that switches back behind the top of the falls, and then toward a narrow ledge just off the approved path. I sidestep along the rock face, the spray soaking through Blake's flannel shirt in seconds. The roar is deafening now, a constant white noise that somehow makes it easier to concentrate on the scent.

"Found somethin'?" Mina shields her eyes against the spray, squinting from the trail thirty feet behind me.

"Maybe!" I point to the spot I'm investigating.

The ledge opens into a small alcove hidden away just as Mina had suggested. Blake's eyes adjust quickly to the dimmer light, revealing a patch of disturbed soil near the back wall. I crouch down, running fingers through wet earth. Something cold and rough touches my fingertips.

"Bingo," I murmur. I grab the protective cloth, now soaked, and gently remove what looks like a silver chain.

Mina appears at the entrance to the alcove, her face flushed. "What is it? What did ya find?"

I lift the object from the dirt, holding it up to catch what little light filters through the waterfall. It's a silver pendant, about the size of a half-dollar, crafted into the shape of a wolf's head. The detail is exquisite. Each strand of fur is etched into the silver. The tiny eyes not only gleam but seem to track my movement. There are fresh scratches in the metal, as if something clawed at it from the inside.

"It's beautiful," Mina breathes, stepping closer. "And creepy as hell."

I turn the pendant over. Symbols are etched into the back. Runes similar to those we found at the circle.

"Another power collector, like the charm at Moonstone Circle."

"Does it feel especially cold in here to ya?" Mina asks, hugging herself despite the mild day. "Like, unnaturally cold?"

She's right. The air feels like we stepped into a walk-in freezer. My breath mists, and goosebumps rise along my arms, making the furry blonde hair wrestle with goose pimples.

"It's the magic," I explain. A shiver runs up Blake's spine. "Whatever spell she cast here must be pulling energy from the falls. Falling water is a powerful energy source."

Mina nods, keeping her distance from the pendant. "So she's tappin' into natural energy points."

"Smart witch," I admit grudgingly. I seal the bag and place it in my backpack. "She's creating a network of energy channels, all feeding back to the amulet under the apothecary."

As I finish securing our evidence, a chill breeze sweeps through the alcove, making the mist off the waterfall dance and sway. For a second, it almost looks like a curtain, hiding something behind it. Something that might be watching.

"We should go." Blake's protective instincts have flared. "I don't like the feel of this place."

Mina doesn't argue, already backing toward the ledge. "Right behind ya, pet."

We make our way carefully out from behind the falls, the sunshine feeling warmer after the unnatural cold of the alcove. As we start down the trail, my thoughts shift from magical pendants and evil witches back to Blake.

How did we go from childhood teasing to mortal enemies, to living in each other's bodies? And why can I suddenly not stop thinking about him? More importantly, what will we do if we can't switch back?

"Penny for your thoughts?" Mina asks, breaking into my reverie. "You've gone awfully quiet, and you're smilin' like you've just remembered a good joke."

"Just thinking about the evidence we've gathered. I'm hoping it's enough to convince the council."

"Uh-huh." Mina's knowing tone makes heat rise to Blake's cheeks. "And that dreamy look has nothin' to do with a certain werewolf currently borrowin' your body?"

"I don't do dreamy looks," I lie.

"Oh, please." She elbows me lightly in the ribs. Well, she tries to, but Blake's height means she mostly hits my lower arm. "You've been moonin' over him since we left the shop. Every time his name comes up, your face does this adorable little twitchy thing."

I drag Blake's hand across his jaw, the scratch of his stubble weirdly grounding. "It's complicated."

"Love usually is."

"I didn't say anything about love!" A nearby squirrel flinches and dashes up a tree.

Mina laughs. "You didn't have to, pet. It's written all over your scruffy little face."

Rude. Accurate, but rude.

"If your heart's telling you something," she says, going gentle in a way that always precedes sage advice, "why are you arguing with it?"

I don't answer, mostly because I'm very busy suddenly caring a lot about where I put my feet and also making sure that Mina doesn't tumble headfirst off the side of this very steep trail. But the question gets in anyway. Why *am* I fighting it? Because Blake drives me insane on a molecular level, and witches and werewolves aren't supposed to mix. And the last time I let someone in they walked all over my heart and literally told me to my face that I wasn't good enough.

We make it down to the parking lot and I've got the pendant in my pack and nothing resolved in my chest

If your heart's telling you to go for it, why fight it?

I don't have an answer yet. But for the first time, I'm willing to consider the question instead of dismissing it outright. I'll call that progress and leave it at that.

For now.

***

The bell sounds wrong when we push open the apothecary door. It tends to match the mood in the room, and the mood says worried.

Blake looks up from behind the counter, my auburn curls looking like he lost a fight with a wind machine. Calvin stands nearby pretending to study a jar of bones.

"You're back," Blake says, voice warm with relief. The tension drops a couple of notches, but something is still off.

"Where's La'Tasha?" I peel off the wet flannel and immediately feel twenty pounds lighter. It was like wearing a piece of furniture. "Isn't she supposed to be elbow-deep in salt right now?"

Blake shrugs and shakes his head. "No idea. It was all locked up when we got here. No note or anything."

"That's not like her." I place my backpack with our magical artifacts on the counter. I reach for my phone, checking for a text from La'Tasha. Nothing. "Did you guys have any luck?"

Calvin nods, pulling out his own collection of evidence bags.

"Found a weird setup at the mill. Star pattern with stones, leather pouch in the center. Wolf fur mixed with something else."

"Flower petals," Blake adds.

I grind out a text, *Where r u?* and then glance down at what they found.

"Hmm, probably nightshade or foxglove. Something toxic to dial up the negative energy."

"We found something similar at Moonstone circle. But then we found this at Whispering Falls." I carefully extract the silver pendant. "It was buried behind the falls."

Blake reaches for the pendant, and when his fingers brush against mine, that spark jumps between us again, but this time it's like touching a live wire. I feel it in my molars.

"This is old." He takes the pendant and traces the wolf's head design with one finger. "Like, generations old. Look at the details."

Mina peers over his shoulder. "Creepy little thing, isn't it? Makes my skin itch just lookin' at it."

"I'm pretty sure it was pulling energy from the falls," I say. "I'm beginning to think she's tapping into natural power sources around Moonridge. Which makes sense. If you need to power a big spell, you're going to tap into key places along the ley lines"

"The whosie?" Mina asks.

"Ley lines. They're basically like nature's Wi-Fi, but for magic and vibes instead of internet and social media. It keeps magical monuments in sync."

"Interesting."

I check my phone to see if La'Tasha responded. Nothing. "What else did you guys find?"

"Nothing. Our office was clean," Calvin says, perching on the edge of a display table. I wait for it to crumble beneath him, but it holds just fine. He's not quite as tall as Blake, but he's at least twenty pounds heavier.

"So there was nothing there? At all?"

Blake and Calvin both shake their heads. "Nope."

"That's odd," I frown. "She mentioned five points when we overheard her. And she can't complete a Pentagram without five points." I walk back to the map spread out on the work table. "The apothecary at center, and then the mill, the circle, the falls, the fountain, your office."

Blake looks up sharply. "Oh shit. It's not our office. It's Town Hall. The fifth point is Town Hall. Has to be. It's across the street from our office. We were off a few hundred feet."

A thousand hot pokers needle their way up my spine. The council meeting is tonight.

At Town Hall.

"She's definitely going to pull some shit at the meeting." Calvin says what we're all thinking.

Before anyone can respond, the back door crashes open, bouncing off the wall. La'Tasha staggers in, one shoulder against the doorframe for support, looking like she's gone ten rounds with a yeti. And lost.

"La'Tasha!" Mina rushes to her side, helping her to a chair. "What happened to ya?"

"Mason," she gasps, collapsing into the seat. "The salt circle must have weakened. He freaked out again. Next time one of y'all gets to play werewolf-wrangler. I'm done being his chew toy."

Blake grabs the first aid kit from behind the counter. I love watching him take care of people. Will he still be like this when this is over?

"I thought the containment salt was working." I move closer to examine La'Tasha's arm. The scratch is deep but clean. Definitely claw marks.

"It was," she winces as Blake dabs antiseptic on the wound. "Until about an hour ago. He was fine one minute, talking about how hungry he was, then his eyes went yellow and he just changed. Like a little half-human demon dog."

"Did he say anything?" Calvin asks.

La'Tasha nods grimly. "That's why I rushed back. He finally calmed down after I dumped a big-ass pile of containment salt around him. He said Ravena was calling to him again." She looks up, her eyes wide with urgency. "She wants him at Town Hall. Tonight."

I can't stop pacing. "Just like we thought. If she can orchestrate another incident at the meeting itself . . ."

"Game over," Calvin finishes. "The vote to relocate the pack would be unanimous."

Blake finishes bandaging La'Tasha's arm. "How much containment salt do we have left?"

La'Tasha shakes her head. "Almost none. I used most of it on Mason. And before you ask, no, I can't just whip up more like it's instant coffee. My ingredients are spent."

The room falls silent except for the ticking of the old clock above the register.

"Why don't you just take the wolves to Amethyst Beach?"

The voice comes from the back room, making us all jump. Coco stands in the doorway, looking intently at all of us. The neon pink tracksuit she wears is the spot of color this drab room needs. Her curly black hair is piled on top of her head in a high ponytail, a sprig of rosemary stuck through it. I'm not even going to ask why.

I look at her like I've never seen her before. "When did you get here?"

She shrugs, twirling a pencil between her fingers. "Like, ten minutes ago? I came in through the back to look for some mugwort for my energy cleansing spells. Then I heard all the drama and figured I would see if I could help."

"What's this about Amethyst Beach?" Blake asks. For once Coco's presence hasn't completely thrown him.

"It's the perfect safe spot," Coco explains, as if it's the most obvious thing in the world. "The whole beach is made of crushed amethyst and salt. Nature's biggest protection circle."

We all stare at her.

"How do you know that?" La'Tasha asks slowly.

Coco spins the rosemary sprig. "Geology elective last semester? Professor Harris went on these epic rants about local mineral formations. Like, passion-level obsessed. I mostly took it for the easy credit, but there was some good stuff in there. I guess it stuck. Amethyst is a major protective stone, and the beach has like, tons of it mixed with the sand. Plus salt from the lake. It's basically a twelve-mile safe zone."

Could it really be that simple?

"Why didn't I think of that?" La'Tasha asks. "It's so obvious."

"Would it block Ravena's influence?" Hope creeps into Calvin's voice.

"It should." Coco shrugs. "Amethyst blocks negative energy, and salt seals the deal. That's why nothing weird ever happens at that beach, even during full moons. Haven't any of you noticed?"

Coco's explanation makes perfect sense. I can't believe the new witch in town knew more about this than La'Tasha or me. Maybe Coco isn't as spacey as I thought.

"So we'll send the entire pack to the beach," Blake says slowly. "Keep them there through the full moon, away from Ravena's influence."

"Yeah." I say, excitement building in Blake's chest. "But we can't send everyone at once. Calvin can you spread the word? Try and get everyone up there during the meeting when she's preoccupied. But don't tell Mason what the plan is. We can't chance Ravena getting inside his head and figuring out what we're up to."

"We need to get changed," Blake says. "The meeting starts in an hour."

"I'll start getting the word out," Calvin says. "I'll just tell them it's an emergency pack gathering. A camping trip for safety."

"I'll go with you," La'Tasha says. "I can patrol and make sure Ravena hasn't planted anything around there."

"Can I come, too?" Coco asks. "I can help strengthen the

natural barriers."

Blake turns to me, my green eyes meeting his blue ones. "Yeah, you all get everyone up to the beach and we'll go to the council meeting. We'll present our case . . ."

"And hope it's enough to convince them," I finish, feeling both terrified and oddly confident. I somehow believe we might pull this off.

"And I need to get back to the B&B. Call me after the meetin'?" Mina says before heading out.

As they prepare to leave, Blake moves closer, lowering my voice until it's almost a whisper. "Are you sure about this? Once we walk into that meeting, there's no backing down. Ravena will know we're onto her, and she won't hesitate to use everything she's got against us."

"Getting cold feet, Carter?" I tease.

"Concerned," he corrects, but a small smile tugs at his lips—my lips. "For both of us."

The sincerity in his voice makes something sparkle in Blake's chest. Maybe Mina's right. Maybe it's time to stop fighting whatever this is between us.

I so want to kiss him. But I'd just be kissing myself, and that feels weird. If we pull this off, there'll be plenty of time for that later. Right now, we have a town to save and a witch to expose.

"Let's go crash a council meeting."

Suddenly, I feel more like myself than I have since this whole body-swap adventure began.

town over the past few weeks."

Understatement of the year.

He shuffles papers in front of him. "Reports of aggressive werewolf behavior have increased, along with sightings of strange lights around historical sites outside of town."

No one responds, which is odd. Most everyone sits stone still, like they're watching a movie. I scan the faces around us, recognizing most (Moonridge isn't that big of a town). Everyone's expression appears off. No one smiles, and there's an edge to the crowd.

"Before we hear from the council," Sheriff Harlow says, "we'll open the floor to community concerns."

Hands shoot up across the room like meerkats. The Sheriff points to Mrs. Alberts, who runs the flower shop and whose husband was friends with my father for decades.

She clutches her pink cardigan, pulling it tight around her shoulders. "I was walking my dog near the edge of town last night, and I saw two werewolves." Her voice hitches. She takes a sip from a Ravena-branded water bottle and clears her throat. "At least I think they were werewolves. They were stalking through the trees. They looked wrong somehow. Their eyes were glowing yellow, and they were making these horrible growling sounds."

More murmurs. I glance at Hazel, whose expression has gone tight. Who could it have been? We were focused on keeping Mason safe, but had Ravena influenced someone else?

Mr. Garcia from the hardware store stands next. "Three nights ago, I saw blue lights hovering over the Old Mill. Like fireflies, but bigger and brighter. When I went to investigate, I saw blue and red lights flashing in the windows. Someone was performing magic. I thought we banned magic for two weeks?"

All eyes turn on me. I don't move. If I speak up, no one will believe me anyway. No need to make myself look guilty. Especially when I already know who it was.

One by one, townsfolk rise to share similar stories. Werewolves acting strangely aggressive. Mysterious lights around town. Magic being performed in secret. Witches controlling wolves. As each person speaks, I notice the same inflection. They pause before certain words like they are trying to remember their lines.

But there's something else happening here, too. I notice people sipping from water bottles and travel mugs, many bearing the distinctive white and mint-green logo of Ravena's wellness brand. A woman in the front row takes a supplement capsule, washing it down with what looks like a bottle of one of Ravena's special tea blends.

Her products are everywhere. How did I not notice before how thoroughly Ravena's "health" products have infiltrated Moonridge?

Right on cue, the demon herself stands and turns to address everyone. She pauses, looking at all of us with a look of pride, like we all came tonight specifically to see her. She has on a white pantsuit that makes her look like a high-powered businesswoman who moonlights as a cult leader, which, when I think about it, is pretty on brand. Her hair is yanked back into a severe knot that looks like it might pop her eyes out of her head if it got any tighter.

"Sheriff, if I may address the council?"

Sheriff Harlow nods, gesturing to the podium. "The floor is yours, Ms. Mayweather."

Ravena glides to the podium like a shark moving toward dinner. Her smile is practiced, perfect, revealing just the right amount of teeth.

"Friends. Neighbors."

My skin crawls with agitation. Her voice is like honey drizzled over a dog turd. "What we've seen the last few days isn't just a series of random incidents. It's a pattern. And patterns always have a source."

She pauses, letting her words hang. Hazel squeezes my knee.

"For generations, Moonridge has allowed supernatural beings to walk among us. We've been led to believe that they're helpful.

Witches heal minor illnesses and help us sleep better or banish evil pests from our gardens. Even the werewolves are helpful with their brute strength. We've been led to believe that coexistence was possible, even safe."

She shakes her head sadly, as if disappointed by a child's naivety. "But the evidence speaks for itself. The werewolves are becoming more aggressive, more unpredictable. The magic in this town is destabilizing, creating dangerous phenomena that threaten us all. We have to face the facts. Supernatural creatures are dangerous. They're different. They're unpredictable. This is no longer a safe place for humans. We have to think about the children."

I watch in growing horror as heads nod throughout the audience. Even council members are leaning forward, hanging on her every word.

"I've consulted with experts," she says, though I'd bet my construction company that these "experts" are her imaginary friends. "And I believe I have a solution that will restore peace to Moonridge once and for all."

She pauses for dramatic effect, then delivers her killing blow.

"We must strip the witches of their power. Permanently. And we must require all werewolves to relocate at least fifty miles from our town borders."

Several audience members nod immediately, murmuring in agreement as if the idea makes perfect sense.

She holds up a hand. "Now let me be clear. This isn't about hatred or fear. It's about safety. About preserving what makes Moonridge special while eliminating the dangers that threaten it."

Before she can continue, Hazel surges to her feet beside me, towering over the seated crowd. "That's bullshit. And I can prove it."

All eyes turn to us. Ravena's smile doesn't falter, but her eyes narrow dangerously.

Sheriff Harlow straightens. "Mr. Carter? You have something

to add? And please, watch the profanity. There are children here."

Hazel pushes past people as she moves toward the center aisle. I follow, clutching the backpack, heart pounding so hard I wonder if everyone can hear it.

"What's threatening Moonridge isn't werewolves or magic. It's her." Hazel points directly at Ravena. "She isn't who she claims to be. Her real name is Ravena Blackwood, and she's an immortal witch using blood magic to control werewolves. She's using her products to drug and manipulate all of you."

The room erupts. Ravena's smile finally slips. It's replaced by an expression of wounded innocence that might have won her a best performance award if this were a movie.

Her voice turns sickeningly sweet. "Blake, I understand you're upset about the proposed relocation, but these wild accusations—"

Hazel moves toward the podium. "They're not accusations. They're facts. We have evidence."

I notice Ravena's hand slip into her pocket. The movement lightning quick. When she pulls it out, I notice a fine powder on one of her fingers.

"Wait—" I start to call out, but it's too late.

As Hazel passes Ravena, she leans forward as if to offer words of encouragement. Instead, she purses her lips, and blows, sending a fine glittering powder straight into Hazel's face.

Hazel flinches slightly but continues walking to the podium. At first, I think maybe the powder is harmless, or won't work on a body swap victim. But then I notice how Hazel's movements become slightly jerky. She reaches the podium and grips its edges like it's the only thing holding her up. "We found evidence of blood magic at multiple sites around Moonridge," she begins. Her voice is steady, but her eyes grow large, the blue irises briefly flash a sickly yellow. "Charms and artifacts . . ." she takes a deep breath, "designed to channel power toward the amulet . . ." she coughs and clears her throat, "were hidden beneath the Blue Moon Apothecary."

Ravena returns to her seat, the picture of calm interest, but her eyes never leave Hazel's face. I start moving toward the front of the room, a sick feeling building in my gut. Something's definitely wrong.

"This pendant," Hazel continues, pulling out the silver wolf's head with trembling fingers, "was found at Whispering Falls." She doubles over in pain. She breathes deep, then stands upright again. "It's a power collector, designed to . . . to . . ."

The words cut off as if someone hit the pause button. Her muscles lock up. Then a shudder runs through her like an electric current.

"Blake?" Sheriff Harlow steps closer, concern replacing suspicion. "You okay, son?"

Hazel opens my mouth to say something, but the sound that emerges is pure wolf. A growl that vibrates through the entire room like a revving engine.

"He's shifting!" someone shouts from the crowd. "The werewolf is changing! He's going to kill us!"

Panic explodes through the room. People leap from their seats, scrambling toward the exits. Council members push back from their table, faces pale with terror.

"No." My words are too quiet for anyone to hear over the chaos. "No, no, no."

Whatever powder Ravena used is forcing a transformation that Hazel has no training to resist. She's not a werewolf. She doesn't know how to fight the change or control it. This could kill her.

I watch in horror as her hands begin to change. Fingernails lengthen into claws. The muscles in her arms bulge and twitch beneath her shirt while blonde hair begins to sprout. Worst of all, fangs elongate in her mouth, pressing against her lips as she fights to keep them contained.

"Everyone back!" Sheriff Harlow shouts, drawing his Taser. "Blake, I need you to calm down now, son."

But Hazel's caught in the grip of a transformation she has no control over. Her eyes find me in the crowd, filled with confusion and terror. She struggles, fighting against the magic. But it's too strong.

"It's not—it's not me—it's—" Another growl tears free, and she doubles over, clutching at her stomach. When she straightens, her expression has completely changed.

She's no longer in control.

She lunges at Mrs. Henderson, the elderly librarian. Sheriff Harlow moves with impressive speed for a man his age. He positions himself between them. He fires his Taser before I even realize he'd drawn it.

The electrodes hit. Currents of electricity ripple through her. She convulses. Electricity courses through her nervous system while the wolf magic still tries to complete its transformation. The scream that tears from her throat almost brings me to my knees. It's part agony, part howl, and completely heartbreaking.

I shove my way through the panicking crowd, desperate to reach her. "Stop!" I shout. "She's being controlled! It's not her fault!"

Sheriff Harlow doesn't hear me. He's too focused on the threat. He kneels beside Hazel in my fallen body, cuffing her wrists behind her back as she continues to twitch and growl.

"I need backup at Town Hall," he barks into his radio. "Got a wolf going feral. Need containment, now."

I finally break through the crowd, reaching the front just as two deputies burst through the main doors.

"Sheriff, wait!" I grab his arm. "This isn't what it looks like. Hazel— Blake would never—"

Sheriff Harlow shakes me off. "Hazel, I understand he's your friend, but you need to step back. This is for everyone's safety. Including his."

"But—"

"One more word and you'll be joining him in a cell." His

patience level is clearly at negative ten. "Now, back up and let us do our job."

Helpless, I watch as the deputies lift Hazel and half-carry, half-drag her toward the exit. The transformation seems to be receding now, her movements more human than wolf, but the damage is done. Everyone saw "Blake Carter" try to attack a council member.

Ravena steps forward, her face a mask of concern. I want to scratch her eyes out.

"I hate to say I told you so," she says to the shaken council members, "but this is exactly the kind of unpredictable violence I was warning you about. If the pack leader himself can't control his shifts, you know his pack won't be able to."

She surveys the room, taking in the fear-glazed eyes and the nodding heads.

"She did this!" I shout, Hazel's voice cracking with the strain. "*She* is controlling the werewolves! *She's* been drugging her wellness products, and she's controlling you, too!"

All eyes turn to me, but with looks of pity, not belief, and I realize with sinking dread that I've just accused them of being under mind control.

"Hazel," Mrs. Henderson says gently, "I know you're upset, dear. But we all saw what happened."

"No. You saw what she orchestrated," I insist.

Ravena steps back to the podium like she owns it, which, at this point, she basically does. "In light of what we've witnessed, I move we vote immediately. The safety of Moonridge can't wait another day."

The council nods.

Of course they do.

And I stand at the edge of the room and watch it all go down.

CHAPTER NINETEEN

Blake

I grip the steering wheel of Hazel's Jeep like it might fly away if I loosen my grip. I keep replaying the disaster at Town Hall on an endless loop. I thought for sure we had her. But once again, she was six steps ahead of us.

I'm grateful I had the foresight to grab Hazel's keys from her purse before we left for the meeting. One of those "just in case" decisions that seemed paranoid at the time. Turns out, that paranoid, just-in-case thinking pays off when your body gets arrested with someone else wearing it.

I check my phone for the tenth time. No messages. I'd texted Calvin right after sneaking away from Town Hall.

Meeting a total disaster. H arrested. Need help. Coming to beach.

His reply? **Shit.**

After leaving Town Hall, I went straight to the sheriff's station where they'd taken Hazel. I'd barely made it through the front door when Deputy Miller blocked my path.

"Sorry, Hazel," he'd said, not sounding sorry at all. "Sheriff's orders. No visitors for Carter, especially not you."

"What? Why?" I'd asked. This guy was one of my best friends

in high school. He knows I'm not a threat, which means Hazel in my body would also not be a threat.

Miller crossed his arms. "Because that Bianca lady warned us you two might be working together. Said you'd probably try to help him escape. Orders are orders."

And that told me everything about how thoroughly Ravena had worked her influence into the department. The influence she holds over this town is terrifying. One accusation, and people believed the worst.

"When can I see him?" I'd asked, feigning casualness despite the panic bubbling in my chest.

"After the council votes tomorrow. There's nothing I can do for you now."

The weathered wooden sign announcing Amethyst Beach catches me by surprise. The narrow dirt road jostles the Jeep, making the silver charm bracelet around my wrist jingle against the steering wheel. The dense maples and birches finally thin, giving me glimpses of the dark, glass-calm water sparkling under the almost-full moon.

I park next to Calvin's truck and jump out, using my hip to shove the door shut with a metallic *thunk*. The night air is crisp, carrying the scent of campfire smoke and . . . Is that singing? I follow the sound, shouldering through a stand of white pines until the shoreline opens up.

I freeze.

My serious, disciplined pack of werewolves is sprawled around a massive bonfire like they're at some lakeside team-building retreat. Lyle's girlfriend, Lisa, plays her guitar while at least eight wolves sing along, arms linked, bodies swaying. Even grumpy-ass Marcus hums along while building a sand castle.

What in the actual hell?

If I'd known this place was a werewolf sedative, I would have brought them up here as soon as the trouble started.

"Weird, right?" Calvin's voice materializes next to me, making me nearly jump out of my boots. "They've been like this since we arrived. It's like they're all high or something."

"But they're okay?" I scan the surrounding woods for the shimmer of Ravena's magic or a hidden threat.

"Better than okay. They're like big puppies."

Part of me wants to be horrified. This isn't a retreat for a strong, protective pack. It's a summer camp. But then it hits me. Maybe Hazel is right. I've been holding the leash so tight I forgot they needed to breathe.

"La'Tasha thinks it's the amethyst combined with the salt. Says it's like one big collective joint for werewolves."

I watch the scene with a combination of relief and bewilderment. "So no shifting? No aggression? No weird yellow eyes?"

"Nope. Coco was right. Ravena can't touch us here."

That's one piece of good news. One thing out of what feels like several hundred, but I'll take it.

"Blake!" La'Tasha's voice carries over the noise, and I follow it to a campsite set up at the beach's edge, where the trees provide some shelter from the wind. Coco waves, surrounded by a mess of open books and a bubbling cauldron. I can only imagine what she's cooking up. Mina's here too, stirring a large pot of what could be chili over a small camp stove. The smell makes my stomach growl. I haven't eaten since lunch.

La'Tasha squeezes my arm. "Thank the goddess. We were about to send out a search party after that cryptic-ass text. What went down at the meeting?"

I drop onto a log beside her and immediately deflate. The adrenaline crash has turned my bones to lead.

"Total disaster." I launch into the whole mess, from the first sideways glance to the moment the handcuffs clicked shut. By the time I'm done, the only sound is the happy, oblivious singing from the main bonfire drifting over the trees.

Coco twirls a strand of her curly hair. "Te cogió de pendejo." She shakes her head. "Sorry. I mean, you got played, bestie."

"No kidding," I mutter, staring into the dark. "And now Hazel's locked up, and the council's probably voting to force us to change our zip code. I feel like we're seconds away from losing everything."

"Speaking of time," La'Tasha says, her voice unusually serious, "there's something else we need to discuss." She glances at Coco, who nods encouragingly. "It's about the body swap."

A knot forms in my stomach. "What about it?"

La'Tasha pulls a thick book from her bag. "I've been researching while you were at the meeting. About magical transfers of consciousness, body swaps, all that jazz."

"And?" I prompt when she hesitates.

"And most sources agree that these things have . . . expiration dates."

Hope fills my chest. "So, we'll just pop back into our bodies when a timer runs out?"

Wouldn't that be nice? But La'Tasha's face says otherwise. She shakes her head as she flips to a marked page. On it is a diagram of two figures with arrows between them. "The longer two souls remain in swapped bodies, the more they adapt. Settle in. Eventually, the swap becomes permanent."

My heart—Hazel's heart—skips several beats. "Shit."

"It seems there's always a catalyst that speeds things up exponentially. Something that forces the borrowed body to fully express its nature."

"Like shifting." The words come out barely audible, horror crystallizing in my chest. "Hazel shifted in my body. She's not supposed to be able to do that. Ever. Which means—"

La'Tasha closes the book. "The bodies are adapting. Accepting their new inhabitants."

"That also explains why you've gotten better at using Hazel's magic," Coco adds brightly, then wilts slightly under our stares. "Which is, um, not great news for the whole getting-back-to-normal thing."

I pull the ponytail over my shoulder and mess with the end, a gesture that's become almost natural. "How long do we have?" My fingers drum against the log.

La'Tasha closes the book. "If I had to guess? Until the full moon. It's the night you have no choice but to shift, right? If Hazel shifts . . ."

"That's tomorrow." The irony isn't lost on me. I spent years dreading full moons, seeing them as a loss of control. Now the full moon might be the night I lose myself entirely. And worse, the night Hazel becomes trapped in a world she never chose, in a body that will betray everything she believes about herself.

I drop my head in my hands. "We're so fucked."

Calvin places a firm hand on my back. "It's not over yet. We just need to prioritize. We'll break Hazel out, then figure out how to reverse the swap. We'll wait out the full moon up here and then figure out how to get rid of Ravena."

"Don't give up. You're not in this alone," La'Tasha says. "Coco and I will keep working on fixing the body swap issue while you two criminals focus on the jailbreak."

"I'll stay up here with this lot. I closed the B&B for the weekend. Just until we get this sorted out," Mina adds. "I'll keep everyone fed and entertained. I can text ya if anything gets suspicious."

"And I'll hold down things at the construction office," Calvin says. "Make it look like we're going about business as usual."

I'm not comfortable with him leaving the lake. "But what about the energy she is sending out to affect werewolves? What if you freak out?"

"I can wear this," he says, pulling a leather cord from his pocket. Hanging from it is a small silk pouch. "Filled with amethyst sand and salt from the beach. Should help keep me clear-headed in town."

I nod, a plan forming. "Good. Yes. We need to look normal tomorrow. Nothing to tip her off. And she absolutely cannot know the wolves are up here."

"Will you be okay manning the apothecary?" La'Tasha asks.

"I'll be fine." If Ravena notices that the shop is closed, it would tip her off.

"Once everyone's focused on the festival in the park," Calvin says, "you and I will break into the jail and get Hazel out."

Our little group falls silent, the weight of what we're facing settling over us. The singing from the bonfire continues, a cheerful soundtrack to our grim planning session.

"We should rest," La'Tasha finally says. "Tomorrow's going to be intense."

"I'll drive back with you," Calvin tells me. "I rode up here with Leo."

I nod, rising from the log. My legs feel steadier now that we have a plan. I let my eyes drift to the main bonfire and watch my pack for a moment. They look happy. Carefree.

Lisa notices me and waves, calling out, "Hazel! Come sing with us!"

For a second, I'm tempted. To sit by the fire and pretend everything's okay. Pretend my town isn't being manipulated by a vengeful blood witch and the woman I'm falling for isn't locked in a cell wearing my face.

"Another time," I call back with a smile. "Keep an eye on them," I add quietly to Mina as she walks me back to the Jeep.

"Like watchin' a litter of puppies," she assures me. Then, more seriously, "We'll get her back, Blake. And La'Tasha will figure out the swap."

I nod, not trusting my voice not to crack if I speak. The thought of never returning to my own body is terrifying. But somehow, the thought of Hazel being trapped in mine, forced to live as a werewolf forever because of my failure to protect her, is infinitely worse.

As I slide behind the wheel, Calvin climbs into the passenger seat, his large frame making the Jeep feel even smaller.

"She'll be okay," he says, reading my expression. "Hazel's tough."

"I know." I start the engine, taking one last look at the peaceful scene playing out at the edge of the lake. "That's what scares me. She'll fight back if provoked. It's who she is. But she doesn't know that my body has reflexes she can't control. She now possesses strength that responds to adrenaline in ways that could hurt someone. What if she tries to defend herself and accidentally proves Ravena right about werewolves being dangerous?"

The Jeep's headlights cut through the darkness as we pull away, illuminating the road back to Moonridge. Back to a town being slowly poisoned by fear. Back to a jail where Hazel waits, trapped in my skin.

Less than twenty-four hours until the full moon.

Not even a full day to fix everything, or lose ourselves forever.

But as I drive through the darkness toward town, toward whatever tomorrow brings, I realize that somewhere along the way, 'losing myself' stopped being about being stuck in the wrong body.

It's about losing her.

CHAPTER TWENTY

Hazel

I wake up to thin cotton pressing against my cheek and every muscle screaming in protest. The cell is freezing, and there's this crazy leftover sizzle of electricity dancing through my limbs. Getting tasered, it turns out, is exactly as awful as it looks on TV. Maybe worse. TV doesn't capture the lingering smell of singed werewolf hair. Or the metallic taste of blood because I bit my tongue during the convulsions.

I groan and push myself upright on the narrow cot, wincing as I uncurl these long-ass legs. Everything hurts. My joints feel like they've been taken apart and reassembled by a toddler, my head throbs along with my heartbeat, and somewhere deep inside my chest, there's an unsettling buzzing sensation like the wolf inside is pacing behind my ribs, waiting for another chance to break free.

That's what terrifies me most.

I shifted last night. Not fully, but enough to grow claws and fangs and scare a room full of people, then get arrested and thrown in this freezing concrete box.

Sounds drift in through the small windows in the hallway. Voices call instructions as booths are set up, and upbeat pop music blasts from a nearby speaker. It's far too peppy for my current mood. I pace the cell, six steps one way, six steps back. Outside, someone laughs, the sound carrying clearly through the thin walls of the sheriff's station. The whole town is preparing for the biggest celebration of the summer while I'm stuck in here. In the wrong body. What will happen if I shift in here? Will I go absolutely apeshit? Probably. Is this cell even big enough for a wolf? How big do they get? I swear, if I shift in here and I can't get out, I'm totally dropping a hot, steamy dog turd right on that uncomfortable cot. They deserve it. Of course, if Ravena succeeds, there may not be anyone around to care. There'll be bigger issues to deal with.

Snippets of conversation from the deputies in the front office bring me out of my werewolf revenge fantasy.

"—extra security for tonight—" "—after what happened at the meeting—" "—I'm ready for the wolves to go—"

I flinch at this. They're talking about me. About the pack.

The outer door creaks open, followed by familiar heavy footsteps. Has to be Sheriff Harlow. I'd recognize his walk anywhere. I move to the edge of the cell and wrap Blake's fingers around the cold metal bars.

Harlow appears, coffee in hand, his warm brown skin set in grim lines. The bags under his eyes look heavier than usual. He pulls up a folding chair and settles into it with a sigh. "Morning, Blake. How're you feeling?"

I almost go off. He tased me! I guess he had good reason, but still. "Like I got hit by a truck. Then the truck backed up and hit me again for the hell of it. Any chance of some aspirin?"

He nods to a deputy hovering nearby, who disappears and returns moments later with pills and water. I swallow them, though I doubt they'll do much.

Harlow studies me, running a finger down one side of his

mustache. "You remember what happened last night?"

I press my fingers against my eyes and nod. "Some of it. Not all." I roll my shoulders. "It's like static. I remember pieces, but nothing that makes complete sense."

That's not entirely a lie. My memories of the transformation are overlaid with a red haze of panic and rage.

Harlow leans forward. "You tried to attack Martha Henderson. Seventy-eight years old and about as threatening as a bunny slipper. What happened?"

I grip the bars tighter, leaning forward. "I didn't want to attack anyone. It wasn't me . . . I mean, it wasn't under my control. Bianca—Ravena—she blew something in my face. Some kind of powder. It triggered the shift."

Harlow's expression doesn't change, but his eyes narrow slightly. "Hazel was saying something similar. About Bianca being this . . . Ravena person. About mind control." He doesn't believe any of it.

"It's true." Blake's voice comes out as a low growl. I take a breath, trying to calm down. Getting angry won't help. "Sheriff, you've known Blake—known me—for years. Have you ever seen me lose control like that? Ever?"

Doubt crosses Harlow's face. He quietly sets his coffee aside.

"Your dad never lost control. Not once in all the years I knew him. Man had iron discipline when it came to his wolf. I'd have figured that he would have taught you boys how to do the same."

The mention of Blake's father sends an unexpected pang through my chest. I'm not sure how to respond, so I just nod.

Harlow leans forward, elbows on his knees. "Listen. I've got a town to keep safe and right now, you're in here and your pack is missing. My deputies did a sweep of the usual spots this morning, and the only wolf they found was Calvin, and he played it coy. Said he had no idea where anyone was. This looks awfully suspicious."

I keep my face carefully neutral. "Oh. Uh . . . Monthly camping trip. Bonding. Team-building exercises. Figured it would be better that way with all that was going on."

He's not convinced.

"Look, Sheriff." I have to get through to him. "Something's happening in Moonridge. Something bad. Like Blake—like Hazel said, Bianca isn't who she says she is. She's using blood magic to make the wolves aggressive. She wants to turn the town against us."

Harlow cocks an eyebrow. "And why would she do that?"

"Because the magical protection around town requires both wolf and witch magic to maintain. If the wolves are gone . . ." I let him fill in the blank.

The sheriff studies me for a long moment, and I can practically see the wheels turning behind his tired eyes. Finally, he sighs and stands. "Here's the situation. The council has called an emergency meeting to take place tomorrow after the festival. They're voting on Bianca's proposal—a temporary relocation order for all werewolves, effective immediately."

My heart sinks. "Sheriff—"

He holds up a hand. "I'm not finished. She was fighting really hard for a permanent ban, but I think we talked her down. The Blue Moon Festival goes on as planned tonight. It's been a Moonridge tradition for over a hundred years, and the council doesn't want to cancel it. But they've made it clear. If there's as much as one more wolf showing aggression toward humans or anyone else, the temporary order becomes permanent. No werewolves in Moonridge. Period."

"They can't do that," I protest, though I know full well they can. "This is our home."

"It's my home too," Harlow says quietly. "This town has had its share of troubles, but we always get through them. And we do because we believe in something that I'm starting to think we've forgotten. That Moonridge works because we choose to make it work. Because wolves and witches and humans find a way to live together. Even when it's hard. Or at least we used to. Somewhere along the way, we seem to have forgotten that." He picks up his chair, folding it closed with a sharp snap. "Your dad would be ashamed of what's happening. This isn't the Moonridge he believed in."

The words scrape at something raw inside me. Not because they're directed at me, but because I can feel how they would devastate Blake. This body carries his love for his father in its very bones, and hearing that his dad would be ashamed . . .

I make one last plea. "Sheriff, please. Just look into Bianca. Check her background. Where she came from, what she was doing before she showed up here six months ago. And if you need more proof, ask Mina. Or La'Tasha. We've found things."

Harlow pauses, his back to me. "I'll ask some questions. That's all I can promise."

It's more than I expected, honestly. "Thank you."

He grunts in acknowledgment, then nods to the deputy waiting by the door. "Get him some breakfast. And a blanket. It's cold in here."

The deputy returns minutes later with a tray holding a sad-looking breakfast sandwich, a tin cup of coffee, and a thin wool blanket. Not exactly five-star service, but it'll do for now.

I inhale the flavorless sandwich in two bites and take one sip of the tar that they call coffee. I wrap the blanket around Blake's broad shoulders and return to the cot, back against the wall, knees pulled to my chest.

I've never felt so powerless. Not when Evan broke up with me, or Grandma Agnes died. Not even when I first realized I was stuck in Blake's body.

Now I'm stuck in here with nothing. I can only hope that Blake and the others have figured out a way to fix this. I close my eyes, trying to calm the storm of emotions, and in the quiet of my mind, there's a shift. A comforting presence.

"Gran?" I whisper, not actually expecting an answer.

A feeling of warmth spreads through my chest like honey in tea, gentling the wolf's restless energy until it curls up like a contented dog. I know better than to think my grandmother's spirit is literally visiting me in jail. But there's magic in memories, in the lessons she taught me that live on in my heart. And right now, those memories are speaking to me.

You've always looked to others for acceptance, Hazel. You always let them lead you instead of your heart.

I can almost hear her saying it, in that gentle but no-nonsense way she had. It was her favorite criticism of my magic. I relied too much on impressing others with my tricks. "There's more to you than magic, and there's more to magic than flashy tricks," she'd say, tapping my chest. "The power you possess can be dangerous. Never lose sight of who you are or what this magic means."

But it's what's inside that guides you back to yourself.

I press my hand against my heart.

Your heart knows the way. Follow it.

My heart? Or Blake's? Or both?

Love is the key, not just magic.

The thought stops me cold, like walking into a glass door I didn't see coming. Love? I don't love Blake Carter. I like him, and feelings have surfaced, but I don't love him. Not yet.

Do I?

Sure, there's attraction. It's kind of impossible to ignore when you're literally wearing someone's skin. And trust me, from what I've seen the last few days, there are definitely parts of this man I am attracted to. But love?

And maybe it's time you stop running from what that love really is.

Oh!

Okay, Grandma.

The realization unfolds slowly. Each petal of understanding makes me want to curl up and hide. Because admitting this changes everything. Because once I acknowledge it, I can't turn back. I've been fighting this connection with Blake because I'm scared. Because after Evan left me for being "too much" with my magic and my quirks, I built walls. Because it's easier to keep Blake at arm's length than to admit that maybe, just maybe, what I feel for him isn't just physical attraction or magical prophecy. Maybe it's something real. I hated him as a kid. My God, he was so mean, and I've carried that bitterness with me into adulthood. The wolf inside quiets at this thought, like it's been waiting for me to finally catch up.

Footsteps in the corridor snap me back to reality. Quick, light steps, not a deputy's heavy tread. I rise from the cot, expecting . . . I'm not sure what, but it's definitely not La'Tasha's face appearing before me on the other side of the bars.

"Tash?" I whisper, stunned.

"Shh!" She glances nervously over her shoulder. "I snuck in during shift change. I need you to listen."

"How's Blake?" The question escapes before I can stop it.

La'Tasha's eyebrows rise, but she doesn't comment on my obvious concern. "He's fine. Pretending to be you at the shop. But that's not why I'm here."

She pulls a small velvet pouch from her pocket and passes it through the bars. "While you've been enjoying being a criminal, Coco and I pulled an all-nighter looking for a way to get you out of that big, hairy body. There's a way to undo the swap, but the window is closing fast. It has to happen during the Blue Moon tonight."

I clutch the pouch and almost collapse with relief. "How do we do it?"

"It's complicated, and I don't have time to explain now." She glances behind her again. "But there's bad news and I don't mean to chap your ass, but you need to know. I'm pretty sure if we don't swap you back by midnight, the change becomes permanent."

My throat tightens. "Because of the shift?"

"Not because of that, exactly. It's just . . . weird shit is happening. Sis, you shouldn't have even been able to partially shift in Blake's body. The fact that you did means . . ." She hesitates, biting her lip.

I take a step back. "Means the bodies are adapting to their new occupants," I finish for her. "Becoming truly ours."

She nods grimly. "That pouch contains a protective amulet. Wear it. It might help prevent further shifts until we can get you out of here."

"Get me out? How?"

A small, fierce smile curves her lips. "Blake and Calvin have a plan. Just be ready tonight, okay? And Hazel . . ." She reaches through the bars, squeezing my hand. "Whatever happens, remember that the prophecy is about two becoming one in purpose. In choice. Not because they feel like they have to, but because they want to. And it's perfectly okay to want to."

My cheeks heat at her knowing look. "I don't—"

"Girl, please. I've watched you secretly moon over that boy for the last twenty years." Amusement dances in her eyes. "Even now when he's wearing your face." Her expression softens. "It's okay to care about him. Maybe even love him."

Before I can respond, voices sound from the front office. La'Tasha squeezes my hand once more, then vanishes down the corridor. I open the velvet pouch. The amulet is simple yet beautiful. A small moonstone wrapped in silver wire, strung on a leather cord. I slip it over my head, tucking it beneath the T-shirt. The change is immediate. The restless energy that's been clawing at my insides since the forced shift settles into a feeling of peace. The wolf doesn't disappear; I can still feel it there, but it no longer fights for control.

I close my eyes and breathe.

Hold on, I think, pressing my hand against the amulet and sending the thought out like a prayer.

Hold on, Blake. I'm ready. Ready for whatever comes tonight.

Ready to fight for us.

Because maybe, just maybe, I'm starting to understand what it means to be both of us at once. And what it means to love someone enough to become part of them.

CHAPTER TWENTY-ONE

Blake

If one more person comes in here asking for "Bianca's Vitality Boosting Supplements", I'm going to throat punch them. I'm starting to think I've stumbled into some kind of wellness twilight zone complete with eerily polite zombies begging for Ravena's overpriced, underperforming magic pills. I plaster Hazel's best customer service smile on and hand over the bottle of gleaming capsules, wondering when exactly the entire town decided to join the same cult.

"Will that be all today, Mrs. Henderson?" My inflection still sounds wrong after five days in this body. It's impossible to sound exactly like Hazel and I've pretty much given up.

Her eyes have a glazed look and they're fixed on something just over my shoulder. I turn, but there's nothing there. Whatever it is, she finds it utterly captivating.

"Yes. Just the supplements." Her voice is almost robotic. "Bianca says they'll align my chakras and boost my immune system."

I seriously doubt "Bianca" knows what a chakra is, but I keep that thought to myself.

I ring up the sale. "Of course."

While Mrs. Henderson digs through her purse for her wallet,

I reach under the counter. La'Tasha helped me make tiny pouches of rowan berries, basil, and mugwort this morning. They're designed to break minor enchantments and protect from evil influence. I slip the pouch between the supplement bottle and receipt, hoping the simple magic might break through whatever hold Ravena has on her.

"And I've included a free sample of our new, uh, energy-aligning herbs."

Mrs. Henderson barely glances at the bag. "Thank you, Hazel." She turns and walks out, her usual shuffling gait replaced with a strangely confident stride.

I drum Hazel's fingers against the counter, anxiety bubbling in her stomach. That's the fourth person today with that same blank stare, flat voice and single-minded focus on Ravena's products. This isn't normal. Even for Moonridge, which has a pretty flexible definition of "normal" to begin with.

I glance at the clock. Only 10:30, and already the shop has been busier than I've ever seen it. Is this normal for a Saturday?

The bell jingles again, and Mr. Garcia from the hardware store steps in. His eyes immediately lock onto the display of Ravena's products that were set up by the register.

"Morning, Hazel." He doesn't quite make eye contact. "Just need to grab some of those Clarity Capsules. The wife says they're helping with her, uh, memory issues."

"Right. The Clarity Capsules," I repeat, reaching for the shelf behind me. My skin crawls just touching the sleek packaging with its mint-green logo. "You know, if your wife is having memory problems, Hazel—I mean, I—have an herbal tea that might work better. No artificial ingredients."

Mr. Garcia seems to look right through me. "No thanks. Bianca's products are the only ones that work for us now."

The word 'now' sends a chill down my spine. It's like he's stating a fundamental law of physics rather than expressing a preference.

"Of course." I place the bottle on the counter. "That'll be twenty-eight dollars."

While he counts out cash, I grab another protection sachet and slide it into his bag. "Here you go. The herbs are a festival promotion. For prosperity and health."

He takes the bag without looking inside. "Thanks."

The bell jingles again as the elementary school principal and the town's only dentist enter. Both make a beeline for Ravena's display.

I force brightness into my voice. "Hi there. How can I help you?"

"Immunity Boosters," the principal says.

"Sleep Enhancers," the dentist says at the exact same time.

They don't look at each other, don't acknowledge my presence beyond the bare minimum required to complete their transaction. Their focus is laser-sharp on the bottles, like everything else in the world has simply ceased to exist.

They're like those creepy dolls my grade school friend's mom used to collect. I stayed the night one night and I had to sleep in the room with them and I know at least two of them moved. I've never been comfortable around dolls since.

I fill their requests, adding protection sachets to both bags. Neither notices or comments. They just pay (exact change, both of them) and leave with the same measured steps I've seen all morning.

The next two hours continue in the same vein. A steady stream of Moonridge residents all requesting Ravena's products. Every one of them has the same vacant stare and unnervingly polite demeanor. All ignore my attempts at normal conversation.

By one o'clock, I've gone through almost all the protection sachets La'Tasha and I prepared this morning. My stomach growls, reminding me that I haven't eaten since nibbling on a banana for breakfast. I grab a granola bar from her stash behind the counter and chew it thoughtfully, watching the door. The post-lunch rush should be starting soon. If it's anything like the morning traffic, I'll need reinforcements. I pull out Hazel's phone and text La'Tasha:

Shop crazy busy. Everyone wants R's products. Made it through a lot of sachets. Need more. Everyone in town is under her spell.

No immediate response. She's probably up at the beach.

The bell jingles again and this time a young mother enters with a toddler on her hip. The woman's eyes have that now-familiar glazed look, but the child appears normal. Cranky, squirming, and very much alive behind the eyes.

"Hello, Hazel." The woman's voice is not quite right. "I need more of Bianca's Growth Gummies for my little one here."

The child whines and buries his face in his mother's neck. "No gummies," he mumbles.

"They're good for you." Her voice takes on a strange, singsong quality that raises the hair on the back of my neck. "Miss Bianca says they'll help you grow big and strong."

I hesitate, hand hovering over the jar of colorful gummies. These are meant for children. Kids who can't consent to whatever Ravena's doing to their minds. If her supplements are turning adults into compliant zombies, what might they do to developing brains? The thought makes my stomach turn.

I search for a lie. "Actually, we're out of the Growth Gummies today. Festival rush. Cleared us right out."

That's the best you can do? There are three bottles on the counter in front of you.

The woman's cheerful expression doesn't change, but something cold and dangerous flickers in her eyes. "I can see them right there, Hazel." Her voice remains light. "Don't be a liar. What kind of example are you setting for my child?"

The words are spoken in that same cordial tone, but underneath lies a threat wrapped in silk.

"Oh, those?" I force a laugh. "Those are, um, the adult version.

Different formula. Not suitable for children under twelve." I move the bottles out of sight. "Can I offer you one of my, uh . . . one of my special children's tonics instead? All natural, much gentler."

The child peeks at me, his little face hopeful. "No gummies?"

"No gummies," I confirm, giving him a small smile.

For a moment, the woman just stares at me. Her cheery expression never wavers, but the temperature in the room seems to drop by several degrees. Then she shakes her head, the movement slightly too fluid to be natural.

"That won't do at all. Bianca said the gummies are essential for proper development. We'll try one of the other pop-up locations."

She turns and walks out, the boy looking back at me with wide, frightened eyes. The door closes behind them with a cheerful jingle that feels wildly out of place given the situation.

I slump against the counter. The exchange left me feeling dirty. Something is deeply, horrifically wrong in Moonridge, and it's spreading through those supplements.

I glance at the clock again. Almost two o'clock. The streets outside are getting busier as festival preparations ramp up. I can see people stringing lights across the town square, setting up booths for tonight's celebration. It looks so cheery. If someone were to drive by, it would look like nothing more than a community coming together to celebrate. Not one that is about to get ripped apart by a crazy witch.

The next hour passes in a blur of identical transactions. When Mr. Hartwell, the high school chemistry teacher, comes in for his "Brain Boost Elixir," I ring him up and then walk him to the door.

"Sorry, folks!" I call to the three people approaching the shop. I flip the sign to CLOSED and offer my best apologetic smile through the window. "Closing early for festival preparations! Blue Moon tradition!"

They stare at me without expression for several uncomfortable seconds. Then, as if responding to some silent command, they turn in unison and walk away. I shudder and pull the blinds down. I lean against the door and let out a long breath. I push away from the door and move through the shop, checking that all the windows are locked. Then I go to the display of Ravena's products and examine them more closely.

The packaging is slick and professional, white with mint-green accents. The logo kind of resembles a rune if you look at it closely enough. The ingredient lists are vague: "proprietary herbal blend," "natural energy enhancers," "ancient wellness secrets."

I unscrew one of the Vitality Boosting Supplement bottles and shake a capsule into Hazel's palm. It looks ordinary enough. Just a transparent gelcap filled with fine green powder. But when I hold it up to the light, I notice something odd. Tiny flecks of red gleam with an oily sheen that makes my skin crawl. They're too dark to be herb fragments.

Wait. Is that . . .? Yes. It is. Dried blood mixed into the supplement powder.

My stomach lurches. I quickly cap the bottle and step back, wiping Hazel's hand on her jeans as if the mere touch of the capsule could contaminate me. Ravena's been feeding the entire town blood magic in pill form. I need to get these to La'Tasha for analysis, and then warn the council, and—

"Finding my products interesting, are we?"

I whirl around, nearly knocking over the display. Ravena stands in the doorway, one perfectly manicured hand resting on the frame. She wears white again today. Shocker. Her dark hair is pulled back in another severe bun and I'm beginning to think she's shellacked it in place.

"How did you get in?" The words come out as more squeak than demand, my voice betrays the fear coursing through my body. "The door was locked. The windows—"

Ravena smiles, her teeth very white against her red lipstick. "Oh, Blake. So many questions, always. But never the right ones."

My blood freezes in Hazel's veins. She called me Blake.

She knows.

She knows I'm not Hazel.

"I don't know what you're talking about." I try to remain cool. Slowly edging toward the counter where I know Hazel keeps a protection charm under the register.

Ravena laughs, the sound like ice cracking. "Let's not play games. I know exactly who you are, Blake Carter. Just as I know that Hazel Thornton is locked in a jail cell." She takes a step toward me. "I know this because I planned this."

My heart sinks. We were never in control.

"I got to the amulet, reversed its effects, and charged it for exactly this purpose. It was just waiting for the right moment. I figured that with your powers limited, it would be easier for me to execute my plan. I just didn't expect you two to actually work together. You're tenacious."

She has to be lying. "You couldn't have known—"

"That the son of John Carter and the granddaughter of Agnes Thornton would find themselves drawn to each other? That they would discover the amulet precisely when I needed them to? Oh, but I did know." Her smile widens, triumph gleaming in her eyes. "I've been planning this for decades, Blake. Since before you were born. Since before your father was born. This town has wronged my family for generations, and it was one of your ancestors who started it all."

She glides closer, each step deliberate. "Generations of Carters and Thorntons have poisoned this town. And then that *stupid* pact."

"I know about the pact." My hand inches toward the register.

"Do you? Do you really?" She tilts her head, studying me like a curious specimen. "Do you know that it requires balance? Equal power from both sides? To ensure that witches and wolves will always live here in peace?"

I don't answer, but she doesn't seem to expect me to.

"Before I was even born, the witches of Moonridge held the power. This was our land. And then werewolves arrived, promising peace. And then the wolves grew in number and tried to overthrow us. The town agreed on a pact to align the magic and allow both witches and wolves to live here in peace. My grandmother fought it. This land belonged to the witches, and it should stay with the witches. And do you know what they did to her?"

I shake my head, still inching my hand toward the register.

"They burned her alive in the town square. Made the whole town watch while my grandmother screamed. And do you know what your precious ancestors did? They howled. They celebrated. They treated it like entertainment." She has the story all wrong. Of course she thinks her family is the victim. "The witches and their pet wolves—your ancestors—burned Elowen Blackwood for daring to speak the truth. For trying to keep what was rightfully hers. And then years later, another of my ancestors—Adeline Blackwood—was once again scorned by a werewolf, and she too was banished."

"And let me guess. Now you want revenge." My fingers finally brush the small carved box under the counter. "An eye for an eye."

"Oh no, Blake. Not an eye for an eye." She shakes her head, her smile returning. "I want the whole town. I want Moonridge. I want the power that comes from breaking the pact in exactly the right way, at exactly the right time. I'm taking what belongs to me. I'm cleansing the town of witches and wolves so I can start fresh. I'm also ending the stranglehold the Carters and Thorntons have held over this town for centuries. By morning, you both will be gone. Permanently, if I'm lucky."

Permanently?

Desperation makes me clumsy. I grab the box with shaking hands, nearly dropping it as I flip the lid open. The small protection crystal inside seems pathetically inadequate against the power radiating from Ravena, but it's all I have. I snatch it up and point it at her like a weapon.

She laughs again. "A protection charm? Really? How cute." With a flick of her wrist, the crystal flies from my hand, shattering against the wall. "I've spent fifty years planning this moment. Did you think I'd be unprepared for a few parlor tricks?"

"The pack is safe," I tell her, desperately looking for another weapon. "They're protected. You can't hurt them."

"Ah yes, your little beach vacation. Clever, I admit." She nods appreciatively. "But unnecessary. I never wanted to hurt the pack, Blake. I need them."

"For what?" My voice cracks on the question. She thinks she has the upper hand. I need her to spill her guts. I need to know everything so we can fight her.

"To break the pact, of course. At midnight, when the Blue Moon reaches its zenith, my power will be unstoppable. With the Wolfsbane Amulet to control the pack, and my supplements controlling the town, I'll channel the combined energy into shattering the pact completely."

She extends her hands in my direction and they begin to glow. Behind her, shadows gather and twist like they're alive. "And when the dust settles, Moonridge will finally be returned to the power of the Blackwoods."

"You're insane," I say.

Ravena's smile doesn't falter. "Genius is often mistaken for madness. Now, enough talk."

She raises her hands above her, pulling in a cloud of red light that smells of blood and sulfur. She blows gently, sending it scattering into sparkling motes that drift toward me like crimson snowflakes.

It's kind of pretty, and the lights look harmless—until they touch my skin. They burn as they sink beneath the surface. I can feel them spreading through my bloodstream like poison, turning my body against me one nerve at a time. The paralysis starts in my toes and races upward. I try to run, but Hazel's legs won't respond.

"What . . ." My tongue grows heavy, the word slurred. "What did you do to me?"

"Blood-binding." Ravena smirks as I struggle to remain standing. "Very old magic. *Very* effective."

Hazel's legs give out, and I collapse to the floor. The paralysis reaches my chest, making each breath a struggle. I can only watch as Ravena steps over me and moves to the center of the shop.

"Now, let's see about that amulet." She kneels on the worn wooden floor, running her hands over the boards until she finds what she's looking for. "Ah, here we are."

With surprising strength, she pries up a section of floorboard, the same spot where Hazel and I first found the amulet days ago. Of course, that's what she came for. She needs it for tonight. She withdraws the amulet, and peels back the layers of protective fabric. A dim, red glow illuminates her triumphant face.

"Beautiful, isn't it?" Ravena breathes, holding it up. "My ancestor's greatest creation. The perfect tool for controlling werewolves."

I try to speak, to move, to do anything, but the paralysis is complete now. I can only blink and breathe shallowly as Ravena rises to her feet, the amulet clutched in her hand.

She towers over me, admiring her prize. "I should thank you and Hazel, really. Without your little body-swap adventure, I might never have confirmed the amulet was still here. Agnes hid it well."

With a sigh that sounds almost regretful, she tucks the amulet into her pocket. "Well, I'd love to stay and chat, but I have a ritual to attend to, and you've given me quite enough trouble already."

She grabs my arms and starts dragging me across the floor. Even though I can't feel the sensation of being moved, I can see the ceiling sliding past above me. She pulls me into the back room and continues to a small storage closet tucked under the stairs. The small space smells of dust and old herbs, scents that should be comforting in Hazel's shop but now feel like the inside of a tomb. With another impressive display of strength, she props me up against the shelves like a discarded mannequin.

"Comfortable?" she asks with mock concern. "You'll be here a while."

She steps back, surveying her work. "Such a shame. You and Hazel could have been quite the power couple. That prophecy wasn't entirely wrong, you know. Wolf and witch united in love . . . it could have been beautiful. Or something."

Her expression hardens. "But some wrongs can't be forgiven. Some debts must be paid."

She closes the closet door partway, then pauses. In the sliver of light still reaching me, I see her smile one last time.

"By morning, your wolfy friends will be gone. Or dead. The choice is theirs, really. They can leave Moonridge forever, or they can stay and burn like my grandmother did. Either way, they won't be my problem anymore."

The door closes with a final click, plunging me into darkness. A key turns in the lock, and then Ravena's footsteps fade away.

I'm alone. Paralyzed. Locked in a closet while a vengeful witch prepares to destroy everything and everyone I care about.

In the darkness, I try to fight the paralysis, to wiggle just one of Hazel's fingers.

Nothing responds.

The blood magic holds me completely immobile, a prisoner in a body that no longer obeys me.

CHAPTER TWENTY-TWO

Hazel

Festival music drifts through the cell window. Some upbeat, cheery crap that's currently making me want to rip my own ears off. Or Blake's ears. Whatever.

Where are they?

Everything is turned up to eleven tonight. I'm starting to get claustrophobic, and I'm tempted to rip the bars off the window and haul ass out of here. I feel like I'm trapped in a body that's being rewired by a toddler with a soldering iron. The power of La'Tasha's amulet has been thinning out, leaving behind something twitchy and wild that's scratching at the inside of my ribs.

Seriously, though. Where the hell is he?

A kid shrieks with delight somewhere outside, and the sound pierces my skull. It's loud and obnoxious and it's making me want to rip off my clothes and this skin and go absolutely batshit on everyone.

A door clangs shut somewhere in the building, followed by muffled voices. The night deputy making his rounds, probably. I squeeze Blake's eyes shut, trying to find a "happy place" that isn't currently vibrating with predatory intent. I need to calm down.

Keys jingle in the corridor outside. I move toward the bars just as the deputy appears, but something's off about his movements. Calvin is behind him, a finger pressed to his lips in a shushing gesture.

I'm a hot mess of relief. "What's going on? Where's Blake?"

Calvin motions for me to stay quiet as the deputy mechanically unlocks my cell door. "Later," he mouths, gently guiding the zombie-like deputy aside.

I step out of the cell. Calvin nods at the deputy, who locks the empty cell and then shuffles away.

"Did you steal his brain or something? What the hell is wrong with him?"

Calvin leads me toward the back exit. "Nothing permanent. La'Tasha whipped up a quick mind-control potion, and I slipped it into his coffee. He won't remember you were ever here."

"Smart. But where's Blake? He was supposed to—"

Calvin's expression grows grim. "He never showed. We were supposed to meet at the hardware store at six. He's not answering his phone or responding to texts. I drove by the apothecary and it was all locked up, lights out."

My gut knots up. "That's not like him."

"Tell me about it." Calvin pushes open the back door and peers carefully into the alley behind the station. "La'Tasha, Mina, and Coco are looking for him now. But we need to get you to the lake."

I plant my feet. "I'm not going anywhere without Blake."

Calvin turns back to me, frustration and worry battling on his face. "Look at the sky. The moon is rising. You're in a werewolf's body with zero experience controlling the shift. If you lose control in the middle of town tonight, with everyone already on edge about wolves . . ."

He doesn't need to finish the sentence. I get it. I'm a walking time bomb in this body. I relent. "Fine. But as soon as I'm safe, we find Blake."

"I already told you, we have people looking for him." Calvin leads me down the alley, keeping to the shadows. "My truck's around the corner."

Moonridge has transformed for the festival. Lanterns strung between lampposts throw flickering light across the cobblestones. The air is thick with fried dough and cotton candy. On any other night, it might feel magical. But half the crowd wanders with glassy stares. The rest shout, or twitch with restless energy.

"What's happening to them?" I whisper as we skirt the edge of the square. We pass a group of teenagers who stare at us with unblinking eyes. Their synchronized tracking makes my skin crawl. They're like those weird animatronic dolls you see in store windows at Christmas.

"I don't know. It's like they're in a trance. Don't make eye contact," Calvin mutters. "Just keep moving."

We hop into his truck and I catch sight of myself in the side mirror. Blake's face stares back, eyes already glinting with hints of yellow as the wolf responds to the rising moon.

Calvin pretends not to notice. "How are you holding up?"

"I'm okay." A muscle twitches in my jaw. "Everything feels a little overwhelming. Too many sounds and smells."

"That's normal for a full moon," Calvin says, peeling away from the curb. "The fact that you're still talking in complete sentences is impressive."

"Yay me," I mutter, rolling down the window for fresh air.

As we drive through town, I notice more weirdness. A woman stands perfectly still in the middle of the sidewalk, staring at something only she can see. A man walks in small, precise circles around a lamppost.

"This is so much worse than this morning," Calvin says, knuckles white on the steering wheel. "It has to be the supplements."

We leave the town behind, turning onto the winding forest

road that leads to Amethyst Beach. The trees seem to close in around us, branches reaching over the road. As we climb into the hills, restlessness consumes me. My skin feels hot. Itchy. I feel like a giant, walking rash. My fingernails ache in their sockets and my teeth feel three sizes too big for my jaw.

"Calvin," I strain to say. "I think something's happening."

He glances at me with wide eyes. "I know. Just hold on. We're almost there."

"What if I can't stop it?"

"Then this is going to be a very weird insurance claim." He tries to joke.

I try to breathe and remain in control, but Blake's wolf has a different plan. It wants the moon. It wants to run until its lungs burst. I grip the dashboard so hard the plastic groans. My fingertips are ghost-white.

Then I smell it.

Smoke.

My nostrils flare. "Do you smell that?"

"Yeah. Is it from the festival?"

"No. It's too close. Something's burning up ahead."

Calvin floors it and the truck lurches forward on the uneven road. We round a bend and the gray haze hits the headlights like a wall.

"This can't be good," Calvin mutters.

The higher we climb, the thicker it gets.

"Almost there, and then we'll be in the clear." Calvin's voice lacks conviction.

We crest the final hill before Amethyst Beach, and the world is orange.

Fire.

Not a small campfire gone wrong. It's a literal wall of flame cutting through the woods in a perfect, deliberate arc. Trees are being eaten alive. Tongues of fire lick the trunks and jump from branch to branch.

The pack is scattered across the hillside, running in our direction. Some are fully human, helping injured pack members down the slope. Others have partially shifted. A few have shifted completely, their wolf forms darting between trees, eyes reflecting the firelight like demons.

"Oh my God." I can barely breathe. "The pack . . ."

"She drove them out," Calvin says, his voice hollow with disbelief. "She knew exactly what would force us back to town."

A howl rips through the night. It sounds like pure panic. Another one answers. Then another. The sound vibrates inside Blake's chest. It pulls a howl out of my own throat before I can even think to stop it.

Calvin curses and slams the brakes. Two wolves streak across the road right in front of the bumper. The truck skids into the gravel.

"We have to help." He stares at the chaos. "We have to move them somewhere safe."

I'm already out the door. My feet hit the dirt and I'm moving.

"Hazel, wait!"

But I'm already rushing toward the scattered pack. The smoke stings my eyes and burns my lungs, but I push forward. I cup Blake's hands around his mouth and call out, "Here! This way! Follow me!"

Some of the wolves turn at the sound of their alpha's voice—my voice now. Relief flashes in their eyes as they change direction, racing toward me. But others are too far gone in panic, racing blindly away from the fire, deeper into the night.

Leo appears from the smoke, helping a limping young woman. Lisa follows, her flannel shirt smudged with soot, her eyes wide with fear.

"What happened?" I demand, scanning the hillside for more pack members.

"I don't know," Leo says, soot streaking his face. "The fire started in three places at once. There was literally no warning.

We were singing and swimming when suddenly the whole hill-side just erupted."

Several of the pack members jump into their vehicles and drive off. Others are on foot. A crash sounds from the burning forest as a tree in the distance succumbs to the flames. Sparks explode skyward.

"We need to round up anyone who didn't already drive off," I decide. "Get them somewhere safe."

"Where?" Leo asks. "The beach is cut off, and the town isn't safe with Ravena controlling everyone. That's exactly where she wants us."

I think fast, Blake's sharper instincts guiding me. "Skipper Lake. Blake told me you all go there for training, right? It should be far enough from town that Ravena can't reach us. Granted, we'll have to cut right through town to get there, but it's our only option."

Calvin nods approvingly. "Good thinking."

We split up, calling to the wolves we can see, herding them toward Calvin's truck and two other vehicles I now notice parked farther down the road. A sandy-colored wolf, I think it's Marvin from the construction crew, gives me one regretful look before bolting into the darkness. Two more follow him, disappearing between the trees.

"Let them go," Calvin says when I move to follow. "We can't waste any more time. The fire is coming."

He's right, but it tears at my heart to abandon any of Blake's pack. They're his responsibility. Which makes them mine, at least for tonight.

We manage to gather about fifteen wolves into the vehicles. Some are injured with minor burns or smoke inhalation. All are frightened. The fully human pack members crowd into the truck beds while those partially shifted are coaxed into the back seats, away from curious eyes, should we pass other cars.

I scan the hillside one last time, hoping for a glimpse of the missing pack members. Or better yet, Blake.

Nothing. Just smoke and the orange glow.

"We'll find him," Calvin promises. "Blake's survived worse."

I nod, but the knot in my stomach tightens. Where is he?

As we make our way back down the hill, I feel the inner wolf tensing, rising closer to the surface. The amulet La'Tasha gave me pulses, hot against my skin.

I squeeze my eyes shut. I breathe deep even though the smoke shreds my lungs.

Hold on, Blake. Wherever you are. Whatever's happened, just hold on. I'm coming.

We will find our way back to each other.

If we can just survive this night.

CHAPTER TWENTY-THREE

Blake

I can't move. I can't even blink. I'm stuck with my thoughts screaming inside the prison of this paralyzed body while dust floats through the sliver of light under the closet door. Time slips by while Ravena's blood magic keeps me frozen against the shelves. And somewhere out there, Hazel is in my body, about to experience her first full moon shift with no idea how to control it.

Things are beginning to look very, very bleak.

The moonlight filtering through the tiny window above me has grown brighter as the moon rises in the sky. Something skitters behind the wall. Festival sounds penetrate the floorboard. The whole town is celebrating while Ravena prepares to tear everything apart.

And I'm stuck in a damn broom closet that smells like crushed herbs and wet mops. Couldn't she have at least picked a different closet to stuff me in? How long have I been here? An hour? Two? I try again to move something, anything. A finger. An eyelid. Maybe my mouth, to scream for help. Nothing responds.

Then, something moves on the other side of the door. Soft footsteps, the rustle of fabric. Ravena, back to gloat?

The footsteps pause, then continue with purpose.

"Hello? Hazel? Blake? Whoever you are. Anybody here?"

Coco! I never thought I'd be so happy to hear that little weirdo's voice. I try to yell, but my voice is as frozen as the rest of me.

She's right outside the door, but I can't do anything to alert her. I will the mop to fall over, or a bottle to fall off the shelf. Come on, magic, don't fail me now!

The doorknob rattles.

"That's weird," she mutters. "Why is this locked?"

She chants, and then I see sparks and the door swings open, flooding the small space with light. Coco appears, backlit like a mismatched guardian angel in green leggings and an oversized pink sweater.

"Hazel?" She blinks, then narrows her eyes. "I mean, Blake-in-Hazel's-body? Why are you just standing there in the dark like a weird broom? We've been looking everywhere for you!"

Her eyes widen as she realizes I can't respond. She steps closer, waving a hand in front of my face.

She flips on a light and looks me over. "Ay! Oh no. Oh no no no. You're paralyzed, aren't you? Oh, that evil, evil, bad, bad, witch."

Coco stands abruptly, yanking her phone from her pocket. "Don't worry, I'm calling La'Tasha right now. She'll know what to do. Just . . . hang in there?" She winces at her own words. "Sorry, not like you have a choice."

She presses the phone to her ear, pacing in the small space. "Tash? It's me. I found him—her—Hazel—whatever. In the storage closet at the apothecary. Paralyzed. Ravena magic, for sure . . . No, completely frozen . . . Hurry!"

She hangs up and walks back toward me. "La'Tasha's coming." She enunciates each syllable. I want to tell her I'm not deaf, but I can't speak, so I just let her do her thing.

"She was just down the street at the festival, looking for you. She'll be here in like two minutes."

She fidgets with the dried chamomile. "Good thing we ran

out of supplies and needed more, huh? You might have been in here all night."

In less than two minutes, quick, decisive footsteps cross the shop floor. La'Tasha appears in the doorway. She takes one look at me, and her expression hardens.

"That nasty ho," she mutters, brushing past Coco. I can smell her floral perfume when she leans in to examine me. "Damn, she paralyzed your ass."

"Can you break it?" Coco asks, worrying her lower lip.

"Yeah, but I might need your help." La'Tasha leaves, then comes back with a small vial of clear liquid, a chunk of black stone and a feather. "I'm gonna need a second witch's blood to counter the binding."

"I'm not really comfortable with—" Coco starts.

"Just a drop." La'Tasha pulls out a tiny silver pin. Coco looks terrified, but her face relaxes when La'Tasha pricks her own finger. She lets a few drops of her blood fall into the bowl, and the liquid immediately begins to glow a sickly green color.

La'Tasha dips her fingers into the bowl and draws symbols on my forehead, cheeks, and the backs of my hands, the liquid cool against my skin.

"Ready?" La'Tasha looks at Coco, who nods nervously.

They begin to chant. Their voices weave together in a language I don't recognize, but my skin tingles with recognition. Green sparks dance from their fingertips. The symbols on my skin grow warm, then hot until the binding spell snaps like a wire breaking. I gasp. My fingers twitch, then my toes. The paralysis melts away like ice under hot water, leaving behind a pins-and-needles sensation that hurts like hell.

"It worked!" Coco claps her hands.

La'Tasha rolls her eyes. "Please. Like I'd let that crusty-ass wannabe blood witch get the best of me."

She glances toward the window where blue moonlight streams through the stained glass. "We need to move. Now. Calvin and

Hazel are headed to the lake."

I flex Hazel's fingers, then her wrists, working life back into her stiff limbs. "Ravena has the amulet. She's going to use it tonight to break the pact."

La'Tasha takes my hand. "We know. And we need to stop her. Mina's waiting outside."

I wobble forward, and La'Tasha reaches out to steady me. "Hazel. Is she okay?"

La'Tasha nods. "Calvin broke her out. He was taking her up to the lake. We need to hurry. We need to get you two back in your own bodies before midnight."

Outside, Mina's little SUV idles beneath the apothecary's ivy-covered sign, its headlights cutting through the gathering twilight.

"Oh, thank heavens," Mina breathes as we stumble toward her truck. Her bright red hair is pulled back in a ponytail, and she's dressed all in black. She looks ready for a fight. "I was about to come in after you lot."

I climb into the passenger seat, muscles still tingling as the last of the paralysis wears off. La'Tasha and Coco squeeze into the back.

Mina grimaces as she pulls away from the curb. "Festival traffic is brutal. Every tourist within fifty miles showed up tonight."

She's not wrong. Sidewalks teem with people streaming toward the town square. Most locals move with an eerie calmness, but tourists bounce and chatter, oblivious to the shitshow around them.

Coco stares out the passenger window. "What's wrong with their eyes?"

Mina curses as we hit a wall of pedestrians crossing the street. "This is hopeless. We'll never get through the main roads."

"Take Mitchell," I suggest, pointing toward a narrow side street. "It runs behind the stores."

She nods, cranking the wheel hard. The truck bounces down

the alley, scraping past dumpsters and stacks of empty boxes.

"Stop!" I hiss. "Pull over."

Mina obeys, sliding the truck behind a parked delivery van. I point through the gap between vehicles. There, next to the Raven & Rye gastropub, stands Ravena. Two women in similar white outfits flank her, handing out small paper cups filled with some glowing blue liquid.

"What are they doing?" Coco asks, peering between the front seats.

"Handing out free samples of her devil juice, probably," La'Tasha says in disgust.

A smiling tourist accepts a cup, downs it in one gulp, then freezes. The smile remains fixed on his face, but his eyes glaze over.

"She's building an army," I murmur. "We need to find another way around."

Mina nods, putting the truck in reverse and turning toward the diner. "I'll try the delivery entrance behind Midnight Stack. It connects to the west road."

We back up carefully, then detour down another side street. We're three blocks from the café when Mina curses and hits the brakes. "They're everywhere."

Sure enough, a group of Ravena's glossy-suited assistants block the intersection ahead, distributing cups of blue liquid. The scent of artificial citrus wafts through the open window. It must be some kind of mist they're spraying to attract people.

"Cut through the alley behind the library."

Mina flips another U-turn. We're halfway down the alley when shadows appear at the other end. Another line of people mills before us. It's like they're purposely blocking us.

Coco rolls down her window and sticks her head out. "¡Saca el culo del medio!"

The people in the street turn and look at us.

Coco sticks her head out the window again. "I said move your asses! Nooooooow."

Slowly, the people begin to disperse, clearing a path for us. "You go, Coco," La'Tasha says.

Coco settles back into her seat. "We have places to be, and they were in the way."

***

Mina's SUV groans up the steep mountain road like it's personally offended that she's forcing it up the mountain again. Through the windshield, I can just make out the glow of the Blue Moon, impossibly large tonight, casting silver light across the forest. Somewhere ahead is Amethyst Beach, and hopefully, Hazel and the other wolves. Safe.

The truck rounds another switchback, headlights briefly illuminating the rusted water tower of the abandoned sawmill. I roll down my window, letting the cool mountain breeze rush over Hazel's face. That's when I smell it.

"Is that smoke?" I sit up straighter. "And not campfire smoke."

Mina sniffs, then nods grimly. "Forest fire."

Headlights appear around the bend ahead, barreling down the mountain toward us. The approaching vehicle swerves wildly across the narrow road.

"That's Calvin's truck!" I shout, recognizing the distinctive outline of his sleek new truck.

Mina pulls to the side, barely avoiding a collision as Calvin screeches to a halt alongside us. The back of his truck is filled with pack members. Some are fully human, others show signs of partial shifts.

The driver's door flies open, and Calvin jumps out, rushing to my window. "Blake! Thank God!"

"What happened?" I demand, taking in his soot-smudged face and the panicked expressions of the wolves in his truck bed.

"Ravena set the forest on fire!" he shouts over the roar of both engines. "Cut off access to the beach completely. We couldn't go forward, couldn't stay put. The whole pack's scattered. Half of them ran off into the woods in a panic."

My heart sinks. "Hazel?"

Calvin looks over his shoulder, and that's when I see her leaping down from the truck.

"Blake!" She grabs the door frame, her knuckles white. My face looks strange. Eyes wild, pupils dilated, sweat beading on the forehead. I can see the struggle happening beneath the skin.

I reach out and touch her face. "You okay?"

She doubles over, wincing. "It's getting worse. I can feel the wolf fighting to get out."

I want to hold her. Protect her. But we don't have time right now.

"We need to move. We have to get them out of town," La'Tasha interrupts. "As far away as we can."

"Yeah, I know," Calvin says. "I was going to take them to Skipper Lake, but we have to cut through town to do it, and the closer we get to Ravena, the more difficult it is for the pack to keep it together."

A howl cuts through the night. Another answers. One of the wolves in the bed of Calvin's truck whimpers, then growls, his features beginning to elongate.

La'Tasha snaps into action. "We don't have a choice. Get them out of here. Avoid town center. Stick to Elm and then Maple, and then take the service road. Don't stop for anyone."

Calvin glances back at his truck full of increasingly agitated werewolves. "Alright. Let's go."

Calvin leads, his truck's taillights glowing red in the darkness. Behind us, the forest fire paints the night sky orange, the blue moon hanging like a 3D object in the sky. Every few minutes, howls echo through the forest on both sides of the road.

"Is that Mason?" Coco points at a large figure standing in Calvin's truck bed.

La'Tasha leans forward, squinting. "Yes. And he's not looking good."

He stands like a statue while others around him fidget and whimper. His head turns slowly, face catching the moonlight, eyes yellow and glowing.

"Ravena has him," I mutter. "The containment spell didn't hold."

We close in on downtown. Festival lights glow ahead, but the air feels eerily still. Calvin slams on his brakes.

"What the hell is he doing?" La'Tasha yells in my ear. "I told him to keep driving."

"Somethin's wrong," Mina says, popping her truck into park.

I watch in horror as Mason suddenly throws back his head and lets out a guttural howl. The other wolves respond instantly, their own half-shifted forms tensing.

"No," I breathe.

Mason vaults over the tailgate, landing on the asphalt with predatory grace. Three others follow him immediately. And then they shift.

"Stop!" Calvin shouts, jumping from the driver's seat.

Too late. Mason takes off toward the town square, the others following like missiles locked on a target. Calvin sprints after them, then stops. I leap out of Mina's truck.

"The pack—" Calvin gasps, the amethyst charm at his throat glowing faintly. "I can't control them. Ravena's pull is too strong."

In the distance, screams rise from the festival.

"What happened to the fountain?" La'Tasha points toward Central Park. "It's dry!"

She's right. The fountain that anchors the park sits empty, its stone basin cracked. How had that happened? We were literally just here, and it was fine.

A crash echoes from the direction the wolves ran, followed by more screams. That's when I notice Hazel trembling violently beside Calvin's truck. Her hands clench and unclench, face contorting in a grimace of pain and concentration.

"Hazel!" I run to her. Our fingers brush, and a spark jumps between us.

"I can't—" she gasps, voice rough. "Blake, I can't hold it back—"

"Look at me." I grip her shoulders. "Focus on me. Not the moon, not the wolf. Me."

For a moment, her eyes clear. Then they shift to bright, unnatural yellow. A growl builds in her chest. Her muscles bunch under my hands.

"No," I whisper, knowing what's coming. "Hazel, please."

But it's too late. Bones crack and reshape. Coarse fur erupts across her face. Her stance changes. She throws her head back and howls.

And then she runs.

"Hazel!" I scream, but she's already gone, following the other wolves toward the center of town.

"This is bad." Calvin stares after her. "If they reach the town square . . ."

La'Tasha snorts. "No. Don't stand there wringing your hands. Move. I didn't do all that research while y'all were running around playing adventure time for nothing. Let's go kick some ass."

"Yeah. Come on." I'm already moving toward the lights. "We have a town to save."

And a witch to find.

Both the vengeful one with her ancient grudge and the one I've fallen for.

CHAPTER TWENTY-FOUR

Blake

The park is a goddamn battlefield. Overturned taco carts, smashed crafts, and trampled decorations litter the ground. The air is jagged with people screaming and wolves howling. And one of those wolves is Hazel.

"Split up!" I yell over the chaos. "Calvin, La'Tasha, get the wolves under control. Coco, Mina, help anyone injured if you can. I'm going for Hazel. And if you see Ravena, try to corner her, but only if it's safe."

They nod and scatter.

I shove through a crowd of tourists who are losing their minds. Deputy Miller fires his Taser at a partially shifted Leo. He hits the cobblestones like a convulsing bag of bricks. A fully wolfed-out Marvin leaps onto an ice cream cart, shattering the glass top. There's a literal explosion of glass and ice cream. Nearby onlookers scream.

"No, no, no." I scan frantically for any sign of Hazel.

My bones rattle as a gunshot cracks through the air. I whirl toward it, heart in my throat.

Sheriff Harlow takes to the gazebo steps, bullhorn pressed to his lips. "Goddammit, I said no guns! Tasers only! These are our people!"

A wolf darts past me, shoulder fur matted with blood. My blood boils. Magic crackles at my fingertips. I've never been able to access her power so easily before. Evidently, rage helps pull it forward.

"Blake!" Calvin's voice cuts through the chaos. He points across the square to a pocket of people scattering like pigeons.

There she is.

She's hunched and dangerous, moving with predatory grace. Half-shifted. Face stretched into a partial muzzle. Hands curved into deadly claws. Muscles bulge beneath torn clothes and eyes burn yellow in the moonlight.

And she's stalking straight toward Sheriff Harlow.

"Ben!" I scream, but my voice doesn't reach him.

I shove past frozen onlookers.

"Ben! Be still!"

Harlow turns too late. He sees the wolf and fumbles for his Taser. Hazel launches. She's a blur of muscle and fur and teeth. They collide. Hard. Harlow hits the gazebo floor with a sickening thud. Claws press against his throat.

"No!"

Harlow doesn't struggle. He doesn't make eye contact. Good. No threats. No aggression. Harlow remains calm despite the teeth inches from his face. "Blake," he says calmly, "I know you're in there, son."

But Blake isn't in there. Hazel is. And she's drowning in wolf instincts. I reach into the pocket of Hazel's jacket and pull out my only protection sachet. It's the only card I have left to play. I squeeze it once. The magic surges. I hurl it, and it hits the floor. It splits, letting loose a cloud of purple smoke that swallows them both. And for one heart-stopping moment, nothing happens.

Then, Hazel flinches.

Her head pivots. Nostrils flare. Yellow eyes track across the square and lock onto me. Recognition flickers. Her claws retract, just slightly, from Harlow's throat.

I step closer. "That's it. Come on. Leave him."

The wolf growls, confused. The muscles bunch and release, caught between instinct and the woman inside that fights to regain control.

"Get clear!" someone shouts to Harlow.

I counter, stepping closer. "No. Don't move. She's fighting it. Give her a chance."

I step onto the gazebo one slow step at a time. The wolf watches me, head tilting in a distinctly canine gesture of confusion. I recognize the internal struggle taking place.

"Hazel." My voice is soft. Steady. "Hazel, it's me. It's Blake."

A growl rumbles deep in her chest.

"I know you're in there," I continue, taking another step. "I know the wolf is strong. Trust me. I know better than anyone. But I also know that you're stronger."

Harlow remains still. He clamps his eyes shut as a string of drool drops onto his face and slides down his cheek.

"Remember the promise?" I put one hand out, palm flat. "We said if we get stuck like this, we wouldn't pretend. Right? We'll live our truth as ourselves. Together. But we can't do that if you hurt these people. That's not who we are. Okay?"

Her ears prick forward.

"Your intent matters. Your actions make you who you are." I take the final step. I'm close enough to touch her now. "Don't let Ravena win."

I reach one hand forward. She tenses. She watches my hand like it's a threat.

"Come back to me," I whisper.

Something breaks. She whines, a sound of raw pain. She shudders. Claws retract. Teeth shrink.

"Blake?" Her voice is rough and uncertain. "I can't . . . it's too much . . ."

"No no no. It's okay. I've got you."

I touch her face. An electric shock slams through us. Magic crackles over our skin. Harlow uses this moment to roll sideways and clear the gazebo. He gives me a quick nod before backing away.

"I'm scared," Hazel admits. Her voice cracks. "The wolf wants out. I can't hold it back much longer."

The park is still a riot of charging wolves and screaming humans. But on the gazebo, time seems to slow. I cup her furry face in my small hands. "I'm here. And if we get stuck in these bodies, it's okay. We'll make it work. Together."

Her eyes flicker again. Blue. Yellow. Blue again. Her muscles spasm as she controls the shift.

"Hazel." My voice drops to a whisper. "I need to tell you something."

She half-laughs, half-growls. "Now?"

"Yeah. Now." I slide my hands to her shoulders. "Because if we don't make it through this, you need to know."

Her eyes focus on mine.

"I love you," I say simply. "Not because of some old-ass prophecy. No magical destiny. I loved you well before all this shit went down. I was just too stubborn to admit it."

Her expression shifts. "Blake . . ." Another wave of the shift hits her and she winces. Her spine arches. Bones crack as they try to reshape.

"I can't hold on," she gasps, panic edging her voice.

I do the only thing left to do.

I pull her close.

And I kiss her.

Our lips meet, and for a heartbeat, nothing happens. Then magic erupts between us like a dam breaking. Light spills outward, brilliant white shot through with electric blue and hot pink. Wind whips around us in a cyclone of pure energy, lifting loose leaves and festival debris. The kiss deepens, and the magic responds. It flows between us, through us, around us. Witch magic and wolf spirit, darkness and light.

The wind picks up, and the light intensifies until I can see nothing but Hazel's soul superimposed over my own. We lift off the ground, suspended in a storm of magic and energy. Then, just as suddenly, everything stops. We drop like boulders.

We hit the gazebo floor hard, rolling apart with the impact.

"Oh my God! It's like *Beauty and the Beast!*" Coco exclaims.

I groan. The sound is deep. My body feels more full. I flex my fingers. They're much longer and stronger than they'd been just a few seconds ago.

Holy shit, these are my fingers. I'm in my body. I sit up with a jolt and stare down at my hands. My actual fucking hands. Finally!

"Blake?" Hazel pushes herself upright. Auburn curls tumble around her freckled face. Green eyes blink at me in wonder. "We're back," she whispers.

"We're back," I echo, my voice rumbling in my throat. God, I've missed this body.

I move to embrace her just as Coco starts to sing a song about tales as old as time. Then another scream cuts through the air. The chaos around us hasn't stopped. If anything, it's intensified.

Across the square, Mason and two other wolves scramble to the roof of the apothecary. They howl, and it echoes across Moonridge.

And right behind them, in all her white, hawk-faced glory, is Ravena, the Wolfsbane Amulet glowing red in her hand.

CHAPTER TWENTY-FIVE

Hazel

Being back in my own body is like slipping into a favorite pair of pajamas after wearing nothing but someone else's itchy, oversized clothes. I'm not even going to stress about my hair. It's still slicked back in that god-awful low ponytail. I'll deal with that hot mess later.

I flex my fingers just to make sure they're still mine. "We did it."

Blake smiles so big his dimple pops. "We did."

He reaches for me, and our fingers brush. The touch sends a shiver up my arm. His whole "I love you" confession is still ringing in my ears. As much as I'd like to drag him back to my bedroom and make him prove just how much, we still have one more thing to do.

My eyes scan the park for my fellow witches. "I need La'Tasha and Coco."

He groans, and I turn to look at him. His face contorts, every muscle locked in a grimace. A growl rumbles from his chest.

"Blake?" My stomach drops as I step closer. "What's happening?"

His eyes flash yellow. He hunches over, hands curling into claws at his sides. He clenches his teeth, barely able to get the words out. "Something's wrong. I can't—"

Another growl tears through his throat. The swap back didn't fix everything. Ravena's curse is still very much alive.

I spin toward the square. "She's still controlling you."

Ravena hovers over the apothecary roof, white suit gleaming under the blue moon. The Wolfsbane Amulet dangles from her hand. It pulses with sick red light. Mason and two other wolves pace across the roof behind her like demonic guardians.

Blake's voice is rough with strain. "I need to get to her. Grab the amulet—"

He stumbles, then falls to one knee. His spine arches unnaturally.

"Blake!" I reach for him.

Harlow's arm blocks me. His free hand moves to his Taser. "Stand back. I don't want to hurt him, but I will if I have to."

"No!" I push against Harlow's arm. "He's fighting it. It's not his fault. It's Ravena. She's using that amulet to control all the wolves."

Around us, the festival grounds are still a nightmare version of a wildlife documentary. Wolves race between overturned booths and scattered decorations. Some still partially human, others fully transformed. Their eyes all glow with the same unnatural yellow. Puppets on Ravena's bloody strings.

A group of tourists huddles beneath a table, filming everything on their phones. Deputies fire Tasers. Probes streak toward the advancing wolves. And through it all, Ravena watches from her perch.

My voice cracks with desperation. "We have to stop this. The full moon peaks at midnight. Once that happens, Ravena's magic will hit, and we'll be cooked."

"And that means what exactly?" Harlow asks, eyes still trained on Blake.

"It means the wolves will lose their shit. They'll be under her control. And every protection we've put in place. All this—" I gesture around us at our beautiful, weird, magical town, "—will be destroyed."

Blake groans. Muscles ripple. He's about to burst out of his clothes.

He looks up at me, eyes flickering between blue and yellow. "Go. Find La'Tasha. I'll . . . try to hold on."

Sheriff Harlow nods. "I'll stay with him. But make it quick. My deputies can only hold back these wolves for so long before someone panics and does something stupid."

I squeeze Blake's shoulder once, then dart into the swirling madness of the square. I duck under a flying string of festival lanterns and sidestep a running child.

I cup my hands around my mouth. "La'Tasha! Coco!" The screams and growls completely swallow my voice.

I spot a flash of bright fabric through the crowd. Never have I been so glad for Coco's obsession with highlighter-colored outfits. She sits huddled with Mina behind an overturned popcorn cart. Her hands glow as she maintains a protection spell around them.

"Coco!" I slide to my knees beside them.

Coco's face brightens. She pulls me into a quick hug. "Hazel! I'm so happy you're you again! Your hair is so much prettier when it's actually yours."

What is she talking about? My hair is still a mess.

"Where's La'Tasha?"

Mina points toward the bandstand. "Tryin' to calm the Lawrence twins. They got separated from their parents."

I peer over the cart. I spot La'Tasha on the far side of the square. She's created a protective ring around herself and the twins. She has to be hating this. Nothing makes her more uncomfortable than needy children.

I stand, already moving in La'Tasha's direction. "We need

to get to her. The three of us need to cast a containment spell to rope in the wolves. Kind of like what we did with that ghoul a few weeks ago. We have to neutralize the amulet's effect on the wolves."

"Like magical Xanax for the entire pack?" Coco reasons.

I grab her hand. "Exactly. Big, magical Xanax. Come on."

We weave through the crowd, dodging panicked festival-go-ers and snarling wolves. Halfway to La'Tasha, Blake's agonized howl tears through the night. I whip around to see him fully shifted now, a massive sandy-blonde wolf standing where my boyfriend had been moments before.

Wait. Boyfriend? Is that what he is now? The thought should feel strange, but it feels perfect.

Not now, Thornton.

Blake's howl snaps me out of my thoughts.

Sheriff Harlow backs away slowly, Taser raised. Wolf-Blake shakes his enormous head, as if trying to clear fog from his brain. His yellow eyes lock onto mine across the square, and I see recognition there. He's fighting the amulet's influence, holding onto himself through sheer force of will.

"Hurry!" I urge Coco, pulling her through the crowd.

We reach La'Tasha just as the Lawrence twins' parents show up. Relief floods La'Tasha's face the moment she sees me. "Oh my hell, it's really you, isn't it? Are you okay? I mean, aside from that hairdo?"

"I know, right? But, yeah, I'm fine, but not for long if we don't stop Ravena."

Ravena still hovers above the apothecary roof, tracing symbols in the air. Complex, ancient signs that glow red against the night sky. The amulet pulses in rhythm with her movements, each beat sending visible waves of energy across the square. With each pulse, the wolves grow more frenzied, their attacks more coordinated.

La'Tasha's eyes narrow as she studies the glowing symbols.

"She's amplifying the amulet's power."

"Can we stop it?" Coco asks.

I look between my two closest friends. "We have to try."

La'Tasha nods, understanding immediately. "A circle of three. We've done it before."

"We need to expand your containment spell," I explain. "Make it cover the whole square, calm all the wolves at once."

"Easy enough." La'Tasha looks around at the chaos. "I think. It's gonna take a shit-ton of magic, though."

"I know, but if we don't do this, Moonridge is finished."

Coco slips her hand into mine, then grabs La'Tasha's. "We got this, chicas. I have supplies."

Coco digs through her oversized backpack, packets of herbs and vials of liquid spilling onto the bandstand. "I've got salt from the pretzel stand. I always grab extra for emergency protection spells." She tosses handful after handful of white packets at my feet. "And herbs! Lavender, mugwort, rue . . ." Each name comes with a small packet.

"How much of that stuff do you carry with you?" I ask, amazed despite our desperate situation.

"It's my emergency witch kit." Coco's grin is fierce. "La'Tasha has her never-ending bag, and while I can only aspire to that level of power, for now I just have a backpack full of . . . well, pretty much everything."

La'Tasha nods and winks. "Mama didn't raise no unprepared witch."

We form a circle immediately. I sketch a triangle with La'Tasha's emergency charcoal while Coco trails salt and herbs along the lines. La'Tasha presses her fingers to the cut on her hand and adds drops of her blood to each point. Coco tosses one of her raspberry-shaped earrings into the center as an offering. I unclip my charm bracelet and drop it next to the plastic fruit.

"Ready?" I ask. The air hums between us.

They grip my hands tightly. And we begin to chant.

"Peace to the wolves who hunt the night," I start.

"Calm to hearts that rage and fight," La'Tasha continues.

"Love will fill their souls with light," Coco finishes.

The words loop and weave. They gain strength with each repetition. The herb lines begin to glow. My charm bracelet rises from the floor, spinning so fast the charms blur into a solid ring of light.

"Now!" La'Tasha yells.

We shove the collected energy outward. A perfect blue sphere races across the square, passing through humans. The effect on the wolves is immediate.

Yellow eyes fade. Fierce snarls transform into confused whines. One by one, the wolves stop and drop onto their haunches as the magic wrings out the rage that had taken hold.

Blake's blue eyes find mine across the chaos. He tips his head slightly in a gesture of thanks.

On the apothecary roof, Ravena's expression goes from smug to pure fury. The red symbols she's been tracing flicker and fade as our protective shield thrashes her spell. The Wolfsbane Amulet pulses like a dying heart in her hands.

"No!" Her scream slices through the suddenly quiet square. "What have you done?"

She raises the amulet higher, pouring her own energy into it. The red glow flares brighter, fighting desperately against our blue magic. She traces new symbols in the air. Her movements are sharp and frantic. Sweat beads on her forehead.

The two energies war in the air between us. Sparks clash like miniature lightning strikes. The amulet's red light seems to regain strength and the wolves become restless again.

"Oh, she wants to play rough? Fine by me," La'Tasha grits her teeth.

"Hold the circle," I command, squeezing their hands.

We pour more power into the spell. The blue light surges. Ravena staggers back. Her face contorts with rage, eyes wild.

"You think this is over?" she snarls. She clutches the amulet to her chest like a shield. "I've waited way too goddamn long to be stopped by three useless witches playing with forces they don't understand!"

Desperate fury twists her features as she realizes she's losing. With a final scream of frustration, she gestures sharply. The air around her ripples and tears like fabric and a doorway of darkness opens behind her. She steps backward into the void.

"This isn't over," her voice echoes. The portal snaps shut with a crack like thunder.

She's gone.

Our circle of magic continues to pulse. It's calmed the wolves but hasn't reversed the forced transformation. It's still not over.

"She's gone somewhere else to complete the ritual." La'Tasha's voice is strained. "Somewhere we won't easily find her."

"We need to warn everyone," I say. "Rally the town to help us search."

Coco nods toward the festival stage. The band equipment still stands despite the chaos. "Use the mic to get their attention."

We dismantle the circle without breaking the calm we've created. My bracelet drops back into my palm. The chalk lines fade, but the blue energy remains.

I climb onto the stage and grab the microphone. The festival crowd huddles in small clusters at the edges of the square. They whisper, watching the docile wolves with total terror.

"Everyone, please listen to me!" My voice booms through the speakers, startling several people. "I know you're scared. I know this looks like something you'd see in a horror movie. But there's an explanation."

Faces turn toward me. Fear. Confusion. Outright hostility.

"For those who don't know me, my name is Hazel Thornton. I own the Blue Moon Apothecary. I am Moonridge's Virtus Suprema."

"Head witch in the house," Coco mutters behind me.

I ignore her. "What you saw tonight wasn't an attack. It was a setup by the woman calling herself Bianca Mayweather."

Mr. Whitaker, the mailman, blinks fast. He presses a hand to his head like he's fighting a migraine. Mrs. Wu from the electric company shakes her head. She looks lost. I feel a flicker of hope. Maybe we can break the spell.

"Bianca is a lie. Her real name is Ravena Blackwood. She's been using blood magic to weaponize the werewolves. And she's been drugging all of you with her supplements."

Lillian Drake clutches her mint-green thermos. "She wouldn't," she whispers. She takes another sip from the thermos. Her posture straightens. Eyes go hard. "No. That's not . . . Bianca warned us about her." She points a finger at me.

"Look at the wolves now." I gesture to where they sit calmly. "They're not attacking anyone. They're victims, just like you. Ravena has been planning this for decades. She wants to—"

"She's lying!" Ellen Baskins from the bank pushes forward. Her face twists with fake rage. Her eyes dull. She must have been mainlining those supplements because she is strung out on Ravena juice. "Bianca said the witches would try to turn us against her."

A ripple passes through the crowd. Tom Bradley, who's bought herbs from my shop for years, starts to nod. But then he jerks like someone pulled his strings. His typically friendly smile twists into a sneer.

"Wait," Mrs. Wu calls out, pressing both hands to her temples. "This doesn't feel right. I can't—"

But her husband grabs her arm, pulling her back into the crowd. His eyes hold that same empty glaze. "Don't listen to the witch. Remember what Bianca said."

I can't get through.

"It's the witches doing this!" someone shouts from the back. It came from someone I don't recognize, probably a tourist. "She's the one controlling the wolves!"

"No!" I lean into the microphone, desperation cracking my voice. "You're being manipulated. Fight it! Think for yourselves!"

But it's too late. The few clear voices are drowned out as the chant begins.

"Burn the witch! Burn the witch!"

Milton Grigsby, who makes it a point to pop his head into the shop every day to say hello, raises his fist with the rest. Mrs. Wu has stopped fighting, her husband's hand still locked around her arm. Even some of the tourists have joined in, swept up in the mob's fury.

Sheriff Harlow moves to the base of the stage, hand on his gun, but not drawing it. "Folks, calm down now. This isn't the Salem trials. Nobody's burning anybody."

But his reasonable voice can't penetrate the wall of artificial rage. A bottle missiles through the air and smashes against the stage near my feet.

La'Tasha and Coco appear at my sides, their presence giving me strength.

"This isn't working," La'Tasha leans into the microphone. "Everyone, listen up. What you're feeling is a lie. That woman is poisoning you."

More bottles fly. More pissed-off shouting. The crowd starts to surge.

Blake bounds onto the stage beside us. He plants himself between us and the angry mob. The other wolves follow his lead. They form a protective circle around the stage. They don't attack. They don't even growl. They simply stand firm. A boundary that even the angriest townsperson wouldn't dare cross.

Sheriff Harlow climbs onto the stage and grabs the microphone. "That's ENOUGH!" His voice booms across the park. It cuts right through the chemical rage. "This stops now. Everyone, get out of here. The festival is over."

The crowd wavers. They're caught between Ravena's influence and ingrained respect for the law.

"Go home," Harlow repeats. He's quieter now but he's not budging. "Lock your doors. Stay inside until the sun comes up. That is a direct order."

Slowly, they start to scatter. A few people throw one last glare our way. Others just look confused, like they're waking up from a fever dream.

When the square has mostly emptied, Harlow turns to us. "You've got about five minutes before they come back. Ravena's hold is too strong to break with just words."

"Then we find her." Determination hardens my voice. "We find her and destroy that amulet before midnight."

La'Tasha checks her watch. "That gives us fifty-three minutes."

Blake nudges my hand with his muzzle, his blue eyes intent. Even without words, I understand what he's saying. He wants to help. All the wolves do.

"Are you ready for this?" I ask him.

He dips his furry head in a nod.

"Then let's go."

Harlow helps me down from the stage. He looks like he's aged ten years in the last hour.

"Watch your back," he says. "If even half of what you said is true, this woman is playing a game we don't know the rules to."

"I know," I say. My shoulders feel like I'm carrying the weight of the whole damn town. "That's exactly why she can't win."

Blake presses against my side. I bury my fingers in his coat and just breathe for a second, trying to find my center. We managed to un-brainwash the wolves, but the town is still under her thumb.

For now.

CHAPTER TWENTY-SIX

Hazel

I run my eyes over this weird-ass collection of witches and wolves standing in the wreckage. This is it. This is who will save Moonridge. Or at least try to.

"We need to find Ravena. Now. Before she pulls another disappearing act." My voice sounds like I've been eating gravel.

Coco's already elbow-deep in her backpack. "I might have some stuff in here we can use."

I swear, this girl is like a walking witch supply store. I really need to up my game.

Calvin steps up, annoyingly composed. "And what do we do if we find her?"

That right there is the question of the day. I look at our "army." Three witches and maybe fifteen wolves. We aren't exactly an unstoppable band of superheroes, but we're all Moonridge has left.

I place my hands on my hips and try to sound like I might have a plan. "We hit her with every bit of juice we have. Witches will punch her in the throat with as much magic as we can. Wolves form a perimeter and keep her contained."

Blake lets out a deep, grumbling sound. It sounds like he tried to say "hell yes."

La'Tasha waves her hand, and a map of Moonridge shimmers into existence across the bandstand floor. "I want to try a tracking spell. I need something connected to Ravena."

Coco grabs a mint-green thermos from the ground. "Will this work?"

"Perfect. The liquid will be laced with her blood." La'Tasha dumps one of Coco's herb packets onto the map and smears it around. Nothing happens.

"Try adding something connected to the town's original magic," I suggest. "Something that might be on the same frequency as the amulet."

Calvin jogs off and comes back with a smooth stone from the fountain. "How's this?"

I drop the stone in the map's center and pour three drops of the glowing liquid on top of it, making damn sure I don't get any of it on me or anyone else.

"Circle up." La'Tasha and Coco move in, forming a triangle around the map.

I close my eyes. "Seek what is hidden. Find what is lost."

La'Tasha and Coco pick up the beat. "Reveal the path, whatever the cost."

The herbs start to smoke, and a green mist swirls above the paper. The stone vibrates. Light ripples across the map. The drops of yellow liquid turn black and begin to migrate toward the forest's edge.

"The Old Mill," Calvin says as the drops stop and expand into a circle.

La'Tasha studies the location. "Of course. It sits on a convergence of ley lines. Perfect for major magic."

I get to my feet. "Let's move."

The humans pile into Calvin's truck while the wolves run ahead, the streets eerily empty as our strange procession moves through town. Lights burn in windows, but curtains are drawn tight. Without the terror from a few minutes ago, it's strangely quiet.

Calvin shifts the truck into fourth gear, then touches the amethyst at his throat. It still glows. It makes me wish we'd had about thirty more of them for the rest of the pack. It's done a lot to protect him against the forced shift.

Calvin glances at me. "You okay?"

"Ask me when this is over." I attempt a smile, but I can feel it cracking at the edges. The truth is, I'm terrified. Not just of Ravena and her power, but of failing. Of letting down Blake, the town. My grandmother's legacy. "And you?"

"I'm okay." He sounds surprised. "It's weird not being in wolf form, but I feel like I can be of more use in my human skin. This pendant really helped. You may have changed my mind about magic."

We round a bend, and the Old Mill looms before us. Calvin kills the engine so we don't tip her off. We'll go the rest of the way on foot.

Stone walls rise three stories high in front of us. The east side of the mill is a burned-out skeleton against the sky. Windows gape like empty eye sockets. The whole place hums with intense energy. A low, vibrating buzz that makes the air feel thick enough to chew. So much so that it makes my nipples perk up. That's not embarrassing at all.

"She's in there," I say.

La'Tasha steps up beside me, her expression grim. "That heifer set up at least three protection circles. Powerful ones."

Calvin shifts next to me. "Can we break through?"

Coco's spacey vibe is gone. She's hyper-focused. "Not without alerting her. But maybe we don't want to be sneaky. Maybe we want her to know we're coming. Send the wolves first. Maybe she'll think she managed to reverse our spell and they're coming to help her."

"Could work," I nod. "Wolves come in loud from the front. We circle around the back and hit her from the sides."

Blake growls. He herds the pack into a V-shape. He takes the point. He's ready to wreck this bitch.

"Wait!" I grab a handful of herbs from Coco's bag. I quickly trace protection symbols on each wolf's forehead, murmuring words of safety. "Not perfect, but it should help keep you from getting your fur singed off."

"Be careful," I whisper as I smudge Blake. I press my forehead against his. "I just got you back in your own body. I can't lose you now."

He makes a soft sound, almost a purr. He pulls away, ready for battle.

We split up, wolves charging toward the mill's main entrance. Coco, La'Tasha, and I circle around to approach from the sides. Calvin, still in human form, goes with the wolves.

The abandoned mill yard is littered with old machinery and stacks of rotting timber. It makes for great cover. I catch a flash of movement through the gaping holes in the burned-out east wing. There. A streak of red among the blackened stone.

The witch herself.

I whistle. The wolves charge. They howl in one long, jagged chord that makes my skin crawl. A crimson flash erupts from the mill. A blast of energy ripples out like a shockwave.

Guess she realized her puppets cut their strings. Oops.

La'Tasha, Coco, and I slip through the back while the pack keeps Ravena's eyes on the front door. The mill looks like a hollowed-out cavern. Shadows crawl across the floor. Rusted machinery sits in the dark like dead giants. Ravena stands in the center. A circle of glowing red symbols surrounds her.

Her white suit has been replaced with robes made of living shadows. Her dark hair whips around her head. But it's her eyes that stop me cold. They burn red like embers in a furnace.

"Right on schedule." Her voice slices right through the howling. "I was hoping you'd—"

La'Tasha doesn't let her finish. She brings her hands up and out. A shimmering dome drops over us. "Game over, ho. Your puppet show's canceled."

Ravena laughs. The sound is like ice cracking. "You may as well give up now." The red symbols around her flare. "I have a legacy of power that is stronger than the three of you combined."

I circle to flank her. "Your grandmother was a murderer. The town didn't burn her for being a witch."

"LIES!" she screams. A bolt of crimson energy sizzles toward my chest. I duck. It screams over my head like a subway train.

"It's the truth," I shout back. I pull my own power up from the floorboards. "She broke the covenant. She tried to wipe out the packs when—"

Ravena's face twists. "And now I finish the job!" Another blast of red light sends me diving behind a rusted gear.

Coco launches an illusion. Suddenly, the mill fills with duplicates of the three of us.

Ravena's head whips around, tracking the imaginary witches. I hurl a burst of energy at her. She counters and blocks it. She sends it screaming back at me. La'Tasha intercepts the hit and shoves it back at Ravena. It knocks her off her feet.

"What are you really after?" I yell.

"With the pact broken—" Ravena spins. Coco's illusions have her confused. "—I can anchor demonic energy to this world!"

So that's the endgame. It's not just a grudge. She wants to turn Moonridge into a hostel for demons.

La'Tasha hurls golden sigils at Ravena's barrier. "Girl, you need therapy. Seriously."

"No. I'm owed this!" Ravena deflects the hit. Her voice goes up to a shriek. "After what my ancestors went through—"

The front doors explode. The wolves burst in with Blake in the lead. Ravena spins toward them. She holds out both hands. "Yes, my pets. Come to Mama."

The amulet pulses. Waves of visible darkness wash over the pack. A few wolves hit the dirt. They whimper. Their bodies twist. Mason turns and snaps at Leo.

Calvin steps forward. His hand clamped over the amethyst at his throat. "Hold the line!" he roars. "Remember the pack!"

Blake throws back his head and howls. It's a primal, bone-vibrating sound. One by one, the other wolves join in. The chorus drowns out Ravena's chanting.

It's my chance. I launch myself forward. Power flows through me like an electrical current has been opened. I hurl everything I have at Ravena's barrier. Witch-fire. Cutting wind. Pure, blinding white light. La'Tasha's magic ripples around mine. Eventually, we sync up.

Ravena turns on me. She sends a wall of shadow racing across the floor. It hits me like a truck. I fly backward and land hard. Stars explode in my vision. Everything goes bright and fuzzy at the edges, like I've been flash-banged.

"Hazel!" La'Tasha's voice sounds like she's underwater. My magic flickers. It's weak.

I try to stand, but my body won't cooperate. My vision tunnels. The dark creeps in.

Then something warm and wet hits my face. Blake's thick fur tickles my chin. He licks my cheek. His blue eyes meet mine, and our connection ignites. Energy flows between us. Wolf to witch. Strength for strength. I feel his power.

And I know exactly what to do.

"The amulet!" I grasp his fur with one hand. "It's a conduit. Just like we were during the body swap. It moves energy both ways."

He dips his head in a nod. I push myself to my feet, drawing strength from our connection.

"La'Tasha! Coco!" I call. "Hit the amulet!"

They respond instantly. Magic floods the air. All of it converges on the red gem at Ravena's chest.

She laughs, though it's not a confident one. "Fools! The amulet can't be destroyed. It's bound to the blood of every wolf and witch in this town!"

"We don't need to destroy it," I reply, stepping closer. "Just change its connection."

I reach deep inside myself, finding the well of magic that's been my birthright. And then I reach beyond it. I draw on a new power. The residual connection to Blake's wolf energy. It still lingers in my soul after our time in each other's bodies. Together, Blake and I hold the perfect balance. Witch and wolf.

Power erupts from my hands. A swirling vortex of blue and silver roars across the mill. It swallows the amulet. The blood-red glow turns a vibrant, electric blue.

Ravena screams. She claws at her throat. "No! What are you doing?"

"Changing the channel, bitch," I yell. My knees shake, but I press forward. "Connecting it back to what it should have been tuned in to."

Blake presses against my leg. The other wolves move closer, forming a tight circle around us.

Ravena's face goes purple. She plunges her hands through the rotting floorboards. She sucks dark energy straight out of the dirt. Her body convulses as the power hits her.

But it's too much power. Too raw.

Her skin cracks. Glowing red veins ripple over her body.

"If I'm to go, I'm taking you all with me!" she shrieks. She gathers the energy for one last nuke.

Blake moves to my side. I put my hand on his head. The connection expands until it's everything. White-hot. Unstoppable. One mind. One heart.

Ravena launches a massive wall of darkness that blots out all the moonlight streaming through the ruined roof.

And we respond as one.

The combined blast of our energy meets hers in the center

of the mill. Two forces of nature colliding. For one breathless moment, they war against each other. Darkness versus light. Hatred versus love. The mill shakes. The space fills with blinding yellow light.

And then the amulet at Ravena's throat explodes.

The backlash strikes with bone-jarring force. She's lifted off her feet. Thrown into the crumbling wall. Her body collapses to the stone floor. The dark robes dissolve. She's back in her torn and bloodstained white suit.

The mill creaks, settling back into stillness. Silence fills the space. All I can hear is the sound of my ragged breathing.

"Did you kill her?" Calvin steps forward cautiously.

La'Tasha kneels beside Ravena's still form. "Nope. She's just out cold and magically castrated. Good job, friends."

Around us, the wolves begin to shift. Fur recedes. Bodies straighten. Blake is the last to transform, his naughty bits on full display. I should be embarrassed, but I've lived in that body. I've seen it all. Just not from this angle.

He covers himself, suddenly aware that he has an audience. "You did it." His voice is rough from howling.

I shake my head, reaching for his hand. "We did it. Together."

His fingers intertwine with mine. We stand there, shaken but victorious, surrounded by our strange family of witches and wolves. And for the first time since this whole mess began, I feel like we might actually be okay.

CHAPTER TWENTY-SEVEN

Blake

I'm still white-knuckling Hazel's hand. I'm not ready to let go yet. Around us, the pack is a mess of shifting bodies. Fur slinks back into pores like a reverse-motion car wreck.

"Is she actually dead?" Marvin asks. Like the rest of my pack, he's now completely naked with his hands over his wang. He looks equal parts confused and embarrassed.

Hazel answers for me. "No. Just unconscious. We cut her power cord. At least for now."

Coco glances around at all the naked people in front of her. I can't tell if she's impressed or unnerved. "Wow. This is a lot of naked. And it's a little overwhelming because I don't know where to look. Like, I don't want to be rude, but I'm not gonna lie, I kind of want to look because of, you know, curiosity and intrusive thoughts . . ." She puts her hands over her eyes.

"Get a grip, kid." La'Tasha snaps her fingers and all of us are draped in simple hooded cloaks. Not exactly high fashion, but definitely better than standing around with our nips and balls out.

I look down at Ravena's crumpled form. Her once-pristine suit is spattered with soot and blood. I'd hate to be her dry cleaner.

La'Tasha starts yanking gear out of her bottomless bag. "Time to truss up Sleeping Psycho before she decides to rejoin the party."

I nod and let go of Hazel's hand so I can help. I grab some old rope from a corner of the mill and begin fashioning restraints.

La'Tasha shakes her head, handing me chains that hum with magic. "Normal rope won't hold her. These have binding spells baked in."

"And you just carry these around with you everywhere you go? Do I even want to ask why?"

"You can ask, but I can't guarantee you'll like the answer," she deadpans. "Seriously, though. It's an enchanted bag. I can pretty much pull anything out of it that I need."

Calvin helps me lock down her wrists and ankles while La'Tasha starts sketching symbols on the floor in blood-ink. I've seen enough of this crap over the last few days to know exactly what she's doing. She's building a cage.

Sirens wail in the distance, growing closer.

La'Tasha glances toward the approaching sirens. "I called them. They need to know what happened so they can help us decide what to do with her."

"The Sortium, too?" Hazel asks. She seems panicked.

"No, I called Hattie."

Hazel goes stiff. "The Regency? Tash!"

"She was bound to find out, and I figured it was best if she heard it from us, rather than hearing about it second-hand." She places an arm on Hazel's shoulder. "She wants us to call her tomorrow. You'll be fine. I got you."

"What are we going to do with her?" Calvin nods toward Ravena's still unconscious form. "We can't just leave her here."

Before anyone can answer, headlights swing across the mill's broken windows, casting long shadows across the floor. Car doors slam. Several footsteps crunch against the gravel outside.

"Blake? Hazel?" Sheriff Harlow's voice calls from outside.

I call toward the entrance. "In here, Sheriff. We stopped her, but . . . it's complicated."

Harlow appears in the doorway, flanked by two deputies. Both have their hands on their holstered weapons. Behind them are several members of the town council. Mayor Peterson, Melanie Perkins, looking like she was dragged out of bed, and Dr. Whitman still in his hospital scrubs. Their eyes widen as they take in the scene. We have a dozen people in makeshift cloaks, three battle-worn witches, and an unconscious woman bound with magic chains and glowing symbols. It's safe to say Moonridge's assembled leadership is a little overwhelmed.

"What exactly happened?" Harlow asks.

"Ravena came to Moonridge with a plan," I begin. "She's been poisoning the town with her supplements. They contained blood magic, meant to make humans susceptible to her influence and agitate werewolves into violence."

Mayor Peterson's mouth hangs open. "So you're trying to tell me she was the one who made the wolves go rogue? She seemed so helpful. And her products—"

Hazel cuts him off. "You were under her spell *because* of those products. All of you. Except the Sheriff. He was the only one who didn't buy into her wellness crap."

The mayor falls silent, his mouth a tight line.

"Five days ago," I say, trying to keep my voice steady, "Hazel and I found an artifact under the shop. The Wolfsbane Amulet. Hazel tried a spell, it backfired, and—"

I stumble over the words. Do I even attempt to explain the body swap?

Calvin sees me struggling and steps in. "Ravena planned the whole thing. She rigged the deck to tank the magical balance in Moonridge. Tonight, during the Blue Moon, she tried to break the pact for good. She wanted to strip the witches of their power. And she wanted the wolves to attack the humans so the council would ban them. With our powers broken, she could have taken over."

"And let demons into our world," La'Tasha adds solemnly.

"Like the real-ass, eat your grandma, kind of demons."

Sheriff Harlow rubs his forehead like he's fighting the mother of all headaches. He studies his surroundings. He doesn't speak for what feels like forever. Then he looks at Ravena, wrapped in those humming chains.

"God help me," he finally mutters. "Never a dull moment in this town. But this definitely takes the cake."

A groan from the center of the room pulls every eye to the floor. Ravena stirs. Her eyelids flutter open. The demonic red glow is gone from her eyes.

"Well, well," she says. Her voice is rough but still has that "I'm better than you" edge. "The whole gang is here. How very democratic."

She lunges, but the chains hold.

La'Tasha steps closer to the binding circle. "Don't try anything. We burned you out. And these chains will hold anything short of a full demon."

She lets out a dry, hollow sound like bones rattling. "Is that what you think? That I'm finished?"

"You failed," Hazel says firmly. "Your ritual was ruined. It's over."

"Naive little witch." Ravena sits up. The chains clink against the stone floor. "This wasn't my first attempt—"

"And it won't be your last, we get it," I cut her off. I don't have time for another one of her monologues. "Save the defeated villain speech. You're done."

Her smile is a slash of red. "Did you think I acted alone? That I concocted this plan on a whim?"

Mayor Peterson finds his spine. "What are you talking about?"

"I sold my soul decades ago," Ravena starts.

La'Tasha snorts. "Let me guess. A demon?"

Ravena's eyes flash with a spark of red. "*The* demon. Azrael, Lord of the Seventh Gate, will—"

"Okay, stop." Sheriff Harlow holds up his hand. "I don't care about your evil history. I don't need your resume. I just want to know how we're going to deal with you."

"You can't kill me," Ravena hisses. "I'm immortal."

"We'll see about that," Calvin mutters, but Dr. Whitman takes an involuntary step backward.

"She's immortal?" he whispers.

Melanie makes a strangled sound.

"So what do we do with her?" Harlow looks at Hazel and La'Tasha, cutting off whatever else Ravena planned to say. "If she can't be killed . . ."

Hazel and La'Tasha lock eyes. It's a silent conversation that lasts way too long.

"The caves under the mill," Hazel says. "The original witches used them for things that couldn't be destroyed. They'll contain her."

"They *should*," La'Tasha corrects.

"Should?" Melanie squeaks from the back.

"It's our best option," I say, looking straight at Harlow. "Unless you've got a jail cell that can hold immortal demon-witches."

Harlow stays silent for a beat, then nods. "Lead the way."

It takes six of us to carry Ravena and her magical chains through the old trapdoor that leads to the caves. The passage is narrow and we have to move single-file down rough stone steps that go on for so long I'm pretty sure we're delivering her directly to Satan himself.

The stairs finally open into a huge underground chamber. The space is easily the size of Moonridge's town hall. Maybe bigger. The ceiling just disappears into blackness. Runes cover every inch of the walls. In the center, there's a stone pit. It looks like a sarcophagus carved directly into the floor.

The space confuses the hell out of me. I've helped build foundations all over this county. No chamber this massive should exist without someone knowing about it.

"This is it." La'Tasha's voice echoes strangely in the cavernous space.

"How did you know this was here?" Sheriff Harlow asks, his flashlight beam darting nervously around the cave.

"Gran told me," Hazel replies, her eyes never leaving Ravena. "She brought us down here once and explained the things the original witches had to deal with. It wasn't pretty."

Coco moves around the room. She flicks her fingers and ancient torches roar to life. The light reveals things I didn't want to see. Bones embedded in the stone, crystals growing like teeth from the ceiling.

Ravena's gaze follows each of us, lingering on the witches the longest, then shifting to study the cave entrance behind us. Her fingers twitch against the chains. She's measuring them. Testing their strength.

"We need to prepare the binding ritual." La'Tasha pulls yet more supplies from her bag. I thought Coco's backpack was crazy, but this is nuts. Why didn't Hazel give me a big-ass bag of magic to use?

I step closer to Hazel as she joins the other witches, my protective instincts in overdrive. "Are you sure about this? This place feels wrong. And locking her up in a tomb for what? Ever? It seems kind of dark."

She nods, eyes hazy with exhaustion. "It is dark. But so is she." She glances at Ravena, who watches us with that unsettling smile. "The best way to fight a fire is to contain it."

I guess I can't argue with that. "What do you need me to do?"

"Watch her." She squeezes my arm briefly before joining La'Tasha.

The witches work fast. They draw symbols with chalk and salt. I stand guard with Calvin and the rest of the pack. We form a circle of muscle around the pit. Harlow and the council stay by the entrance, looking like they want to bolt.

"Almost ready," La'Tasha announces after what feels like hours. "Bring her to the center."

We half-carry, half-drag Ravena to the edge of the pit. She doesn't fight us. Doesn't speak. She just watches with those calculating eyes.

"Into the sarcophagus," La'Tasha instructs.

We lower her into the stone coffin. It fits her perfectly, like it was made specifically for her.

La'Tasha, Hazel, and Coco position themselves around the pit, forming a triangle. Each witch holds a small silver knife.

"The binding requires a sacrifice," La'Tasha explains solemnly. "Blood. Truth. Magic."

One by one, they slice their palms. It drips onto the runes surrounding the pit. Each drop sizzles on contact. The symbols flare a deep, bruised purple then settle into a hot gold.

"I am La'Tasha Morehouse," she begins. Her voice echoes through the ancient chamber. "I give my blood to bind what won't die."

"I am Coco Montoya," Coco adds. Her spacey vibe is gone. She's all business. "I give my truth to trap what shouldn't walk."

"I am Hazel Thornton," Hazel finishes. Her voice is the strongest of the three. "I give my magic to seal the broken."

Together, they chant words I don't recognize. The air gets heavy. My ears pop from the pressure. The blue light spreads toward Ravena, and the stone under her starts to shift. It looks like it's turning into liquid.

"Let what cannot die be buried," they chant. "Let what should not walk be stilled. Let what remains unbroken be sealed."

The stone walls of the sarcophagus start to rise. They flow over Ravena's body, and her mask finally breaks. Her eyes go wide. She looks like she's about to scream.

"This isn't over," she hisses. She struggles against the chains, but the stone is already up to her chest. "You think you won? The gate is already cracked. You aren't ready for what's coming next."

The stone hits her neck.

"Immortality is patient," she says. Her voice is eerily calm now. She looks right at me. "We'll meet again, wolf."

Her eyes glow red one last time before the stone completely swallows her. The surface of the sarcophagus goes still. A deep hush fills the cave.

"Did it work?" Sheriff Harlow asks from the edge of the chamber, his voice small in the vast space.

La'Tasha leans against the wall. She looks wrecked. "She's bound. The cave will hold her."

"For how long?" Mayor Peterson demands.

La'Tasha shakes her head. "No clue. We've never had to deal with anything like this."

We make our way back to the surface in silence. The mill seems different when we emerge. It's darker somehow, though the night outside has begun to give way to the first hints of dawn. I stay by the trapdoor for a second, looking back into the dark.

"I have a feeling this isn't over," I say to nobody in particular.

Hazel appears at my side, her hand finding mine again. "It's not," she agrees. "But maybe it's a beginning. Of something different. And better."

Her fingers intertwine with mine, warm and certain. After days in her body, feeling her hand in mine seems both strange and perfectly right. I close the trapdoor with my foot, shutting away the darkness below.

"So." I look down at the woman I fell in love with while literally walking in her shoes. "What happens next?"

A small smile curves her lips. "Breakfast? I'm starving."

I laugh, the sound startling in the solemn aftermath of all we've been through. Trust Hazel to bring us back to the basics, to remind me that even after body swaps and demon witches, life goes on.

"Breakfast for sure," I agree. I steer her toward the exit. Morning light hits the broken doors in dusty streaks. "I'll head home, scrub the funk off me, and put on actual pants. Then maybe we can hit the diner?"

"A shower and a change of clothes is a must," Hazel says, glancing at her phone. "I just got a text from Mina. She said all of her guests checked out after last night, and she has a ton of food she needs to get rid of. She wants us all to come for breakfast."

"Mina's it is then."

Outside, the ground vibrates. Just a twitch. It's so faint I almost dismiss it. But then it comes again. A rhythmic thud like a massive heartbeat buried deep underground.

Did we just put her exactly where she wanted to be?

I push the thought away, but my gut tightens. Ravena's voice keeps looping in my brain.

You're not ready for what comes next.

CHAPTER TWENTY-EIGHT

Hazel

Mina's B&B smells like heaven after a night of magical battles and demon witches. Cinnamon and butter float through the air, wrapping around us like a hug as we stumble through the front door. Dawn light streams through lace curtains, turning everything golden and soft-edged. After the darkness of the mill and whatever hellish dimension Ravena was trying to tear open, this cozy B&B dining room feels like the sweet comfort I needed.

"You lot look like you've been through a war." Flour dusts Mina's cheeks and apron, making her look like she's been caught in a snowstorm. "Sit. Eat. Then tell me everything."

Nobody argues. We collapse into chairs around oak tables. Every muscle in my body feels like overcooked pasta. Even my fingernails ache. Magical hangovers are brutal.

Calvin rubs his eyes, the amethyst charm no longer glowing around his neck. "Is it really over?"

Blake's broad shoulders finally relax. "For now."

"Breakfast time," Mina announces, setting down a platter

stacked with pancakes that steam in the cool morning air. "Eat all ya want. I have enough food here to feed an army."

My stomach growls loudly enough for Blake to shoot me an amused glance. "Someone's hungry."

"Try spending a few days in your enormous body," I retort. "You burn calories like a furnace."

His smile is so big it crinkles the corners of his eyes and makes my heart flutter in my chest.

Mina returns with platters of crispy bacon, fluffy eggs, golden biscuits, and coffee.

"The festival grounds are destroyed." Sheriff Harlow looks more rumpled than I've ever seen him. When did he even get here? "And there's the aftermath of that forest fire to deal with."

"And half the town thinks we're monsters," Mason adds gloomily, still looking a bit dazed.

Blake straightens his shoulders. "We'll fix it." His unshakable calm settles the anxiety flitting around in my chest. "Together. It'll be a good bonding exercise for the town. Remind us that we are all friends and neighbors, and we can get through anything."

My hand finds his under the table. A spark jumps between us. This time it's not magic. Just us. That excitement of something new. Something hopeful. Something right.

Coco suddenly tilts her head like a curious puppy. "Are you guys in love now? Is that what saved us? True love's kiss breaking the spell, just like the prophecy predicted?"

I nearly choke on my orange juice. Blake's ears turn crimson.

La'Tasha groans. "Coco, my dear. There's this thing called subtlety. Look it up."

"What? It's a fair question! They kissed and got zapped back into their own bodies. Then they did that weird glowy thing at the mill. Seems pretty love-powered to me."

The entire table stares at us. Even Mina pokes her head out of the kitchen to hear our answer.

"We, uh . . ." I start.

"It's complicated," Blake finishes, his hand squeezing mine under the table.

"Hmm." Coco narrows her eyes. "Well, I still think it was love magic that saved us."

Calvin snorts into his coffee. "My brother. Saved by love magic. Never thought I'd hear those words."

"Shut up," Blake mutters.

The conversation mercifully shifts to other topics. The town cleanup, how to explain everything to the tourists who witnessed the chaos, whether Ravena's supplements will permanently affect anyone. I half-listen, too aware of Blake's thumb tracing circles on the back of my hand. Of how right it feels to be sitting next to him in our own bodies.

An hour later, plates are cleared, and the first real yawns start making the rounds. We've been up all night saving the world. Even superheroes need sleep.

"I should probably head home," La'Tasha says, gathering her bag. "Make sure my house is still standing after all that magical fallout. You two lovebirds try not to body-swap again while I'm gone, okay?"

One by one, everyone says their goodbyes. Coco bounces off with promises to check on her protection spells around town. The wolves disperse in groups. Sheriff Harlow leaves to start damage control with the mayor. Soon, it's just Blake, Calvin, and me left at the table, nursing the last of our coffee.

Calvin jingles his truck keys. "Ready to go?"

Blake hesitates, looking at me. "In a minute."

Calvin rolls his eyes but smiles. "I'll wait in the truck. Don't be all day about it." He gives me a friendly nod before heading out the door.

Alone at last. Well, except for Mina humming in the kitchen.

Blake shifts in his chair to face me directly. "So." He looks nervous.

"So," I echo. "It's going to be weird, not sharing a bedroom with you tonight after this past week."

"Yeah." He runs a hand over his face. "About that . . . I was wondering if maybe I could stay over tonight. You know, so we can figure out what this feels like when we're both in our own bodies."

"You sure you just don't want to see me naked, Carter?" I poke him in the ribs.

He shrugs. "Already seen that."

"True. And I've seen *all* of you, too." I lean in close, whispering in his ear. "I touched it, too."

"Yes." He looks away. "I'm sure you did." The blush creeping up his neck is possibly the most adorable thing I've ever seen on big, tough Blake Carter.

"What can I say? I was curious. But to answer your question, yes, you can come over. I was hoping you'd ask." I can't keep the smile from my face. "I think we have some reacquainting to do."

Our fingers brush again as we stand to leave, and that familiar spark flares to life. Honestly, who needs magic when a simple touch can make the world spin like this?

***

Moonridge looks like it survived a battle between giants. Festival decorations hang like wounded soldiers from lampposts, food carts lie overturned with their contents splattered across the cobblestones, and the fountain at the center of Town Square sits dry and cracked as an old man's lips in winter. Blake and I pick our way through the debris, our fingers loosely linked as we take in the aftermath of our supernatural showdown.

"Wow," I say, eloquent as ever. "This is going to take some serious cleanup."

Blake nods, his expression grim as he surveys the broken gazebo. "At least no one died. Buildings can be rebuilt, but people can't be replaced."

A pretzel cart lies on its side next to a popcorn stand that appears to have exploded. Salt packets and popcorn kernels litter the ground like confetti. Broken glass glitters in the morning sunlight. The scent of spilled beer and sugary soda fills the air, the contents of said liquid making the pavement sticky under my boots.

"Look," Blake points toward the hills where a dark plume of smoke still rises from the forest. "Fire crews are up there. They said it's going to take another day or two to get it fully contained."

My stomach twists. "How bad is it?"

"Calvin got a call from someone on the fire crew while we were at breakfast. The fire took out about two hundred acres around Amethyst Beach." He squeezes my hand. "The beach itself is okay. Something about the amethyst in the sand created a natural firebreak. But the hiking trails, the campgrounds . . ."

"Gone," I finish for him. Moonridge isn't just physically damaged. Its heart is wounded. The forest, the lake, downtown. These are the places where our community comes together.

"We'll replant. The pack can help with clearing the burned areas. Seeds from the untouched forest will spread naturally, and we can speed things along."

"I can help heal it. I know a thing or two about earth magic," I add, already mentally cataloging what I'll need. "Nature magic is pretty straightforward."

We turn down Main Street, where shopkeepers sweep glass from sidewalks and nail plywood over broken windows. Mrs. Drake, now free from Ravena's influence, sweeps outside the diner.

"Morning, Hazel. Blake," she calls, her normally perfect perm now a frazzled halo around her head. "Quite a night, wasn't it?"

Blake nods. "Everyone okay here?"

"Shaken up, but we're Moonridge folk." She straightens her spine. "Takes more than a little magical chaos to keep us down for long."

I bite back a smile. Even after witnessing werewolves running wild through the festival and being mind-controlled by a demon witch, folks here will still act like it's just another day. Some things never change.

"We should organize a town meeting," I suggest as we continue toward the apothecary. "Get everyone working together on repairs."

"Good idea. Nothing brings people together like a common enemy," Blake says. "Or a common disaster."

"It'll be like a team-building exercise. But with less trust falls and more magical repairs."

He laughs, the sound warming me from the inside out. "You're something else, Thornton."

The destroyed festival grounds fade behind us, and I find myself dreading what we might find at my shop. My smile fades as we round the corner and the apothecary comes into view. The ivy-covered stone building looks mostly intact, but someone spray-painted "WITCH" across my front door in angry red letters.

"Well, they're not wrong." I try to make it sound light, though a chill settles in my chest. How many times throughout history had my ancestors seen that same word scrawled on walls and doorways as both accusation and death sentence?

Blake's jaw tightens. "I'll help you clean it off."

I fish my keys from my pocket, the familiar weight comforting in my palm. "Let's see what else got wrecked first."

The bell jingles as we step inside, and at first glance, things seem normal. Morning light streams through stained glass windows, painting rainbow patterns across the wooden floor. Shelves of herbs and tinctures stand undisturbed. The ancient cash register sits on the counter, dented but functional.

Then I notice the mint-green thermoses arranged in a perfect pyramid by the tea display. Supplement bottles organized by "benefit." Brochures with Ravena's face smiling up at potential victims. My blood turns to ice water in my veins. I'm across the room before I realize I've moved, staring down at the last physical evidence of Ravena's presence in my shop.

"Hazel?" Blake's voice sounds far away.

Heat rises in my chest, molten and powerful. Magic sparks at my fingertips.

"Get back," I warn Blake, raising my hands toward the display.

He steps back without question. This is something I need to do.

I close my eyes, drawing power from deep inside. Powers of cleansing and renewal that have been passed down through generations of Thornton witches. "What was poisoned, now be pure. What brought darkness now brings light. What was false and harmful, now be gone forever."

The words flow naturally as my fingers dance in familiar patterns. I open my eyes. Blue flames erupt from my hands to engulf Ravena's stand. They burn impossibly bright but produce no heat or smoke. It's a magical fire that consumes only what needs to be destroyed. This is the first time I've been able to do that without a book. It's like whatever happened last night removed a blockage in my abilities. I feel free.

The thermoses melt like cheap plastic. Supplement bottles dissolve into dust. The brochures curl and vanish. Within seconds, there's nothing left but a clean, empty space where Ravena's influence once stood.

I let the fire burn a moment longer, drawing circles with my fingers to spread the cleansing energy throughout the shop. Eventually, the scent of lavender and sage replaces the artificial citrus of Ravena's products.

When the flames finally fade, I sway slightly, light-headed from the release of power. Blake is there immediately, his hand steady at my elbow.

"Feel better?" he asks, a smile playing at the corners of his mouth.

I look at the now-empty corner, clean as if nothing had ever been there. "Much."

In the sudden quiet of my shop, the weight of everything we've been through, and everything we've avoided talking about, settles between us. The air shifts, becoming thick and charged. Blake gnaws at a fingernail and catches me staring. Heat creeps up my neck, and suddenly I can't seem to find a comfortable place to look. His blue eyes watch me with a mixture of nervousness and desire. It makes my stomach flip.

"So," I say, because someone has to break this silence before I combust.

"So." The hint of a smile tugs at one corner of his mouth.

I pick up a couple of bottles and move them to a different shelf. Anything to keep my hands busy. Why did things suddenly get awkward? I finally crack. "This is weird, right? Like, good weird, but still weird."

"Definitely weird," he agrees, crossing his arms. His biceps bulge against the hem of his T-shirt, and it makes me wish they were wrapped around me. "But you're right. Good weird."

The morning sunlight streams through the stained glass, painting him in blues and greens. Blake Carter. Werewolf and eternal thorn in my side, is looking at me like I'm something precious.

"Can I tell you something ridiculous?" I ask, finally turning to face him.

"Always."

I take a deep breath. "I was completely smitten with you in third grade. Like, embarrassingly so."

His eyebrows shoot up. "What?"

"Yep." My cheeks burn, and I duck my head, letting my hair fall forward to hide the blush I know is spreading down my neck. My fingers twist together. "Ever since you helped me find my lost guinea pig. Remember that? I had her outside in a makeshift pen, and she escaped. You tracked her all the way to the Johnsons' shed next door."

A slow smile spreads across his face. "I remember. You were crying so hard your face was all blotchy."

"Gee, thanks."

"It was cute." He nudges me. "I remember you promising the universe you'd never ask for another birthday present if you could just have your guinea pig back."

I'm surprised he remembers so much detail. "After that, I was convinced you were my personal hero. I used to practice writing 'Hazel Carter' in the margins of all my notebooks."

He pushes off from the counter, taking a step closer. "And then what happened?"

I laugh, but it comes out a little hollow. "Then we got older. You made fun of me. You called me Sparkles. You started pulling my pigtails and making fun of my freckles. Classic boy behavior, I know, but little Hazel didn't understand that. So . . ."

"So you hexed me," he finishes. I look up to meet his gaze. "Don't deny it."

I shrug. "Nothing serious! Just little things. That time, your shoelaces kept coming untied during the fifth-grade relay race? That was definitely me. The mysterious green tint to your hair before the eighth-grade dance? Also me."

Blake runs a hand through his hair, as if checking that it's the right color now. "I thought you did all of that because you hated me."

"I wanted your attention, but I thought *you* hated *me*," I counter. "The teasing got more intense, and I just assumed . . ."

"That I was being a jerk because I didn't like you," he supplies, taking another step closer. "When really I was just a clueless werewolf kid who had no idea how to tell the brilliant, pretty, mysterious witch girl that I thought she was amazing."

My heart does a little somersault. "You had feelings for me? Back then?"

He nods, looking almost sheepish. "Since about fifth grade. I picked on you because it was the only way I could think to get your attention without admitting I thought you were cute."

We stare at each other for a moment before bursting into laughter. It bubbles up from somewhere deep, washing away years of misunderstandings and hurt feelings.

"We're idiots," I laugh.

"Complete morons," he agrees, now close enough that I can smell him. Pine and cedar and a little bit of sweat. It's different experiencing it with my own senses rather than his wolfed-out ones.

When our laughter dies down, he reaches out to tuck a strand of hair behind my ear. His fingers linger on my cheek. "Can I tell you something else?"

I nod, not trusting my voice.

"I have wanted to ask you out for years, but I thought you'd turn me down. I fought my attraction. Told myself it was complicated. Wolves and witches don't mix. Agnes would turn me into a toad. You'd hex my tail off."

"I would never," I protest. "Your tail is one of your better features."

He smiles, but his eyes stay serious. "The truth is, I was scared. Not of hexes or magical backlash. I was scared of how much I wanted this. How right it felt, even when everything else said it should be wrong. And I was terrified you'd turn me down because witches don't date dirty werewolves."

Something raw flickers across his face. My throat tightens, and I have to resist the urge to reach for him, to smooth away the uncertainty creasing his forehead. I know exactly what he means. I've spent so long fighting with Blake Carter that the idea of being *with* Blake Carter is terrifying.

"I know," I whisper. "It was easier to keep hexing your coffee to turn cold than admit I still watched for you to appear at the diner every morning."

"Knew it," he mutters. "No coffee gets cold that fast naturally."

I laugh softly. "Sorry. Old habits."

"Don't be sorry." His thumb traces my cheekbone, feather-light. "Every cold coffee, every magical mishap . . ." he sighs. "It all led us here."

"Here being . . . ?" I prompt, because after years of miscommunication, I need to hear him say it.

"Here being me, standing in front of the most frustrating, beautiful, powerful witch in Moonridge, hoping she'll let me kiss her properly. In our own bodies and without magical threats surrounding us."

My heart hammers against my ribs like it's trying to escape. "I think that could be arranged."

He leans down slowly, giving me time to back away if I want to.

As if I would.

His lips brush against mine, tentative at first, then with growing confidence when I slide my arms around his neck and pull him closer. His lips are warm and surprisingly soft, tasting faintly of coffee and maple syrup. Unlike last night's desperate collision of need and magic, this kiss unfolds slowly, tentatively. It's a question asked and answered with the gentle press of our lips. Last night was survival, adrenaline, necessity. This is choice. This is Blake's hands cradling my face like I'm the most precious treasure he's ever touched. This is me sharing a moment with him I'd only ever dared to dream about. This is us. Finally, purely us. No magical chaos or body swaps or ancient vendettas threatening what we feel.

We break apart just enough to breathe, foreheads touching.

"That was . . ." I begin.

"Yeah," he agrees, eyes slightly dazed.

"Do you want to see my bedroom?" The words tumble out before I can overthink them. "I mean, while you're in your own body."

His smile is slow and sweet and just a little bit wicked around the edges. "I thought you'd never ask."

He kisses me again, deeper this time, and I melt against him like one of Ravena's thermoses in magical fire. We stumble toward the back stairs, unwilling to stop touching long enough to walk properly. Sometimes, it turns out, you have to walk a mile in someone else's body before you can find your way back to your own heart.

CHAPTER TWENTY-NINE

Hazel

The morning sun spills through the stained-glass windows of the apothecary. Puddles of orange, green, and blue paint the floor. It's been two weeks since Ravena's smackdown, and life has settled into something kind of like normal. Well, if openly dating the werewolf I used to detest can be called normal.

"One sleeping potion. Extra strength." I slide a small blue bottle across the wood to Mrs. Henderson. Her eyes look sharp today. No more of that vacant, glassy stare. I think she's finally completely detoxed. "Two drops in tea before bed. Not three. Three will have you sleeping until Christmas."

She nods, tucking the bottle into her purse. "Thank you, Hazel. My insomnia's been worse since . . . well, you know."

I do know. Half the town is dealing with nightmares about wolves, fire, or being puppets to a demon witch. Trauma does that. But at least they're coming to me for real help now instead of Ravena's magical mind-control juice.

"Come back if it doesn't help," I tell her.

I think the biggest change I've noticed since the Ravena business is that I'm no longer treated as just a quirky shop owner. I'm Hazel Thornton, witch who helped save the town. People take my magic more seriously now.

As Mrs. Henderson leaves, the door chimes draw my attention back to the front door. Blake enters, ducking his broad frame under the low doorway. My heart does that stupid flutter thing it always does when I see him. Two weeks of officially dating, and I still get butterflies.

"Morning, witch." His voice is warm with affection. Sawdust clings to his hair. His T-shirt sticks to his shoulders in a way that makes me want to flip the 'Closed' sign and see how fast I can get him out of those jeans.

I lean over the counter and steal a kiss. "Morning, wolf." He tastes like coffee and mint gum. "Rebuilding again today?"

He nods. He rubs his hand over his head, and a cloud of cedar dust hits the air. "Town Square's almost done. Finishing up the park this afternoon."

Blake and his pack have been working overtime to help rebuild. The town that was terrified of them at the beginning of the month now depends on them. I gotta admit, it's a great PR move.

"I brought breakfast sandwiches." He lifts a paper bag that smells like bacon and cheese and maple syrup. "Got time for a food break?"

Shared meals and stolen kisses between his rebuilding shifts and my steady stream of customers have become our new normal. Our first official date after the whole saving-the-town adventure wasn't anything fancy. Just sandwiches at Skipper Lake, Blake's favorite place. We just sat and talked and watched the sunset turn the water to fire. He'd brought a blanket. I'd brought wine. We'd talked until stars peppered the sky, filling in all the gaps from our time in each other's bodies.

The shop bell chimes again, pulling me from the memory. La'Tasha sweeps in, arms laden with fresh herbs from her garden. Her bright pink, floral print blouse makes her flawless mahogany skin pop.

"Morning, lovebirds." She nods at Blake as she sets her harvest on the counter. "Got that feverfew you wanted. And some lemon balm for those anxiety potions everyone's been asking for."

I inhale the citrusy scent of the balm. "You're a lifesaver. The way people are going through calming potions, we'll need to plant more next spring."

"Already ahead of you." She taps her temple. "Coco's working on some super-growth soil mix. Says she can make plants grow twice as fast with the right enchantment."

Speaking of Coco, she's become something of a town celebrity with her protection charms. Every house in Moonridge now sports one of her colorful creations above the door. It's funny how nearly being taken over by a demon witch changes one's perspective about "the weird little witch".

I flick crumbs from my skirt. "Any word on the caves?"

Blake shakes his head. "Nope. Nothing. Calvin's driven by pretty much every day and said he hasn't seen anything weird. Leo and I drove by on the way to a site yesterday and all was quiet. I think we're good. I think we got her."

We don't say her name much. It's like we're afraid we'll summon her if we do, and nobody wants to risk that.

"Do you want to drive up to the lake together tonight?" I ask, changing the subject to something lighter.

"The New Moon Festival, forest healing thing? That's tonight?"

I nod, feeling a flutter of nervousness. It's big magic, what we're planning. But if it works . . . No. When it works, it'll be the final step in Moonridge's healing.

"I'll be there," he promises, leaning in for another kiss. This one lingers, sweet and full of promise.

The bell chimes again, breaking our moment. More customers. Always more customers these days.

"Duty calls," I sigh, getting to my feet. My pulse hitches when

I see Evan standing at the register. I can't help but laugh. Three weeks ago, I thought I'd never move on from him, yet here I am, completely in love with someone else.

Evan shifts nervously. "Hello, Hazel. Can I have a word? Alone?"

"Um, sure." I can't help but notice the look that passes between Blake and La'Tasha. "What's going on?"

"Did you, um . . ." Evan starts, lowering his voice to barely above a whisper. He blushes and can't seem to get out what he wants to say.

"Did I?" I prod.

"Did you put some kind of hex on me? Every time I try to kiss Missy, I get . . . digestive issues."

"Um, no. Why would you think that?" I glance toward La'Tasha and Blake and see them laughing hysterically. And then I know.

"Every time our lips touch, I get violently gassy. Like, room-clearing, relationship-ending gas. Missy won't even hold my hand anymore. Last week at dinner, she sat on the other side of the table so I couldn't kiss her. Her friends think I have some kind of medical condition." His face flushes red, and he can't meet my eyes.

"Evan, do you really think I would do something like that?"

He looks at me very pointedly.

"I can assure you that I most certainly did not curse you to fart any time you kiss Missy." It's technically true. I didn't curse him. Though I have a pretty good idea of who did.

"Make. It. Stop." He turns on his heel and stomps out of the shop.

As soon as the door closes, I turn and look at the responsible parties.

"What did you two do?" I ask, placing a hand on my hip.

"Please. That man deserves every unexpected fart that drops from his ass. Consider it community service," La'Tasha says.

"Oh, I'm not mad at you. I'm mad that I didn't think of it first."

Blake gives me a kiss. "You're welcome," he says as he walks toward the door. "I'll pick you up at closing. We can head to the lake together."

I watch his broad shoulders disappear through the doorway, a smile tugging at my lips. Two weeks ago, I was trapped in his body, fighting for our lives. Now we're planning festival dates, sharing meals, and making my ex fart whenever he kisses his new girlfriend. You know. Just like a normal couple. Well, as normal as a witch and a werewolf can be.

And honestly? I wouldn't have it any other way.

***

I flip the sign to "Closed" three hours early. My fingers tingle with anticipation. Tonight is our first New Moon Festival. A chance for the community to heal. We need this after Ravena tried to shred the town's sanity and pull us apart.

The idea for the New Moon Festival came to me during a late-night gab session at Mina's. We were huddled around her kitchen table, brainstorming ways to help Moonridge move forward. And then it dawned on me. We needed a do-over. A new moon was in a couple of weeks. These things always symbolize new beginnings and healing and rebirth and all that. Of course, we needed the town to agree that another festival would be a good thing. And convince them that the wolves wouldn't try to tear them apart again. Little details, but important ones.

Shockingly, the town council signed off faster than I could blink. They were definitely ready to put all this behind us.

A curt honk comes from outside. I grab my bag and step outside to find Blake's truck. He's so punctual it almost hurts. His truck idles at the curb, windows down to let in the fresh evening air.

I jump in, and he leans over the center console for a kiss. "Ready for some magic?"

"Born ready." The words melt between our lips.

The drive to Amethyst Beach takes less than twenty minutes, and the transformation we see when we pull up takes my breath away. Two weeks ago, this shoreline was a hellscape of charred stumps and drifting ash. Now, the wreckage is gone. The blackened trees still stand, but someone wrapped them in strings of twinkling lights. They look like weird, glowing skeletons. It actually works for what we have planned.

The new dock stretches into the water. Paper lanterns hang from poles along the shore. Their light hits the lake and shatters into a million gold pieces. A couple of guys have turned it into a stage. They tune their guitars, and the notes drift over the sound of the waves lapping at the shore.

Blake's voice drops. "Wow. Calvin said they were busy up here, but I didn't think they'd pull this off."

"It's beautiful, right?" I squeeze his hand. "Hope looks good on Moonridge."

We make our way down to the shore. It looks like the entire zip code showed up. Harlow talks shop with the Mayor near a table full of food. Mina and Mrs. Henderson sling apple cider like it's their job. Kids sprint through the crowd, screaming in that way that usually annoys me, but tonight it's just . . . noise. Good noise.

Mina spots us and waves like she's trying to direct a plane. Next to the cider stand is a table with enough baked goods to feed a small army.

"There's our magical saviors!" she calls. "I've saved ya spots on the beach next to me."

We settle onto the sand as the sun begins to set in a mess of gold and pink. It's a hell of a view. The two guys with the guitars start playing folk music, and a few people sing along.

"How's the B&B?" Blake asks Mina. "Has business picked up?"

"Not at all. The summer is windin' down, though, and business usually slows this time of year. I'm hopin' things will pick back up in October when we have our big fall festival."

Fall. My favorite time of year. I'm hoping that tonight goes well, and the Council will allow Coco, La'Tasha, and me to head up the committee for the week-long Halloween festival. I just need tonight to be a success.

I glance over my shoulder and see Hattie Lawrence and a couple of the Regency members speaking with Sheriff Harlow. Hattie meets my eye and nods. We'd spoken a week ago when I'd debriefed her on the Ravena situation. I got my hand slapped for not alerting them sooner. They are supposed to be alerted to any magical danger—magical law and whatnot. I played dumb, and got away with a minor scolding. She seems to be over it now. Plus, after she sees what we have cooked up tonight, all will be forgiven.

"Nervous?" Blake must have noticed my fingers drumming against my knee.

"A little," I admit. "It's big magic. If it works . . ."

"*When* it works," he corrects, kissing my temple.

La'Tasha finds us just as the sun disappears behind the mountains. She wears a flowing, white cotton dress that makes her look radiant. Coco is right behind her, practically vibrating. She wears a lime green dress over pink leggings. My little chaos fairy.

La'Tasha motions to us. "Let's do this."

I stand, feeling the weight of every eye turning our way. The music stops. Conversations fade. Even the kids settle down next to their parents.

Mayor Peterson steps forward, clearing his throat. "Friends, neighbors, we gather tonight to celebrate new beginnings. Our town has faced darkness and emerged stronger. Tonight, we'll witness the healing of our beloved forest, thanks to the combined magic of three extraordinary women."

He gestures to us. My palms go sweaty, and my heart becomes

a flopping fish in my chest. But then Blake catches my eye from the crowd. He smiles.

I've got this. This is what I was meant to do.

The three of us move to the edge of the burned area. Ash still covers the ground like dirty snow, capturing our footsteps. I pull a small box from my bag and open it to reveal three seeds. One silver, one lavender, one emerald. They pulse with the magic we spent all week cramming into them. I take them in my hands.

"One seed for the wisdom of what came before." My voice carries across the silent crowd as I hand La'Tasha the silver seed.

"One seed for the strength we hold today." I give the lavender seed to Coco.

"And one seed for the growth that's yet to come." I hold the emerald seed in my own palm.

We form a triangle, standing just far enough apart that our outstretched hands don't quite touch. Together, we kneel, pressing our seeds into the ash-covered soil. The second they touch the soil, the connection snaps into place. Three witches. Three seeds. One purpose. We begin to chant. Our voices weave together like a single chord.

"What was burned, be green,
What was lost, be seen,
What was broken, be whole,
New life will rise. Take control."

At first, nothing happens. The seeds are gone. The earth doesn't stir. But then there's a pulse of light. The ground shudders. Coco's eyes grow wide. The ground shifts. Cracks rip through the soot, and silver light bleeds out. The magic we poured into the seeds spreads through roots and soil.

"Keep going," La'Tasha urges.

We hit the chant again. Louder. More sure.

The silver light spreads like veins across the entire forest. Where it touches, the ash dissolves. Rich soil with tiny signs of green life appears.

At first, it's just the tiniest shoots of green. Thin as eyelashes. They unfurl into a velvet carpet of grass right before our eyes. Vines crawl up the charred tree trunks like they're hugging an old friend. Wildflowers explode out of the dirt, petals opening for the stars. Blackened tree husks crumble into dust. New saplings rip through the dirt. Each pulse of magic drags more life out of the ash. The transformation spreads. A ripple of green. A splash of bright colors where flowers bloom. It won't fix everything. A few massive oaks are beyond repair and the deepest burns still show. But it marks a start. A promise.

When the last verse of our chant fades, the silver light sinks into the earth and stays there. Silence holds for one heartbeat. Then a gasp. A slow clap. Then the whole crowd just loses it. Coco kicks her shoes into the weeds and starts dancing barefoot through the new grass. La'Tasha's eyes fill with tears.

We did it.

Blake wraps his arms around my waist from behind. He hooks his chin over my shoulder. His chest feels like a radiator against my spine.

"You did it," he murmurs, breath tickling my ear.

I turn around and look into his eyes. "*We* did it. All of us."

The festival kicks back into gear. The music picks up, something fast and loud. Mina hands out sweet buns while kids sprint after fireflies by the lake.

Blake's lips hit mine, and the rest of the town just blurs out. It's a quiet kiss, but it feels like home.

*****

The festival thins as midnight hits. Families with sleepy children drift home. Blake and I find a patch of grass away from the noise. I rest my head on his shoulder, his arm heavy and warm around my waist. The stars look like someone spilled glitter across a black table. It's perfect. Almost too perfect.

"You killed it tonight," Blake says. His voice vibrates through my cheek. "I've seen you do magic, but this was a whole different level."

I smile, watching the moonlight dance across the water. "It felt different. Like something clicked into place when we stuck Ravena in the ground."

"Or maybe spending a week in a wolf body rewired your brain."

"And how were you changed after your week as a witch?" I tease.

"Well, I definitely learned the importance of wiping front to back. And that I'm happy I never have to wear a bra again." He catches my finger, bringing it to his lips for a quick kiss. "Best worst experience of my life."

Music drifts across the lake, and Blake wraps his arms around my waist. We sway a bit to the music, lost in this perfect moment.

"Did you ever think we'd end up here?" I ask.

"Three weeks ago?" His fingers lace with mine. "Absolutely not. You are the last person I thought I'd be sitting with like this. Funny how things change."

"Well, I think the whole 'living in each other's bodies' thing probably helped," I add. "Nothing builds intimacy quite like washing someone else's genitals for a week. I mean, if we can get through that, there's nothing that could come between us. Amirite?"

He leans down to kiss me again. "You're so romantic. Poetic even."

I close my eyes and lose myself in how perfect this all feels. I almost lose myself in the quiet when Blake goes rigid. I feel his muscles lock.

"What's wrong?"

He scans the darkness on the far shore. His nostrils flare. "I don't know. Something feels off."

My skin prickles.

"There." He points toward the mountain road winding along the far bank. "See it?"

I squint. An SUV sits in the thick shadows of the pines. Sleek. Black. The headlights stay off, but the running lights glow. It looks almost predatory.

"Looks like one of those limo-sized SUVs. I don't know anyone in Moonridge who has one of those. Do you?"

"No." A chill creeps up my spine. "Why is it just sitting there?"

I can't make out movement or shapes through the windshield, but the sensation of being watched unsettles me. My magic pulses. Even with Blake right here, I feel like a bug under a microscope.

He pulls me tight against him. "Could be a tourist," he offers.

"At midnight? Parked in the trees?"

"Point taken."

We watch. It watches back.

The festival noise feels miles away now. I try to tell myself it's just the trauma talking, that after Ravena, I see monsters in every shadow. But this feels deliberate.

"You know," Blake says slowly, "we never did figure out who that guy was. The one with Ravena that night."

My stomach tightens. I'd totally forgotten about him.

"You think it's him?"

Blake shrugs, but his jaw is tight. "Could be. Ravena said she wasn't flying solo."

I remember her threat in the cave. I thought it was just an empty threat. Now, I'm not so sure.

"Should we go check it out?"

Blake shakes his head. "Not without backup. If it is one of Ravena's people, they might have powers we're not prepared for."

He's right, of course. We barely survived our last magical showdown. We're in no shape for another. At least not tonight.

"I should call La'Tasha." I reach for my phone.

"Wait." He places a hand on my wrist. "Look."

The SUV's headlights flick on. Twin beams sweep across the pines as the car turns toward the main road. For a second, the lights hit us directly. I squint, but the glare hides everything.

Then the car glides away and vanishes around the bend. The silence it leaves behind feels ten times heavier.

"That was weird, right?" My voice sounds small. "That wasn't just me being twitchy?"

Blake pulls me closer. "No. That was definitely weird."

I shiver. The car is gone, but the unease stays behind like an oil slick on a perfect night.

"You think they were watching us?" I ask. "Or just the party?"

"I don't know," Blake says. "But I don't like either answer."

I lean into him. I want to feel safe, but for the first time since we buried Ravena, I feel like the clock just started ticking again. "Should we at least tell Sheriff Harlow, maybe?"

"And tell him what? That we saw a car that didn't do anything wrong?" Blake sighs, running a hand through his hair. "We don't have much to go on. But I'll have the pack keep an eye out for unfamiliar vehicles. Maybe increase patrols around town for a while."

I nod, knowing he's right. Without proof, without even a license plate, there's little we can do. Still, the knot in my stomach refuses to unwind.

"She said it wasn't over," I murmur, more to myself than to Blake. "Ravena. In the cave. She said it wasn't over."

"Hey." Blake turns my face gently toward his. In the moonlight, his eyes are more silver than blue. "Whatever this is—if it's even anything—we'll handle it."

I try to smile, but I can't stop staring at the spot where the SUV was parked. "You're right. I'm probably overreacting."

Yet even as I say it, I know I'm not. That car wasn't there by chance.

Blake hits me with a quick kiss on the forehead. "Come on. Let's head back to the festival."

We head back toward the music and the noise, but I glance over my shoulder at the empty road anyway. That "being watched" vibe refuses to fade. It clings to me. Our hands stay locked together. Fingers tight. It's like we're both afraid the other one will vanish if we let go. The night doesn't look as bright now. That car just smeared grease all over the perfect evening.

Moonridge is healing. The forest is regrowing. Blake and I have found each other through the strangest of circumstances. Everything is supposed to be perfect. But as I gaze up at the star-filled sky, I can't escape the certainty that we've only won the first battle. Somewhere in the darkness, something else is brewing.

And I wouldn't expect anything less, because that's how we roll around here.

Welcome to Moonridge.

ACKNOWLEDGEMENTS

Every book is a team effort, and this one would never have made it into your hands without some truly incredible people behind the scenes.

First, to Ally, Susie, Ilona, and "Brick", my forever partners in crime, thank you for your editing wisdom, sharp eyes, design skills, and for talking me off more than one metaphorical ledge. And to Gloria, thanks for checking my Spanish. This book is cleaner, tighter, and far more readable because of all of your generous help (and occasional tough love).

To my beta and sensitivity readers: Corey, Lonnie B, Raelynn, and Claudia, thank you for your unfiltered, thoughtful, and sometimes hilariously blunt feedback. You pointed out what wasn't working, celebrated what was, and gently pointed out how I randomly changed side characters names and occupations throughout the novel. You really helped shape this story into something I'm proud of. You saw the messy, early version and still came back for more. That deserves a medal.

To my friends not directly mentioned here (there are many), thank you for letting me disappear for hours and sometimes days without too many questions or interruptions. This is what I was doing when I turned down dinners, canceled plans and left texts unanswered. Your patience with me and my quirks means more than I can say. I often wonder what I did to deserve you all.

And finally, to you, the reader. Thank you for taking a chance on an indie author. I hope you fall headfirst into Moonridge and love these weird, wonderful characters as much as I do. Trust me, this is only the beginning. There's a lot more where this story came from.

ABOUT THE AUTHOR

Avery Arujo is the pen name of a socially anxious, awkward, and proudly introverted author of the paranormal mystery/romance series *Welcome to Moonridge*. Avery lives in the northern U.S., where the scenery is beautiful, the weather perfect, and the food divine. When not writing, you'll find Avery watching a horror movie or trashy reality TV or reading under a blanket with a cup of coffee, and the world's sweetest dog trying to prove that they are more interesting than any old book.

For more information about the *Welcome to Moonridge* series, or to sign up for the newsletter, visit welcometomoonridge.com.

COMING SOON

Welcome to Moonridge, where the ghosts have come out to play and Death just checked into the local B&B.

Running a B&B in a town cursed by magical drama wasn't Mina Cartwright's dream job, but it's home. After all of the werewolf debacle over the summer, business has flatlined and she's barely holding on financially. Her last hope? A surprise booking from the cast of *The Real Vampire Wives of Obsidian Hills*, who are bringing their reality-show chaos (and impeccable fashion) to Moonridge just in time for the Halloween festival.

But the real trouble begins when Dex Grimm, a mysterious, breathtakingly aloof man with a cane and a suspiciously deathly aura, checks into Room Ten. He says he's a writer. Mina suspects he's hiding something... like the fact that he might actually be the Grim Reaper.

As ghostly activity spikes, magical boundaries fray, and her guests (living and otherwise) cause mounting mayhem, Mina finds herself caught between a brewing supernatural crisis and a man known primarily as Death who somehow makes her feel more alive than she has in years.

Add in a reality TV crew, rampaging ghosts, and the underlying danger of an ancient evil reawakening in Moonridge, and Mina's fall season is about to be to die for.

Date Night With Death will be released in the fall of 2025.

Keep reading for a sneak peek at Date Night With Death.

CHAPTER ONE

Mina

The booking software sits open on my laptop. Rows of empty slots stare at me like missin' teeth. Twelve rooms, and only three have been booked in the last two months. I tap my pen against the desk and wince as another headache blooms behind my right eye.

Outside my window, orange and yellow leaves skitter across the lawn like they're runnin' away from summer. October in Moonridge is one of my bread-and-butter months. I normally have guests booked three months in advance for the Haunted Fall Festival. This year? I can't pay people to stay here.

I snap the laptop shut and dig my thumbs into my eyes. The headaches have grown more frequent, almost unbearable. And I know what it means. Dr. Patterson didn't mince words when she showed me the MRI scans six weeks ago.

The grandfather clock in the hall hammers out six chimes. Its deep toll rattles the floorboards of this empty cage of a home. Halloween is a week out. By rights, these rooms should be packed with guests, all of them sippin' apple cider and leavin' crumbs of pumpkin bread on the rugs. Instead, it's just me and the dust bunnies, and even they don't want much to do with me.

I rise and stretch. My spine cracks like a dry branch. Too much time hunched over the laptop looking for money I don't have has me all dried up like a dead tree.

Six years ago, I poured every cent I had into this place. A fresh start, I thought. Away from all that troubled me in Scotland. And for the first few years it was exactly what I needed. Now I'm the proud owner of a three-story Victorian that's fallin' apart faster than I can patch it up.

She's not listening again.

The voice is soft and feminine. It floats on a draft across the room. I freeze. My heart stutters and I scan the parlor. No one else is here.

"Hello?"

Silence.

There I go talkin' at empty rooms again. It has to be the stress. The doctor said stress could make the symptoms worse.

Someone should tend to the flowers. They're dying. Like everything else around here.

The scent of wet roses drifts through the room and then vanishes.

The whispers started a few weeks back. Always at night. Always when I'm on my own. It happens every year, like clockwork, but usually the dead have the decency to wait until a day or two before Halloween. Not this year. They showed up about a month early, and they really have somethin' to say.

My phone pings. I pick it up and see it's another notification from the Trippa app. I swipe it open even though I know it's just lookin' for a way to make my mood worse.

Moonridge used to be charming, but after what happened with those werewolf attacks this summer, I wouldn't risk bringing children here. The B&B owner was nice enough, but one star for safety concerns.

One star. Brilliant.

I toss my phone onto the desk. My B&B did nothing to encourage what happened, so why am I getting negative reviews? Hell, it wasn't even the wolves' fault. That witch Ravena was the one stirrin' the pot, and we stopped her. There's nothin' to worry about now. But try tellin' that to a tourist from New Jersey.

I check the clock again. Already six-fifteen, which means Lily and Jasper Brooks will be here any minute. I tuck a stray bit of red hair behind my ear and head toward the kitchen. I catch my reflection in the hall mirror and have to do a double-take. My appetite's been absolute shite lately and it shows. My cheekbones are sharp enough to cut glass and my eyes look far too big for my head. I pinch some color into my cheeks and yank my sweater straight. Not much else I can do about it now.

The kettle starts its screamin', pulling me away from my reflection. I'll get Lily's chamomile ready and have Jasper's black coffee waitin', his doctor's orders be damned. Some battles just aren't worth the breath ya waste fightin' 'em.

I arrange homemade shortbread cookies on a blue ceramic plate. My hands tremble as I set out the teacups. Another new symptom to add to the pile. Dr. Patterson says it'll get worse before . . . well, before everythin' stops for good.

The doorbell chimes, and I plaster on my best hostess smile. Show time.

"Mina, my dear!" Lily Brooks throws her arms around me, her floral perfume a welcome reprieve from phantom flowers. At seventy-nine, she's still a beauty. And a relentless hugger. "Don't you look lovely!" Lily steps back, hands still on my shoulders.

"She needs to eat more." Jasper emerges from behind his wife. He leans heavily on his cane. "Too skinny."

If only he knew. Stage IV doesn't leave much room for appetite. Not for food or for the future I'd once had planned.

"Jasper!" Lily swats at him. "Don't be rude!"

I laugh and usher them inside, away from the bite of the

autumn air. "It's so good to see ya both. Room two is all ready for ya, just how ya like it."

"With the view of the garden and the maple tree?" Jasper's bushy eyebrows climb toward his nonexistent hairline.

"With the view of the garden and maple tree," I confirm with a pat on his arm. "And I've put extra blankets in the chest. I know how ya like to sleep with the window cracked, even when it's cold enough to freeze the ears off a brass monkey."

Jasper grunts, but I see the corner of his mouth twitch. He's a grumpy old bastard, but he's got a heart in there somewhere. He and Lily spent their honeymoon here decades ago and they haven't missed a festival since. They're as reliable as the seasons, these two. Bickerin' one minute and finishin' each other's sentences the next. I guess sixty years of marriage'll do that to ya. I used to want that. That shared history. The comfort of someone knowin' exactly what ya need before ya even ask.

But that was before. No use gettin' sappy now. Dr. Patterson's diagnosis stole all those dreams with three words: *glioblastoma multiforme*. Inoperable. A death sentence wrapped in fancy words.

Lily takes my arm as we walk toward their room. "Are you doing okay, dear? How's business?"

I hesitate. Lyin' to Lily feels like a sin, but there's no reason to burden her with my problems. "Oh, ya know. It's been a bit quiet since the summer festival."

"Since those wolf boys lost their marbles?" Jasper asks from behind us. "You all have a reputation now. Must be bad for business. Should've seen the news coverage. We know better, but other tourists don't."

"It wasn't the wolves' fault." I feel the need to defend the pack. I was there, and I know what really happened. I know the mess Ravena made.

"Tell that to the tourism board." Jasper shakes his head. "Salem's probably loving this. Getting all your October business."

I sigh. "You're not wrong. Things have been rough. Honestly,

I'd probably be sittin' here talkin' to the wallpaper right now if it weren't for the two a ya."

"I wish there were more we could do. You won't close down, will you?" Lily clutches my arm.

"That's the last thing I want to do, love." I pat her arm. "I'm hopeful things will turn around. I just had a last-minute bookin' last week that could help fix our reputation." I can't keep the excitement out of my voice. "*The Real Vampire Wives of Obsidian Hills* is filmin' their cast trip here. They'll be here for six nights."

And if this doesn't work, I'm out of options. Not the legacy I'd hoped to leave.

Lily's eyes widen. "The reality show? With the—" She mimes fangs with her fingers.

"The very one." I can't stop the grin from rearrangin' my face. "They've booked eight rooms for cast and crew. They arrive day after tomorrow. Can ya believe it?"

"Those trashy shows." Jasper wrinkles his nose.

"Those trashy shows might just save my B&B." I help them down the hall to their room. "Once people see Moonridge on TV, and see that we're not the mess the media made us out to be, business will bounce back. It has to."

Because, and what I don't say is, I don't have time for a backup plan.

The Vampire Wives reservation came by way of a desperate email from a location scout lookin' to house cast and crew. She'd heard about Moonridge's 'authentic New England haunted town vibe' and wanted to film a cast trip here. I'd said yes before I even finished readin' the email. I practically threw my details at them. Now, with only three rooms available, I feel a flicker of somethin' dangerously close to hope. I don't have a staff and I'm runnin' on fumes, but I'll find a way to make it work. My livelihood, or what's left of it, depends on it.

I head for the door to let them get settled, but Lily stops me. "Mina? Remember that first year we came after you bought the place? We were your first guests after you reopened. You were a nervous wreck."

I smile and lean against the doorframe. "Aye. I remember."

"You've come so far since then. Don't let a rough patch get you down."

I step into the hall, her words of encouragement like a supportive hand at my back. I take a breath and steady myself. The house doesn't feel so much like a tomb anymore. The clock ticks and the floorboards groan under the weight of real guests. This place will spring back to life yet, and that spot of hope warms up the parts of me that have been frozen solid for weeks.

I'm halfway through thumpin' the sofa cushions back into shape when the front door practically flies off its hinges and a wall of noise hits me.

"Knock knock, hermit!" Hazel's voice enters the room before she does. She steps inside and unwraps herself from her pink puffer jacket. "We've come to drag you back into society!"

Coco bounces in right behind her, grinnin' like she's won the lottery. La'Tasha brings up the rear. She hooks the door shut with the toe of her boot while she balances a massive fall bouquet.

My shoulders finally drop. These three are a colossal pain in the arse, but they're *my* pains. I never thought I'd find a group of people who'd actually notice if I went missin' for a day. Who'd call me up just to say hi and make sure I'm okay. They're the sisters I never asked for and definitely don't deserve. And I wouldn't trade them for nothin'.

"You lot are a sight for sore eyes," I say, huggin' them one by one. Coco's bulky, purple hand-knit sweater is soft against my cheek. La'Tasha's flowy green top smells faintly of sage and lavender. "Did I mention lately how fond I am of ya?"

"You have, but you can say it more, Mami." Coco plops down on the couch, her bright eyes full of mischief. "And since you're so fond of us, that means you have to join us at every festival event this year."

I let out a groan and sink into the chair next to her. "Aye, not this again."

"Yes, this again." La'Tasha nudges her glasses up on her nose. "You cannot keep hiding in this B&B. It's been three weeks since you joined us for a proper night out."

"I've been busy," I mumble. "Runnin' this place on my own isn't exactly easy work."

Why don't you tell them?

"But not networking is also bad for business," Hazel says. "We're not asking for every night, but you need to be seen. Blake and the other wolves have been asking about you. Blake misses your fresh scones."

You really should tell them.

What? That I'm not long for this world? That this might be the last Halloween festival I'll ever see? That every headache could be my brain givin' up? No. Not now.

I stand and slice the pumpkin bread I'd baked earlier and pour mugs of hot cider. The spicy-sweet aroma warms the room. "Well then, tell that great wolfy boyfriend of yours to get his hairy arse over here to see me. The man's got two good legs, hasn't he?" I hand out the mugs, savorin' the scent that reminds me of fall. "And besides, I do show my face. Someone has to pick up supplies for this place."

"Going to the market once a week doesn't count," Coco says through a mouth full of pumpkin bread.

"Look, we're worried about you." La'Tasha pulls a branch of burnt-orange maple leaves from the bouquet and arranges it carefully in the vase.

I open my mouth to protest, but she cuts me off, tuckin' a sprig of goldenrod into place.

"And before you say 'I'm fine,' just know we all recognize that as code for 'I'm drowning but too stubborn to ask for help.'"

She always gets to the point.

"That said," she adds a dusky sunflower to the vase, "we need help with the Spirits and S'mores booth on Thursday. Would you be willing? Two hours tops."

I sip my cider, stallin'. These women could guilt a saint into sinnin'. "Fine," I relent. "But no costume."

"Half costume," Hazel negotiates. "At least some cat ears or something."

"We'll see," I say, which is code for *not bloody likely.*

Coco perks up, changin' the subject. "Oh my God, you won't believe who's coming to town!" She wiggles in her seat like a kid at Christmas. "*The Real Vampire Wives of Obsidian Hills!*"

I laugh. "Aye. I know. They've gone and booked nearly every room I have."

La'Tasha's jaw hits the floor. "Wait, hold up. You're for real? The whole damn cast is crashing here? Under this roof?"

"Cast and crew and most likely, their egos, too," I confirm, unable to keep the pride from my voice. "Eight rooms for six nights."

"Oh my God, *Mami!* I think I'm gonna faint." Coco places her hand on her chest and breathes deep. It's like she's havin' a religious experience. "I. Cannot. Believe. This! I'm gonna breathe the same air as Vivienne St. James. She gives me life. And her fashion? Literally unmatched! Did you see the episode where she turned that pendejo to stone for a week just for breathing on her? She left him in the garden so the crows could poop on him. Iconic."

"That was staged," La'Tasha says with an eye roll. "But I get it. I love Vivienne, too, but Ayana is the real deal. She's my melanin sister. That woman is allegedly almost 300 years old and still slaying. If that's for real, I'm gonna need that skin care routine. And you *know* she has tea on important people in history. I'd kill for an hour with her."

Hazel shrugs. She leans against the counter, unimpressed. "Are we sure they're even legit vampires? Not just actors with expensive veneers?"

"Of course they're real!" Coco looks like Hazel just offended her soul.

"I'm leaning toward real," La'Tasha says.

Hazel shrugs. "Well, either way, this is a massive win for you. Exactly what you needed."

"Tell me about it," I say. "One more month like I've had, and I'd be turnin' off the electricity and eatin' nothin' but bread and water."

"We would not let that happen," La'Tasha says as she places the finished vase of flowers in the entryway.

And I believe her.

Hazel glances toward the window, her brows pinched. She tucks a curl behind her ear, her nervous tell.

"What's that stuck in your head?" I ask.

She sighs and runs a hand over her forehead. "The energy around town is really off. We spent most of the day reinforcing the barriers just to be safe. For some reason the veil feels thinner than normal this year."

La'Tasha nods and takes a seat at the table. "It's almost unsettling."

So it's not just me, then. I'm a hair's breadth from spillin' the truth about the whispers I've been hearin' in the walls, but I bite the words back. I don't need them worryin' about me when they've already got plenty on their plates.

"Do ya think it's connected to what happened with Ravena?"

"I don't know for sure." Hazel shrugs and shakes her head. "She stirred some shit up, no question. Blake's been patrolling near the abandoned mill, but he hasn't seen anything that seems off." She takes another sip of cider. "Still, her threats before we entombed her really rattled me. And I could have sworn I saw her standing under a tree in the park the other day."

"I think we all have a little PTSD after this summer," La'Tasha says, helpin' herself to a slice of pumpkin bread. "But I'd rather be paranoid than dead. And I don't want to risk her crazy ass getting loose and rampaging again. Especially with the festival. This town can't take another hit."

The veil cracks. She knows it cracks.

The voice comes from across the room. I look around, but none of them seem to have heard it.

"Exactly," Hazel nods. "Plus, I've got Penny Fisher testing my last damn nerve. She wants to learn and do *all* the magic. I'm like, girl, just because you can *read* a spell, doesn't mean you can *do* a spell. We have rules in place for a reason."

"Oh, the new librarian? I met her a couple of months ago. She seemed sweet." I force myself to concentrate on the conversation. Push back the static crowdin' my thoughts.

"That's her," Hazel sighs. "She's got ability. I'll give her that. But it's all over the place. Her adoptive parents hated magic and never let her practice, and now that she's on her own, she feels she can just do anything she wants. She has no focus, no training. It's like giving a toddler a flamethrower."

"That bad?" I wince.

La'Tasha pours herself another round of cider. "Last week, she tried a basic light spell and nuked her eyebrows right off her face."

"Yikes."

Death will come to Moonridge.

The voice slithers into my ear. I nearly drop my mug.

Tell them to ask the witch about what sleeps below the library.

I set down my mug carefully and try to focus on Hazel's voice, but the whispered words keep comin'. It's a pile-up in my head. Too many voices at once.

The Mortician walks among you . . .

The Anchor wants her child . . .

Warn them!

"Mina?" Hazel's hand clamps onto my arm. "You're really pale right now. You good?"

I blink and use her touch as an anchor to stop the room from spinnin'. "Sorry, pet. Just tired. Been a hell of a day."

She studies me, eyes narrowed. She's far too perceptive.

"We should probably let you rest." La'Tasha begins to gather the empty dishes and takes them to the sink.

Though several hours have passed, I don't want them to go already. I don't want to be left alone with the voices.

"Promise you'll come to the 5K Festival kickoff on Tuesday?" Hazel asks as she puts on her coat.

"If the TV vampires are playin' nice and not breakin' wine glasses or raisin' hell, I'll try to make an appearance." It's the best lie I can manage.

We exchange hugs, and I usher 'em out. The house feels twice as big and three times as empty as soon as the door clicks shut. Then the phone rings, and I nearly hit the rafters. Who would call the landline at 9:00 PM? Either a scammer or a drunk lookin' for the pub, probably.

I should just let it ring and let the voicemail earn its keep, but, no. My hand betrays me. "Moonridge Bed and Breakfast."

There's a pause. Static crackles like a bad radio. Like someone is callin' from inside a wind tunnel. Then a voice, deep and strangely formal, cuts through the fuzz.

"Yes. Hello. My name is Dex Grimm. I'm looking for accommodations beginning tonight."

His voice. It's deep. Mysterious. The voice of someone used to not bein' told no. It makes my skin prickle.

"Oh! Well. You're in luck. I actually have a vacancy." I straighten my posture, even though he can't see me. "How long would ya be stayin'?"

"I'm uncertain of the duration. I'm a writer finishing a project that requires . . . solitude."

The way he says it feels like he's hidin' a body in the trunk. And who uses words like *solitude* anymore?

"A writer, eh? What's your flavor?"

Another pause. "Ghost stories primarily. I was told by an old friend that Moonridge would provide an inspiring atmosphere."

My gut says *hang up now*. My bank account is tellin' my gut to shut the hell up. There's somethin' oily about this man, but I'm bleedin' cash and need every penny I can make. And for some reason, his voice seems very familiar.

"We'd be glad to have ya, Mr. Grimm," I say, ignorin' the dragons in my gut. "I've got a quiet room on the third floor. It's on the east side of the house, very peaceful. When can we expect ya?"

"This evening," he answers cryptically. "Thank you, miss."

The line goes dead before I can ask for details. I stare at the receiver a moment before hangin' up.

Creepy bastard.

Death comes to Moonridge . . .

I shut out the ghostly voice. I don't need another reminder of the time bomb in my head.

I squeeze my eyes shut and push the whispers back along with the pressure building behind my eyes. Keep busy. That's what I need to do. If this Grimm fella is showin' up tonight, I suppose I should get his room ready.

Room Ten is my favorite room in the house, tucked at the end of the east hall with bay windows that look out over the garden. The wallpaper is a posh damask that looks expensive when the light hits it just right. It's meant to give the room an air of elegance, but it's been so long since anyone's stayed in here, it's more of a dust collector. I've just started to wrestle fresh sheets onto the four-poster bed when the house starts its nonsense. A floorboard screeches down the hall. Then the slow, heavy grind of a door hinge.

I go stone still.

The air grows heavy, pressing down on me like I'm under water. Then come the footsteps from the floor above. Who the hell is in the attic? Every step sucks the warmth out of the room until I can see my own breath cloudin' the air.

"Hello?" I call out, my voice a pathetic croak.

No answer.

The temperature continues to plummet. It's like the entire house decided to turn into an iceberg. I drop the pillowcase on the bed, and my hands begin to tremble again. I step into the hallway just as a sconce flickers. Once. Twice. A scent trails past, thick and sickly sweet, like old roses left to rot in a vase. But there haven't been flowers on this floor in months. Goosebumps scatter across my arms.

"Jasper? Lily?"

My footsteps thud against the hardwood as I make my way down to the second floor. I pause. Still quiet. Only thing I can hear is my bloody pulse hammerin' my eardrums. The silence feels out of place. The house is always makin' some kind of noise as old houses do. But this feels purposeful. It's like it needs to say somethin', but doesn't know how to say it.

A soft thump hits the back porch. I spin around so fast I nearly get tangled in my own limbs. The rotten flower smell hits me again. My heart hammers against my ribs as I scramble to the window at the end of the hall. My breath fogs the glass instantly. The porch below is empty, bathed in the silver beam of the motion light I installed last spring. The light flickers once.

"Pull yourself together, you daft woman," I mutter to myself. I force my breath to slow. "It's an old house. Old houses make noise."

I head back downstairs, determined to finish washin' up and not let my imagination get the better of me, but as I reach the foyer, the wind picks up outside, and the porch swing groans in protest. And then they come.

Three sharp, deliberate knocks on the front door.

I jump and a startled squeak escapes. I press a hand to my chest as I inch toward the peephole.

My breath catches.

A tall man stands on the porch, face half-swallowed by shadow. He holds a single bag in one hand, and in the other, somethin' that looks suspiciously like a cloak draped over a cane or walkin' stick. Is this the mysterious Dex Grimm? Certainly not. It's been less than fifteen minutes since the phone call. I don't see a car, and I would have seen headlights had someone dropped him off. The train and bus stations are on the other side of town.

I hesitate, hand on the doorknob. My heart pounds in my chest. For one wild moment, I consider pretendin' I'm not home.

His eyes meet mine through the peephole. It's ridiculous, but I feel like he can see me.

"Hello? Is someone there? We just spoke on the phone."

That voice.

Deep. Familiar.

I take a breath to steady my nerves and open the door, one hand still braced on the frame, ready to slam it shut if I have to.

He stands perfectly still. Dark eyes that don't blink nearly enough. Medium-length black hair, stylishly cut. Pale skin that doesn't reflect moonlight so much as absorb it. Chiseled features. Hands folded over a sleek black cane topped with a silver skull.

He's like a work of art. Beautiful, the way carved statues are: cold, flawless, and a little bit off. Too perfect. Like a wax figure that got tired of the museum and walked out.

"Good evening," he says. Why is his voice so familiar? "I believe you were expecting me."

I swallow, suddenly aware of just how vulnerable I am in this big, mostly empty house.

Well. Not empty anymore.

Read the rest of Dex & Mina's story now.
Date Night With Death *is available on Kindle, hardcover and paperback.*